PENGUIN

ARKANA

ATLANTIS – MYTH OR REALITY

Journalist, teacher, lecturer and a former professional classical singer, Murry Hope is one of England's foremost authors on metaphysics, ancient magical religions and parapsychology. She was co-founder of The Atlanteans in 1957 and served as the society's president, principal teacher and healer for twenty years. In 1977 her psychic abilities were tested by Dr Carl Sargent of Cambridge University under the auspices of the BBC, and she achieved an extraordinarily high percentage of accuracy. Her recent work and studies have been concentrated on effecting a bridge between ancient and metaphysical beliefs and the new approach to physics and allied disciplines which is now being espoused by many scientists of repute.

OTHER BOOKS BY MURRY HOPE

Ancient Egypt: The Sirius Connection
The Psychology of Healing
The Psychology of Ritual
The Way of Cartouche
Essential Woman: Her Mystery, Her Power
Olympus: An Experience in Self Discovery
The Paschats and the Crystal People
Time: The Ultimate Energy
The Greek Tradition
The Nine Lives of Tyo
The Lion People

Atlantis
– Myth or Reality?

Murry Hope

ARKANA
PENGUIN BOOKS

ARKANA

Published by the Penguin Group
Penguin Books Ltd, 27 Wrights Lane, London W8 5TZ, England
Penguin Books USA Inc., 375 Hudson Street, New York, New York 10014, USA
Penguin Books Australia Ltd, Ringwood, Victoria, Australia
Penguin Books Canada Ltd, 10 Alcorn Avenue, Toronto, Ontario, Canada M4V 3B2
Penguin Books (NZ) Ltd, 182–190 Wairau Road, Auckland 10, New Zealand

Penguin Books Ltd, Registered Offices: Harmondsworth, Middlesex, England

First published 1991
3 5 7 9 10 8 6 4

Copyright © Murry Hope, 1991
All rights reserved

The moral right of the author has been asserted

Printed in England by Clays Ltd, St Ives plc
Filmset in Monotype Bembo

Except in the United States of America, this book is sold subject
to the condition that it shall not, by way of trade or otherwise, be lent,
re-sold, hired out, or otherwise circulated without the publisher's
prior consent in any form of binding or cover other than that in
which it is published and without a similar condition including this
condition being imposed on the subsequent purchaser

To 'He of the Old Ones',
who has been my teacher and mentor
through Inner and Outer Time,
with gratitude and love

Contents

Acknowledgements   ix

Introduction   1

CHAPTER 1.   The Atlantis Legend   5

CHAPTER 2.   Plato's Atlantis   12

CHAPTER 3.   Question Marks   30

CHAPTER 4.   Alternative Sites   48

CHAPTER 5.   The Atlantic Ocean   66

CHAPTER 6.   Asteroids, Moons and Axis Tilts   92

CHAPTER 7.   Cycles, Time Scales and Dates   126

CHAPTER 8.   Atlantis and Her Peoples   157

CHAPTER 9.   Religion and Science in Atlantis   184

CHAPTER 10.   Colonies, Missions and Safe Havens   205

CHAPTER 11.   Atlantean Heritage   244

CHAPTER 12.   Torch-Bearing Collectives   270

CHAPTER 13.   Akashic Anomalies   300

CHAPTER 14.   Is Chaos Returning?   320

Notes on Sources   338

Bibliography   344

Index   349

Acknowledgements

My gratitude and sincere thanks to Ian Wright for specialist advice and for trusting me with the loan of rare books; to Maureen Ballard for the loan of books and tapes; to Tom Clarke (Magis Books) and Martin Jones, who also supplied me with much-needed works of reference; and to Jed Collard, for his typing and editorial assistance.

Acknowledgements and thanks are also due to the authors and publishers who have kindly granted permission to use illustrations and quotes from the following books:

Bristol Classical Press. *Plato: The Atlantis Story* by Christopher Gill; Carol Publishing Group (University Books, Inc.) *The History of Atlantis* by Lewis Spence; William Collins Sons & Co. Ltd and Econ-Verlag GmbH, Düsseldorf. *The Secret of Atlantis* by Otto Muck; C. W. Daniel Co. *The Other Atlantis* by Robert Scrutton; Element Books Ltd. *The Great Pyramid Decoded* by Peter Lemesurier, and *The Psychology of Ritual* by Murry Hope; *The Greek Myths, Vol. 1* by Robert Graves (by permission of A. P. Watt Ltd, on behalf of the Executors of the Estate of Robert Graves); Robert Hale Ltd. *Atlantis: From Legend to Discovery* by Andrew Tomas; William Heinemann Ltd. *Cosmic Blueprint.* Reprinted by permission of William Heinemann Ltd. Copyright Paul Davies, 1987; Penguin Books Ltd. *Plato: Timaeus and Critias*, translation by Desmond Lee; The Putnam Publishing Group, New York. *Atlantis* by Charles Berlitz; Quartet Books Limited. *Atlantean* by Bob Quinn; Random House, Inc. *Serpent in the Sky* by John

Acknowledgements

Anthony West; *Sacred Science* by R. A. Schwaller de Lubicz, published in 1982 by Inner Traditions International, Rochester, Vermont. Distributed by Harper & Row, Hagerstown, Maryland, USA; Souvenir Press Ltd. *We are Not The First* by Andrew Tomas and *Colony: Earth* by Richard Mooney; Thorsons Publishing Co. Ltd. *Maps of the Ancient Sea Kings* by Charles Hapgood, and *The Earthquake Generation* by Jeffrey Goodman; Warner Books Inc. (Reprinted by permission of Warner Books/New York from *Edgar Cayce on Atlantis* by Edgar Cayce. Copyright 1968 by the Association for Research and Enlightenment, Inc.).

Additional artwork by Martin Jones.

Every effort has been made to contact the Baton Press, without success, in connection with the use of additional material from *Genisis* by David Wood.

Introduction

> Where chaos begins, classical science stops. For as long as the world
> has had physicists inquiring into the laws of nature, it has suffered a
> special ignorance about disorder in the atmosphere, in the turbulent
> sea, in the fluctuations of wildlife populations, in the oscillations of
> the heart and the brain. The irregular side of nature, the discontinuous
> and erratic side – these have been puzzles to science, or worse,
> monstrosities.

So writes James Gleick in his enlightening book *Chaos –
Making A New Science*. The overturning of many of the
established laws of physics and allied disciplines that has
followed the advent of 'chaos science' has opened the door to
the resolution of many enigmas both past and present, not the
least of which is the much debated and highly questionable
subject of the lost continent of Atlantis. The anti-cataclysmic
schools, which to date have constituted the bulwark of the
opposition in their insistence that large land masses do not
disappear suddenly or in a comparatively short space of time,
will have to rethink their arguments, while their historian
allies may find themselves in the position of having to consider
the possibility that civilization might conceivably have commenced in some place or time other than that proposed by
currently favoured academic schools of thought.

It is amazing to what irrational lengths people will go to
disprove something they find difficult to accept, or to prove

that which takes their fancy. The psychological connotations of this are cleverly noted and commented upon by Professor Hans Eysenck and Dr Carl Sargent in their book *Explaining the Unexplained*, fear and insecurity being the basic underlying themes. Since the subject of Atlantis appears to evoke strong feelings in the camps of both pro and con, questioning the views of either side is guaranteed to highlight the ego-orientated nature of favoured hypotheses, prejudice being ever fruitfully spawned in the turgid waters of dogma. Such considerations have rendered the study of Atlantology somewhat intellectually hazardous, as many past students of the subject have discovered to their chagrin.

Reconciling left-brain logic with right-brain intuition has always proved a Herculean task for those who endeavour to steer an unwavering course through the labyrinth of uncertainties that inevitably confront the thinking person. For my own part, while the closed attitudes of the more orthodox disciplines represent academic strait-jackets from which one struggles to free oneself, my credulity is equally strained by some of the outlandish 'revelations' from those psychics or sensitives who claim *carte blanche* entrée to what is described in metaphysics as the 'Akashic Records'.

I do not dispute the fact that we all have access in varying degrees to what Carl Jung described as the 'collective unconscious', which could be compared to computer data, the input of which has been programmed by the experiences of past generations. Taking the computer analogy one stage further, it is logical to assume that if Atlantis had existed, those who had lived there would have effected the encoded input of their experiences, which would be available to anyone sufficiently sensitive to press the appropriate command keys. However, it is not that simple, as we shall see.

Intellectual conclusions that tend to accommodate the prevailing political and national ethos are frequently accepted in later times as conventional wisdom, so that the somewhat questionable views of earlier scholars end up as the canon of later sacrosanct social or philosophical credos. Likewise, those who call themselves psychics, sensitives, channellers (or whichever term is in current use to denote the faculty of sensitivity, or psi) are programmed by their own social, cultural, religious and political backgrounds. Unless they are able to break with that programming, ancient myths and legends may be subconsciously rationalized to accommodate the individual's belief in a patriarchal or matriarchal society, Sun worship, sea worship, racism, socialism, spacemen, Jesus, the Bible, eastern mysticism, or whichever, and presented (or channelled, as the case may be) to the listener or reader as Atlantean gospel. An unbiased assessment of the evidence available from both intuitive sources and serious research and scholarship is therefore called for if a balanced perspective is to be achieved.

The fact that innumerable books have been written about Atlantis over the ages designates it an important watershed in the evolutionary history of this planet. In the ensuing pages I shall be bringing to the reader's notice a broad array of the theories and conjectures proffered by the many students of Atlantology, the data presented in their support and the opposing views. As there is such a wide variety of opinions from which to choose, however, I feel the evidence should be allowed to speak for itself, although my own views may tend to surface on occasion.

Although much of the information here has been culled from what the more stalwart supporters of orthodoxy might refer to as the ramblings of the lunatic fringe of academe, the authorities in question are mostly highly qualified in their own disciplines, as we shall see. For my own part, my conclusions are based on forty years of intensive study of the subject, plus the fact that I was (for my sins!) born with what is broadly termed the 'psychic faculty', the combination of which, I trust, places me in a position to comment on both sides of the picture. I have, however, endeavoured to confine psychic speculations and impressions gained via ESP or other psi-related practices to the final three chapters. Should the odd metaphysical allusion slip through the net earlier, *mea culpa*!

I have no doubt that science will eventually crack the time code, making this facility available both as an energy and as a vehicle for viewing the past and future (a process that our right-brain hemisphere was, I believe, designed to accommodate in the natural course of somatic evolution). Mastering the intricacies of time will, one hopes, provide us with the wherewithal to study Atlantis and allied mysteries from the Earth's past in a more rational, generous and civilized light. Until the advent of such merciful times, however, we are confined to the negotiation of the maze, the entrance to which is named 'Reason', and the exit, 'Intuition'.

CHAPTER I

The Atlantis Legend

In some green island of the sea
Where now the shadowy coral grows
In pride and pomp and empery
The courts of old Atlantis rose.

JOHN MASEFIELD

Atlantis! The very name is evocative of poetry, of an Edenic existence before the legendary 'Fall', when 'bird and beast and flower were one with men'. The human race has ever been haunted by the idea of a Golden Age, an instinctive knowledge or far memory of a time in days long past, in some mysterious, hidden location, when all was perfect. The Utopia concept, so patently obvious in the Atlantis story, encapsulates our inner yearnings for a state of bliss where suffering, strife and death are non-existent — the Avalon of the west, the Blessed Isles, Erewhon, Arcadia — longingly expressed in *Ulysses*:

... for my purpose holds
To sail beyond the sunset, and the baths
Of all the western stars, until I die.
It may be that the gulfs will wash us down:
It may be we shall touch the Happy Isles,
And see the great Achilles, whom we knew.

ALFRED LORD TENNYSON

A poetic illusion, perhaps, but one cherished by artists,

mystics and philosophers over the centuries. Nor are such fancies limited to the creatively inclined. The scientific disciplines have spawned their own share of dreamers, as we shall shortly see – men and women who have made it their business to substantiate those dreams and point the direction to a quality of life, fortified by true knowledge and unprejudiced learning, from which all peoples could benefit.

But where did the name 'Atlantis' originate, what are its roots and what relationship, if any, does it share with the ocean whose present title echoes to its name? We owe much of the information from the past to the writers of the Graeco-Roman world, most of whom seemed familiar with the Atlantis concept and the likely location of the lost continent in the ocean of that name. Indications of earlier Atlantean colonization are to be found in ancient references to the tribes of north-western Africa as Atalantes, Atarantes and Atlantioi. The North African Berbers have their own legends of Attala, a kingdom rich in gold, silver and tin, which now lies buried beneath the ocean but, according to an ancient prophecy, will one day rise again.

The ancient Celts of Gaul, Ireland, Wales and other parts of Britain maintained that their ancestors hailed from a land to the west, sometimes known as Avalon, which was ultimately annexed by the sea god. The Basques of south-western France and northern Spain subscribe to the belief that they are the descendants of the ancient Atlanteans, whom they refer to as Atlaintika, while a popular theory among the Portuguese proposes that Atlantis, or Atlantida, the southern mountain peaks of which the Azores formed a part, once existed in the ocean to the west of Portugal. The Iberians of southern Spain also believe they have Atlantean connections; the Canary Islands, which are owned by Spain to this day, are considered another small section of the Old Country (as Atlantis is sometimes affectionately termed) that managed to survive the Deluge. In fact, Atalaya is still in common use there as a place name, while the original inhabitants laid claim to being the only survivors of a world-wide cataclysm that rent their land apart.

The Phoenicians referred to a secret island of great wealth, which they called Antilla. An Arabian legend tells of a land called Ad located in the western ocean, which was believed to have been the cradle of civilization. Even the ancient sacred writings of India, the *Puranas* and *Mahabharata*, make reference to the 'White Islands', a continent called Attala, located in the ocean half a world away from the shores of their own sub-continent.[1] In fact, an approximate location is given for Attala, which accords with information from other sources as to the position of the legendary site for Atlantis. The term Atyantika also appears in these and other texts in reference to a final catastrophic destruction.

On the other side of the Atlantic there are an equal number of confirmatory indications. On their arrival in Central and South America the *conquistadores* were told by the Aztecs that their race originated on a large island called Aztlan, which lay in the ocean to the east. Similar sounding names are also to be encountered all along the coast of Mexico, Central and the northern parts of South America. Lemesurier, the well-known researcher in pyramidology and allied subjects, tells us that:

(i) In the name Quetzalcoatl, the last syllable – *atl* is the Nahua word for water. A related word, *atatl*, means arrow.
(ii) The god Atlaua is thus known as Master of the Waters – a name oddly reminiscent of the function of the early pharaohs . . .[2]

Certain North American Indian tribes have retained traditions of their ancestors coming from a large island in the sea to the east, while early settlers in Wisconsin discovered a village known to its inhabitants as Azatlan. Ignatius Donnelly tells us that the Toltecs traced their migrations back to a place called Aztlan, and the *Popol Vuh* contains references to the comings and goings of royal princes between Aztlan and its colony in the west.

Among the Norse and Scandinavian legends the most interesting references are to be found in the *Oera Linda Book*, which purports to be a history of the Frisian race from the time when a major catastrophe of global proportions caused their main land mass to sink beneath the waves. The land in question (see Figure 1), which housed a matriarchal society of fair, blue-eyed people averaging 7 feet (2 metres) tall, was known as Atland. The legend states that prior to the cataclysms that precipitated the sinking of this land, the climate in those parts was far warmer and more hospitable than that in corresponding latitudes today. But more of the *Oera Linda Book* later, as its contents serve as an aid to the confirmation of other dates and events in the chronicle of pre- and post-diluvian events. Another Viking tradition tells of a strange and magical land called Atli, which lay to the south-west.

The German scholar Pastor Jurgen Spanuth seems to find further evidence of the Atlantis connection with these northerly parts in the *Eddas*, a collection of traditional poems recorded around AD 1200 but deriving from much earlier times. The *Eddas* refer to the northlands as Atalland (Thule?) and the sea as Atle's Path. Atle (or Atal) was the name of a sea king who, we are told, 'ruled over the sea and from whom the whole island and surrounding ocean took their designation of Atlantic'.[3]

In his brilliant work *The Secret of Lost Atlantis*, the Viennese scientist Otto Muck refers to the giant Atlas, who, according to Greek mythology '. . . has the great columns that keep earth and sky apart . . .' as holding the key to the names Atlantis and Atlantic.[4] Muck comments that although the Greek for Atlas appears to differ slightly from that for the name of the island and the ocean, the genitive in classical

Fig. 1. Arctic Crater caused by the explosion of a great asteroid followed by volcanic activity and earthquakes which sank Atland and broke up ancient northern continents.

9

Greek – Ατλαντου – indicates the same etymological root. It was the island of Atlantis, Muck asserts, that received its name from the high mountains that dominated its impressive land-scapes, and gave it, in turn, to the surrounding ocean. Its first king was designated the son of Poseidon, god of the sea, and paralleled with Atlas, bearer of the heavenly vault.

Another writer to mention Atlantis is Theopompus of Chios, a Greek historian of the fourth century BC, whose work has survived in the *Varia Historia* of Aelian. He tells us of a conversation that purportedly took place between King Midas of Phrygia and Silenus the satyr, who was tutor to the godling Dionysus. Although there are several perhaps more sober renderings of this legend, the following by Robert Graves clothes the tale in a poetic garb.

MIDAS, son of the Great Goddess Ida, by a satyr whose name is not remembered, was a pleasure-loving King of Macedonian Bromium, where he ruled over the Brigians (also called Moschians) and planned his celebrated rose gardens. In his infancy, a procession of ants was observed carrying grains of wheat up the side of his cradle and placing them between his lips as he slept – a prodigy which the soothsayers read as an omen of the great wealth that would accrue to him; and when he grew older, Orpheus tutored him.

One day, the debauched old satyr Silenus, Dionysus's former pedagogue, happened to straggle from the main body of the riotous Dionysian army as it marched out of Thrace into Boeotia, and was found sleeping off his drunken fit in the rose gardens. The gardeners bound him with garlands of flowers and led him before Midas, to whom he told wonderful tales of an immense continent lying beyond the Ocean's stream – altogether separate from the conjoined mass of Europe, Asia, or Africa – where splendid cities abound, peopled by gigantic, happy, and long-lived inhabitants, and enjoying a remarkable legal system. A great expedition – at least ten million strong – once set out thence across the Ocean in ships to visit the Hyperboreans; but on learning that theirs was the best land that the old world had to offer, retired in disgust.[5]

Nowhere, however, is the legend of Atlantis more graphically related than in two works of Plato, the *Critias* and *Timaeus*, which also embody the ancient Egyptian beliefs concerning their Atlantean heritage. Many writers on Atlantology have tended to select those passages from Plato that they judge to be supportive of their favourite theories, a practice that has tended to attract criticism from more orthodox scholastic sources. However, as the work in its entirety would occupy too large a portion of this book, I have elected to reproduce the abridged translation that has been bequeathed to us by that most revered of Atlantean scholars, Ignatius Donnelly (1831–1901), and appeared in his original work *Atlantis – The Antediluvian World*. So popular was Donnelly's book when it was published in the last century that a poll undertaken by the British press at the time accorded the news value of Atlantis as second only to the Second Coming of Christ!

CHAPTER 2

Plato's Atlantis

Amicus Plato, sed magis amica veritas.
(Plato is dear to me, but dearer still is truth.)
GREEK ORIGINAL ASCRIBED TO ARISTOTLE

Critias. Then listen, Socrates, to a strange tale, which is, however, certainly true, as Solon, who was the wisest of the seven sages, declared. He was a relative and great friend of my great-grandfather, Dropidas, as he himself says in several of his poems; and Dropidas told Critias, my grandfather, who remembered, and told us, that there were of old great and marvellous actions of the Athenians, which have passed into oblivion through time and the destruction of the human race – and one in particular, which was the greatest of them all, the recital of which will be a suitable testimony of our gratitude to you. . . .

Socrates. Very good; and what is this ancient famous action of which Critias spoke, not as a mere legend, but as a veritable action of the Athenian State, which Solon recounted?

Critias. I will tell an old-world story which I heard from an aged man; for Critias was, as he said, at that time nearly ninety years of age, and I was about ten years of age. Now the day was that day of the Apaturia which is called the registration of youth; at which, according to custom, our parents gave prizes for recitations, and the poems of several poets were recited by us boys, and many of us sang the poems of Solon, which were new at the time. One of our tribe, either because this was his real opinion, or because he thought that he would please Critias, said that, in his judgment, Solon was

12

not only the wisest of men but the noblest of poets. The old man, I well remember, brightened up at this, and said, smiling: 'Yes, Amynander, if Solon had only, like other poets, made poetry the business of his life, and had completed the tale which he brought with him from Egypt, and had not been compelled, by reason of the factions and troubles which he found stirring in this country when he came home, to attend to other matters, in my opinion he would have been as famous as Homer, or Hesiod, or any poet.'

'And what was that poem about Critias?' said the person who addressed him.

'About the greatest action which the Athenians ever did, and which ought to have been most famous, but which, through the lapse of time and the destruction of the actors, has not come down to us.'

'Tell us,' said the other, 'the whole story, and how and from whom Solon heard this veritable tradition.'

He replied: 'At the head of the Egyptian Delta, where the river Nile divides, there is a certain district which is called the district of Sais, and the great city of the district is also called Sais, and is the city from which Amasis the king was sprung. And the citizens have a deity who is their foundress: she is called in the Egyptian tongue Neith, which is asserted by them to be the same whom the Hellenes called Athene. Now, the citizens of this city are great lovers of the Athenians, and say that they are in some way related to them. Thither came Solon, who was received by them with great honor; and he asked the priests, who were most skilful in such matters, about antiquity, and made the discovery that neither he nor any other Hellene knew anything worth mentioning about the times of old. On one occasion, when he was drawing them on to speak of antiquity, he began to tell about the most ancient things in our part of the world – about Phoroneus, who is called "the first"; and about Niobe; and, after the Deluge, to tell of the lives of Deucalion and Pyrrha; and he traced the genealogy of their descendants, and attempted to reckon how many years old were the events of which he was speaking, and to give the dates. Thereupon, one of the priests, who was of very great age, said, "O Solon, Solon, you Hellenes are but children, and there is never an old man who is an Hellene." Solon, hearing this, said, "What do you mean?" "I mean to say," he replied, "that in mind you are all young; there is no old opinion handed down among you by ancient tradition, nor any science which is hoary with age. And I will tell you the reason of this: there have been, and there will be again, many destructions of mankind arising out of many causes. There is a story which even you have preserved, that once upon a time Phaëthon, the son of Helios, having yoked the steeds in his father's chariot, because he was not able to drive them in the path of his father, burnt up all that was upon the earth, and was himself destroyed by a thunderbolt. Now, this has the form of a myth, but really signifies a declination of the bodies moving around the earth and in the heavens, and a great conflagration of things upon the earth recurring at long intervals of time: when this happens, those who live upon the mountains and in dry and lofty places are more liable to destruction than those who dwell by rivers or on the sea-shore; and from this calamity the Nile, who is our never-failing savior, saves and delivers us. When, on the other hand, the gods purge the earth with a deluge of water, among you herdsmen and shepherds on the mountains are the survivors, whereas those of you who live in cities are carried by the rivers into the sea; but in this country neither at that time nor at any other does the water come from above on the fields, having always a tendency to come up from below, for which reason the things preserved here are said to be the oldest. The fact is, that wherever the extremity of winter frost or of summer sun does not prevent, the human race is always increasing at times, and at other times diminishing in numbers. And whatever happened either in your country or in ours, or in any other region of which we are informed – if any action which is noble or great, or in any other way remarkable has taken place, all that has been written down of old, and is preserved in our temples; whereas you and other nations are just being provided with letters and the other things which States require; and then, at the usual period, the stream from heaven descends like a pestilence, and leaves only those of you who are destitute of letters and education; and thus you have to begin all over again as children, and know nothing of what happened in ancient times, either among us or among yourselves. As for those genealogies of yours which you have recounted to us, Solon, they are no better than the tales of children; for, in the first place, you remember one deluge only, whereas there were many of them; and, in the next place, you do not know that there dwelt in your land the fairest and noblest race of men which ever lived, of whom you and your whole city are but a seed or remnant. And this was unknown to you, because for many generations the survivors of that destruction died and made no sign. For there was a time, Solon, before that great deluge of all, when the city which now is Athens was first in war, and was preeminent for the excellence of her laws, and is said to have performed the noblest deeds, and to have had the fairest constitution of any of which tradition tells, under the face of heaven." Solon marvelled at this, and earnestly requested the priest to inform him exactly and in order about these former citizens. "You are welcome to hear about them, Solon," said the priest, "both for your own sake and for that of the city; and, above all, for the sake of the goddess who is the common patron and protector and educator of both our cities. She founded your city a thousand years before ours, receiving from the Earth and Hephaestus the seed of your race, and then she founded ours, the constitution of which is set down in our sacred registers as 8,000 years old. As touching the citizens of 9,000 years ago, I will briefly inform you of their laws and of the noblest of their actions; and the exact particulars of the whole we will hereafter go through at our leisure in the sacred registers themselves. If you compare these very laws with your own, you will find that many of ours are the counterpart of yours, as they were in the olden time. In the first place, there is the caste of priests, which is separated from all the others; next there are the artificers, who exercise their several crafts by themselves, and without admixture of any other; and also there is the class of shepherds and that of hunters, as well as that of husbandmen; and you will observe, too, that the warriors in Egypt are separated from all the other classes, and are commanded by the law only to engage in war; moreover, the weapons with which they are equipped are shields and spears, and this the goddess taught first among you, and then in Asiatic countries, and we among the Asiatics first adopted.

'"Then, as to wisdom, do you observe what care the law took from the very first, searching out and comprehending the whole order of things down to prophecy and medicine (the latter with a view to health); and out of these divine elements drawing what was needful for human life, and adding every sort of knowledge which was connected with them. All this order and arrangement the goddess first imparted to you when establishing your city; and she chose the spot of earth in which you were born, because she saw that the happy temperament of the seasons in that land would produce the wisest of men. Wherefore the goddess, who was a lover both of war and of wisdom, selected, and first of all settled that spot which was the most likely to produce men likest herself. And there you dwelt, having such laws as these and still better ones, and excelled all mankind in all virtue, as became the children and disciples of the gods. Many great and wonderful deeds are recorded of your State in our histories; but one of them exceeds all the rest in greatness and valor; for these histories tell of a mighty power which was aggressing wantonly against the whole of Europe and Asia, and to which your city put an end. This power came forth out of the Atlantic Ocean, for in those days the Atlantic was navigable; and there was an island situated in front of the straits which you call the Columns of Heracles [Hercules]: the island was larger than Libya and Asia put together, and was the way to other islands, and from the islands you might pass through the whole of the opposite continent which surrounded the true ocean; for this sea which is within the Straits of Heracles is only a harbor, having a narrow entrance, but that other is a real sea, and the surrounding land may be most truly called a continent. Now, in the island of Atlantis there was a great and wonderful empire, which had rule over the whole island and several others, as well as over parts of the continent; and, besides these, they subjected the parts of Libya within the Columns of Heracles as far as Egypt, and of Europe as far as

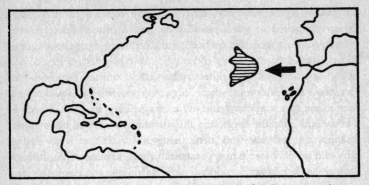

Fig. 2. The approximate position of the island of Atlantis according to Plato's description.

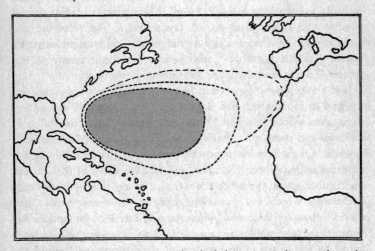

Fig. 3. Map of the Sargasso Sea (the shaded portion indicates where the weed is thickest).

Tyrrhenia. The vast power thus gathered into one, endeavored to subdue at one blow our country and yours, and the whole of the land which was within the straits; and then, Solon, your country shone forth, in the excellence of her virtue and strength, among all mankind; for she was the first in courage and military skill, and was the leader of the Hellenes. And when the rest fell off from her, being compelled to stand alone, after having undergone the very extremity of danger, she defeated and triumphed over the invaders, and preserved from slavery those who were not yet subjected, and freely liberated all the others who dwelt within the limits of Heracles. But afterward there occurred violent earthquakes and floods, and in a single day and night of rain all your warlike men in a body sank into the earth, and the island of Atlantis in like manner disappeared, and was sunk beneath the sea. And that is the reason why the sea in those parts is impassable and impenetrable, because there is such a quantity of shallow mud in the way; and this was caused by the subsidence of the island.''

'But in addition to the gods whom you have mentioned, I would specially invoke Mnemosyne; for all the important part of what I have to tell is dependant on her favor, and if I can recollect and recite enough of what was said by the priests, and brought hither by Solon, I doubt not that I shall satisfy the requirements of this theatre. To that task, then, I will at once address myself.

'Let me begin by observing, first of all, that nine thousand was the sum of years which had elapsed since the war which was said to have taken place between all those who dwelt outside the Pillars of Heracles and those who dwelt within them: this war I am now to describe. Of the combatants on the one side the city of Athens was reported to have been the ruler, and to have directed the contest; the combatants on the other side were led by the kings of the islands of Atlantis, which, as I was saying, once had an extent greater than that of Libya and Asia; and, when afterward sunk by an earthquake, became an impassable barrier of mud to voyagers sailing from hence to the ocean. The progress of the history will unfold the various tribes of barbarians and Hellenes which then existed, as they successively appear on the scene; but I must begin by describing, first of all, the Athenians as they were in that day, and their enemies who fought with them; and I shall have to tell of the power and form of government of both of them. Let us give the precedence to Athens. . . .

Note: At this point in Plato's tale Critias digresses from the

Atlantean theme to an account of life in prehistoric Athens, in which he enumerates various legendary heroes such as Cecrops, Erechtheus and Erichthonius, who featured in the narratives of Atlantean/Athenian conflict, the subject matter of which is dealt with in Chapter 10.

'Many great deluges have taken place during the nine thousand years, for that is the number of years which have elapsed since the time of which I am speaking; and in all the ages and changes of things there has never been any settlement of the earth flowing down from the mountains, as in other places, which is worth speaking of; it has always been carried round in a circle, and disappeared in the depths below. The consequence is that, in comparison of what then was, there are remaining in small islets only the bones of the wasted body, as they may be called, all the richer and softer parts of the soil having fallen away, and the mere skeleton of the country being left. . . .

'And next, if I have not forgotten what I heard when I was a child, I will impart to you the character and origin of their adversaries; for friends should not keep their stories to themselves, but have them in common. Yet, before proceeding farther in the narrative, I ought to warn you that you must not be surprised if you should hear Hellenic names given to foreigners. I will tell you the reason of this: Solon, who was intending to use the tale for his poem, made an investigation into the meaning of the names, and found that the early Egyptians, in writing them down, had translated them into their own language, and he recovered the meaning of the several names and retranslated them, and copied them out again in our language. My great-grandfather, Dropidas, had the original writing, which is still in my possession, and was carefully studied by me when I was a child. Therefore, if you hear names such as are used in this country, you must not be surprised, for I have told you the reason of them.

'The tale, which was of great length, began as follows: I have before remarked, in speaking of the allotments of the gods, that they distributed the whole earth into portions differing in extent, and made themselves temples and sacrifices. And Poseidon, receiving for his lot the island of Atlantis, begat children by a mortal woman, and settled them in a part of the island which I will proceed to describe. On the side toward the sea, and in the centre of the whole island, there was a plain which is said to have been the fairest of all plains, and very fertile. Near the plain again, and also in the centre of the island, at a distance of about fifty stadia,* there was a mountain, not very high on any side. In this mountain there dwelt one of the earth-born primeval men of that country, whose name was Evenor, and he had a wife named Leucippe, and they had an only daughter, who was named Cleito. The maiden was growing up to womanhood when her father and mother died; Poseidon fell in love with her, and had intercourse with her; and, breaking the ground, enclosed the hill in which she dwelt all round, making alternate zones of sea and land, larger and smaller, encircling one another; there were two of land and three of water, which he turned as with a lathe out of the centre of the island, equidistant every way, so that no man could get to the island, for ships and voyages were not yet heard of. He himself, as he was a god, found no difficulty in making special arrangements for the centre island, bringing two streams of water under the earth, which he caused to ascend as springs, one of warm water and the other of cold, and making every variety of food to spring up abundantly in the earth. He also begat and brought up five pairs of male children, dividing the island of Atlantis into ten portions: he gave to the first-born of the eldest pair his mother's dwelling and the surrounding allotment, which was the largest and best, and made him king over the rest; the others he made princes, and gave them rule over many men and a large territory. And he named them all: the eldest, who was king, he named Atlas, and from him the whole island and the ocean received the name Atlantic. To his twin-brother, who was born after him, and obtained as his lot the extremity of the island toward the Pillars of Heracles, as far as the country which is still called the

---

* Stadia: it is generally believed that a stadium was 607 feet (185 metres), so 50 stadia would be 5.8 miles (9 kilometres), 3,000 stadia would equal 345 miles (555 kilometres), and so forth.

region of Gades in that part of the world, he gave the name which in the Hellenic language is Eumelus, in the language of the country which is named after him Gadeirus. Of the second pair of twins, he called one Ampheres and the other Evaemon. To the third pair of twins he gave the name Mneseus to the elder, and Autochthon to the one who followed him. Of the fourth pair of twins he called the elder Elasippus and the younger Mestor. And of the fifth pair he gave to the elder the name of Azaes, and to the younger Diaprepes. All these and their descendants were the inhabitants and rulers of divers islands in the open sea; and also, as has been already said, they held sway in the other direction over the country within the Pillars as far as Egypt and Tyrrhenia. Now Atlas had a numerous and honorable family, and his eldest branch always retained the kingdom, which the eldest son handed on to his eldest for many generations; and they had such an amount of wealth as was never before possessed by kings and potentates, and is not likely ever to be again, and they were furnished with everything which they could have, both in city and country. For, because of the greatness of their empire, many things were brought to them from foreign countries, and the island itself provided much of what was required by them for the uses of life. In the first place, they dug out of the earth whatever was to be found there, mineral as well as metal, and that which is now only a name, and was then something more than a name – orichalcum – was dug out of the earth in many parts of the island, and, with the exception of gold, was esteemed the most precious of metals among the men of those days. There was an abundance of wood for carpenters' work, and sufficient maintenance for tame and wild animals. Moreover, there were a great number of elephants in the island, and there was a provision for animals of every kind, both for those which live in lakes and marshes and rivers, and also for those which live in mountains and on plains, and therefore for the animal which is the largest and most voracious of them. Also, whatever fragrant things there are in the earth, whether roots, or herbage, or woods, or distilling drops of flowers or fruits, grew and thrived in that land; and again, the cultivated fruit of the earth, both the dry edible fruit and other species of food, which we call by the general name of legumes, and the fruits having a hard rind, affording drinks, and meats, and ointments, and good store of chestnuts and the like, which may be used to play with, and are fruits which spoil with keeping – and the pleasant kinds of dessert which console us after dinner, when we are full and tired of eating – all these that sacred island lying beneath the sun brought forth fair and wondrous in infinite abundance. All these things they received from the earth, and they employed themselves in constructing their temples, and palaces, and harbors, and docks; and they arranged the whole country in the following manner: First of all they bridged over the zones of sea which surrounded the ancient metropolis, and made a passage into and out of the royal palace; and then they began to build the palace in the habitation of the god and of their ancestors. This they continued to ornament in successive generations, every king surpassing the one who came before him to the utmost of his power, until they made the building a marvel to behold for size and for beauty. And, beginning from the sea, they dug a canal three hundred feet in width and one hundred feet in depth, and fifty stadia in length, which they carried through to the outermost zone, making a passage from the sea up to this, which became a harbor, and leaving an opening sufficient to enable the largest vessels to find ingress. Moreover, they divided the zones of land which parted the zones of sea, constructing bridges of such a width as would leave a passage for a single trireme to pass out of one into another, and roofed them over; and there was a way underneath for the ships, for the banks of the zones were raised considerably above the water. Now the largest of the zones into which a passage was cut from the sea was three stadia in breadth, and the zone of land which came next of equal breadth; but the next two, as well the zone of water as of land, were two stadia, and the one which surrounded the central island was a stadium only in width. The island in which the palace was situated had a diameter of five stadia. This, and the zones and the bridge, which was the sixth part of a stadium in width, they surrounded by a stone wall, on either side placing towers, and gates on the bridges where the sea passed in. The stone which was used in the work they quarried from underneath the centre island and from

Fig. 4. The cross of Atlantis, a very ancient symbol recurring in prehistoric stone circles and on sacrificial altars suggesting, perhaps, a surviving memory or emulation of the Atlantean original. It contains the three circular walls surrounding the island city and the canals traversing them. The shaft of the cross is the large entrance canal.

underneath the zones, on the outer as well as the inner side. One kind of stone was white, another black, and a third red; and, as they quarried, they at the same time hollowed out docks double within, having roofs formed out of the native rock. Some of their buildings were simple, but in others they put together different stones, which they intermingled for the sake of ornament, to be a natural source of delight. The entire circuit of the wall which went round the outermost one they covered with a coating of brass, and the circuit of the next wall they coated with tin, and the third, which encompassed the citadel, flashed with the red light of orichalcum. The palaces in the interior of the citadel were constructed in this wise: In the centre was a holy temple dedicated to Cleito and Poseidon, which remained inaccessible, and was surrounded by an enclosure of gold; this was the spot in which they originally begat the race of the ten princes, and thither they annually brought the fruits of the earth in their season from all the ten portions, and performed sacrifices to each of them. Here, too, was Poseidon's own temple, of a stadium in length and half a stadium in width, and of a proportionate height, having a sort of barbaric splendor. All the outside of the temple, with the exception of the pinnacles, they covered with silver, and the pinnacles with gold. In the interior of the temple the roof was of ivory, adorned everywhere with gold and silver and orichalcum; all the other parts of the walls and pillars and floor they lined with orichalcum. In the temple they placed statues of gold: there was the god himself standing in a chariot – the charioteer of six winged horses – and of such a size that he touched the roof of the building with his head; around him there were a hundred Nereids riding on dolphins, for such was thought to be the number of them in that day. There were also in the interior of the temple other images which had been dedicated by private individuals. And around the temple on the outside were placed statues of gold of all the ten kings and of their wives; and there were many other great offerings, both of kings and of private individuals, coming both from the city itself and the foreign cities over which they held sway. There was an altar, too, which in size and workmanship corresponded to the rest of the work, and there were palaces in like manner which answered to the greatness of the kingdom and the glory of the temple.

'In the next place, they used fountains both of cold and hot springs; these were very abundant, and both kinds wonderfully adapted to use by reason of the sweetness and excellence of their waters. They constructed buildings about them, and planted suitable trees; also cisterns, some open to the heaven, others which they roofed over, to be used in winter as warm baths. There were the king's baths, and the baths of private persons, which were kept apart; also separate baths for women, and others again for horses and cattle, and to them they gave as much adornment as was suitable for them. The water which ran off they carried, some to the grove of Poseidon, where were growing all manner of trees of wonderful height and beauty, owing to the excellence of the soil; the remainder was conveyed by aqueducts which passed over the bridges to the outer circles: and there were many temples built and dedicated to many gods; also gardens and places of exercise, some for men, and some set apart for horses, in both of the two islands formed by the zones; and in the centre of the larger of the two there was a race-course of a stadium in width, and in length allowed to extend all round the island, for horses to race in. Also there were guard-houses at intervals for the body-guard, the more trusted of whom had their duties appointed to them in the lesser zone, which was nearer the Acropolis; while the most trusted of all had houses given them within the citadel, and about the persons of the kings. The docks were full of triremes and naval stores, and all things were quite ready for use. Enough of the plan of the royal palace. Crossing the outer harbors, which were three in number, you would come to a wall which began at the sea and went all round: this was everywhere distant fifty stadia from the largest zone and harbor, and enclosed the whole, meeting at the mouth of the channel toward the sea. The entire area was densely crowded with habitations; and the canal and the largest of the harbors were full of vessels and merchants coming from all parts, who, from their numbers, kept up a multitudinous sound of human voices and din of all sorts night and day. I have repeated his descriptions of the city and the parts about the ancient palace nearly as he gave them, and now I must endeavor to describe the nature and arrangement of the rest of the country. The whole country was described as being very lofty and precipitous on the side of the sea, but the country immediately about and surrounding the city was a level plain, itself surrounded by mountains which descended toward the sea; it was smooth and even, but of an oblong shape, extending in one direction three thousand stadia, and going up the country from the sea through the centre of the island two thousand stadia; the whole region of the island lies toward the south, and is sheltered from the north. The surrounding mountains he celebrated for their number and size and beauty, in which they exceeded all that are now to be seen anywhere; having in them also many wealthy inhabited villages, and rivers and lakes, and meadows supplying food enough for every animal, wild or tame, and wood of various sorts, abundant for every kind of work. I will now describe the plain, which had been cultivated during many ages by many generations of kings. It was rectangular, and for the most part straight and oblong; and what it wanted of the straight line followed the line of the circular ditch. The depth and width and length of this ditch were incredible, and gave the impression that such a work, in addition to so many other works, could hardly have been wrought by the hand of man. But I must say what I have heard. It was excavated to the depth of a hundred feet, and its breadth was a stadium everywhere; it was carried round the whole of the plain, and was ten thousand stadia in length. It received the streams which came down from the mountains, and winding round the plain, and touching the city at various points, was there let off into the sea. From above, likewise, straight canals of a hundred feet in width were cut in the plain, and again let off into the ditch, toward the sea; these canals were at intervals of a hundred stadia, and by them they brought down the wood from the mountains to the city, and conveyed the fruits of the earth in ships, cutting transverse passages from one canal into another, and to the city. Twice in the year they gathered the fruits of the earth – in winter having the benefit of the rains, and in summer introducing the water of the canals. As to the population, each of the lots in the plain had an appointed chief of men who were fit for military service, and the size of the lot was to be a square of ten stadia each way, and the total number of all the lots was sixty thousand.

'And of the inhabitants of the mountains and of the rest of the country there was also a vast multitude having leaders, to whom they were assigned according to their dwellings and villages. The leader was required to furnish for the war the sixth portion of a war-chariot, so as to make up a total of ten thousand chariots; also two horses and riders upon them, and a light chariot without a seat, accompanied by a fighting man on foot carrying a small shield, and having a charioteer mounted to guide the horses; also, he was bound to furnish two heavy-armed men, two archers, two slingers, three stone-shooters, and three javelin men, who were skirmishers, and four sailors to make up a complement of twelve hundred ships. Such was the order of war in the royal city – that of the other nine governments was different in each of them, and would be wearisome to narrate. As to offices and honors, the following was the arrangement from the first: Each of the ten kings, in his own division and in his own city, had the absolute control of the citizens, and in many cases of the laws, punishing and slaying whomsoever he would.

'Now the relations of their governments to one another were regulated by the injunctions of Poseidon as the law had handed them down. These were inscribed by the first men on a column of orichalcum, which was situated in the middle of the island, at the temple of Poseidon, whither the people were gathered together every fifth and sixth years alternately, thus giving equal honor to the odd and to the even number. And when they were gathered together they consulted about public affairs, and inquired if any one had transgressed in anything, and passed judgment on him accordingly – and before they passed judgment they gave their pledges to one another in this wise: There were bulls who had the range of the temple of Poseidon; and the ten who were left alone in the temple, after they had offered prayers to the gods that they might take the sacrifices which were acceptable to them, hunted the bulls without weapons, but with staves and nooses; and the bull which they caught they led up to the column; the victim was then struck on the head by them, and slain over the sacred inscription. Now on the column, besides the law, there was inscribed an oath invoking mighty curses on the disobedient. When, therefore, after offering sacrifice according to their customs, they had burnt the limbs of the bull, they mingled a cup and cast in a clot of blood for each of them; the rest of the victim they took to the fire, after having made a purification of the column all round. Then they drew from the cup in golden vessels, and, pouring a libation on the fire, they swore that they would judge according to the laws on the column, and would punish any one who had previously transgressed, and that for the future they would not, if they could help, transgress any of the inscriptions, and would not command or obey any ruler who commanded them to act otherwise than according to the laws of their father Poseidon. This was the prayer which each of them offered up for himself and for his family, at the same time drinking, and dedicating the vessel in the temple of the god; and, after spending some necessary time at supper, when darkness came on and the fire about the sacrifice was cool, all of them put on most beautiful azure robes, and, sitting on the ground at night near the embers of the sacrifices on which they had sworn, and extinguishing all the fire about the temple, they received and gave judgment, if any of them had any accusation to bring against any one; and, when they had given judgment, at daybreak they wrote down their sentences on a golden tablet, and deposited them as memorials with their robes. There were many special laws which the several kings had inscribed about the temples, but the most important was the following: That they were not to take up arms against one another, and they were all to come to the rescue if any one in any city attempted to overthrow the royal house. Like their ancestors, they were to deliberate in common about war and other matters, giving the supremacy to the family of Atlas; and the king was not to have the power of life and death over any of his kinsmen, unless he had the assent of the majority of the ten kings.

'Such was the vast power which the god settled in the lost island of Atlantis; and this he afterward directed against our land on the following pretext, as traditions tell: For many generations, as long as the divine nature lasted in them, they were obedient to the laws, and well-affectioned toward the gods, who were their kinsmen; for they possessed true and in every way great spirits, practising gentleness and wisdom in the various chances of life, and in their intercourse with one another. They despised everything but virtue, not caring for their present state of life, and thinking lightly on the possession of gold and other property, which seemed only a burden to them; neither were they intoxicated by luxury; nor did wealth deprive them of their self-control; but they were sober, and saw clearly that all these goods are increased by virtuous friendship with one another, and that by excessive zeal for them, and honor of them, the good of them is lost, and friendship perishes with them.

'By such reflections, and by the continuance in them of a divine nature, all that which we have described waxed and increased in them; but when this divine portion began to fade away in them, and became diluted too often, and with too much of the mortal admixture, and the human nature got the upper-hand, then, they being unable to bear their fortune, became unseemly, and to him who had an eye to see, they began to appear base, and had lost the fairest of their precious gifts; but to those who had no eye to see the true happiness, they still appeared glorious and blessed at the very time when they were filled with unrighteous avarice and power. Zeus, the god of gods, who rules with law, and is able to see into such things, perceiving that an honorable race was in a most wretched state, and wanting to inflict punishment on them, that they might be chastened and improved, collected all the gods into his most holy habitation, which, being placed in the centre of the world, sees all things that partake of generation. And when he had called them together he spake as follows:'

[Here Plato's story abruptly ends.][1]

CHAPTER 3

Question Marks

> We dwell apart, afar
> Within the measured deep, amid its waves
> The most remote of men; no other race
> Hath commerce with us.
>
> HOMER, *The Odyssey*

Recent students of Atlantology have tended to lean heavily on new discoveries and developments in the fields of archaeology, oceanography, ethnology, anthropology and allied disciplines for evidence to support their beliefs. One has to bear in mind, however, that for many centuries there were no carbon-14 or dendrochronological datings to confirm or deny Plato's story or other subsequent accounts of the Atlantis drama, which naturally left the field wide open to speculation and debate. It is, therefore, essential that some of the incongruities that have plagued would-be believers and sceptics alike are taken into consideration at this point.

The *Timaeus* and *Critias*

A number of rather obvious anomalies in Plato's narration, notably the date given for the foundation of ancient Athens, have resulted in some classical scholars discounting the entire narration either as a figment of his imagination or, at the kindest, a flight of poetic fancy. On the other hand, serious research undertaken by equally qualified men and women has tended to support the philosopher. Since it has been commonly observed in psychology that when people are illogically troubled about something, they are often consumed with an irrational compulsion to denigrate it or, to use the popular vernacular, 'knock it', care must be taken to distinguish between personal opinion, irrational prejudice and genuine critique.

Criticism is, as any rational person will agree, both psychologically healthy and necessary in the intellectual growth of any culture or community. What we have to consider as far as the Atlantis question is concerned is the nature and motivation of the people making the criticism. I would classify them as follows:

1. Individuals suffering from personal insecurity arising from some inner fear or conflict.

2. Professional debunkers. (I was once quite friendly with such a man. His idea was to find a subject – any subject that was proving popular with the general public – wait for the 'pro' books to saturate the market, and then gleefully set about debunking them with no personal involvement in their subject matter whatsoever, a practice that is also referred to by some cynics as 'laughing all the way to the bank'.)

3. Scholarly types who are on the look-out for a suitable vehicle for the furtherance of their academic careers.

4. Genuine inquirers and critics who are seeking the answers to life's incongruities, and to whom we should all be grateful for having exposed both

uncalculated errors in scholarship or science and
deliberate hoaxes, such as Piltdown Man.

Although I am adopting the role of devil's advocate, and
plead innocent to 1, 2 and 3, I will endeavour to effect an
approach as eclectic and objective as possible. However, I do
have my own views on the subject, which will become
obvious. So, having said my piece, let us return to Plato.

Before we set about highlighting the possible areas of error
in his story, let us take a look at the background against
which it was penned. The first part of the long drawn out
Peloponnesian War had just ended in a truce, which allowed
Thucydides the much needed time to prepare for his great
history. The dramas of Euripides and Aristophanes entertained the populace, while Democritus considered life's
follies and the great Hippocrates thought up new ways of
curing sickness.

It was the third year of the eighty-ninth Olympiad, 421
BC; the month, Hecatombaeon; the day, the twenty-ninth,
when four men of distinction, each a master in his own field,
met at the house of Socrates in Athens. They were: Timaeus,
of Locris in Italy, a rich aristocrat, Pythagorean philosopher
and astronomer; Hermocrates of Syracuse, a man of great
learning, whose expertise lay in the fields of politics and
strategy; Critias, a distinguished Athenian statesman, orator
and writer, and the great Socrates himself (470–399 BC). Also
present was a tachygrapher, whose job it was to record the
discourses on wax-coated wooden tablets so that none of the
wise words uttered by these great minds of the Classical age
should be forgotten.

On the first day of the meeting the subject matter included
politics, cosmology, physical science and how citizens would
be likely to behave under conditions of a national emergency;
much the sort of items that senior statespersons and specialist

scholars might place on their agendas today. The second day began with the reading of the minutes of former discussions, after which Timaeus was invited to give his talk. Before he could begin, however, Hermocrates interjected:

Yesterday, when Timaeus and I arrived at the house of Critias, with whom we are staying, or, to be more exact, on our way there ... our host told us of a remarkable old tradition which I am sure you, Socrates, would also be interested to hear ...[1]

The Syracusan then suggested that Critias be called upon to tell the story and, as the philosopher had no objection and the others all agreed, Critias proceeded to relate the legend of Atlantis that Plato was later to record for posterity.

None of the aforementioned appear to be fictitious figures. Critias the Younger was the great-grandson of Dropidas, grandson of Critias the Elder – who passed Solon's story on to him – and the maternal uncle of Plato. A famous conservative statesman, poet, orator, philosopher and pupil of Socrates, he lived to the age of 90 before falling in the Battle of Aegospotami.[2]

Completing the ranks of *dramatis personae* involved in the Atlantis saga is Solon (639–559 BC), whose life reads like an epic heroic tale. Of noble Attic descent, this merchant adventurer took Salamis for the Athenians from the Megarans, and later effected constitutional changes in Athenian laws, which were concerned with the mitigation of differences between the hereditary nobility and the common people. In 571 BC he left Athens for Egypt, where he was entertained at the priestly colleges of Sais and Heliopolis, after which he travelled to Cyprus as the guest of King Philocyprus. The latter, on Solon's advice, moved his city of Aepia to a more favourable site and renamed it Soloi in his guest's honour. In 563 BC Solon visited Croesus at Sardis, returning in 561 BC to Athens, where a year later Pisistratus established his unpopular rule.

Solon passed the last ten years of his life in retirement, a man greatly respected for his experience and achievements. Regretfully, few of his numerous poems have been preserved for us and, saddest of all, his incomplete comment on the Atlantis account, verified by Plutarch, has been lost. Of the Seven Sages of Greece, Solon of Athens was considered the wisest. The other six were Thales of Miletus, Pittacos of Mytilene, Cleobulus, Chilon, Periander and Bias.

Plato (427–347 BC), whose account of the proceedings appears to have come under such fire, was the scion of a noble Athenian family. His youthful writings were mostly tragedies until Socrates introduced him to philosophy during the eight years he was his teacher. After the death of Socrates, Plato travelled to Megara to seek the wisdom of Euclid, and later to Cyrene and Egypt, where he imbibed the doctrine of the Pythagoreans. Following an adventurous episode as a prisoner and slave, he returned to Athens, where he founded the Academy some time after 387 BC. After several more journeys to Sicily he devoted himself entirely to the teaching of philosophy.

An understanding of the integrity of the characters and personalities upon whom judgement is being passed is, I believe, essential to a valid assessment of the work. For example, was Plato a man given to fairy stories, or the men from whom he obtained his story the kind of people whose fantasies dominated their lives to such an extent that they either deliberately or unconsciously employed them to deceive their followers? I think not!

Christopher Gill, a lecturer in Classics at the University of Aberystwyth, raises an interesting point in suggesting that much of the political and social structure attributed to the island continent echoes Plato's own views and those of the Pythagorean school generally. He tells us:

Plato's account of a division of the world between gods follows Greek tradition, e.g. Homer *Iliad* 15.187 ff., except in his insistence on the absence of strife in the division (cf. *Republic* 378b ff.). In particular, he denies the well-known legend of the contest between Athena and Poseidon for possession of Attica, and denies Poseidon any place in the cult of ancient Athens. Poseidon is the god of maritime Atlantis, not of the land-power, primaeval Athens . . .[3]

The time span of 9,000 years (see p. 16) also comes in for criticism on purely historical grounds, and Gill cogently suggests that the whole episode could be nothing more than pure political allegory clothed in mythical garb. In fact, it would be quite easy for anyone who has made a study of Classical and pre-Classical Greece to recognize the philosopher's own views, prejudices and hopes, which he has, albeit unconsciously, projected on to the peoples of his Atlantean state. After all, as Gill points out, it is ancient Athens and not Atlantis that is the hero of the tale.

Gill makes another valid point in his assertion that the war initially described emphasizes the central theme of the *Republic*: 'that a ruling-class without private wealth is stable and united, and its state can defeat any enemy, however rich, whereas the possession of wealth by individual rulers creates disunity, and leads to political degeneration and political defeat.'[4]

Examining the theories other scholars put forward, Gill considers the suggestion that it was Minoan Crete to which Plato (or Solon) was referring, which might make sense in the light of the Thera episode, which we will be examining in Chapter 4. However, Gill questions how Plato came to have access to information regarding the extent of Minoan civilization and its ultimate fate, which was not generally known in his time. He notes that the Thera apologist J. V. Luce asserts that the story was indeed told to Solon by the Egyptians and that divergences between Minoan Crete and Atlantis obviously arose due to slight misunderstandings when Solon was receiving the information. Gill argues the implausibility of Luce's assumption on the grounds that the Athenians of the Classical period would have recognized a description of Minoan civilization for what it was, as they appear to have had a much clearer picture of Minoan Crete than did the Egyptians.

The technological innovations emphasized in the *Critias* seem to disturb many scholars, probably because the concept of a prehistoric civilization sporting some kind of advanced technology strains their credulity, to say the least. Magic, shamanism and allied practices were what went on in ancient times, and that was all, or so it is popularly believed in certain circles. However, my own research into early history and prehistory has tended to confirm the conclusions of lawyer and Cambridge Classics scholar John Ivimy, who wrote: 'Classical historians traditionally dismiss tales of magic as unworthy of scholarly attention, but to us any mention of a witch's broomstick or a wizard's wand evokes the smell of the scientist's laboratory.'[5]

Gill's book is entirely taken up with a critical dissection of the *Timaeus* and the *Critias* and, to be fair, many of the points he raises deserve consideration if one is to make an unbiased assessment of the Atlantis story. However, as the text itself (aside from his comments) is reproduced in the original Greek, those untutored in this language are advised to obtain a reliable English translation and apply Gill's observations thereto.

The Importance of Mythology

In spite of scholastic doubts and queries, correlations for Plato's claims are to be found in the ancient writings and traditions of other lands. There is, in general, evidence that seems to confirm the growing belief that myth, as such, is far from the fairy-tale it was formerly believed to be. While there is not enough space here to enumerate the many discoveries that have converted past myths to present realities, the following are significant examples: Herodotus's report of a treasure guarded by griffins, which Soviet scientists have located in the valley of Pazyrka; Petra, the desert city described by Eratosthenes, Pliny, Eusebius and others, which melted into legend; Heinrich Schliemann's Troy, which was housed on the site of an even older settlement; the fantastic walled city south of China, dismissed by Western scholars as pure fiction until its remains were stumbled upon in Angkor Thom in Kampuchea by French naturalist A. H. Mouhot.

The importance of myth as representing a vital strand in the web of consciousness that links us with the all-important collective unconscious is summarized by the great psychiatrist Carl Gustav Jung in the following words:

What we are to our inward vision, and what man appears to be *sub specie aeternitatis*, can only be expressed by way of myth. Myth is more individual and expresses life more precisely than does science. Science works with concepts of averages which are far too general to do justice to the subjective variety of an individual life.[6]

All myths, in fact, would appear to contain a grain of truth. The *Oera Linda Book*, rated as pure mythology by some authorities, contains the history of the ancient Frisian peoples prior to and after the Flood. The text tells us: 'Everywhere about the Rhine the people dug holes, and the sand that was got out was poured with water over fleeces to get the gold . . .'[7] So much for the Jason myth!

Among the other claims made in this extraordinary document are that:

● The Tex, the law of Atland, was the origin of democracy, and that subsequent laws became the basis of Old English common law.

● The Roman goddess Minerva was originally a real person – a Frisian princess, who founded the Athenian state.

● The Roman Temple of Vesta, with its attendant virgins, indirectly derived from Atland's first 'Earth Mother', Fasta, a high priestess who attended a perpetually burning lamp with magical qualities.

● The Druids – called Golen by the Frisian adventurers – were missionaries from Sidon.

● The Greek hero Ulysses visited Europe after the seige of Troy to wrest the 'magic lamp' of the Frisians from the priestess Kalip (Calypso).

● The Cretan law-giver Minos was none other than a Frisian sea king named Minno.[8]

These and other startling revelations are contained in Robert Scrutton's book *The Other Atlantis*, the author being careful to verify the authenticity of the *Oera Linda Book* and provide a history of its whereabouts to date. The Frisians also referred to the ancient Athenians as acknowledging the ascendancy of women and their equality before the law, the Frisians themselves being a matriarchal society whose women bore arms and often led their armies, as did the queens of ancient Celtica. Plato's reference to the worship of a mother goddess in the form of an arms-bearing effigy appears to be borne out by the Frisian account – the principal Frisian female adviser, who was responsible for all decisions of state, being referred to as the 'Mother'. These and other accounts in the *Oera Linda*

Book accord with Plato's narration, while also throwing a new light on many Classical writings.

Verification of the sinking of much of what was once the country of the ancient Frisians has been made public recently, although the dates given by geologists suggest that it took place much earlier than the 2193 BC date calculated from the ancient scripts. Apparently the land mass in question subsided in the second of two major upheavals that caused gigantic floods. A British television programme in 1989 showed that a layer of sand has been discovered in the North Sea off the coast of northern Scotland sandwiched between two layers of peat that were *above water* around 7,000 years ago, just as the Frisian legend describes. Needless to say, when the old Frisian manuscript, which was purportedly penned in AD 1256 from a compilation of ancient Frisian records, made its first appearance in 1871, the usual academic controversies raged. But, as is the case with most questionable antiquities that are brought to public notice after years of residence in some private archive, the polemic was soon forgotten and today the early Frisian and Dutch versions are out of print. Scrutton's comment is well worth study, however, and although the racial exaggerations in the original texts are highly obvious, the work does suggest that a great deal of mythology might in future years become transferred to the realm of fact.

I opened this chapter with a quote from Homer, which referred not to Atlantis but to Scheria, the island of the Phaeacians, as described in the *Odyssey*, which is defined as being somewhere in mid-ocean. Odysseus, it seems, was strangely connected with the Atlantic, and the description of the walls, harbour, ships and palaces in the Phaeacian city where Alcinous held court are vaguely reminiscent of Plato's Atlantis. Mention is made, for example, of the hero lingering spellbound before the palace, not daring to cross its 'golden threshold':

The palace ceilings shone like the sun and moon. Its walls were covered with copper. The gates were gold with silver lintels, silver posts and gold doorhandles. The great banqueting hall was lit by the flare of torches held in the hands of golden youths. Outside the palace was a marvellous garden . . . The Phaeacians were the best sailors in the world; but when they sailed Odysseus back to Ithaca, they aroused the wrath of Poseidon, who had already done his best to drown him on the voyage from Calypso's island and would have succeeded but for the timely intervention of Athene. Alcinous realized that Poseidon had his knife into the Phaeacians because the Phaeacian ship which was returning to Scheria after taking Odysseus back to Ithaca was 'smitten in to a rock of her own size and shape quite close to the shore'.[9]

Shades of some seismic disturbance, which, no doubt, left the ship in question either embedded in lava or buried by falling rocks!

The island of Calypso, which is well referenced in the *Oera Linda Book*, also appears to have been in the Atlantic Ocean, a twenty-day sail from the Phaeacian isles. Odysseus, when journeying to the traditional land of Hades, the abode of the dead, 'reached the far confines of Oceanus' beyond the Pillars of Hercules.[10] Odysseus's wanderings, in fact, appeared to involve a prolonged struggle with Poseidon, who was credited with being the founder and principal god of Atlantis. Perhaps Homer is recalling poetically a vague memory of a much earlier drama, in which he casts his hero in the leading role? In fact, James Bramwell comments on this very point when he draws our attention to the fundamental, as well as the superficial, resemblance between Homer's Scheria and Plato's Atlantis, which he sees as indicative of a considerably older convention that could not have come to Plato's attention through Greek tradition and must therefore have originated, as Solon said, in Egypt.

Plato's Dilemma

When he was nearing the end of his life, Plato apparently wrote a letter to some friends in Sicily in which, Ivimy tells us, he declared that 'the truths he had at heart he had never written down because they could not have been understood except perhaps by a few who might be intelligent enough to discover them for themselves.'[11] From this we may gather that the truths referred to were those inner mysteries that Pythagoras taught his *mathematici*. Pythagoras, known to his contemporaries as 'the Master of Samos', and reputedly the inventor of the words 'philosophy' and 'cosmos', achieved a unique union between science and religion that metaphysicians would probably argue was unconsciously brought through from Atlantis. Pythagoras divided his pupils into two classes, the initiated and the uninitiated. To the second category he applied the term *acusmatici*, which has been freely translated as 'those who hear with their ears but do not understand', while to the fully initiated he applied the term *mathematici* – 'those who learn and understand'. All men of wisdom in ancient times took great care to ensure that metaphysical secrets were never explicitly revealed. Could it be that this late statement of Plato's encapsulates his reason for the precipitous cessation of the Atlantis dialogues?

There has been much speculation as to why the philosopher ceased his narrative so abruptly and at a point in the story that leaves the reader suspended, in much the fashion that modern episodic television dramas tend to end their weekly offerings with a situation calculated to retain the curiosity of the viewer for the following week. Did Plato deliberately leave his readers hanging in this way? I hardly think so.

Let us consider a few alternatives for Plato's sudden abandonment of a fascinating tale at a point where the continuance of the story might equally well apply to the situation today:

- Political expediency;

- Prevention of the disclosure of certain metaphysical secrets;

- An illness (or even the advent of his demise) that obliged him to rest, after which he never returned to completing the work;

- He did actually complete it, but some person or persons unknown saw fit to remove the explanation.

I feel intuitively inclined to suggest the last option, but as there is not a shred of evidence to support my feelings, the reader is left to draw his or her own conclusions.

It has been suggested that one problem with which both Plato and Solon might have wrestled and that could, perhaps, account for the fact that both men left it rather late in life to tell their story, was that the traditional Greek underworld, or Hades, was believed to exist in the far west, where the Sun sank into the sea. So how could that location house an entire solid continent, peopled by ordinary human beings, far removed from the world of spirit? The sacrosanct dogmas of the old Greek religion also maintained that the Earth, which lay in the centre of Okeanos, was the only abode of life as we know it, all realms beyond constituting part of the regions of Hades, or the dead. This may also have accounted for the Atlantis story receiving little sympathy from Plato and Solon's contemporaries, although the historiographers Theopompus and Herodotus, the geographer Poseidonius and the natural scientist Pliny saw fit to salute their flag.

However, in a series of lectures entitled 'Astrology and Religion among the Greeks and Romans', which later appeared in book form, Professor Franz Cumont places Plato's eschatological beliefs in a rather different category. Citing the

Epinomis (which he concedes might well have been composed by Plato's pupil Philip of Opus) to support his views, Cumont comments on the fact that the Master obviously possessed a deep understanding of the metaphysical nature of the sidereal cults of his time, indicating a freedom from the limitations of traditional Greek religious dogma.

The Roman poet Ovid, who wrote about the great Flood, continues the unfinished chronicle for Plato:

There was such wickedness once on earth that Justice fled to the sky, and the king of the gods determined to make an end to the race of men . . . Jupiter's anger was not confined to his province in the sky. Neptune, his sea-blue brother, sent the waves to help him. Neptune smote the earth with his trident and the earth shivered and shook . . . Soon there was no telling land from sea. Under the water the sea nymphs Nereides were staring in amazement at woods, houses and cities. Nearly all men perished by water, and those who escaped the water, having no food, died of hunger.[12]

Nor is Ovid alone in his account. Flood legends among the peoples of many lands are indeed legion, and written references exist in the records of subsequent nations. King Assurbanipal of Assyria left to posterity on tablets of baked clay the statements that at his order his scribes had translated from books written *before* the Flood, in long dead languages, details of very ancient history. The Greek historian Strabo tells tales brought back by travellers 2,600 years before his time of Tartessos, a rich and powerful city and seaport on the south-western coast of Spain, whose written records went back 7,000 years before *their* time, which takes us to a period long before conventional history accepts the invention of writing!

Egypt

Some 900 years after Solon, the philosopher Proclus (AD 412–

85) commented at some length on the *Timaeus*. He states that 300 years after Solon's voyage to Egypt, which took place around 560 BC, a Greek by the name of Crantor also visited Sais and was shown the column in the temple of Neith, complete with its hieroglyphics recording the history of Atlantis. The Egyptian scholars made a translation for him and testified that their account was fully in agreement with Plato's, with which they were familiar. Although Egyptologists claim that they know of no such pillar or, in fact, the existence of any texts relating to the Atlantis episode, this is hardly a conclusive argument since Atlantis could have been mentioned many times in the innumerable documents that were lost when the vast libraries were pillaged and burned by the fanatical zealots of the new faiths that ultimately took hold in Europe and the Middle East. Dare we hope that some priceless scroll that will supply us with the necessary details may yet be found in the ruins of an ancient mud- or sand-covered temple or tomb? If there is any truth in the time-capsule theory, so beloved of modern metaphysicians and fringe scientists, the answer must be yes!

Regarding this theory, the Roman historian Ammianus Marcellinus (AD 330–400) wrote:

There are also subterranean passages and winding retreats, which, it is said, men skilful in the ancient mysteries, by means of which they divined the coming of the Flood, constructed in different places lest the memory of all their sacred ceremonies should be lost.[13]

The early origins of the Egyptian civilization have always been hotly debated by specialists. The historian Diodorus Siculus, writing in the first century AD, tells us:

The Egyptians were strangers, who, in remote times, settled on the banks of the Nile, bringing with them the civilization of their mother country, the art of writing, and a polished language. They had come from the direction of the setting sun and were the most ancient of men.[14]

Diodorus's comment was to receive confirmation in much later times by Professor W. B. Emery in his book *Archaic Egypt*:

... towards the end of the fourth millennium BC we find the people known traditionally as 'The Followers of Horus' apparently forming a civilized aristocracy or master race ruling over the whole of Egypt. The theory of the existence of this master race is supported by the discovery that graves of the late predynastic period in the northern part of Upper Egypt were found to contain the anatomical remains of a people whose skulls were of a greater size and whose bodies were larger than those of the natives, the difference being so marked that any suggestion that these people derived from the earlier stock is impossible ... The racial origin of these invaders is not known and the route they took in their penetration of Egypt is equally obscure.[15]

The legends of the Phoenicians, preserved by Sanchoniathon, speak of Taut or Thoth as being the inventor of the alphabet or art of writing. A passage in Manetho confirms this, telling of how, prior to the Deluge, Thoth (or Hermes Trismegistus) inscribed on stelae, or tablets, in hieroglyphics, or sacred characters, the principles of all the old knowledge. After the inundation, his successor translated the contents of these stelae into the language of the common people. Likewise, Josephus reports:

The patriarch Seth, in order that wisdom and astronomical knowledge should not perish, erected, in prevision of the double destruction by fire and water predicted by Adam, two columns, one of brick, the other of stone, on which this knowledge was engraved, and which existed in the Siriadic country [Egypt].[16]

Other Historical References

One modern critic observed that Atlantis was mentioned only by Plato and those who have read him. But as ethnological, archaeological, linguistic and allied disciplines extend their researches even farther back into the mists of prehistory, it has become increasingly evident that many earlier cultures independently have preserved in their traditions the memory of some great island continent whose peoples had achieved a state of technological advancement comparable to or even ahead of our own, albeit along different lines, and which suffered a major disaster, the effects of which registered across the entire planet.

Pomponius Mela (AD 80–?) strongly affirmed his belief in Atlantis, but placed it in the southern hemisphere, which is interesting in the light of evidence of a different nature that we shall be considering later. In his work entitled *Ethiopic History* Proclus mentions one Marcellus, of whom little else is known, as having spoken of ten islands situated in the Atlantic Ocean close to Europe, the inhabitants of which preserved the memory of a considerably larger land mass, Atlantis. Of these islands, seven were consecrated to Proserpina (Persephone), one to Pluto (Hades), one to Ammon (Jupiter?) and one, which was a thousand stadia long, to Poseidon.

Arnobius, a Christian apologist of Sicca, in Africa, in waxing poetic to the Christians of the period on the subject of previous calamities that had overcome nations and reduced great civilizations to ashes commented:

Did we bring it about, that ten thousand years ago, a vast number of men burst forth from the island which is called the Atlantis of Neptune, as Plato tells us, and utterly ruined and blotted our countless tribes?[17]

So much knowledge has indeed become lost!

Mercifully, the days have passed when individualistic specu-lation regarding the nature of our planet or the universe of which it constitutes an infinitesimal part could condemn one to the horrors of the torture chamber or stake. The dark curtain of ignorance that descended upon the civilized world after the fall of Rome could be blamed on the censorship imposed by new religions on the one hand, and the destruction of the great libraries of antiquity – Athens, Alexandria, Per-gamon, Syracuse, Carthage and Rome – on the other.

And so we have emerged from our caves of nescience to re-explore the world of our ancient ancestors in the light of a new religion, whose dogma is logic and whose white-coated priests conduct their sacerdotal affairs in the laboratories, re-search establishments and universities of life. The thumbscrews and racks of the past have been replaced by more subtle ways of seeing that we do not step out of line with established modes of thinking. Regretfully, there is still a line to be toed, and to neglect the required observances can cost a man or woman his or her means of livelihood, or at least self-respect. On the optimistic side, many people from all walks of life are daring to think for themselves, thus severing links with both the dogmas of the past and the socio-political demands of the present. May their lamps be illuminated by the Eternal Flame.

CHAPTER 4

Alternative Sites

Roll on, thou deep and dark blue Ocean – roll!
Ten thousand fleets sweep over thee in vain;
Man marks the earth with ruin – his control
Stops with the shore.

LORD BYRON, *Childe Harold's Pilgrimage*

Ian Wright, a design engineer and amateur archaeologist who I am privileged to count among my friends, has dedicated many years of research to the Atlantean project, including the investigation of several of the sites mentioned in this chapter. His findings, which he has obtained through a combination of normal scientific procedures and psychometry, accord with those of many of the other researchers to whose work I shall be referring. A statement made in one of his articles deserves mention, as it would seem to apply to many who have contributed to the Atlantean scenario from Plato to the present day:

In many of the natural sciences, the student is frequently faced with questions and situations to which, it may appear, there is little hope of answer or resolution within the confines of orthodoxy. However, there are two categories of seekers to whom these restrictions may not apply – firstly, the amateur, and secondly, the non-conformist. As an amateur he does not risk being professionally ostracised, or his career prejudiced by unconventional activity. Being a non-conformist he is probably well prepared to state an unorthodox case or follow a heretic path by weight of sheer conviction and personal faith. Such is the dividing line on one matter of antiquity, that of Atlantis – was it or wasn't it?

There would appear to be just as many people who do believe that Atlantis once existed as sceptics who do not, although there is a wide divergence of opinion as to where it was located. Let us assume, therefore, that Plato's legend did contain more than an element of truth and examine a few of the likely places that have been suggested as the original site of the vanished continent.

Thera (Santorini)

Thera, an island in the Greek Cyclades north of Crete in the Aegean, was the subject of much publicity in the late 1960s, when Professor A. G. Galanopoulos, an archaeologist and seismologist, and another archaeologist, Dr Spiridon Marinatos, announced their theory that it was the legendary Atlantis. The volcanic eruption that shook the island around 1500–1400 BC is believed to have contributed to the decline of the Cretan maritime empire, which seemed to bear many similarities to Plato's sunken civilization. The theme was later expanded by Dublin Classical scholar J. V. Luce in his book *The End of Atlantis – New Light on an Old Legend.*

Crete was at the peak of its power and prosperity when disaster dramatically struck, destroying the palace of Minos and many other Cretan cities and providing one of the great mysteries of prehistory. The Thera discoveries are believed to furnish the final solution to this historical enigma and, according to the above-mentioned authorities, lay the Atlantean ghost once and for all. Only a crescent-shaped shell of the former island now remains, but even assuming its original size, it hardly tallies with the dimensions given by Plato, while it would be difficult to reconcile the date proposed for its cataclysmic demise with that suggested by him.

Various excuses are given for this anomaly. The Egyptian priests, for example, are blamed for confusing the hieroglyphs for 100 and 1,000 when relating the story to Solon. Even taking this possible error into account, there are other details from Plato's narrative that do not fit into the Thera idea, notably the fleet, harbours, military power and population. Nor is Thera a new discovery. Ignatius Donnelly, considered by many as worthy of the Platonian mantle of 'father of Atlantology', wrote in the last century:

The Gulf of Santorin, in the Grecian Archipelago, has been for two thousand years a scene of active volcanic operations. Pliny informs us that in the year 186 BC, the Island of 'Old Kaimeni', or the Sacred Isle, was lifted up from the sea; and in AD 19 the island of 'Thia' (the Divine) made its appearance. In AD 1573 another island was created, called 'the small sunburnt island'. In 1848 a volcanic convulsion of three months' duration created a great shoal; an earthquake destroyed many houses in Thera, and the sulphur and hydrogen issuing from the sea killed 50 persons and 1,000 domestic animals. A recent examination of these islands shows that the whole mass of Santorin *has sunk, since its projection from the sea, over 1,200 feet* [457 metres].[1]

In fact, Donnelly devotes a whole chapter to the many islands and larger land masses that have risen and disappeared. One particular reference caught my eye, in which he mentions the history and growth of the European continent as recounted by Professor Geikie, who gave some instructive illustration of the relationship between geography and geology. The earliest European land, Professor Geikie claimed, appears to have existed in the north and north-west, comprising Scandinavia, Finland and the north-west of the British area, and to have extended thence through boreal and arctic latitudes of North America (see Lurasia p. 71).

Andrew Tomas also produces a similarly impressive catalogue of geological comings and goings, including Krakatoa, which exploded in 1883; the Etruscan city of Spina in the Adriatic, which, according to Pliny the Elder and Strabo, was once a thriving metropolis; Dioscuria in the Black Sea, which was visited by the Argonauts; Phanagoria, an old Greek maritime city also in the Black Sea, and many, many more. No doubt this list could be considerably extended in the light of more recent knowledge.

I do not for one moment doubt the worthy professor's claim that Thera, or Santorini, was partly destroyed by a seismic disturbance about 1500 BC, as this is attested to in the records of surrounding cultures, quite a few other areas also having experienced the rumblings of Vulcan around that time. Nor do I dispute his claims that the island once housed an advanced culture, the evidence of which has been found under 130 feet (40 metres) of volcanic ash. The date given suggests a Minoan rather than an Atlantean connection, however, but as many students of the subject believe that the Minoan civilization was founded on the teachings of Atlantean colonists who arrived in the Aegean several thousand years earlier, an Atlantean connection could broadly be implied.

Tartessos, Southern Spain – Northern Morocco

Referred to in the Bible as Tharshish, Tartessos possessed a fine fleet, which supplied luxury goods to the kings and potentates of the period, notably Solomon himself. 'Once in three years came the navy of Tharshish, bringing gold, and silver, ivory, apes, and peacocks. So King Solomon exceeded all the kings of the earth for riches . . .'[2]

Herodotus (fifth century BC) also referred to a great city called Tartessos, beyond the Pillars of Hercules, which must have at some time been considered a colony, if not an actual part, of Atlantis itself. The city mysteriously disappeared, however. Whether this was caused by some natural catastrophe or the result of sudden conquest and annihilation by the Carthaginians is open to conjecture. I doubt very much if Tartessos was Atlantis or even a part of it; more likely a minor colony that grew rich through trading with the surrounding nations.

Tunisia

More than one explorer has eyed Tunisia as a possible site for Atlantis. In 1926 the German archaeologist Dr Paul Borchard placed it in the region that was formerly known as 'Little Syrta' in the Gulf of Gabes. Borchard deduced the salt lake Schott el Hammeina to be one and the same as a place known in earlier times as both the Lake of Atlantes and Lake Tritonis, the latter title suggesting an association with the legend of Triton, son of Poseidon and Amphitrite, who, Hesiod tells us, dwelt with his parents in a golden palace under the sea. Near the seaward side of Lake Tritonis was an island called Poseidon's Island, which convinced Borchard even further that he was on the right track. Some of the ruins he took to be remnants of a prehistoric city, however, were subsequently proven to have been of Roman origin.

Another Tunisian protagonist, German archaeologist Dr Albert Hermann, undeterred by Borchard's disappointment, continued to look for Atlantis in southern Tunisia. Working on the assumption that the measurements given by Plato were erroneous due to a translation error, the central plain of Tunisia, which was once believed to have been an island, appeared to fit. The lofty cities, grand canals and great harbours were reduced to the status of village dwellings, irrigation ditches and small inlets. It is amazing to what lengths some people will go to prove their pet theories! To be fair to both the aforementioned scientists, however, there is a local tradition of a powerful kingdom that disappeared under the sea in the distant past, but it would be surprising if this were not so, since there is ample evidence to suggest that most of that area underwent drastic changes in prehistoric times.

West Africa and East Africa

Olukun, the Yoruba god of the ocean, shares many of the attributes of Plato's Poseidon. This, among other facts, led German archaeologist Leo Frobinius to believe that it was Yorubaland and other sites along the Nigerian coast that fuelled the imaginations of the Phoenician sailors who returned from their voyages with strange tales of mysterious civilizations across the oceans.

According to Egyptian records, the legendary lands of Punt and Ophir, to which both the Phoenicians and Hebrews sent their fleets in search of rare jewels, exotic oils and other trading goods, were situated down the east coast of Africa. Although the tales of these cities might be seen by some as placing them in the Atlantean category, there would seem to be little evidence to suggest that they suffered the kind of catastrophic ending usually associated with the disappearance of the old island continent. Besides, the sources from which these stories derive would appear to place them at a much later period than that suggested by Plato and most other Atlantologists, which obliges me to dismiss them from the serious Atlantean scene.

The North Sea

In 1953 German pastor and scholar Jurgen Spanuth organized a diving expedition to search for evidence of Atlantis under the North Sea in the firm belief that Plato's story related to a great northern civilization that sank beneath those icy waters. The people of these long-lost lands were, Spanuth believed, those same seafaring people who sent an expeditionary force to invade Egypt around 1200 BC, details of which were depicted on the temple walls at Medinet Habu. The *Oera Linda Book*, which contains the traditional, if unattested, history of the Frisian peoples, appears to agree with this premise and other claims Spanuth makes in his book *Atlantis of the North*. But to return to Spanuth's divers: did they find anything of consequence? Parallel rock walls coloured black, white and red were sighted near Heligoland at a depth of 45 feet (13.7 metres), and flint implements of Stone Age type were later brought to the surface by the divers. The colour combination of the rocks confirmed Spanuth's belief that he had, in fact, located Plato's Atlantis, as the red/white/black rock description also appears in the legends of other lands, notably in parts of America, when old tales of Atlan or Aztlan are recounted. Spanuth tells us:

The 'pillars of heaven' stood – as I have shown – under the pole star. The god of these world-pillars was known to the Egyptians as 'Tat', to the Greeks as 'Atlas', and to the German peoples as 'Irmin' (who is called Iormun in the *Eddas*). All these people believed that the heaven-bearing god stood in the far north. This is why the Egyptians said of him: 'I am Tat, son of Tat, born in the distant darkness.' The Greeks said of Atlas:

> '. . . And here stand the terrible houses
>   Of dark Night,

> . . . Before them
> Atlas, son of Iapetos, stands
>   Staunchly upholding
> The wide heaven upon his head
>   And with arms unwearing
>   Sustains it . . .'
>
> HESIOD, *Theogony*, 746f[3]

Spanuth continues to make his point with various Classical quotes concerning the land of the Hyperboreans, which was said to lie in the Atlantic 'opposite the land of the Celts' to the north. The events related by Plato he sees as also taking place in the second half of the thirteenth century BC, when severe natural catastrophes, precipitated by the approach of a comet (Plato's Phaëthon?), caused dramatic changes in climate. Therefore, the great invasion at the end of the thirteenth century BC (supposedly carried out by Atlanteans), which extended as far as Egypt, and the successful resistance of the Athenians mentioned by Plato could well relate to the arrival of the 'sea people from the north', or Frisians, who were, according to W. Witter, an expert in prehistoric metallurgy, among the first to use iron weapons.[4]

Spanuth's deductions appear to confirm the views of many Classical scholars that Plato's narrative relates to *two different periods of history*. In other words, the philosopher (or Solon, perhaps?) superimposed episodes from the annals of Athens over the ancient tale told by the Egyptian priests. The Egyptian invasion referred to therefore accords with history and accounts for the warring people whom Plato believed to be Atlanteans, while also accommodating the stories of the Frisians, who purportedly founded Athens and made their presence felt in Egypt, Crete and other flourishing towns and cities of that period.

The fact that the sinking of the Frisian lands in the north (and the simultaneous sudden change of climate in those parts)

has been confirmed scientifically to have taken place around
5000 BC lends credence to Richard Mooney's suggestion that
although what is referred to as Würm Glaciation has been
estimated to have ended some 10,000 years ago, in Antarctica
glaciation appears to have commenced some 6,000 years ago.
he tells us:

We have theorized, from the evidence, that there was no Ice Age,
or Ice Ages; that, on the contrary, *the present is the period of glaciation*
due to a deterioration in the earth's climate. From the evidence at
hand, we can approximate a time scale for the date of the catastrophe.
The upper limit can be set at 8000 BC and the lower limit at around
4000 BC. It would seem that we could narrow it down to around
6000 BC, for the first traces of settled urban communities date from
that time: the oldest so far excavated are the town sites of Catal
Huyuk and Jericho on the Anatolian plain in Turkey.[5]

The explanation of this is contained in the astonishing
results of the research undertaken by Dr Charles Hapgood,
Professor of Geology at the University of New Hampshire,
and published in his book *Maps of the Ancient Sea Kings*. The
poles, it seems, have moved on more than one occasion, and
the positions they occupied during the Würm period are not
the same as those we know today. In fact, at that time the
South Pole was not located in Antarctica, nor was the North
Pole in its present position. But now we are talking about
axis tilts, which form the subject matter of Chapter 6, in
which the picture will, I hope, be made abundantly clear.

Spanuth's Hyperborean Atlantis and the Atland of the *Oera
Linda Book* are obviously one and the same place, which
flourished as a maritime nation up to and following the late
thirteenth millennium BC, and can possibly be equated with
the legendary Thule. However, according to the *Oera Linda
Book*, the estimated time of the sinking of their main land
mass was 2193 BC. How exactly did they arrive at this date?
To quote from Robert Scrutton's book *The Other Atlantis*:

The *Oera Linda Book* begins with two introductory letters, each intended for its subsequent custodians. I give them here in full. The first, is by Hiddo Over de Linda and is dated AD 1256:

Okke my son –
'*You must preserve these books with body and soul. They contain the history of all our people, as well as of our forefathers. Last year I saved them in the flood, as well as you and your mother; but they got wet, and therefore began to perish. In order not to lose them, I copied them on foreign paper. In case you inherit them, you must copy them likewise, and your children must do so too, so that they may never be lost.*
'*Written at Liuwert, in the three thousand four hundred and forty-ninth year after Atland was submerged – that is, according to the Christian reckoning, the year 1256.*
> '*Hiddo, surnamed Over de Linda – Watch.*'

It is this first letter which establishes clearly the date of the sinking of the Atland continent – 2193 BC (3449 – 1256 = 2193).[6]

Having read the account as Scrutton has presented it, which obviously spans a period of many thousand years, I find the precision of this date questionable, recent archaeological evidence, which I have already mentioned in Chapter 3, indicating that the area in question was above water around 7,000 years ago. This would suggest that the old Atland of the Frisians actually went down around 5000 BC, a date that will prove both interesting and evidential as my inquiries slowly unfold.

According to the *Oera Linda Book*, these early Frisians were exceptionally tall, fair and blue-eyed. Their society was matriarchal and highly law-abiding, the progenitor of their race, whose name was Frya (Freya?) having taught them self-control, the love of virtue and the value of liberty. Other rules laid down for this early Frisian society have a decidedly Atlantean ring about them, although more in keeping with the golden days of Cronus's rule than the latter-day degeneracy described by Plato. We are told that after the sinking of their land many of the inhabitants fled south and intermarried with the races that lived in 'Twiskland' (Germany), 'Schoonland' (Scandinavia) and 'Magy' (the land of the Magyars). It was the descendants of these people who became the 'sea peoples of the north' and were responsible for the later invasions and attacks chronicled by Plato and other historical sources. The original Atland was probably a colony of old Atlantis, its people bearing a striking resemblance in height and colouring to those 'tall, fair strangers' who appeared both sides of the Atlantic to teach the indigenous populations the advantages of civilization. But more of that in a later chapter, as we have still a few sites to consider before we finally focus our inquiry on the mid-Atlantic ridge.

The Americas

Francis Bacon, the English philosopher, politician and Lord Chancellor (1561–1626), first Earl of Verulam and Viscount St Albans, was one of the first British writers to associate the Atlantis legend with the Americas. Bacon based his assumption on Plato's reference to an 'opposite continent', while similarities between the languages, customs and architecture of certain parts of America and the Old World, which had been noted and reported by Spanish colonizers, were seen as supportive of this idea. However, although the ocean has reclaimed large tracts of the eastern seaboard, the Americas could hardly be described as 'sunken', being very much in evidence today!

YUCATAN AND CENTRAL AMERICA

Many scholars have observed enough similarities between the

Mayan art forms, culture and science and those of ancient Egypt to conclude that both nations must have drawn their inspiration from a single source – Atlantis. One very valuable document that we have inherited from the annals of the Mayans is the *Codex Troanus*, which is preserved in the British Museum. Two early French *americanistes*, the Abbé Brasseur de Bourbourg and Auguste Le Plongeon, claimed to have deciphered one fragment of this codex, which, according to the Abbé, contains a striking testimonial to the catastrophe that ultimately demolished the island continent. The lands referred to, however, are Mu and Moud, while the date given for this occurrence is 8,060 years before the codex was compiled. The text runs thus:

On the sixth day of Can, in the Eleventh Muluc in the month of Zac, occurred dreadful earthquakes and continued until the thirteenth Chuen. The land of Clay Hills Mu and the land Moud were the victims. They were shaken twice and in the night suddenly disappeared. The earth crust was continually raised and lowered in many places by the subterranean forces until it could not resist such stresses, and many countries became separated one from another by deep crevices. Finally both provinces could not resist such tremendous stresses and sank in the ocean together with 64,000,000 inhabitants. It occurred 8,060 years ago.[7]

This translation was treated with considerable scepticism by the scientific establishment, as was a similar 'discovery' by Le Plongeon, who used old Egyptian hieratic writing to decipher an inscription on the pyramid of Xochicalco, in Mexico, which he claimed read: 'A land in the ocean is destroyed and its inhabitants killed in order to transform them into dust.'[8]

Braghine is of the opinion that in a remote epoch prior to the last glacial period the Earth was inhabited by a world-wide race, which exerted a considerable influence on posterity. He does not consider the Atlanteans to have been this un-known race, and I am inclined to agree. Legend has it that the continent of Atlantis was once part of a greater land mass that stretched across to the Pacific Ocean, which has been given the name of Mu (the Motherland?), later named Lemuria by the scientist Sclater.

TIAHUANACO, BOLIVIA

Some 11–12,000 years ago the Cyclopean city of Tiahuanaco was a thriving seaport that was thrust 2 miles (3 kilometres) up to become part of the Andes plateau. Several experts, notably Arthur Poznansky, put forward this amazing theory, which is well supported by the presence of calcified salt-water marine plants that appear as a watermark on vast stretches of the surrounding mountains. The architecture of the old ruins also suggests a knowledge of astronomy, while the prehistoric animals depicted on pottery and other artefacts would seem to confirm this as one of the world's earliest civilizations. But was it Atlantis? Not really. Surely its present and former locations confirm the information Brasseur de Bourbourg supposedly extracted from the *Codex Troanus*, which prompts one to think that the wily Abbé was neither as simple or deluded as the 'experts' would have us believe!

BRAZIL

I have often wondered what would happen if the Earth's axis tilted yet again, producing a warm climate in lands that are now cold, and vice versa. What a picking there would be for the archaeologists in the jungles of Brazil! Charles Berlitz makes the following interesting observation:

The very name *Brazil* contains a strange memory or knowledge shared with cultures on the other side of the ocean. According to legends current in Western Europe before the discovery of America,

Brazil or Hy Brazil was the name of a land across the unexplored Atlantic. Then, when Brazil was eventually discovered, it was given the name of the legend. But the name seemed to contain a message, as B–R–Z–L means *iron* in Hebrew and also in Aramaic, the one-time general language of Mesopotamia and the Levant. And only much later did it become evident that Brazil possessed the largest iron ore deposits in the world.[9]

In spite of all this, I do not see Brazil as Atlantis. Mu, perhaps, or part thereof.

Antarctica

Strangely, I find this hypothesis quite logical. After all, according to Frisian records, parts of northern Europe and Greenland enjoyed a warm, temperate climate, while Hapgood's maps are evidence that Antarctica was equally free of ice, in which case it would have provided an admirable environment for the growth and development of a maritime culture.

Our present century has witnessed the rediscovery of a number of maps (see Chapter 11) that have been copied and recopied from charts that go back thousands of years, several of which show Antarctica as being ice-free. And why not? If the poles have shifted, and I firmly believe this to be the case, those regions that are now ice-bound might well have been warm, while those much talked of 'ice ages' afflicted what are at present more temperate zones. I am fully aware that this opens up a whole new field of inquiry as far as the location of Atlantis is concerned, but more of that shortly.

The Sahara Desert

The Sahara was once part of an ocean that later became a lake and then a verdant area fit for human habitation, prior to becoming the desert we see today. According to Berlitz, a radar scan taken in November 1981 by the space shuttle *Columbia* over south-west Egypt and the Sudan at an altitude of 125 miles (201 kilometres) and covering a width of 30 miles (48 kilometres) or more, when enhanced by computer techniques, showed some surprising results. There are beds of buried rivers, some as large as the Nile, with smaller, tributaries, but with indications of having flowed from south to west. All this goes to confirm those early 'myths' of a time when the Sahara was a fertile and well-populated area.

Since so many changes, some of which were drastic, obviously took place in northern Africa, it is advisable to keep an open mind when considering what the historians tell us concerning life in pre-dynastic Egypt. New discoveries might yet demand some rewriting of the history books! In spite of this, there is scant evidence of an Atlantean-type civilization in the Sahara area on the scale described by Plato and confirmed by the myths of other lands. Berlitz mentions that Count Byron Kuhn de Porok (*Mysterious Sahara*) led a series of expeditions to the least-known parts of the Sahara in search of Atlantean clues among the desert tribes in those areas, but whether he discovered anything other than the fact that the Tuaregs have knowledge of a language of great antiquity, aside from their spoken tongue, we are not told. Atlantis in the Sahara? I hardly think so.

Many other places and peoples are believed to have Atlantean connections – the Etruscans, for example, whose lands in Tyrrhenia formed part of Plato's great Atlantean empire. In fact, any place with a history of some strange ancient culture or language is a likely candidate for Atlantean or Muan hypotheses. Legends of sunken islands and continents in the Pacific Ocean have also been considered; an old Hawaiian legend tells of how 'our motherland rests . . . at the bottom of the Royal Ocean.'[10]

Ignatius Donnelly speaks of the submergence of Atlantis as being the last of a number of vast changes by which the continent in the Atlantic Ocean slowly sank while new lands were rising on both sides of it. The entire area of Great Britain, he tells us, was once submerged to the depth of at least 1,700 feet (510 metres), only to rise again from the sea, bearing water deposits as evidence of the fact. Donnelly quotes the ominous words of Professor Winchell (*The Preadamites*, p.437):

We are in the midst of great changes, and are scarcely conscious of it. We have seen worlds in flames, and have felt a comet strike the earth. We have seen the whole coast of South America lifted up bodily ten or fifteen feet [3 or 4.5 metres] and let down again in an hour. We have seen the Andes sink 220 feet [67 metres] in seventy years. . . . Vast transpositions have taken place in the coast-line of China. The ancient capital, located, in all probability, in an accessible position near the centre of the empire, has now become nearly surrounded by water, and its site is on the peninsula of Corea . . .

There was a time when the rocky barriers of the Thracian Bosphorus gave way and the Black Sea subsided. It had covered a vast area in the north and east. Now this area became drained, and was known as the ancient Lectonia: it is now the prairie region of Russia and the granary of Europe.[11]

Although this was written in the last century, its message is as valid today and maybe more so in light of the much discussed 'greenhouse effect'. But was it then, as Plato insists, as it is now, humanity rather than nature who stands accused of courting catastrophe?

Dr Bruce Heezen, oceanographer with the Lamont Geological Observatory of Columbia University, draws our attention to the fact that 11,000 years ago the sea-level all round the world was some 300 feet (91 metres) lower than it is today, the eastern coastline of the United States, for example, being 100 miles (161 kilometres) farther out in the Atlantic Ocean. But the sudden ending of the Ice Age caused enormous quantities of snow and ice to melt and run into the oceans, resulting in a dramatic rise in sea-levels world-wide. This rise, Heezen tells us, caused the flooding of many low-level seaside communities.[12] As Berlitz reminds us, it was the Greek historians who suggested that cataclysmic ends to great civilizations occurred approximately once every 10,000 years – a little

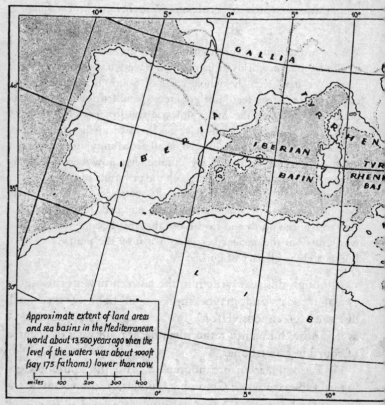

Fig. 5. Probable distribution of land and water before the formation of the Mediterranean.

arithmetic applied here might serve to make us feel a trifle uncomfortable!

But could it *really* happen again today? If we are to place any credence on the new science of chaos, the answer must be yes! Today, tomorrow, the next day, maybe, but most certainly sometime. And when it does, it could occur as swiftly as the catastrophe that caused the raging seas to engulf a thriving island continent all those thousands of years ago. But what have I said? All *how* many thousands of years ago? Read on!

CHAPTER 5

The Atlantic Ocean

> The utmost bounds of earth far off I see
> Where Thetys and Old Ocean boast to be
> The parents of the gods.

HOMER

Having examined several alternative locations for Atlantis, let us turn our attention to the pros and cons of its most popular placing, in the Atlantic Ocean.

Searching for Atlantis in the ocean to which it gave its name (or the other way around according to some authorities) is treated with a degree of amusement and more than a modicum of intolerance from oceanographers and archaeologists in general. Even established scientists with unimpeachable reputations are viewed as having thrown their lot in with the 'lunatic fringe' once they start asking questions or doing serious research into an Atlantis project. This attitude is succinctly summed up in the words of N. Susemihl, a specialist in Platonic studies: 'The catalogue of statements about Atlantis is a fairly good aid for the study of human madness,'[1] the inference being that anyone who does not fall in with his (or the Establishment's) views on the subject is a suitable case for treatment, if not actually highly dangerous to society! I am reminded of a comment made by Professor Hans Eysenck and Dr Carl Sargent in *Explaining the Unexplained* concerning the psychology of irrational belief as pertaining to the attitude of the great scientist Hermann von Helmholtz, who was heard to say:

Neither the testimony of all the Fellows of the Royal Society, nor even the evidence of my own senses, would lead me to believe in the transmission of thought from one person to another independent of the recognized channels of sense . . . My mind is made up, and no evidence is going to change it![2]

On the other hand, Einstein, who was a scientist of a different calibre, was once asked 'How are discoveries made?', to which he replied, 'When all the scientists present have agreed that something is impossible, one arrives late for their meeting and solves the impossible.'[3] The inference is that the majority of people, and that includes scientists, are conditioned (I prefer the term 'programmed') by the collective, and it takes a brave man or woman to break from that group thinking or, as Jung would say, individuate. Another famous saying of Einstein's was 'Imagination is greater than knowledge', which brings us back full circle to Atlantis.

Evidence from the Sea-bed

Reason demands that we accord full acknowledgment to empirical research, so what is the evidence for and against the Old Country lying submerged in the deep caverns of Neptune? Is there, for example, any tangible proof from the ocean floor to suggest that there might conceivably be some truth in Plato's story?

Ignatius Donnelly stated that in his lifetime (he died in 1901) there was ample evidence from the sea-bed to suggest that Plato's island does lie submerged in the Atlantic, and that the islands of the Azores were formerly the peaks of its highest mountains. He tells us:

Deep-sea soundings have been made by ships of different nations; the United States ship *Dolphin*, the German frigate *Gazelle*, and the British ships *Hydra*, *Porcupine*, and *Challenger* have mapped out the bottom of the Atlantic, and the result is the revelation of a great elevation, reaching from a point on the coast of the British Islands southwardly to the coast of South America, at Cape Orange, thence south-eastwardly to the coast of Africa and thence southwardly to Tristan d'Acunha. [See Figure 6.] . . . It rises about 9,000 feet [2,743 metres] above the great Atlantic depths around it, and in the Azores, St Paul's Rocks, Ascension, and Tristan d'Acunha it reaches the surface of the ocean. [See Figure 7.]

Evidence that this elevation was once dry land is found in the fact that 'the inequalities, the mountains and valleys of its surface, could never have been produced in accordance with any laws for the deposition of sediment, nor by submarine elevation; but, on the contrary, must have been carved by agencies *acting above the water level.*' (*Scientific American*, July 28th, 1877.)[4]

William Gladstone, who was Prime Minister of Great Britain when Donnelly's book was published, although already a believer in Atlantis, was so impressed by the book that he sent Donnelly a letter of appreciation, and requested Parliament to approve the use of the Royal Navy to search for the lost continent. However, as luck would have it, Her Imperial Majesty's fleet was otherwise engaged on matters of national urgency, which was a great pity since the climate of opinion at that time was decidedly pro-Atlantean.

Continental Drift

The Central American books translated by Brasseur de Bourboug appear to agree that part of the American continent

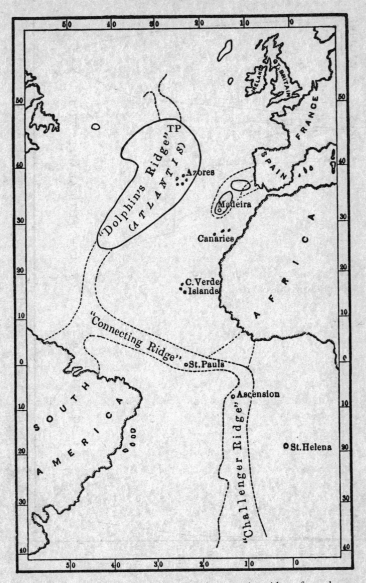

Fig. 6. Map of Atlantis with its islands and connecting ridges, from deep-sea soundings. TP indicates the location of Telegraph Plateau (see p. 76).

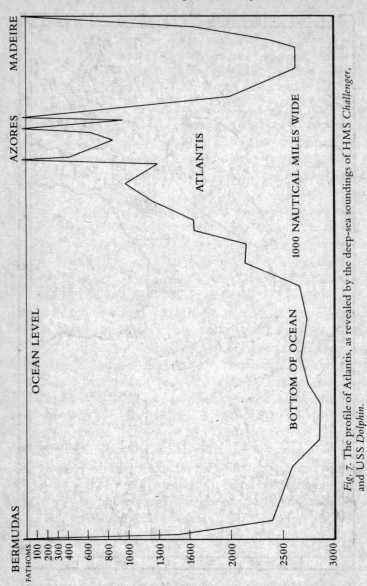

Fig. 7. The profile of Atlantis, as revealed by the deep-sea soundings of HMS *Challenger*, and USS *Dolphin*.

formerly extended far into the Atlantic Ocean, a belief that was confirmed by the explorations of the *Challenger*. These produced evidence that the Dolphin's Ridge was connected with the shore of South America north of the mouth of the Amazon. Donnelly tells us that the geologists of his time were happy to agree that the land from which America and Europe were formed once covered much of the space now occupied by the Atlantic Ocean. This brings us round to one of the major arguments against there ever having been a continent in the Atlantic – the Wegener theory of continental drift.

Geologists believe that prior to their separation some 200 million years ago all the continents of the world were grouped together in a single land mass, which is known in geology as Pangaea (from the Greek word meaning 'all earth'). At the end of the Palaeozoic era, Pangaea split into two sections, Gondwanaland, which is the name ascribed to the hypothetical southern portion, which consisted of Africa, South America, India, Arabia, Australia, Madagascar, New Guinea, the Malay Peninsula, Indonesia and Antarctica; and Lurasia, the northern portion, which comprised North America, Greenland, Europe and Asia (excluding the Indian subcontinent). Lurasia itself split during the Mesozoic era, into North America and Eurasia. The German zoologist Ernst Haeckel saw Gondwanaland as being synonymous with the legendary continent of Lemuria, although it is more likely that the Lemuria or Mu of myth was much smaller and probably lay in the region of, or near, the west coast of South America.

Beneath the Earth's outer shell, or lithosphere, there is a molten layer called the asthenosphere, through which slow convection currents exercised their force on Pangaea, causing it to break into separate pieces. The lithosphere is composed of a number of rigid plates colliding, growing apart or sliding past each other in continuous and measurable movement.

When continental plates collide, the Earth's crust buckles and mountains are formed, while ocean ridges occur where molten rock rises through a rift in the ocean floor to form the new lithosphere. Geologists refer to the oceanic crust, composed mainly of rocks containing silica and magnesia, as sima; and to the continental crust, composed of rocks rich in silica and alumina, as sial.

It was in 1912 that Dr Alfred Wegener (1880–1930), a German geologist, first recognized the clues and put forward his theory of continental drift, which no one seemed to take very seriously at the time. Wegener postulated that in the Early Tertiary epoch there was no wide expanse of water between the Old and New Worlds, but only a single, homogenous continent, which later separated into the platforms now shown as the continents on modern maps. He also hypothesized that changes in the Earth's axial spin from time to time could bring about new directions of continental drift, and pointed to the westerly movements of the continents as evidence of this spin effect.

In 1972 Dr Leon Knopoff and Dr A. Leed, of the University of California at Los Angeles, reported in *Science* the motion of the ten major crustal plates and confirmed the present tendency towards a westerly drift. Apparently, in the past the movements of the continents were northerly or southerly and unrelated to present spin.[5] In his book *The Earthquake Generation*, Jeffrey Goodman writes, 'One of the most important anomalies that pole shift can explain is the periodic reversal of the earth's magnetic axis', and quotes Drs Allan Cox, Brent Dalrymple and Richard Doell, three of the United States Geographical Society's top scientists, as stating: 'After centuries of research the earth's magnetic field remains one of the best described and least understood of all planetary phenomena.'[6]

However, what really worries many modern scientists about

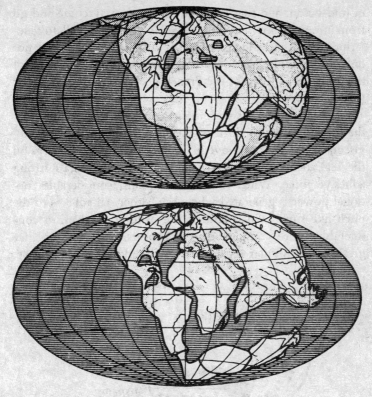

Fig. 8. Map showing Alfred Wegener's theory of continental drift and the origins of the Atlantic Ocean.

the Atlantis theory is the swiftness with which the continent was supposed to have sunk, which runs counter to the concepts of gradualist geology and to Sir Charles Lyell's theory that changes in the Earth's surface are caused solely by minute forces. These ideas have been popularly accepted for nearly a century. Their adherents believe that major subsidences, such as those registered along the Dutch coast, would *never* occur in mid-ocean, and that while small islands may come and go from time to time, anything vaguely resembling Plato's description of the sudden demise of a whole continent is not only unthinkable, but constitutes an irresponsible reversion of the cataclysm theory of the French geologist Georges Cuvier (1769–1832).

Otto Muck concurs with the general scientific opinion that the upper platforms float on the underlying, denser, plastic-viscous sima, and can move in it only slowly, like 'icebergs on the sea', because they are held by the gluey sima's strong adhesive force. When the platforms shift, considerable frictional power is generated where the harder sial adheres to the pitch-like sima, which renders the drifting mechanism considerably more complex than it appears, and its effects far greater. The secular separations of the platforms of Europe,

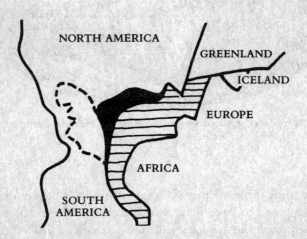

Fig. 9. The shelves match the Atlantic Ridge. In rectangular parallel projection, the map shows the Early Tertiary position of the shelves before the first continental drift began. The shelves are a perfect fit of the edges of the Atlantic Ridge. Only the black patch in the North American basin indicates a subsequent subsidence of the land.

America and Greenland, he tells us, have been accurately measured and show a gradual widening of the Atlantic.

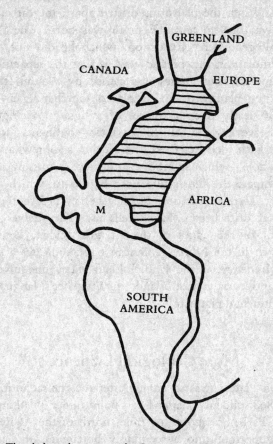

Fig. 10. The shelves do not match. Contrary to Wegener's drawings, the shelves match only in the South Atlantic – South American and Africa – but not in the North Atlantic, which plays a much more important role in the problem of Atlantis. Here a 'black patch', a hole north-east of the structural basin of Mexico (M), is found between Africa and Europe on one side and Canada on the other. The shelves in the North Atlantic cannot be matched without due allowance for the Atlantic Ridge.

According to the Wegener school, the existence of Atlantis would have been simulated only by a pre-Tertiary land bridge between the Canadian shield and the Eurasian platform. When the platforms drifted apart, the direct connection was broken and the myth was born. The theory behind Wegener's reconstruction, which he did not, however, formulate in this precise way, is that the separation of the continental land masses was caused by a clean fracture between the platforms. So, if placed together again, they should fit neatly like the pieces of a jigsaw. As Figure 9 shows, however, the North Atlantic continents do not oblige us with such exactness, there being a somewhat questionable 'hole', which signifies that a piece is missing in this area. Compare this illustration with Figure 10, which shows the Early Tertiary position of the shelves before the first continental drift began. Muck tells us: 'The shelves are a perfect fit of the edges of the Atlantic Ridge. Only the black patch in the North American basin indicates a subsequent subsidence of the land.'[7] Plato states unequivocally that Atlantis was a vast island; in Wegener's language, a small continental platform!

More Geological Evidence

Telegraph Plateau was so named after the transatlantic cable laid in 1898 suddenly snapped at a point under 47°N and 29° 40'W of Paris, i.e. about 500 miles north of the Azores, the ends disappearing into a seemingly bottomless underwater chasm (see Figure 6). A cable-laying vessel searching for the broken cable between Brest and Cape Cod eventually retrieved it, but not without great difficulty. During the course of the operation it was discovered that the sea floor 1,000 miles (1,609 kilometres) north of the Azores at a depth of

10,170 feet (3,100 metres) consisted of high peaks and mountainous valleys. Dredging the ocean floor yielded fragments
of vitreous lava, including a large piece of rock that was
deposited in a Paris museum. Muck notes that fifteen years
elapsed before it was examined by Paul Termier, director of
the Oceanographic Institute at that time and recognized as a
scientist of repute both in his own country and in the world
generally. The specimen turned out to be a tachylite of typi-
cally vitreous structure. Termier proclaimed his findings in
a dramatic lecture entitled 'Atlantis', which he gave in the
Oceanographic Institute. Muck summarizes Termier's conclusions, which were sensational to say the least, as follows:

First, the specimen was of volcanic origin. Large tracts of the ocean
floor were covered with lava. To produce the flow of lava of which the
specimen formed a part, there must have been at some time very
considerable volcanic eruptions in the region of Telegraph Plateau.

Second, the specimen was amorphous, vitreous, and of non-
crystalline structure. It must have solidified in free air, not in deep
water. . . . It could have been ejected only by an above-water
volcano, not a submarine one. The lava covering those vast areas of
ocean floor must have come from former land volcanoes . . . (In this
respect he was mistaken; it has since been established that the
vitreous quality is the result of gases present in lava coming from
the mantle. But the tachylites nevertheless were on the sea-bed as a
result of a major eruption.)

Third, the whole region must have sunk through more than
6,560 feet (2,000 metres) either at the same time as the eruption or
very shortly afterward. The specimen was therefore evidence of a
prehistoric catastrophe in the middle of the Atlantic . . .

Fourth, the specimen was a tachylite according to mineralogical
classification. Tachylite dissolves in sea water within about 15,000
years. But the find had sharp contours and appeared intact. The
catastrophe in the Atlantic must therefore have occurred less than
15,000 years previously. In other words, later than 13,000 BC, and
probably considerably later.[8]

Muck sees this as confirming Plato's dates of '9,000 years before Solon', which would be around 10,000 BC, and corresponding with the mean value of the geological estimates of the end of the Quaternary Age.

The nineteenth-century German geologist Hartung dismissed the validity of Termier's suggestions, basing his counter-argument on observations made during a visit to the Azores in the 1860s when he noticed curious beach blocks consisting of a type of rock not found elsewhere on the island. Hartung concluded that these rocks originated elsewhere and had been carried along and deposited by icebergs. That the rocks had been found on the present shores of the Azores, Hartung said, showed that no major post-glacial change in level could have occurred in that area. The Swedish explorer Högbom and others consequently deduced that a catastrophe could not have taken place in the Azores region, the change in level associated with such an event similarly being ruled out by Hartung's argument.

Hartung's theory hardly disproves (or even conflicts with) Termier's if you care to think about it. After all, by the time the great ice-sheet was fragmenting following the post-glacial melting period, and its icebergs drifting southward, Atlantis had disappeared anyway, leaving only the small Azores archipelago to catch the flotsam.

The geological indications are, therefore, that the subsidence in the Azores region must have been sudden and catastrophic for, as Muck points out,

had the subsidence postulated by Termier been a gradual process over a considerable period during the postglacial age, then the odd blocks transported by icebergs during this long period would have been deposited, not along the present shores of the Azores, but along the earlier shoreline, now submerged.[9]

Rock samples collected by more recent expeditions during

the course of their normal research programmes have tended to support Termier's findings. Dr Maria Klenova, of the Soviet Academy of Science, examined rock samples dredged up from 6,600 feet (2,012 metres) in the same general area north of the Azores. In her opinion, the rock had been formed at atmospheric pressure approximately 15,000 years ago. Likewise, Duke University furnished some fine samples of granitic rocks that their expedition dredged from an underwater bridge between Venezuela and the Virgin Islands. Leading US oceanographer Dr Bruce Heezen, on assessing the find, stated:

Up to now, geologists generally believed that light granitic or acid igneous rocks are confined to the continents and that the crust of the Earth beneath the sea is composed of heavier, dark-colored basaltic rock . . . Thus, the occurrence of light-colored granitic rocks may support an old theory that a continent formerly existed in the region of the eastern Caribbean and that these rocks may represent the core of a subsided lost continent.[10]

What the *Jesmond* Saw

Charles Berlitz, of *Bermuda Triangle* fame, cites a fascinating tale of Atlantean ruins that concerned the vessel SS *Jesmond*, a British merchantman of 1,495 tons bound for New Orleans with a cargo of dried fruits from Messina in Sicily. Its captain was David Robson (Master's Certificate No. 27911 in the Queen's Merchant Marine).

On March 1882 the *Jesmond* passed through the Straits of Gibraltar into the open sea. Upon reaching 31° 25'N, 28° 40'W, some 200 miles (322 kilometres) west of Madeira and a similar distance south of the Azores, the crew observed enormous amounts of dead fish and an unusual amount of mud in the water, as if some underwater explosion had caused the death of the fish and, at the same time, dislodged a considerable amount of sediment from the ocean bed. Late that same afternoon smoke was observed on the horizon, which the Captain took to indicate the presence of another vessel. On the following day, however, the fish shoals were thicker, while the smoke on the horizon could now be seen to be issuing from heights directly to the west, where, according to the charts, there was no land for vast distances. Upon approaching the vicinity of the 'island' Captain Robson cast anchor some 12 miles (19 kilometres) off shore. But although his charts indicated an area depth of several thousand fathoms, the anchor reached the bottom at only seven fathoms.

Robson, being consumed with curiosity, took a landing party ashore. They found themselves on an island covered with volcanic debris, but completely devoid of any sand, trees or vegetation, as though it had just emerged from the sea. As there was nothing to obscure the view, the party were able to see a plateau some distance away with smoking mountains in the background. Although the party tried to make their way farther into the interior, their progress was severely hampered by a series of deep chasms. As one of the sailors found what was believed to be a rather unusual arrowhead, the Captain sent back to the ship for picks and shovels so that the crew could seek out other pieces of archaeological interest.

When the ship docked later in New Orleans, Robson told a reporter from the *Times Picayune* that he and his crew had uncovered crumbling remains of massive walls. A variety of artefacts recovered from two days' digging near the walls included

bronze swords, rings, mallets, carvings of heads and figures of birds and animals, and two vases or jars with fragments of bone, and one cranium almost entire . . . [and] what appeared to be a mummy enclosed in a stone case . . . encrusted with volcanic deposit so as to be scarcely distinguished from the rock itself.[11]

Several reporters apparently examined Captain Robson's unusual finds, which, he informed them, he planned to present to the British Museum. Unfortunately, the log of the *Jesmond* was destroyed during the London blitz of September 1940, along with the offices of the *Jesmond*'s owners, Watts, Watts and Company. The British Museum appears to have no record of ever having received the collection, although it has been speculated that it could still turn up in some dark attic or temporarily forgotten storeroom.

Robson's story of the mysterious island did receive corroboration, however. Captain James Newdick of the steam schooner *Westbourne*, sailing from Marseilles to New York during the same period, reported, on his arrival in New York, having sighted a large, uncharted island at coordinates 25° 30′ N, and 24° W. His report appeared in the *New York Post* on 1 April 1882. Berlitz argues that if the coordinates given by both captains were correct, the mystery island would have covered an area of 20 × 30 miles (32 × 48 kilometres). The floating fish were also reported by several other vessels passing through that area and pronounced by certain hungry sailors as being in good condition and therefore providing excellent food. This would indicate that their demise was sudden, and not the result of some epidemic disease.

The reference to 'bronze implements' does, however, raise some questions. The Bronze Age is designated that period of human culture between the Stone and Iron Ages characterized by weapons and implements made of bronze, which is thought to have been invented about 3000 BC in the city-states of Mesopotamia. As most authorities tend to place Atlantis much earlier in the prehistoric scene, there are two possible solutions to this enigma. First, that the Atlanteans possessed a knowledge of bronze centuries before it made its appearance in Mesopotamia, and second, that the artefacts discovered by

Robson and his crew came from shipwrecks, although the stone sarcophagus tends to discount that probability.

The Bronze Age itself has raised many questions among researchers. Articles of bronze are found over nearly all of Europe, but in especial abundance in Ireland and Scandinavia. They indicate considerable refinement and civilization on the part of their makers, which has resulted in a wide diversity of opinion as to where the knowledge originated. Ignatius Donnelly quotes Sir John Lubbock (*Prehistoric Times*, p. 59) as stating: 'The absence of implements made either of copper or tin seems to me to indicate that *the art of making bronze was introduced into, not invented in, Europe.*'

Since Captain Robson's brief viewing of 'Atlantean' walls, sightings of buildings, walls, roads and other unusual underwater phenomena have been reported with increasing frequency from various parts of the Atlantic. Pilots flying the Atlantic claimed to have seen what appeared to them as groups of buildings or cities, archways and pyramids. It seems that at certain times in the afternoon, when there is a special slant of the Sun's rays and a low rate of diatoms in the sea, parts of the ocean are clear enough for glimpses of former human habitation to be visible at certain angles. Pilots on scheduled flights, however, are seldom in a position to abandon their flight path to investigate such phenomena, and however much they swear to the authenticity of their sightings, being unable to provide any tangible proof is usually guaranteed to evoke comments about flight fatigue, hallucinations or simply wishful thinking.

Despite the fact that aerial photographs have been taken that point to the possibility of former habitation on the Bahama Banks and off the Caribbean coast of Mexico, no such evidence is yet available to support the mid-Atlantic placing of the sunken continent. Convincing material has, however, been supplied by submarine cameras from a research ship, and by oceanographers engaged in their normal work of investigating the ocean bed in this general area. The vessel and oceanographers in question were from the USSR.

Although the various possible causes for the Atlantis catastrophe will come under scrutiny in the next chapter, it is relevant at this juncture to consider that rather than just sinking into the sea the Atlantean continent might have been 'drowned' by rising waters. Whether this rising was caused by the sudden melting of glacial ice or some other cause, perhaps external to the immediate environment of this planet, we shall shortly be discussing, although Soviet underwater research would seem to provide a degree of corroboration for the 'drowning' theory.

The *Academician Petrovsky* Photographs

I was first informed of the Soviet expedition by the late Egerton Sykes, with whom I frequently corresponded. He used to run two small magazines, called *Uranus* and *Atlantis*, in which he regularly reported his ongoing correspondence with Professor Nicolai Zhirov. Although Russia is distanced from the supposed area of Atlantis, a number of erudite Russian writers and scholars have seen fit to comment on the subject. These include Dmitri Merezhkovski who, in tsarist times, saw in the doom of Atlantis a parallel with the forthcoming European situation; Nicolai Zhirov, whose book *Atlantis* (1964) dealt with the historical and geological material available on the subject with special attention to its Atlantic location; and V. Bryusov, who favours the 'single source' theory regarding the beginning of civilization (Atlantis).

The Soviet deep-sea expedition that took place early in 1974 was carried out by the *Academician Petrovsky*, a Soviet research ship engaged in photographing the sea floor in the region of the Horseshoe Archipelago.

This is a U-shaped group of underwater mountains some 300 miles (483 kilometres) west of Gibraltar in the same area that Captain Robson's island had appeared and disappeared with equal rapidity. Berlitz quotes from *The Atlantic Floor* by Heezen, Thorpe, and Young:

Some of them, such as the underwater mountains Ampere and Josephine, rise to a depth of less than 100 fathoms. . . . Photographs taken of the surface of these mountains show cliffs, traces of ripples and isolated living corals. The underwater mountains of the northern half of the Horseshoe, which have not yet been properly studied, stretch from west to east. The southern half of the group apparently resembles volcanic cones, while for the northern half tectonic changes played an important role.[12]

In the past expeditions to this area, notably from the Lamont Geological Observatory, had proven unsuccessful, while Dr Maurice Ewing was heard to complain that after spending thirteen years studying the mid-Atlantic Ridge he found no traces of sunken cities.

It should be noted at this point that the crew of the *Petrovsky* were not searching for remnants of Atlantis, nor had they any plans for so doing, although it would seem that they produced the first photographs ever taken of the legendary island continent.

At first, they were unaware that some of the many photographs they took revealed archaeological relics. The aim and results of the expedition were summarized by M. Barinov and appeared in the Soviet publication *Znanie-Sila*, No. 8, in 1979, at the time when details of the discovery also found their way into the world press. Berlitz reproduces the following extracts:

The purpose of the expedition was to study the sandbanks in the shallow waters of the Mediterranean Sea and of the Atlantic Ocean not far from northwest Africa. On board the ship as part of the team were geologists and biologists. The origin, structure and population of the sandbanks, the peaks of underwater mountains and of the shallows comprised the main scientific interest of the specialists. In the team there was also a researcher from the USSR Institute of Oceanography, Vladimir Ivanovich Marakuyev, who was a specialist in underwater photography.

. . . lighting equipment with special cameras was lowered to a depth of about three and a half meters [11½ feet] above the bottom, after which the lights were switched on and a series of photographs were taken using a simple automatic device. Each series took about an hour to an hour and a half to complete. At the same time other members of the expedition carried out experiments and a series of tests with the aid of other apparatus. The water in the Atlantic near Gibraltar was exceptionally clear and the work of the expedition depended only on the weather. During the winter storms when the ship started to roll from side to side work had to be discontinued and sometimes shelter had to be sought.[13]

When the photographs taken by the *Academician Petrovsky* were developed, the Ampere seamount, which extends from a depth of 10,000 feet (3,048 metres) to within 20 feet (6 metres) of the surface, proved to be full of surprises. Photographer Marakuyev commented:

While still on the expedition, when I had developed the photographs and made the first prints, I realized that I never seen anything like it before. The Institute of Oceanography of the USSR has a huge archive of underwater photographs that have been taken on countless expeditions over many years in all parts of the world's oceans. We also have copies of many thousands of photographs taken by our American colleagues. Nowhere have I seen anything so close to traces of the life and activity of man in places which could once have been dry land.[14]

But what exactly did these amazing revelations consist of? Although the *Znanie-Sila* saw fit to release some information, I am sceptical whether this constitutes the entire find, as the Russians do have a tendency to keep certain facts to themselves. Perhaps *glasnost* might encourage them to let us know a little more. However, here is the information they did decide to share with us:

On the first photograph we can see this wall on the left side of the photograph. Stone blocks on the upper edge of the wall are clearly visible . . . Taking into account the foreshortening of the photograph and the height of the wall, it is curious to examine more closely the strip of vertical masonry. Although the lens was pointing almost vertically downwards, areas of masonry can be seen quite clearly. One can count five such areas, and if one takes into account the deformation of scale caused by the nearness of the lens to the object, one may suggest that the masonry blocks of the wall are up to 1.5 meters [4.9 feet] high and a little longer in length.

'On the second photograph we can see the same wall from directly above. It crosses the picture diagonally. The control disc is in the center. It is not difficult to calculate that the breadth of the wall is about 75 centimeters [29.5 inches]. The masonry blocks are clearly visible on both sides of the wall. Seaweed is visible on all the photographs, thick, reddish brown in color . . .

'The third photograph is from another series taken at the summit of Ampere Seamount. An area over which lava has flowed can be seen on it, and it appears to descend by three steps. If one counts the upper and barely visible lower edges . . . in all we can see five steps. They are broken down, of course, and overgrown with glass-like sponges.[15]

Copies of the photographs are reproduced in Berlitz's book *Atlantis* for those who would like to study them. In my opinion the reproductions are too indistinct for the layperson to make much of, although, no doubt, the originals, if studied with appropriate instruments, are highly informative. They were, however, sufficiently evidential to evoke from Professor Andrei Aksyonov, a leading Soviet scientist and deputy director of the Soviet Academy of Science's Institute of Oceanography, the comment: 'In my opinion these structures once stood on the surface.'[16]

Although the expedition took place in 1974, the Soviets did not see their way to releasing this information until 1978, which again prompts me to suspect them of knowing more than they are prepared to say. An interview with Professor Aksyonov took place in Moscow and appeared in the *New York Times* on 21 May 1978. What puzzles me, and many others no doubt, is why the learned gentleman saw fit to explain to his interviewer that the information had come to his attention only in 1977. 'I don't know why it took him [Marakuyev] so long to get to them.' He was later heard to comment: 'They belong to Marakuyev and he is very sick with a heart condition in a hospital – I think they will be published in one of our scientific journals sometime soon.'[17]

The whole thing sounds totally unprofessional to me and suggests that there might be more to it than meets the eye. Apparently I am not alone in this assumption. Egerton Sykes was also intrigued and, when interviewed by Berlitz in 1982, had a few things to say about it. The main reason for the secrecy, he surmised, was that the Russians were reluctant to divulge the real position where the pictures had been taken, which was probably off the Azores between Santa Maria and São Jorge, as this represented a more strategically interesting location, where they should not have been anyway. According to Sykes, the *Petrovsky* was apparently a highly qualified spy ship.

Sykes proffered his opinion on the stones and platform and suggested that there were probably a lot more steps, maybe a hundred or more, after the style of the Aztec pyramids, below the point where the photograph was taken. He judged the platform to be a landing connecting to another staircase in step-pyramid style. Sykes seemed unaware of any other finds in the Ampere area of Madeira, although he claimed to have seen photographs of sunken walls and pavements several miles out to sea from Cadiz. Donnelly reminds us that:

Plato tells us that the dominion of Gadeirus, one of the kings of Atlantis, extended towards 'the pillars of Heracles as far as the country which is still called the region of Gades in that part of the world'. Gades is the Cadiz of today, and the dominion of Gadeirus embraced the land of the Iberians or Basques, their chief city taking its name from a king of Atlantis . . .[18]

The fact that such a recognized authority as Dr Maurice Ewing has failed to find any evidence of a sunken civilization in the Atlantic, whereas a Soviet ship, purportedly on a scientific mission in no way concerned with the Atlantis project, should come upon such exciting evidence as though by accident has always proved a thorn in the side of both sceptics and believers.

There is an answer, however, which has been supplied to us by parapsychology. It is called the 'Experimenter Effect', which maintains that the experimenter or researcher who believes in something is more likely to find evidence to support that belief than the sceptic, whose searches are orientated towards disproving the proposition or theory in question. In other words, the human mind erects its own barriers, albeit subconsciously, and stays well within their area of reference. This, in turn, sets up a quality of PK (psychokinetic energy) that automatically blocks people from finding evidence to prove what they do not believe in, either by veering them in the wrong direction or causing their experiments to produce the answers *they want*. Likewise with people who believe a particular theory to be true, whose PK will tend to point them in the direction of the evidence for which they are seeking. Einstein probably observed this principle in action during his many years as a physicist, which, no doubt, prompted his famous comment that I quoted earlier in this chapter.

Fig. 11. Physiographic profile of the St Peter and St Paul Rocks, located between Brazil and Africa, considered by Professor Hapgood as remnants of a much larger island, possibly connected with other sunken islands that composed Atlantis.

Summarizing the Evidence

Evidence collected from the ocean bed would seem to indicate that the Azores, Canary Islands, Madeira and the Cape Verde Islands were once part of the old Atlantean continent, with St Peter and St Paul Rocks and Bermuda also being favoured by some authorities. There is also evidence to suggest that a series of smaller islands once existed both east and west of the mid-Atlantic Ridge, which could have been seen by ancient mariners as stepping stones to the larger continent beyond. This would also account for Plato's description of the islands from which one might pass to 'the whole of the opposite continent which surrounded the true ocean'.

Rocks from the vicinity of the Azores show evidence of great explosions and sudden sinkings. In fact, as Berlitz points out, the evidence so far suggests a large continent poised on a series of plateaux, extending into the Atlantic from around 50°N on a line between Newfoundland and northern France,

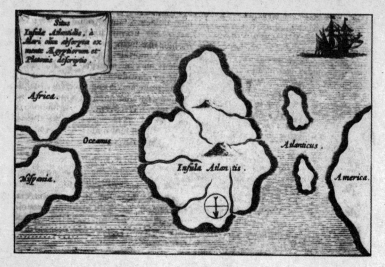

Fig. 12. Athanasius Kircher in his *Mundus Subterraneous* (1678) located the sunken island of Atlantis in the Atlantic, near the Azores.

continuing south through the Azores, turning south-west and passing through the Sargasso Sea down to latitude 20°N on a line between Yucatan and Mauritania in Africa. The corresponding underwater plateau would be roughly the size of France, Spain, Portugal and the British Isles combined, which would suggest that Plato did not get his sums wrong after all!

Many scholars, past and present, have enjoyed the challenge of placing Atlantis where Plato indicated it to have been. The Jesuit Father Athanasius Kircher, whose book *Mundus Subterraneous* was published in 1665, appears to have shown a particular interest in the sunken continent. Kircher discerned summits of submerged Atlantic ridges in the islands of the Azores and drew what must have been for the time an amazingly accurate map of Atlantis, which resembled a pear with the stalk turning downwards. This map is shown in Figure 12 in its inverted form as Kircher originally produced it. How

Kircher arrived at this conclusion remains a mystery to scientists, although the metaphysically inclined amongst us will recognize the coincidence as a flash of far memory.

More recently, David Wood, in providing a geometric solution to the mystery of the valley of Renne-le-Chateau, as popularized by the Baigent-Leigh-Lincoln team (in *The Holy Blood and the Holy Grail*), discovered mathematical connections between several sites of metaphysical importance. These findings suggested to him that there must have been a single source of enlightenment somewhere in the far past from which all knowledge of sacred geometry, mathematics and metaphysics originated, or a centre on the planet's surface that radiated subtle energies that could still be recognized and utilized by the initiated. The mathematics of his discoveries are too lengthy to repeat in this book, but suffice it to say that they resulted in his giving what he believes to be the exact coordinates for Atlantis: 42° 55′ N and 26° 6′W![19]

CHAPTER 6

Asteroids, Moons and Axis Tilts

Atlantis, woe to thy children!
Alas, shall we live to see another dawn?
Our ancestor's words came true one by one;
His Atlanteans, lands and gods are no more.

JACINO VERDAGUER [1]

The haunting lament of the Catalan poem seems to have an eternal quality about it, as though it could apply as much to today's world as to times long past when our planet showed a different face to its celestial brethren. But this statement assumes the former existence of the Atlantis of Plato and countless other scribes world-wide. So let us suppose that there is no fairy-tale, no myth; simply a garbled version of an actual happening that was recorded in the traditions of the distant past.

There are three factors that call for analysis:

1. What could have caused a large land mass of the size described by Plato to disappear so quickly?

2. In view of certain discrepancies in his story, how much can we rely on the measurements he has given us?

3. When did such an event take place?

Extraterrestrial Assaults

Atlantologists who have sought proof of their theories within the disciplines of science appear to have narrowed their choice down to two possibilities. The first of these, much favoured by Otto Muck and supported by several Russian authorities, is that the Earth was struck by a giant asteroid with such force that its axial rotation was affected. Muck uses data concerning the sudden change of climate that took place during the Quaternary Period. During that era, he tells us, the Gulf Stream was deflected westward by a barrier in the centre of the Atlantic Ocean. Palaeoclimatical research has established that the land ice in north-western Europe advanced as far as the fifty-second parallel because there was no warm current flowing towards the European coast that would have melted it. The sudden disappearance of such a land mass allowed the Gulf Stream to flow northwards and so the ice was freed and Europe was therefore able to settle into its present climate. Muck points out, however, that such a large land mass cannot disappear entirely, so it remains for the most part a submarine plateau.

Muck backs his arguments with some sound scientific facts coupled with plenty of logical deduction. The geological and oceanographical evidence upon which he places the following hypothesis centres around a depth chart that shows a great structural basin to the east of what is now the south-east coast of North America, where a sharp abnormality is apparently revealed. Muck tells us:

Near the stump that remains of the fractured Puerto Rico Plateau, there are two great holes of nearly 23,000 feet (7,000 metres) in depth. These holes are in the center of the fragmented coastal area, not very far from the southern edge of the submarine landmass that acted as a barrier to the Gulf Stream before its submergence, and that we have identified as Plato's Atlantis. The Puerto Rico Trench, which has a depth of about 30,000 feet (9,000 metres), encircles the southern part of the central area of catastrophe. A study of the ocean bed in this region will enable us to forge a further link in our chain. From it we will be able to draw far-reaching conclusions, not only about the center of the catastrophe, but about its cause and its wider effects.[2]

Muck seems to have little doubt that the Atlantean catastrophe was centred on these two holes, and that its most violent effects were felt in their vicinity, a theory supported by the American anthropologist Alan H. Kelso de Montigny. The depth chart in the eastern part of the Caribbean Sea bordered by the arc of the Lesser Antilles reveals a deep-sea hole in the centre of the arc, which surrounds it, giving the impression of the rim of a half submerged giant crater. De Montigny postulates that it was caused by an asteroid striking the area some 10,000 years ago. The site of this suspected collision is near enough to the two great holes in the American basin to associate it with the Atlantean catastrophe at the end of the Diluvial Age.

As the two large holes cover some 77,000 square miles (200,000 square kilometres), it would have taken a force of some magnitude to drive them into the sima floor of the Atlantic basin. In fact, Muck likens the impact to a colossal submarine nuclear explosion, and rejects the possibility that they could be 'subsidence craters caused by tectonic earthquakes or enormous sinkholes, elutriation products of submarine vortices'.[3] He favours the likelihood that they are 'unhealed scars left by two deep wounds inflicted on the Earth's crust by the impact of a celestial body of considerable size'.[4]

Muck is not alone in this hypothesis. Earlier researchers, including Braghine, Wyston, and Count Carli de Lalande, have favoured the idea, while in more recent times Professor N. S. Vetchinkin of the Soviet Union declared:

The fall of a gigantic meteorite was the cause of the destruction of Atlantis. Impacts of gigantic meteorites are clearly seen on the surface of the moon. There are craters 200 kilometres [124 miles] in diameter, whereas on earth they are only 3 kilometres [2 miles] wide. Falling into the sea, gigantic meteorites brought about tidal waves which washed away not only the plant and animal kingdoms but also hills and mountains.[5]

Professor Hapgood postulates that the thin terrestrial crust of the Earth slides back and forth on the molten ball of the centre, the weight of the ice-caps on the poles setting the sliding in motion. If this hypothesis is correct and the Earth's shell is movable, the crust could easily be displaced by the impact of a massive body.

Nothing like this having occurred within the period of recorded history accepted by the major establishments of learning, is it really feasible that Earth could have been struck in this way in the distant past? In October 1937 a planetoid missed Earth by only five and a half hours, while early in 1989 an asteroid approximately 1 mile (1.6 kilometres) in diameter missed the Earth by less than 500,000 miles (805,000 kilometres) – approximately four hours! This naturally spawned a barrage of speculative writing as to what would have happened had the asteroid struck. Vast tidal waves would have been caused, the axis of the Earth would probably have been altered, resulting in violent global weather changes, famine, destruction on a world scale and millions of deaths. It would have hit the Earth with a force equal to millions of nuclear bombs and could even have obliterated life as we know it. And while this near disaster loomed, people slept peacefully in their beds, totally unaware of what *might have been* their impending doom!

Had this occurred and a few lived to tell the tale, what sort of vision of our age, with all its technological achievements, would have found its way down several generations hence, let us say to the third or fourth millennium? Assuming that the survivors were thrown back to primitive living conditions from which they were once again obliged to drag themselves, one is tempted to envision the myths that would grow over the centuries only to be dismissed as pure fable when technology and science once again found their feet. Perhaps Professor Efremov of the Soviet Union had this in mind when he insisted that 'historians must pay more respect to ancient traditions and folklore', and accused Western scientists of a certain snobbishness when it comes to the tales of the so-called common people.[6]

Aside from Plato's story, myths and legends that support these past events there certainly are, and far too many of them to be labelled 'tribal imagination'.

But let us return to Muck's asteroid, and the astronomical evidence upon which he bases his theory. Muck explains that every cosmic particle, no matter what its size, circles in orbit around its mechanical centre. In our solar system the planets circle the Sun in their respective orbits. Were a cosmic particle to come too close to a large planet, such as our own, whose orbital plane forms a straight line of intersection (the nodal line) with that of the particle, the particle would be drawn even closer by the gravitational pull of the larger body. This pull increases the particle's rate of acceleration, which, in turn, increases the centrifugal force trying to counteract the pull. If the velocity of the particle is sufficiently high, it will merely graze the marginal layer of the atmosphere. It will, however, become extremely hot, causing the rarefied gas surrounding it to become luminous. Thus we see distant 'shooting stars' that appear to flash across the sky.

The fact that meteorites of all shapes and sizes have landed on Earth tells us that not all objects from outer space whose trajectories have brought them within the gravitational pull of our planet have been able to escape its clutches. According to *New Scientist*, some of these have only recently been detected as a result of analysing photographs taken from outer space. In 1988 two scientists from Boston University, Michael Papagiannis and Farouk El-Baz, related at a meeting of the American Geophysical Union that they believed the meteorite that formed the Praha Basin 15 million years ago was about 50 miles (80 kilometres) in diameter. According to Papagiannis, the impact of such a large object would have been equivalent to an explosion a million million times more powerful than the atom bomb on Hiroshima, and would have adversely affected the world's climate at the time. The city of Prague is near the centre of the basin, the diameter of which is about 199 miles (320 kilometres) and covers much of western Czechoslovakia.[7]

Nor are these extraterrestrial assaults essentially a phenomenon of the past, several having made their appearance this century. One such fall of meteorites occurred in the Sichota-Alin mountains north-east of Vladivostok in Siberia in 1947, devastating the forests in an area of over 5 square miles (13 square kilometres) and producing circular craters up to 82 feet (25 metres) in diameter and 50 feet (15 metres) deep. In contrast to this comparatively small display, the extraterrestrial material that landed near the Podmanen Naya Tunguska River, also in Siberia (61° N, 102° W of Pulkov) on 30 June 1908 created an explosion that was heard up to 900 miles (1,448 kilometres) away and within a circle of 4,200 miles (6,757 kilometres). The powerful seismic shock wave produced traversed the Earth at the speed of 317 miles (510 kilometres) per second. These and many more instances of bombardment from extraterrestrial sources are evidence of the magnitude of destruction and material displacement that can be visited on our planet even to this day.

What size of object would it take to gouge the two deep-sea holes in the south-western part of the North Atlantic? If a large meteorite explodes and disintegrates into two main parts and innumerable fragments, the greater part of its total mass will doubtless be in the heavier metals of its core. Working on this basis, and taking into consideration other knowledge concerning the behaviour and effect of meteorites, even large ones, Muck discards the idea that the Atlantis catastrophe could have been caused by anything so small, and puts his money on an asteroid. Asteroids are mini-planets that are almost as old as some meteorites. Their orbits are normally confined to what is known as the asteroid Belt, although some extend beyond it.

Between Mars and Jupiter there is an unusually large gap in which Johannes Kepler indicated there should be another planet. The existence of this planet has never been substantiated, although according to the Titius–Bode Law there might well be an invisible body in that vicinity. Many small bodies, identified as asteroids or minor planets, have been detected in that area by astronomers, the first, named Ceres, in 1801. Since then more than 2,000 asteroids have been identified. One group of seven seems to be particularly drawn to major planets. One of this group, Adonis, came within 186,000 miles (300,000 kilometres) of the Earth in February 1936, and had our planet captured it the disaster would have been greater than the effects of a giant nuclear explosion.

Muck was convinced that the celestial body that fell into the Atlantic and was responsible for the sinking of the island continent of Atlantis was, in fact, an asteroid, which he called Asteroid A. The damage caused by its impact has enabled him to make some assumptions regarding its orbit. He tells us:

It approached from the northwest, that is, from the direction of sunset. It travelled much faster than Earth and overtook our planet in its rotation and in its orbit round the sun. The orbit of Asteroid

A must therefore have been very flat and elongated. This is a characteristic of all the asteroids in the Adonis group. The smaller body may have approached the larger near a nodal point, that is, a point in which both orbits intersect. Asteroid A would thus have come even closer to Earth than Adonis did in 1936. It was attracted by the Earth's gravitational pull, which bent its orbit into a progressively steeper parabolic trajectory and progressively accelerated it. The asteroid must have entered the hydrogen layer of the atmosphere at a speed of at least 9–12 miles per second (15–20 km per second) (velocity referred to the Earth) in an orbit that intersected that of Earth at an angle of 30°. At a height of about 248 miles (400 km), it began to be surrounded by the red glow of the hydrogen light. The hotter the asteroid became, the whiter and more brilliant was the light that it emitted. Its gaseous tail became immense. This lethal thunderbolt must have struck more violently than any comet could possibly have done, and in a blaze of light that made the sun pale. Eyes that saw it would have been permanently blinded. The temperature of its front surface, where it was exposed to the greatest atmospheric resistance and therefore heated most intensely, would exceed 36,032°F (20,000°C). Its luminosity would be 20–100 times that of the sun's disk. The gases hurled backward would have increased the fantastic appearance of this flaming giant. After entering the nitrogen layer and speeding through the lowest and densest part of the atmosphere, the heat and tensile stress became so great that it burst. As a result of several explosions, the brittle, solid crust shattered into innumerable lethal fragments gouging a trench of deadly devastation across the southeastern part of North America. The core broke in two immediately above the ground, with a thunderclap that ruptured every eardrum. Two giant boulders, each weighing about 10^{12} tonnes, plunged into the sea, which surged to mountainous heights. This stupendous tidal wave rushed in all directions from the vortex around the impact holes. At a height of 2,000 ft (600 m) it caused appalling devastation in coastal regions and extinguished all traces of antediluvian civilizations there.[8]

Muck himself was well qualified to comment on such

matters, having worked as a member of the Peenemünde Rocket Research Team in Germany in World War II.

Legend and mythology appear to back Muck's graphic description. The famous codex *Popul Vuh* ('A Bouquet of Leaves') is the sacred book of the Quiché of Guatemala, sometimes referred to as the Bible of the Mayas. Discovered in 1854 by Dr Scherzer, its four volumes, written in the tongue of the Quiché, give the history and mythology of the Mayas. The *Popul Vuh* asserts that the forefathers of the Quiché originally came from a distant country in the ocean. Later in their history, however, the god Huracan became angry with mankind and flooded the Earth, while simultaneously a great conflagration was witnessed in the heavens, the sea boiled up and sticky substances rained from the sky. The following account, which is also highly confirmatory, has been paraphrased from the mythology and vagaries of another extraordinary book, the *Chilam Balams*, written in the Maya language, but in Roman script:

This happened when the Earth began to awake. Nobody knew what was to come. A fiery rain fell, ashes fell, rocks and trees crashed to the ground. He smashed trees and rocks asunder . . . And the Great Snake was torn from the sky . . . and skin and pieces of its bones fell on to the Earth . . . and arrows struck orphans and old men, widowers and widows who were alive, yet did not have the strength to live. And they were buried on the sandy seashore. Then the waters rose in a terrible flood. And with the Great Snake the sky fell in and the dry land sank into the sea . . .[9]

In their book *The Great Extinction*, Michael Allaby and James Lovelock propose that a meteorite, or planetesimal (see p. 95) was the cause of the extinction of the saurians at the end of the Cretaceous Period 65 million years ago, and present as their evidence the fact that levels of iridium and osmium in the clay deposits that mark the end of the Cretaceous and the beginning of the Tertiary Period are 200–300 times higher than the levels usually found in terrestrial rocks. These high levels of rare metals are believed by scientists to have been caused by an extraterrestrial object, probably a planetesimal, striking the Earth.[10]

Had the destruction of Atlantis also been caused by the impact of a large meteorite or planetesimal, as Muck claims, it would be logical to assume that a similar rise in the occurrence of these rare elements might also be in evidence. However, despite the fact that only some 10,000 years is believed to separate us from this catastrophic event, no confirmation of this has been forthcoming to date from the field of research.

Heezen's statement that the levels of the seas were significantly lower than they are today (see pp. 63–4) would seem to indicate that the ice-caps were significantly larger, which they would have been during an Ice Age. The impact of a large extraterrestrial object generating as much heat as Muck calculates ($36,032°F/20,000°C$) as it passed through the atmosphere could surely have melted the Ice Age glaciers in its path almost instantaneously. A large planetoid striking solid ground would cause a darkening of the sky that could last for months or even years. This exclusion of sunlight would have a strong cooling effect, which would doubtless slow down the melting process. But an object of similar size striking the sea would vaporize a massive quantity of water, creating vast clouds of moisture that would eventually fall as rain in warmer climes and as snow in extreme regions of the north and south, depending on where the object struck.

There is also a strong body of opinion in favour of the extraterrestrial object being a comet rather than an asteroid, which would have some different effects. It is not without good reason that astronomer Fred L. Whipple described comets as 'dirty snowballs'. According to Chandra

Wickramsinghe, another eminent astronomer and comet expert, approximately half a comet's mass is water ice, the remainder being composed of loosely packed dust and other solids and volatile organic gases such as ammonia and methane.[11] A comet the size of Halley (the nucleus is approximately 5 × 10 miles, or 8 × 16 kilometres) therefore contains a vast amount of frozen water. If a comet of this size had passed into the Earth's atmosphere, the outer layer would have melted very quickly in the extremely high temperatures generated by the friction. The inner core, however, might have remained in a frozen or semi-frozen state as it struck the sea with great force. An immense quantity of water would have been vaporized and the solid material would have smashed into the sea-bed, the organic gases would have been released into the atmosphere along with vast amounts of dust and debris, and the ice portion would quickly have melted in the superheated water. This rapid melting of the comet's ice content, the ice-cap and glaciers could also feasibly have caused the sudden rise in sea-level referred to by Heezen and others, and created the enormous amount of vaporized water that eventually fell as rain (the Biblical Flood?). If this had occurred when the Ice Age was nearing its end and the glaciers were in retreat, the deluge on their southernmost edges could have contributed to their melting process.

The comet theory, therefore, presents a viable alternative to Muck's asteroid. Several myths and legends also allude to this type of phenomenon. Chinese records, for example, mention a 'great star with a tail' appearing in the sky and there being no light for four days.

Axis Tilts

The *Oera Linda Book* also describes a cosmic calamity, involving a tilting of the Earth's axis, which caused climatic changes of great severity to take place within the space of three days:

During the whole summer the sun had been hid behind the clouds, as if unwilling to look upon the earth. There was perpetual calm, and the damp mist hung like a wet sail over the houses and the marshes. The air was heavy and oppressive, and in men's hearts was neither joy nor cheerfulness. In the midst of this stillness the earth began to tremble as if she was dying. The mountains opened to vomit forth fire and flames. Some sank into the bosom of the earth, and in other places mountains rose out of the plain. Aldland, called by the seafaring people Atland, disappeared, and the wild waves rose so high over hill and dale that everything was buried in the sea. Many people were swallowed up by the earth, and others who had escaped the fire perished in the water.[12]

Three points arise from this quote. Firstly, no mention is made of a brilliant celestial body with a fiery tail, which must surely have been visible in the area of Scandinavia unless, of course, it approached from a southerly direction. Secondly, the claims that the climate in those parts changed *overnight* from subtropical to the colder temperatures experienced in present-day Scandinavia do not fit in with scientific dating of the interglacial periods, and thirdly, there is the question of an axis tilt.

Axis tilts have intrigued me for many years and I often wondered why the subject carried such a taboo in scientific circles when there were so many loopholes in the supposedly tight web of 'evidence' against it. However, axis tilts have recently assumed a cloak of scientific respectability, which renders it somewhat easier for an interested observer such as myself to chance an occasional probe.

Both the Eskimos and the Chinese have legends that tell how the Earth tilted violently before the Flood, so, if Hapgood's premise holds good and the Earth's shell is movable, a major collision could easily cause the planet to wobble on its axis prior to settling down again at a slightly different angle in relation to the Sun and Moon. What bothers me are these climatic changes. As discussed in earlier chapters, Greenland and its surrounding area is recognized as having enjoyed a subtropical climate in the geological past, while there is now evidence that land in that area of the North Sea was above water around 5000 BC. Likewise, the region of the Sahara was not always the dust-ridden bowl it is today. And what about all those mammoths, whose carcasses are still providing frozen meat for the animals (and some of the people!) of Siberia: what caused them to die so suddenly? Hapgood describes one mammoth that perished while enjoying a meal of fresh buttercups!

THE CLIMATE OF THE PREHISTORIC ERA

Period	Sub-period	Beginning about	Type of climate
Quaternary	Würm glacial	20,000 BC	typically glacial
	Epiglacial	10,000 BC	sub-boreal (raw, cold)
Quinternary	Post-glacial	5000 BC	optimum climate
	Present	2000 BC	decreasing warmth

Source: Otto Muck, *The Secret of Atlantis*, Fred Bradley (trs), London, William Collins Sons & Co, 1978, p. 67.

Mammoths, we are told, lived in the Quaternary Age and became extinct in the Quinternary Age. They were clearly destroyed in some major catastrophe that changed the weather patterns almost overnight. It has been suggested that they were either suffocated in a wave of asphyxiating gases or drowned in floods; but why should they be found buried in the centre of a glaciated region? Muck tells us that during the Quaternary Age the area in question, northern Siberia, was completely ice-free, its mean temperature being roughly 39–41°F (4–5°C), although Hapgood's buttercups rather suggest that it could have been higher. Fresh meat exposed to this temperature for longer than four days would certainly show signs of decay. The mammoth cadavers that are at present being recovered from the ice are in very good condition and show no signs of decomposition. This indicates that the transition from warm to ice-cold must have occurred very soon after their demise. Continental drift cannot account for this phenomenon, *but an axis tilt can*.

Commenting on post-glacial climatic changes, Hapgood states:

This was a very rainy period which geologists call a 'Pluvial' and which lasted for several thousand years. It was described by Edward S. Deevey, a geologist, in a symposium entitled *Climatic Change* edited by Dr Harlow Shapley, the director of the Harvard Observatory. According to Deevey, who reflects the general opinion of geologists, this cold, wet period lasted until about 6,000 years ago, when it was succeeded by a period warmer and drier than now. While it lasted the large supply of moisture resulted in more and larger rivers and lakes not only in Europe but in Africa. The Sahara Desert was then very fertile, with wide grassy plains and great forests. There were large numbers of animals of all sorts, and there was human occupation.[13]

The fact that people were able to observe the Sun rising and setting in a position other than from east to west, as substantiated in the records of the ancient Egyptians and Norsemen, clearly points to a shift in the Earth's axis, which might also account for certain anomalies in climate. That there was an Ice Age is clearly stated by the geological evidence. But what if the whole planet had been in a slightly different position in relation to the Sun, so that some areas that had formerly been warm were overtaken by ice and others exposed to a warmer temperature? In commenting on the mammoth phenomenon in Siberia Muck suggests:

To find trees like these that supplied food for mammoths in the Ice Age one would have to go further south, to the region of Lake Baikal, to travel the same distance as the North Pole possibly shifted in the Atlantic catastrophe. The primeval forest receded southward as the North Pole shifted north.[14]

This accords with Hapgood's polar shift theory.

Scrutton draws our attention to Mooney's comment regarding the last Ice Age, the Würm. At its maximum extent the ice field covered the British Isles as far south as the Thames Valley, North America as far south as the Mississippi Delta, and parts of Scandinavia, France, Germany and Russia. However, it appears to have missed Jutland (Denmark) and spread no further west than Mecklenburg in East Germany while a large part of Siberia escaped. This raises the questions why is there no evidence of a similar spread of ice at the South Pole and why are the kind of geological conditions normally associated with glaciations absent in the present Arctic regions? The movements of ice-sheets usually cause striations (scratches) on rock surfaces. In the Highlands of Scotland, where the evidence of glaciation is most noticeable, there are striations on the north-facing slopes, while on the south-facing slopes there are none. It would be logical to assume that the ice moving down from the north, having ascended the hill slopes on one side, would have made an even deeper impression on the other.[15]

Fortunately, Hapgood is able to present us with some tangible evidence for all this in the study of rock magnetism. He tells us:

It has long been known that particles of rocks made of iron-containing minerals take on the directions of the earth's magnetic

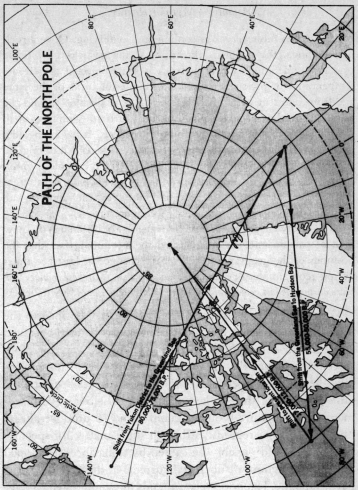

Fig. 13. Three positions of the North Pole.

field at the time of the formation of the rocks. Due to the iron in them they behave like tiny magnets, they are polarized and their north and south poles are aligned with the directions of the earth's magnetic field in that locality. They then tend to point toward the north and south magnetic poles of the earth. They can take on this magnetic orientation only when soft sediments are turning into rock or when molten rock is cooling and solidifying. Once a rock has solidified, the magnetic directions of the particles tend to be preserved indefinitely unless the rock is later subjected to extreme temperatures or pressures. By taking samples of rocks of the same age from different parts of the earth it is now possible to find the positions of the magnetic poles of the earth to within a small margin of error for different geological periods. It has been quite definitely established that the magnetic poles have tended to migrate around the earth's poles of rotation (the geographical poles) within a small radius, so that the positions of the magnetic poles in different periods can be considered true indicators of the approximate positions of the geographical poles. [See Figure 13]

In the last twenty years an immense quantity of research in this new field of paleomagnetism has revealed the astonishing fact that the positions of the geographical poles have changed at least 200 times during geological history, and that *no fewer than 16 of these changes took place during the last geological period, the Pleistocene Epoch* [my italics].[16]

Different positions of the poles were at first ascribed to the hypothesis of drifting continents, but it was latterly observed that this did not apply in all cases. Geologists were therefore forced to conclude that there were other displacements involving the entire outer shell of the Earth, the crystalline lithosphere, over the soft layers of magma below it. Displacements of this nature would certainly tend to produce alterations in the polar regions. Although still a matter for speculation, these could possibly be caused by imbalances developed through the action of subcrustal currents in the magma of the Earth's mantle. Hapgood recommends those interested to refer to his book *The Path of the Pole*, which contains the results of his research and presents evidence to the effect that three displacements of the Earth's crust have taken place over the last 100,000 years. He states:

According to my interpretation of the evidence Hudson Bay was located at the North Pole during the last ice age, and in this way I account for the ice age itself. The North American icecap, covering

108

4,000,000 square miles [10,360,000 square kilometres] of the continent, and reflecting the sun's heat back into space, created a vast refrigerator from which cold winds blowing across the narrow North Atlantic brought about a lesser ice age in Europe, creating the Scandinavian ice sheet and many great mountain glaciers in Britain and in the mountainous regions of Europe.[17]

Hapgood also stresses the fact that the causes of ice ages are not as yet understood; in fact, they present one of the great unsolved mysteries of geology.

Using a combination of radiocarbon dating and other evidence, Hapgood has assessed that a great shift in the Earth's crust began some 17,000 years ago. Being a slow movement, however, it could have taken as long as 5,000 years to complete. The dates become more interesting, do they not? During this shift North America and the whole Western Hemisphere was moved southwards, while the Eastern Hemisphere was shifted northward. As a result the North American great ice-cap was melted and Siberia placed into deep freeze. Likewise, Antarctica would have been affected by this crustal shift by being moved into the Antarctic Circle. When the North Pole was in Hudson Bay, the South Pole would have been located off the Wilkes Coast, which would have rendered the continent ice-free. Assuming these theories to be correct, the originators of the ancient sea maps that show Antarctica ice-free must have lived during the Atlantean epoch!

However, the movements indicated by Hapgood would suggest that any changes in climate took place slowly, over a period of time, which hardly fits in with the cataclysmic concept, unless, of course, the movement of the crustal plates precipitated some seismic disturbances that were sufficiently violent to bring about the gradual disintegration of the Atlantean continent. Some Atlantologists favour this theory in preference to the celestial marauder concept – Spence, for example, who postulated that the major portion

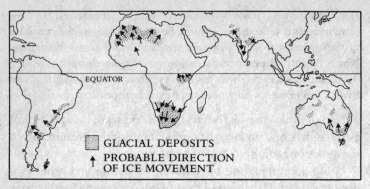

Fig. 14 Erratic ice deposits and movements indicating possible former Pole positions adapted from Gilluly.

of the Atlantean continent may have been destroyed some thousands of years earlier, its remaining portion, to which he gave the name Antillia, having survived until 5000 BC or thereabouts.

Jeffrey Goodman sees axis tilts as having far wider connotations. In *The Earthquake Generation* he writes:

We can approach the possibility of pole shift from still another direction. The earth occasionally tumbling on its axis explains more than only the onset of ice ages, myths and frozen mammoths. It also explains a great number of other correlations and anomalies found in the earth's past. In fact, *sudden pole shift is a unifying explanation for mountain building, volcanic activity, continental drift, magnetic pole reversals, animal extinction, and the erratic occurrence of glaciers.*

Geologists find it difficult to explain why, in the distant geological past, large ice accumulations occurred in what are now tropical and semi-tropical regions. Extensive ice sheets once existed in South America, Australia, Africa and India. By examining the deposits left by these glaciers and the trend of the scratches and grooves etched into the bedrock, geologists have also found that these anomalous glacial sheets moved in directions opposite to what would be expected. Dr William Stokes of the University of Utah, in his text *Essentials of Earth History*, points out,

'In South Africa the glaciers moved principally from north to south – away from the Equator. In central Africa and Madagascar other deposits show that the ice moved northward, well within the tropic zone. Most surprising has been the discovery of great beds of glacial debris in northern India, where the direction of the movement was northward . . . in Australia and Tasmania, where the ice moved from south to north . . . movement in Brazil and Argentina was toward the west.'[18] (See Figure 14)

In his *History of China*, Martinus Martini, a Jesuit missionary in those parts, wrote of ancient Chinese records that mentioned a time when the sky suddenly began to fall northward and the Sun, Moon and planets changed their courses *after the Earth had been shaken*. The tomb of Senmouth, architect to Queen Hatshepsut, presents us with a similar enigma. Of the two star maps painted on the ceiling, one places the cardinal points correctly while in the other they are reversed, the indication being that the Earth had at some point in the past experienced a tilt. The Harris Papyrus mentions the Earth turning in a cosmic cataclysm, and the Hermitage Papyrus of Leningrad and the Ipuwer Papyrus also mention the world as having turned upside down. The zodiacal signs in the famous Zodiac of Denderah are arranged in a spiral and the symbols are easily recognizable. The sign of Leo, however, occupies the point at the vernal equinox, which suggests that a closer examination of the dates involved in the precession of equinoxes might prove fruitful. But more of this in Chapter 7.

Lunar Theories

Although the idea that an asteroid or comet striking the Atlantic Ocean and displacing the tectonic plates or sima could conceivably have been responsible for the sinking of the island continent, there are other equally plausible explanations for the disaster that call for examination and comment. Professor Hans Hoerbiger, whose theories were popular in Europe in the 1920s and 1930s, formulated the concept of a perpetual struggle between the forces of repulsion and attraction. This alternating tension between opposite principles, he postulated, also governs Earth and all living matter and determines human destiny. While the Cosmic Ice aspect of his doctrine has long since been scientifically disproved, chaos science has tended to confirm the basic principles of his argument. In view of the established validity of at least one of his ideas, perhaps it is feasible that some alteration in the distance between our Earth and its satellite could conceivably have been responsible for the kind of axis tilt that would have sent Atlantis to its watery grave and caused the kind of celestial and terrestrial phenomena that have found their way into so many ancient legends and records.

Hoerbiger's Lunar hypothesis was very popular with some writers and scientists in the late 1940s and early 1950s, notably H. S. Bellamy, who wrote several books on the subject, including *The Atlantis Myth* and *Moons, Myths and Man*. Hoerbiger suggested that our planet has known two moons. The first of these, which was smaller than our present satellite, was eventually drawn into the Earth's orbit, and the catastrophe precipitated by its landing caused the sinking of the Pacific continent of Mu, or Lemuria. It was the capturing of our present Moon, however, which he envisaged as originally being a small planet in its own right, that was responsible for the Atlantis disaster.

Before considering whether the Moon could, in fact, have exerted any influence on the Atlantis epic, let us look at the latest discoveries concerning the nature and identity of our satellite. Two articles that appeared in reputable scientific publications in 1989 are germane to this argument. The first of these, which appeared in the American magazine *Astronomy*, concerns the formation of Earth. In the 1950s Nobel Prize-winning chemist Harold Urey uncovered one of the chemical clues concerning the

Earth's origin based on cosmochemical studies alone. The indication was that Earth had formed not from the compression of giant clouds, as had previously been thought, but from small rocky bodies. Urey proposed that solar nebular material aggregated first into small, rocky, asteroid-like bodies called planetesimals, which collided with each other and then clumped together to produce an Earth largely devoid of inert gases. Elsewhere in the solar system other planetesimals also grew as collisions added to their mass until only a handful of major bodies were left – the planets of today.

But what has all this to do with the Moon? To continue with the theory: a giant planetesimal is believed to have struck the newly formed Earth about 4.4 billion years ago, blowing out an enormous cloud of vapour, from which our Moon condensed. This suggests that our satellite is the child of Earth and has therefore never enjoyed a separate orbit, as Hoerbiger suggested. Or does it?

The writer of the article in question, William K. Hartmann, an astronomer known for his work in planetary evolution, ends his article with the following remark:

One prominent planetary geologist remarked that he has lived through two major geological revolutions: the revolution that recognized continental drift and plate tectonics in the 1960s when he was a student and the revolution that recognized possible catastrophic impacts as important in Earth history – a revolution that is happening now.[19]

The second of these articles concerned with the geochemical implications of the formation of the Moon by a single giant impact appeared in the British journal *Nature*. It begins with the statement:

The Earth–Moon system has several unique features. None of the other terrestrial planets possesses a comparable moon – the tiny Martian moons, Phobos and Deimos, are probably captured asteroids. The angular momentum of the Earth–Moon pair is anomalously high compared with that of the other inner planets, and the inclination of the lunar orbit is strange.[20]

An appropriate list of chemical comparisons is then provided for the more technically minded who like to see the facts on paper in front of them.

What we are not told, however, is whether our Moon has ever altered its position, albeit slightly, in relation to Earth. We all know that it is badly pock-marked from continual bombardment by extraterrestrial material, but has there ever been a situation in the past when some of that material has found its way down to Earth, or a glancing asteroid of the proportions envisaged by Muck could have unbalanced the Moon sufficiently to change its position and therefore affect the gravitational pull it exerts on our tidal system? And does the fact that it is a 'child of Earth' mean that it has never enjoyed an orbit other than the one we see in our skies to this day?

Heeding Professor Efremov's advice and turning to anthropology, myth and legend, we must ask ourselves at what point lunar worship actually began. Did it, for example, coincide with the zodiacal Age of Cancer (the Silver Age of Greek mythology), the early days of which are believed by some authorities to have accommodated the many flood legends? The Moon is seen today as representing the feminine principle because of its correspondence with the feminine cycle, but according to some ancient traditions the Moon was masculine and the Sun feminine. Assuming the absence of a Moon, or a change in its proximity to our planet, would our physiological functions have been dictated by a solar cycle? Perhaps the myths of the past will serve to throw some light on these and other questions that are germane to life in antediluvian times.

In contrast to the Earth–Moon relationship postulated by Hartmann, Mooney states that the recent Moon landings and examination of lunar rocks have led scientists to theorize that the Moon was not part of the Earth but *was* a captured body, the capturing process explaining the present axial spin. Since scientists are prone to adjusting their opinions in the light of new evidence, all ideas should be considered as valid propositions until such times as they enter the realms of established fact or are conclusively disproved; of course, even fact has the habit of nonplussing its adherents at times, as is evident in the 'unbreakable atom' concept, among other 'certainties'.

Mooney also dismisses Hoerbiger's theory on the grounds that were the Moon to approach too close to Earth, gravitational forces would shatter the smaller body before actual contact, so that a collision between it and Earth could not happen. Damage to Earth from the shattered satellite would be immense, however, but the planet would survive and would probably be surrounded by the Moon's debris in rings similar to those of Saturn. This hypothesis differs entirely from the theories proposed by Muck and others regarding the entry into the Earth's atmosphere of an asteroid of sufficient size to effect an axis tilt, and the newly popular 'single impact' proposition outlined in the aforementioned scientific articles. So where does that leave us as regards the Atlantean calamity?

According to Braghine, ancient Classical authors affirmed that several millennia before their time a large and heavily populated continent existed in the Indian Ocean between Africa, Arabia and Hindustan, stretching even farther eastwards. As they believed the Moon, or Selene as she was known to them, did not exist in those far distant times, the said authors were disposed to refer to the inhabitants of this legendary continent as 'Preselenites'. Once again the myths tell us of the great bounty, richness of soil and fine climate enjoyed by these prehistoric people, who sadly incurred the wrath of their gods to the extent that their Earthly paradise was sent to the bottom of the ocean. This story, still to be found among the Arabs and Hindus, was dismissed as tribal fable until the famous nineteenth-century zoologist Ernst Haeckel proposed that such a land had once existed millennia early, and had been the birthplace of lemurs, a species of mammal now found in Madagascar. His hypothesis was taken seriously by another scientist, P. Sclater, who saw this continent as the cradle of humankind and named it Lemuria (see Chapter 5).

Braghine was impressed by the British scientist Blandford, in whose opinion both physical geography and palaeontology unanimously confirmed the existence of Lemuria from the beginning of the so-called Permian epoch until the end of the Miocene Period. Other scientists, however, have dated the Lemurian catastrophe nearer 15,000 BC, which coincides with Hapgood's assessment of the beginning of a sizeable shift in the Earth's crust. This would have given the Atlanteans some 6,000 or 7,000 years in which to build up their civilization to the status it achieved prior to its disappearance.

In more recent times Lemuria has been seen as synonymous with Gondwanaland, but at this point Braghine and other Atlantologists find themselves perplexed, as the early legends state that the population of Gondwanaland *did not know the Moon!* If this is the case, someone has their wires crossed somewhere, be it the astronomers, geophysicists, anthropologists or mythologists. Assuming the legends to be correct and that there are things science has yet to discover about the early movements of our satellite, what cosmic perturbation jogged the baleful Selene into our orbit? Too many tribes have analogous legends concerning the recent appearance of the Moon in the heavens, and of times past when there was no moonlight, for this to be attributed to local superstition. Whether it was Muck's asteroid, or some other celestial phenomenon, we cannot prove at this time, but some of the interesting tribal myths about the Moon might help to throw further light on this rather grey area of inquiry. Braghine lists the following:

● The legend of the Greeks concerning the Preselenites, who inhabited Gondwanaland before the appearance of the Moon.

● The myth of the Chibchas of Colombia concerning Bohica, who created the Moon after a great inundation of the Funza valley.

● The myth of the Bushmen, who affirm that a large continent west from Africa disappeared at an epoch when there existed TWO moons.

● The Mayan myth concerning a great calamity, during which the Great Serpent, i.e. a certain celestial body, was ravished from the heavens.

● The myth of the Tupis, who affirm that the Moon falls periodically upon the Earth and a new Moon takes the place of the old one in the heavens.

● The Aravacs of Guyana affirm that the Great Spirit sent a double calamity to the world: at first it was struck by fire and next a great flood covered the Earth.[21]

Braghine sees these vague allusions as falling into two categories: those that suggest that a cataclysm occurred when the present Moon did not exist at all and those that describe the upheaval as having taken place when the Moon as we know it was present in the heavens, but so, also, was another celestial body or satellite (asteroid?) of similar proportions. These legends and conclusions prompt one to think that Hoerbiger was basically correct in his double lunar theory, but erred in its justification.

Evidence from Myths and History

Aside from the lunar connotations, which other phenomena do most of these legendary accounts have in common?

- A celestial fiery phenomenon precipitating a major flood or inundation;

- An object or objects falling from the sky;

- Black rain;

- Dramatic climatic changes for the worse;

- The disappearance of large tracts of land beneath the ocean;

- An alteration of some kind in the Earth's axis precipitating a change in the position or paths of the heavenly bodies;

- Forewarnings of these unpleasant events given by the seers and prophets of the people concerned;

- The catastrophe being sent as some kind of punishment for disobeying the will of God or the tribal gods in question;

- An error on the part of some godling or hero who has misused his power.

The final category includes the story of Phaethon, son of Helios, who wanted to drive his father's chariot but did not possess the necessary skill to handle the fiery steeds. Consequently, the chariot ran out of control and badly scorched the Earth. A confirmatory legend also appears in the *Codex Chimalpopoca*, a Nahua Central American record, which tells that the third era of the world, or 'third sun', is called *Quia Tonatiuh*, or sun of rain, 'because in this age there fell a rain of fire, all which existed burned, and there fell a rain of gravel', the rocks 'boiled with tumult, and there also arose the rocks of vermilion colour'.[22]

There are similar statements in other ancient records, which would seem to indicate that in those remote times this Earth was peopled by beings intelligent enough to make accurate observations of such phenomena, a fact that the bastions of learning are loath to concede. But even assuming that people have existed on this planet for as long as science asserts, they must have experienced many of the great catastrophes that overtook it in its days of comparative youth, and these will be firmly entrenched in both myth and legend, and in the collective unconscious of *Homo sapiens*.

Even within the period embraced by orthodox history, there have been climatic changes that have necessitated large numbers of people moving from their homes and seeking new and more fruitful pastures elsewhere. Recent research using carbon-14 and dendrochronological datings has shown how the sulphur emitted by large volcanic eruptions can affect the weather in certain parts of the world for some time after the event by converting the sulphur to sulphuric acid in the upper atmosphere, blotting out the Sun and causing a severe spell of cold weather. Apparently 1816 was such a year, and it is only recently that scientists have discovered the cause. So perhaps we can dismiss at least a few of the accounts of phenomena such as black rain (volcanic sediments) as falling within this category, but not all.

How many of the myths we have examined relate to the catastrophe that overtook Plato's Atlantis? Maybe not all of them, but there are many that do.

That axis tilts have been witnessed by intelligent human beings in the past, who have recorded them with a reasonable degree of accuracy, is evident in the *Oera Linda Book*. The Norse *Völuspá*, however, which is both graphic and highly informative, claims to contain the most ancient history of man. Three of its verses read:

Verse 2.   First was the time when Ymir raged,
           Sand was not yet, nor sea, nor salty wave,
           I found no earth beneath nor sky above,
           All was a gaping void – and grass nowhere . . .

Verse 3.   Until the sons of Bur raised the ground
           Created her, Midgarth, the myth.
           The sun shone on stone battlements from the south,
           The ground turned green with verdant leek.

Verse 4.   From the south the sun, the moon's companion,
           Touched the edge of the heavens.
           The sun did not know his halls.
           The moon did not know her might.
           The stars did not know their places . . .[23]

Verse 2 is obviously describing the Quaternary period, or Ice Age, while the following lines deal with the terrestrial and celestial changes that ended the Ice Age and heralded the arrival of the warmer weather and its new, more beneficent pantheon of deities.

But what about the allusion to the Sun rising in the south? Verse 4 is even more interesting if taken in the axis-tilt context. The celestial pole is purely a convenient point of reference rather than a set astronomical placing, so should it appear to be displaced, the indication would be that it was the Earth's axis that had altered, and not the positions of the Sun, Moon or fixed stars. However, the verse does afford us a unique reference to some unusual displacement of both the Sun *and* Moon: 'The moon did not know her might' could imply that some movement of that body exerted either an unusual pull on the oceans that had not hitherto been experienced, or caused a monumental catastrophe.

The French scholar Denis Saurat proposed that the proximity of the Moon was connected with the phenomenon of height. The Bible tells us 'There were giants in the earth in those days', which has been interpreted as meaning that at a period in the past some people were, on the whole, much taller than they have been during the time of recorded history. Likewise, the *Oera Linda Book* speaks of the people of Atland as averaging 7 feet (2 metres) tall. Our museums show us that in the age of the saurians many species were of huge proportion, while the Greek poets and sages wrote of giants, Titans and other beings of gargantuan stature. Saurat tells us that fragments of colossal human or pre-human bones have been found in Java, southern China and South Africa, and supplies the appropriate references. Exceptionally heavy stone implements (bifaces) weighing from 4 to 8 pounds (1.8 to 3.6 kilogrammes) have been discovered in Syria, Moravia and Morocco, suggesting that the users must have been at least 9 feet (2.7 metres) tall![24]

Mooney supports the idea that the Earth was nearer to the Sun at some point in its past, and suggests that were this the case, there would have been a greater evaporation of surface water (lowering of sea-levels?), resulting in a high-altitude vapour screen surrounding the Earth. The effect would have been a denser atmosphere, with a slightly higher surface pressure and higher atmospheric pressure in high mountainous regions. Another effect of this screen, he tells us, 'would have been to filter out a great deal of solar radiation and certain cosmic and hard X-radiation from extrasolar regions of the galaxy'.[25] Saurat confirms this view and refers to the theories of the French geologist Edmond Perrier (*La Terre avant l'histoire*), who concluded that in the primary era the Sun was much larger than it is now, and the Earth was then perpendicular to the ecliptic, which would have resulted in a state of perpetual summer!

It has been suggested to me that Mooney's theoretical vapour screen – which is also supported by the arcane teachings of Theosophy and Anthroposophy – could accommodate both the 'absent Moon' myths and the currently favoured scientific view of the Moon's origin. In other words, our satellite was not visible because it was obscured by a dense mist. This lack of visibility would have been even more accentuated had the Moon, as some researchers have suggested, been differently positioned in relation to, or even slightly farther away from, the Earth in those times. What worries me about this theory is that the tribal and cultural sources from which the myths in question originated did appear to be familiar with the galactic and stellar formations, which rather suggests that they did have a clear view of the night sky.

One is reminded of the Hopi legend of the twin gods Poqanghoya and Palongawhoya, guardians of the north and south axes of the Earth respectively, whose task it was to keep the planet rotating properly. They were, however, ordered by Sotuknang, nephew of the Creator, to leave their posts so that the 'second world' could be destroyed because its people had become evil.

Then the world, with no one to control it, teetered off balance, spun around crazily, then rolled over twice. Mountains plunged into the sea with a great splash, seas and lakes sloshed over the land; and as the world spun through cold and lifeless space it froze into solid ice.[26]

The Hopi also insist that their 'first world' was destroyed by fire and their 'third world' by water.

There is a parallel here with the Egyptian twin lion gods, Shu and Tefnut (see Figure 15). The Egyptian Sun-god, Ra, was referred to as 'Ra of the two horizons' ('horizons' is used in this context as a mathematical term denoting a system of dimensions or frame of reference), the Light Horizon and the Life Horizon,

Fig 15. The twin lion gods of yesterday and today.

representing the material and spiritual realms. Ra of the Life Horizon was symbolized by a flattened circle or solar disc mounted on the hindquarters of two lions seated back to back. Some people see the lions as representing the two primordial forces of life – desire and fear – while to others they are the gods of yesterday (the past) and today (the present or future). In other words, the power of time. Their back-to-back position can therefore be interpreted as the masculine 'desire' force and the feminine 'fear' force pulling in opposite directions (chaos?), while the weight of the Ra disc (reason and self-control) holds them in check; or, in the 'time' context, where it can be seen as the solar force that holds our planet in its orbital path and thus creates night and day – the time on our clocks.

But should one or both of those lions move their position, even slightly, then the orb, or Ra, would adjust accordingly and we would see the Sun *from a different angle* than we do today. The irony of this philosophy, however, lies in the idea that if desire and fear do get the better of us, the energies we

Fig. 16. The eye gives access to space, that is to say volume, and therefore to measure. In Egypt, the sections of the eye are the glyphs for the fractions $\frac{1}{2}$ to $\frac{1}{64}$ The parts total $\frac{63}{64}$. (The sum of successive divisions will always fall short of unity except at infinity, which is perfectly consonant with Egyptian thought: only the Absolute is one.)

emit world-wide will cause Shu and Tefnut to rise and dislodge the disc of Ra. In other words, it is the thoughts and deeds of the people of Earth that decide whether the poles will shift, the axis will tilt and calamity will befall us all, as could have been the case in the latter days of Atlantis! A sobering thought for our present age!

The lion symbology also appears in the story of how Ra became angered when men rebelled against the statutes of cosmic law by misusing certain 'powers'. In order to punish them for their misdeeds, he withdrew his divine eye from his forehead and smote the Earth with it. The eye is shown in the hieroglyphics as being synonymous with the Goddess Sekhmet the Powerful, the Lion-headed One, considered by some authorities as a leonine version of Hathor. There were, in fact, two eyes of Ra, as might be expected. The left, or lunar, eye, was 'the Eye of Horus'. The eye that Ra hurled at those who transgressed his laws, however, was his right, or solar, eye. This eye is also symbolized by the uraeus, or Serpent of Wisdom, which adorned the insignia of the ancient Egyptian pharaohs and priesthood. It is also the symbol of the cat goddess Bast, who, according to Herodotus, was the twin sister of Horus.

The Eye of Ra episode is often seen as an allegorical representation of a fiery object falling from the sky, while the mathematical dimensions used in the ancient Egyptian portrayal of the eye are believed to hold some hidden meaning that goes back to the times of Atlantis (see Figure 16).

Let us suppose, then, that an axis tilt did take place at the time of the disappearance of Atlantis, which is highly feasible anyway, and that the Earth had been ever so slightly nearer to the Sun prior to the catastrophe, after which it assumed its present orbit, increasing the solar year from 360 to 365 days – those enigmatic epagomenic, or intercalary, days that have puzzled scholars and metaphysicians for many a century – which leads us neatly into the next chapter.

CHAPTER 7

Cycles, Time Scales and Dates

> What's past, and what's to come is strew'd with husks
> And formless ruin of oblivion.
> The end crowns all,
> And that old common arbitrator, Time,
> Will one day end it.
>
> WILLIAM SHAKESPEARE, *Troilus and Cressida*

The priests of Sais explained to Salon how the myths that were hoary with age in those distant days were but allegories of real facts. The Phaethon story, for example, '. . . really signifies a declination of the bodies moving around the earth and in the heavens, and a great conflagration of things upon the earth recurring at long intervals of time . . .'.[1] Following such cataclysms, humankind lapses into barbarism and forgets the finer arts and sciences it has formerly learned and practised.

Cycles of Periodicity

On what are these 'cycles of periodicity', which seem to feature in all the myths of the past, based and why is it that some people are so unaware of them today? Many cycles have been calculated as being relevant to the Earth and those that dwell thereon. Let us examine some of these, which will demonstrate how *Homo sapiens* and all like forms on Earth are inextricably bound up in the processes of extraterrestrial phenomena to the extent that they do not have the control over their lives that many might believe. Equally, Earth exerts a complementary influence on its celestial neighbours, so that we cannot necessarily blame the stars, asteroids, Sun, Moon or even Gaia herself, if they visit ills upon us, some of which could be avoided were we a little more *au fait* with the subtle cycles of the solar system and universe of which we are each an infinitesimal part.

Astronomers have long recognized that the sequence of solar and lunar eclipses recurs every 18 years $11\frac{1}{3}$ days, or 223 lunations. In other words, the centres of the Sun and Moon return to almost the same relative places, so the eclipses of the next period recur in approximately the same order, but because the length of the cycle includes one-third of a day, the zone of visibility is shifted $120°$ (one-third of a cycle) to the west each time.[2]

The Chaldeans, who were adept at astronomy and astrology, named this the Saros cycle (Greek, from Babylonian *sărŭ*, 3,600 years; the modern use is apparently based on a misinterpretation of the original cycle as one of 18.5 years) and attributed to it magical powers that would one day be instrumental in causing the destruction of the world. Although scientists may dismiss this premise as superstitious nonsense, that does not mean that Saros has no bearing on Earthly affairs. In fact, the French psychologist and statistician, Michel Gauquelin, cites his fellow countryman Le Danois, as emphasizing the great importance that the Saros cycle can have on our lives. Le Danois claimed that the combined gravitational pull of the Sun and Moon acts on the tides, causing widespread disturbances in bodies of water that may account for the changes in climates over the centuries. Although many climatologists were inclined to think that Le

Danois was guilty of stretching fact to suit his fancy, the observations of another hydraulic engineer, E. Paris-Teynac, showed a similar pattern for large rivers, the Nile in particular.

Data available on Nile tides goes back 4,000 years, and from these records some strange facts emerge. Rhythmic variations that coincide with astronomical cycles are clearly in evidence. Paris-Teynac identified an eleven-year variation that accords with the sunspot cycle, and eighteen-year periods corresponding to the Saros cycle that reflect the Sun–Moon eclipse intervals, which suggested to him that Saros really does increase the water-level in some parts of the world. In other words, when Sun–Moon eclipses occur at certain points, the likelihood of some terrestrial drama is increased.

Attempts have also been made to relate the gravitational influence of the planets to the Ice Ages. In 1938, the Serbian astronomer M. Milankovitch tried to use them to explain the succession of glacial epochs. The climatic curves he calculated apparently corresponded rather accurately to the curves of the glacial advances. In 1956 Hans Suess, of the University of California, noted that the same curves also follow the cycles of temperature changes in the oceans over the same geological period.

Although Milankovitch's figures were met with considerable doubt by many in the scientific community, George Gamov, of the University of Colorado, rallied to his defence with the statement:

Despite the objections of some climatologists who claim that a few degrees difference in temperature could not have caused the glacial periods, it seems that the old Serbian was right. Therefore we have to conclude that, although the planets are without influence on the lives of individuals (as the astrologers would have it), they certainly affect the life of men, animals, and plants through the long geological periods.[3]

It is now generally acknowledged that the Sun and Moon can affect health. In 1940 Dr William Petersen noted that deaths caused by tuberculosis were most frequent seven days before the full moon, and sometimes eleven days afterwards. He was able to relate this pattern to the pH content of the blood, the ratio of acidity to alkalinity, which varies according to the lunar cycle of terrestrial magnetism. Since then, evidence of correspondences between lunar phases and various biological phenomena have poured in, while there has also been a deal of confirmatory information regarding the effect of sunspots on both people and weather.

The 'Great Year' is the name given to the period of time (roughly 25,826 years) taken by the pole of the Earth's axis to complete an entire circle round the pole of the ecliptic, the Sun's apparent path among the stars. The gradual changing of direction in space of the Earth's axis is known as the precession of the equinoxes. Each year the point in space where the Sun crosses the celestial equator – referred to by astronomers as the vernal equinox, and by astrologers as Aries – when viewed against the background of the constellations, is seen from the Earth as slightly behind the position it occupied the previous year. Consequently the nearest star to which the axis points, known as the Pole Star, changes through the ages. Some 4,000–5,000 years ago the North Pole pointed to Alpha Draconis, whereas it now points to Polaris in Ursa Minor.

Astrological and Mythological Ages

Confusion arises from the fact that the constellations have the same names as the signs of the zodiac. Astronomers therefore tend to look askance when those interested but untutored in the subtleties of astrology speak of 'being born in the star sign of Leo'. The signs of the zodiac (the word 'zodiac' comes from the Greek and means 'circle of animals') are not synonymous with the fixed stars with whom they share a name, a fact that should be borne in mind when one is thinking in terms of astrological 'ages'.

The constellations that are marked on a stellar chart as definite star groupings are purely terms of reference, as the points of light in question may have taken many hundreds of light-years to arrive and have doubtless moved on long before the light signals reach Earth. At the time when these star groupings were named the 30° of ecliptic, starting from the point of the vernal equinox, was called Aries and the constellations that appeared in its background was also called Aries. The 30° of the ecliptic known as Aries are always the 30° counted from the vernal equinox, and the equinox is slightly farther back each year in relation to the other constellations.

Just as our year is divided into twelve months, the Great Year is similarly divided into twelve ages. These are the periods of time when the equinox is judged as being against the background of each of the twelve constellations that appear to lie roughly around the ecliptic. We are told that these periods cannot be reckoned with any real degree of exactitude, but are roughly 2,000 years each. Nor can the commencement of each period be fixed, because the boundaries of the constellations are not clearly defined. As the movement is backward from the end of a constellation to its beginning, the periods of time are in a backward order through the signs. The last 2,000 years have exhibited characteristics that are decidedly Piscean, while the previous 2,000 years were clearly Arian and the 2,000 years preceding those unmistakably Taurean. Working backwards in this way, we can trace the ages through Gemini to Cancer and Leo, which, according to the ancient zodiacs, appeared to play a key role in the destruction of Atlantis.

The Aquarian Age Estimated commencement around AD 2000 – in other words, we are just about to enter it. Some astrologers believe that we have already done so, or are at least occupying the cuspal position.

The Piscean Age Commenced around 60 BC by astronomical calculation.

The Arian Age Began 2000 BC or thereabouts. A period of exploration and conquest, when empires rose and fell, as might be expected with Mars being the ruler of Aries.

The Taurean Age Began around 4000 BC. The bull featured prominently in the rites, religions and cultures of this era.

The Geminian Age Began around 6000 BC. This is frequently referred by astrologers as relating to twin-god cults, but I am inclined to view it more as a time of confusion or choice, when humanity was poised between two factors. This could be seen in terms of the matrist/patrist dilemma, the onset of the heroic cults or simply a period of movement, communication and the development of new thinking processes.

The Cancerian Age Began approximately 8000 BC. This watery sign is ruled by the Moon, which I believe to be highly significant. I see it as encompassing the Silver Age of Greek mythology and having some definite bearing on the Flood and the sinking of Atlantis, although I cannot agree with those authorities who place the Atlantean cataclysm near the beginning of the sign. I am also prompted to associate this sign with the latter days of Atlantis by the growing influence of the ocean as manifested in the worship of Poseidon, to give the sea god his Greek name.

The Leonine Age Commenced around 10,000 BC. The last great age of Atlantis. The Golden Age of the Greeks, when Cronus ruled and the continent prospered.

Now, working from the earliest days forward, let us compare these approximations and their attendant astrological assumptions with the information that has come down to us from Greek mythology.

THE 'AGES OF MAN'

The Golden Age The people of this era lived like gods while Cronus reigned. Free from worry and fatigue, old age did not afflict them and they rejoiced in continual festivity. Hesiod emphasizes that they were not immortal, but died peacefully as in 'sweet slumber'. All the blessings of the world were theirs; the fruitful earth gave forth its unbidden treasures, and the people ate honey and drank the milk of goats. After their death, they became benevolent genii, protectors and tutelary guardians of the living. They bestowed good fortune, were patrons of music and helped men to uphold justice if their spiritual advice was heard and heeded. Interestingly, the Irish myths apply similar after-life references to the Tuatha de Danaans, or 'fairy people', who were said to have arrived 'from the west in a cloud'.

The Silver Age This age was believed by the sages to have been much inferior, its people resembling those of the Golden Age in neither body nor soul. It equates with the dominance of matrism and has strong lunar connotations. These people were mainly agriculturalists, who did not indulge in war, were vegetarians and consequently lived to a ripe old age. The men were subject to their mothers, which naturally failed to meet with the approval of Hesiod, who described them as disputatious and lacking in manliness. Neither did they offer sacrifice to Zeus, which angered the god to the extent that he eventually destroyed them, after which they sank into the depths of the Earth to appear in later myth as the subterranean blessed, in which capacity they were accorded some small degree of veneration.

The Silver Age is sometimes designated as the Minoan period, although most authorities equate it with the times just prior to, and directly after, the Flood, when goddess worship predominated throughout Europe and the Middle East.

The Brazen, or Bronze, Age The people of this time were entirely different from their predecessors. They 'fell like the fruit from ash trees', were robust and delighted only in oaths, meat-eating and warlike exploits. 'Their pitiless hearts were hard as steel; their might was untameable, their arms invincible.'[4] According to one source they ended by cutting each other's throats, while another account has it that 'black death' seized them all. They were, no doubt, those invaders from the north who worked in bronze, the ash tree (Yggdrasil) holding great significance in their religious beliefs.

The Iron Age Hesiod gives us some variations on this theme, declaring that prior to the Iron Age Zeus created a race of divine heroes, those who fought the famous wars for Thebes or Troy. They were more righteous and better than the Bronze Age people, and after death they came to the Isles of the Blest, which were girdled by Oceanus. In these idyllic islands the life-giving fields bear sweet fruit thrice yearly, and Cronus, set free of his chains by Zeus, rules in peace and harmony.

For the Iron Age, however, Hesiod had nothing but abuse, being obsessed with gloomy prophecies about the birth of grey-haired children and the return of the goddesses Aidos and Nemesis to Olympus, leaving humankind to perish undefended. The Iron Age is generally associated with misery, crime, treachery and cruelty, when 'men respect neither vows nor justice, nor virtue'.[5] This explanation is said to account for what is seen as the progressive degeneracy of people and, as must be obvious, represents the age in which we live now.

Time Scales

If one reads between the lines, it is easy to see where myth has accommodated the prevailing winds of change, while an in-depth study of the legends of many cultures serves to emphasize the 'single source' theory even more strongly.

The Babylonian astronomer and historian Berossus was certainly familiar with the Great Year and precession of equinoxes. The Sumerians, from whom the Babylonians inherited their knowledge, were the first to give names to the zodiacal figures. Their records indicate that they possessed a much wider understanding of celestial phenomena than any succeeding culture up to recent years. As was the case with many other sacerdotally orientated early cultures, however, their most profound truths were inevitably garbed with the cloak of secrecy so as to render them incomprehensible to the profane. Sumerian figurines and graphics displaying astronomical references were often depicted surrounded by twelve stars or planets, although some authorities designate these as representing the Earth, Sun, Moon and *nine* planets, which still makes one more than we recognize at present. According to Sumerian cosmology, this additional planet was visible to observers only once every 3,600 years because of its specialized orbit.

During the writing of this book I attended a talk at the local astronomical society by Patrick Moore, who stated he was quite convinced that there was another planet beyond Pluto, and presented some sound scientific evidence to support his (and other astronomers') belief.

The currently favoured idea that the Earth's development has been a reasonably leisurely affair may be cosy, but is it accurate? We look back through the pages of our history books to the point when geology, palaeontology and allied disciplines take over our thinking processes for us. Ages fold neatly one into another; out go the saurians (the crocodile and a few minor distant cousins excepted) and in comes the human in ape form, gradually evolving to troglodyte status and from thence to agricultural village dweller. The Tertiary and Quaternary eras see Gaia settling quietly down to her new domestic mode, with only the occasional internal hiccup to remind her peoples that she can belch louder should her digestive system take in something she might find hard to stomach. And so the gradualist school of science has held sway for many years, and we have dutifully read our textbooks and applauded the erudition of our tutors.

Professor D. Nalivkin, of the Soviet Academy of Science, commented:

Observations of catastrophic phenomena are limited by the time span of no longer than 4,000–6,000 years. For geological processes this is a short period and it is quite possible that some of the most terrible catastrophes have not been recorded in the chronicles of mankind ... We must not fit into modern standards all that has happened on the Earth throughout ... its existence.[6]

The cosy world of gradualism has finally been completely shattered, and the revolution has come from within the ranks of its own disciplines. The cosmologist Stephen Hawking, occupant of Newton's chair at Cambridge University, chose as a title for a lecture 'Is the End in Sight for Theoretical Physics?', the implication being that predictability is one thing in a cloud chamber where two particles collide at the end of a race around an accelerator, and something else altogether in the simplest tub of roiling fluid, or in the Earth's weather or in the human brain.[7]

Enter the new chaos science, the laboratory mouse of which is the pendulum, its swing from chaos to order and back again being representative of the ever-changing tides of life at all levels, while its sacred geometry is the fractal, as developed by Professor Benoit Mandelbrot. Chaos science and its computerized images are the material of other studies, however, and it is only in their role as freedom fighters against the oppressive strait-jacket of established scientific discipline that we are prepared to welcome them gladly on the Atlantean scene.

The Helmholtz apocalyptic prophecies of a universal demise were based on the second law of thermodynamics. The remorseless rise in entropy that accompanies any natural process could, he felt, lead only to the final cessation of all life-giving activity throughout the universe. Helmholtz envisioned a slowly dying universe, inexorably squandering its finite and irretrievable resources, and so choking on its own entropy. His gloomy prognosis evoked the following reaction from Bertrand Russell:

'... that all the labours of the ages, all the devotion, all the inspiration, all the noonday brightness of human genius, are destined to extinction in the vast death of the solar system, and the whole temple of Man's achievements must inevitably be buried beneath the debris of a universe in ruins – all these things, if not quite beyond dispute, are yet so nearly certain that no philosophy which rejects them can hope to stand. Only within the scaffolding of these truths, only on the firm foundation of unyielding despair, can the soul's habitation henceforth be safely built.'[8]

As Paul Davies, Professor of Theoretical Physics at the University of Newcastle upon Tyne, so wisely remarked:

There exists alongside the entropy arrow another arrow of time, equally fundamental and no less subtle in nature. Its origin lies shrouded in mystery, but its presence is undeniable. I refer to the fact that the universe is *progressing* – through the steady growth of structure, organization and complexity – to ever more developed and elaborate states of matter and energy. This unidirectional advance we might call the optimistic arrow, as opposed to the pessimistic arrow of the second law.[9] ★

This second opinion accords more with my own metaphysical observations concerning the Big Bang theory, the logic of which has always defeated me in spite of the so-called 'evidence'. It would seem more reasonable to suppose that the universe expands and contracts according to some presently incalculable or inconceivable periodicity, a variation of frequencies occurring with each 'exhalation and inhalation', no experience ever being repeated. As time would seem to be the ultimate energy involved in this process, and the metaphysician presupposes all time as existing simultaneously at some ultra-subtle universal frequency, Princeton University physicist John Wheeler's theory of parallel universes, which is also endorsed by theoretical physicist Fred Alan Wolf and

★Reprinted by permission of William Heinemann Limited. Copyright Paul Davies, 1987.

confirmed in the experiments of John Hasted, begins to assume the mantle of feasibility. In fact, *Daily Telegraph* Science Correspondent Adrian Berry, commented in 1989: 'The theory of the existence of an infinite number of parallel universes . . . is gaining overwhelming acceptance among physicists.' This and similarly related issues are to be found in my book *Time: The Ultimate Energy* which offers an in-depth scientific, psychological and metaphysical study of the nature of Time.

Having established that certain periodicities do occur that affect both macrocosm and microcosm, the dates and prophecies of the scholars of old assume a new reality. The Metternich Stele of Egypt refers to the 'Boat of a Million Years' in which the Sun-God Ra makes his regular celestial journey, while Indian scientific philosophers have estimated the age of the universe as approximately 2 billion years. However, the 'Year of Brahma' lasts 311 trillion years, representing the contraction and expansion of the entire cosmos. The Hindu year-count refers to a cycle, each 'cosmic breathing' heralding the commencement of another cycle of trillions of years' duration. The people from whom these early Indian philosophers acquired their knowledge must obviously have been aware of the nature of infinity and the space-time curvature.

The records of several early cultures contain references to their remote ancestors having been supplied with advanced knowledge of astronomy, physics and cosmology by 'aliens' from the stars, as in the case of the Dogons of Mali. Those who are sufficiently unbiased to concede that there must have been, in the distant past, a civilization or civilizations that did possess progressive knowledge, which found its way into primitive tribes balk, however, at the 'E.T.' idea. For my own part, I keep an open mind, as it would seem illogical to suppose that we are the only intelligent life-forms in such a boundless universe!

Returning to the question of the dates of the astrological ages, L. Filipoff, astronomer of the Algiers University, claims to have discovered new facts in old Fifth to Sixth Dynasty pyramid texts that connect the god Thoth with the zodiacal sign of Cancer. Filipoff assumes Thoth to have been a culture bearer from a land in the west, who made his appearance when the vernal equinox was in Cancer, or around 7256 BC. When Thoth (Hermes) arrived on Egyptian soil, he was greatly moved by the people's lack of education and law, so he and his companions set about teaching them science, religion, art and music. This suggests that the world was into the 1,256th year (or thereabouts) of the Age of Cancer at or round the time of Thoth's visit, the intimation being that Thoth and, no doubt, those other people who came from 'a land in the west', who were later deified, were missionaries and colonists from Atlantis. Therefore, the inundation of the old continent more likely took place nearer the end of the Cancerian cycle, as I have earlier suggested.

The learned Thoth and the watery sign of Cancer seem unlikely bedfellows, however, although the second line of Gaius Manilius's (48 BC–AD 20), well-known astrological poem, which allocates the Greek/Roman gods to the zodiacal signs, runs: 'Apollo has the handsome Twins and *Mercury the Crab*', which hints at a tradition known to both cultures. Before supposedly leaving Earth and returning to the stars from which he came, the winged Hermes (Thoth/Mercury) is believed to have bequeathed to humankind the so-called 'Emerald Tables' of Hermes Trismegistus, which, although often seen as a product of the Middle Ages, have, on the basis of research by the eighteenth-century scholar Dr Sigismund Bacstrom, been traced to about 2500 BC.[10]

We would, therefore, appear to be faced with two conflicting views as to which zodiacal sign in the precession of equinoxes the Earth was passing through when Atlantis went down. That the Lion symbolism has some bearing on the event may be evidenced from the Denderah Zodiac, which shows Leo at the vernal point, while the twin lion gods of Akeru also seem to feature in the drama (see Figure 17). Atlantologist Andrew Tomas tells us:

A coptic papyrus *Abou Hormeis* (translated into Arabic in the ninth century) indicates the date of the Atlantean cataclysm: 'The Deluge was to take place when the heart of the Lion entered the first minute of the head of cancer'. From the scholar Makritzi (fifteenth century) we learn that 'fire was to proceed from the sign of Leo and to consume the world'. These ancient sources imply that the zodiacal sign of Leo the Lion was the time, in the precession of equinoxes, when Atlantis came to the end and a new cycle was born.[11]

However, not all authorities are in agreement when it comes to the interpretation of the Denderah Zodiac, and it has been suggested that the real meaning of certain hiero-glyphics might well have eluded Egyptologists. John Anthony West, for example, commenting on the observations of Schwaller de Lubicz apropos of certain anomalies in the Denderah Zodiac, writes:

The Zodiacal constellations are arranged in an irregular circle around the center. Note the curious placing of Cancer, well within the circle described by the others, or perhaps intended as the inner point of a spiral . . . Schwaller de Lubicz thought the signs of the zodiac disposed about an eccentric circle with one center at the pole of the ecliptic (nipple of the female hippopotamus) and the other at the pole star (jackal or dog). This does not seem to me entirely convincing. Note the placement of Libra, for example. But whatever the scheme directing the agreement, it is certain that the sign of Cancer has been singled out for special treatment.[12]

Fig. 17. The circular Zodiac of Denderah.

The Temple of Denderah was erected by the Ptolemys in the first century BC on the site of an earlier temple. Its hieroglyphics declare it to have been constructed 'according to the plan laid down in the time of the companions of Horus', that is, well before the beginnings of dynastic Egypt.

Another corridor in the labyrinth of clues lies in the Egyptian Sphinx, which has the head of a man and the body of a lion. If the leonine, or rear, half signifies that which is 'behind' or has passed, then the front half (man) would relate to Aquarius, the opposite sign to Leo and the only zodiacal sign represented by the male of our species. (See Chapter 10 for more about the sign of Leo and its connection with the binary star Sirius.)

Astrologers and Atlantologists have therefore speculated that the Aquarian Age, which we are just entering, could bring us round to the point at which we might catch up with the knowledge of Atlantis or – the other prospect – be judged by the gods as having broken their laws and therefore suitable victims for the cataclysmic melting pot! There is a body of people, including metaphysicians, psychics, fringe scientists, explorers and delvers into things unusual, who believe that the Sphinx contains a form of time-capsule, although such a notion would doubtless be viewed by some scientists as either pure fiction or wishful thinking!

One of the names of the Sphinx was Hu, or 'protector', while it was also called Hor-em-akhet, or Horus in the Horizon. Horus being a falcon-headed god, intimating the power of flight, the solution could possibly lie in some celestial or astronomical data that is likely to emerge during the Aquarian Age. The name Hu also appears in the Celtic myth of Hu Gadarn, an Atlantean who brought a band of settlers from the Old Country to the shores of Wales, a story we shall also be examining in Chapter 10.

Dates

Dates appear with some frequency in the writings of ancient

scholars. Cicero (106–43 BC), in *De Divinatione*, asserts that the Babylonian priests claimed records dating back 470,000 years, which caused the Roman a degree of both scepticism and amusement. Strabo also mentioned claims made by the Iberians of Spain that the history of their race went back 6,000 years. Diogenes Laertius, writing in the third century AD, mentioned that the ancient Egyptians had recorded 373 solar and 832 lunar eclipses. Taking into account the periodicity of eclipses, these estimations would be seen to cover some 10,000 years. The Gilgamesh epic, dated around 4000 BC, mentions tales of great mysteries and secret knowledge that existed long before the Flood.

This seems as good a point as any to play around with some dates for the Atlantean cataclysm. Muck seems to be in no doubt as to when it all took place and cites zero day at 5 June 8498 BC, according to the Gregorian calendar. The time, 1300 hours. How does he arrive at this figure? He collected a series of data relating to prehistoric cataclysmic changes from various cultures and applied them to known calendars. The most notable data came from the Mayas. The astronomical inscriptions on the Temple of the Sun at Palenque are believed to date back to the first half of the fifth century AD. Professor H. Ludendorff, who was for many years head of the Astrophysical Observatory at Potsdam and made a special study of these, concluded:

The Palenque inscriptions are in themselves evidence that the Mayas knew the sidereal year and the periods of revolution of the planets to a positively uncanny degree of accuracy. It is most unlikely that they had any precision measuring instruments and the observations they made must therefore have extended over extraordinarily long periods of time. This would be the only way to ensure such a high degree of accuracy in these astronomical data.[13]

According to Plato, Herodotus and the *Codex Troanus*, the Atlantean 'event' took place in the ninth millennium, or 8500 BC, while what Muck refers to as 'Zero Day A' may be calculated in the Mayan calendar as 5 June 8498 BC. He also computed that there was a triple conjunction of Sun, Moon and Venus at the time, which played an important role in the 'seduction' of the asteroid:

Venus and Earth revolve in circular orbits around the sun. The moon, in a smaller circle, revolves around Earth. From a geocentric viewpoint, Venus and the moon are near the sun. Heliocentrically this corresponds to an Earth, moon, and Venus conjunction. This was the conjunction on the day the Earth captured Asteroid A. The eccentric elliptical orbit of the asteroid is entered in the diagram [see Figure 18]. As has been calculated, the asteroid approached from its perihelion, that is, from the direction of the sun past Venus. The effect of this triple conjunction was that the asteroid was influenced not only by Earth, but shortly before it had been influenced also by Venus and by the moon in such a way that its orbit was deflected even closer to the Earth's position.[14]

This dating would place Muck's Atlantean catastrophe firmly in the Leo camp, while also defining the date of the Quinternary Period as 8494 BC (Gregorian) as against the previous estimate of 10,000 BC. Cross-checks carried out between radiocarbon dating and dendrochronology have now made it possible to determine with considerable accuracy the date when the inland ice-sheet east and west of the Atlantic advanced for the last time. This was previously deduced as being approximately 25,000 BC. An examination of the snapped-off tree trunks of a pine forest in the state of Wisconsin that had been uprooted by the advancing ice flow, however, tells a different story: carbon-14 datings and tree-ring readings have established that the trunks were severed some 11,000 years ago. This date corresponds to approxi-

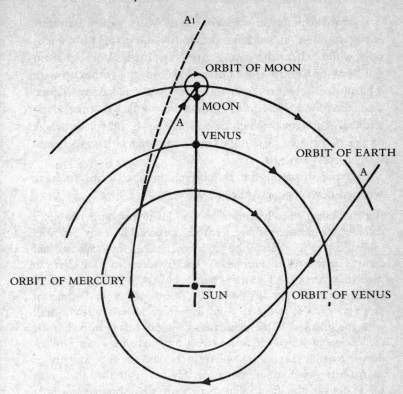

Fig. 18. The celestial constellation on 5 June 8498 BC, 13.00 hours dateline time (1:2000,000,000,000). A_1 undistorted orbit of Asteroid A; a true orbit of A because of deflection by Venus, Moon and Earth. Source: Otto Muck, *The Search for Atlantis*, p. 254.

mately 9050 BC, indicating that the last glacial advance in North America occurred *before* the Atlantean catastrophe.

These and other figures, from which Muck has subtracted an approximated 'mid' period, would again appear to confirm his chosen date. His evidence, though extensive and highly scientific, may well have been countered by more recent discoveries.

Richard Mooney also makes use of Muck's calendar references although, as we have previously discussed, his conclusions differ where the datings are concerned. Working from the Book of Genesis and Sumerian records, he comes up with a period of between 6,000 and 7,000 years as having elapsed since the Flood. He also comments on the fact that the glaciation of Antarctica, which he sees as one of the consequences of the catastrophe, has now been estimated as having begun some 6,000 years ago.

The precise dating of the cataclysm also seems to have worried Lewis Spence, since he wrote:

But did Atlantis finally sink in 9600 BC or thereabouts? Did not a considerable portion of her territory survive for many centuries subsequent to this date, and contrive to send out colonial and cultural influences to Europe, as Antillia seems to have done to barbarous America? I confess the notion has long haunted me. I refer to it as a 'notion' simply because I cannot find sufficient proof to exalt it into a definite hypothesis. I have already dealt with the question of the existence of a great Atlantean prehistoric civilization of which the Aurignacian may have been the 'broken-down' remains. Let us see what can be said for the existence of an Atlantean civilization of considerably later date than that given by Plato for the final submergence of the island-continent, a culture which has either recaptured the ancient spirit of the pre-Aurignacian times, or which has developed from the Azilian type, and continued to exist into the 'historical' period of European archaeology.

The period possibly for the existence of such a civilization must naturally fall many centuries later than Plato's date of 9600 BC, to permit of the development of a civilization more advanced than the Azilian, and, judging from the analogy of the growth of Egyptian culture, it will not be exceeding probability to place it somewhere about 5,000 years BC.[15]

Spence's view is also shared by Ian Wright, who comments: 'The first stage of break-up may have been gradual and we may well be looking at a period of some five thousand years between these earlier occurrences and the final catastrophe.' Nor does Wright dismiss the possibility that a major comet or sizeable asteroid might have disturbed the Earth's mantle to the extent that in areas of geological instability tremendous earthquakes and similar seismic phenomena might well have been precipitated.

Robert Scrutton refers to the Oronteus Finaeus World Map of 1532 (see Figure 19), which shows the coastline of Antarctica *before the continent was ice-bound* and which he sees as corresponding to the same period of temperate climate described in the *Oera Linda Book* for northern Scotland, Greenland/Scandinavia area. He tells us that sediments taken from the bottom of the Antarctic Ross Sea by the Byrd Expedition of 1949 showed that the warm conditions prevailed there 'for a long period up to 4000 BC, during which similar conditions must also have prevailed in the Northern Hemisphere.'[16] This may well have been the case, although Hapgood's explanation of the pole shifts is equally plausible.

Andrew Tomas also turns to ancient calendars for his references, and makes special mention of the writings of Bishop Diego de Landa in 1566 concerning the fact that the Mayas reckoned their calendar from a date that was about 3133 BC in European chronology. The Mayas apparently claimed that 5,125 years had passed in former cycles prior to this date. This would adjust the origin of the early Mayas to 8258 BC, which coincides with the period of the Atlantean cataclysm. On the other hand, had the Mayan civilization resulted from Atlantean colonization, this date could refer to that event rather than to the actual catastrophe.

Braghine cites the work of the scientist R. M. Gattefossé, whose book *The Truth Concerning Atlantis* refutes the views of certain astronomers, notably the Abbé Moreux, that

Fig. 19. The Oronteus Finaeus World Map of 1532.

148

RSI ORBIS DESCRIPTIO

VNIVSTIOLI

REGIO PATALIS.

BRASILIAE REGIO.

TERRA AVSTRALIS RE
center inuenta, sed nondum plane cognita.

MERI
DIES.

CIRCVLVS ANTARCTICVS.

TROPICVS CAPRICORNI.

Iulan

A
ME
RI

AED

raphian
pressam
so vultu
faciem
aria, Flu
neq; Pto
ent, aut
ebris in
tutiq; e
si sapis)
nsulito.

PARS AV STRALI

perturbations in the movements of celestial bodies give rise to great catastrophes. According to Gattefossé, major terrestrial disturbances are brought about by alterations in the positions of the poles of the Earth, which occur every 25,796 years. Braghine sees this argument as establishing that the Earth's axis can never be almost perpendicular to the plane of the ecliptic, and oscillations of that axis could not therefore have been responsible for the Atlantean cataclysm. But what if those oscillations were caused by some other celestial body?

Author and journalist Nerys Dee, writing in *Atlantis Past and to Come*, has this to add to our collection of theories:

Any alteration in the balance of a magnetic field surrounding a planet affects not only that planet but its neighbours, too. Just as astronomers on Earth watch with interest the interplay between the Sun and Jupiter (Jove's red spot responding to certain activity of the Sun) so, too, do they record the influence that passing planets have on us. In 1960 a German scientist, Professor Rudolph Tomaschek of Bavaria, stated that many of the 12,000 people who died in the Agadir earthquake could have escaped if they had been told by astronomers of the position of the planet Uranus. For Uranus, he suggested, exerts a pull on the Earth's crust that helps to cause earthquakes and it was directly above Agadir at the time of the relatively recent disaster. When this statement was published it caused something of a scientific row in the sober and responsible journal *Nature*. Professor Tomaschek claimed that, from a study of 134 great earthquakes he had made over a period of 49 years, at the time of 39 of these the planet Uranus – a giant 46 times the size of Earth – was directly above the earthquakes. And it was directly above Agadir! Uranus was in a critical position in its orbit, he claimed, between 10 and 12 o'clock, and the destruction of the town occurred at 11 p.m. Although there were those in the world of science who felt that Professor Tomaschek's conclusions were based on a series of coincidences, one would need to weigh this up against the question of whether repeated investigations producing the same results over a prolonged period of observation could be so conveniently dismissed! Coincidence or not, there is no doubt about the fact that external influences do play an important part in maintaining a balance throughout the entire universe including our own comparatively small solar system . . .[17]

The Epagomenal Days

My final consideration concerns those enigmatic intercalary days about which Mooney offers the following information:

★ The Reverend Bowles, a nineteenth-century archaeologist and authority on megalithic monuments in Britain, says that the circles of Avebury represent a calendar of 360 days, and that an extra five days were added later.

★ In all the ancient classic writings of the Hindu Aryans there is a year of 360 days. The *Aryabhatiya*, the ancient Indian mathematical and astronomical work, says: 'A year consists of 12 months. A month consists of 30 days. A day consists of 60 nadis. A nadi consists of 60 vinadikas.'

★ The ancient Babylonian year was of 12 months of 30 days each. The Babylonian zodiac was divided into 36 decans, this being the space the sun covered in relation to the fixed stars during a 10-day period. Thus the 36 decans require a year of only 360 days. Ctesias wrote that the walls of Babylon were 360 furlongs in circumference, 'as many as there are days in the year.'

★ The Egyptian year was originally 12 months of 30 days each, according to the Ebers papyrus. A tablet discovered at Tanis in the Nile Delta in 1866 reveals that in the ninth year of Ptolemy Euergetes (*ca.* 237 BC), the priests of Canopus decreed that it was 'necessary to harmonize the calendar according to the present arrangement of the world.' One day was ordered to be added every four years to the 360 days, and to the five days which were afterwards ordered to be added.

★ The ancient Romans also had a year of 360 days. Plutarch, in his life of Numa, wrote that in the time of Romulus the year was made up of twelve 30-day months.

★ The Mayan year was 360 days, called a tun. Five days were later added, and an extra day every fourth year. The Mayans computed the synodal period of the moon as 29.5209 days, as accurately as we can calculate today with our sophisticated equipment. Their degree of accuracy would surely not have been less when they computed the 360-day year. 'They did reckon them apart, and called them the days of nothing; during which the people did not anything,' wrote J. de Costa, an early writer on America. [Author's note: a reference to the five epagomenal days.]

★ The Mexicans at the time of the Spanish conquest called each 30-day period a moon.

★ The Incan year was divided into 12 quilla, or moons of 30 days. Five days were added at the end, and an extra day every four years. The extra days were regarded as unlucky, or fateful.

★ The ancient Chinese calendar was a 12-month year of 30 days each. They added $5\frac{1}{4}$ days to the year, and also divided the sphere into $365\frac{1}{4}$ degrees, adopting the new length of the year into geometry as well.[18]

This list has usually been explained away by scholars as representing errors that were latterly refined as mathematical knowledge increased. One is tempted to ask, however, why so many different cultures, from different parts of the world, would have simultaneously committed the same errors? We have heard of the Law of Synchronicity, but surely this 'coincidence' tends to stretch that one a little too far! An alteration in the Earth's orbital position, or its distance from the Sun, would, however, account for the difference in the length of the year. And if the Earth had been jolted out of its former position, the Moon would also have been affected. As Mooney puts it:

Since the moon is a smaller body than Earth, and the distances between them much smaller than between the Earth and the sun, the differences would have been even more noticeable in the case of the Earth/moon system than in the case of the Earth/sun system.

This would appear to have been the case. In several ancient sources it has been found that there were 4 9-day weeks to each lunar month, making a month of 36 days. This 9-day phase has been found in ancient Greek, Babylonian, Chinese, and Roman sources, among others. As these lunar computations did not fit with a year of 360 days, the calendars were altered to a 10-month year. This was an attempt to regulate the 'new' year to fit the 'old' 360-day year.[19]

Interestingly, the ancient Celts, who were decidedly lunar orientated, ascribed great magical powers to the number nine, which they associated with the three aspects of the Triple Goddess – Maiden, Mother and Crone.

Presuming legend to be the embodiment of past deeds, nowhere is the advent of the epagomenic days better described, albeit allegorically, than in the Egyptian myth of the birth of the five great gods of ancient Egypt. Shu and Tefnut, the twin lion gods of Time, were the children of the Solar Lord Ra (seen by some as representing our Sun, and by others as the binary star Sirius). They, in turn, gave birth to Geb and Nut (Earth and Sky). But Nut, who was also believed to have been the spouse of Ra, offended her husband by cohabiting with her brother. Enraged by his wife's infidelity, Ra swore that she should not be delivered of a child on any of the 360 days of his year, which might have caused her considerable difficulty had not Thoth, god of science, mathematics, Keeper of the Akashic Records, divine advocate and Lord of Time, played his famous game of draughts with the Moon, from which he won a seventy-second part of her light ($\frac{1}{72}$ of 360 is exactly 5!), which he made into five new days called 'epagomenal'. Nut was then able to give birth to the five children she had been carrying: Osiris, Horus the Elder, Set, Isis and Nephthys, in that order. This legend is also reiterated in the Greek myth of Cronus (Time) swallowing five of his own children and disgorging them after taking a potion administered to him by Metis (Justice).

Although various magical and mystical interpretations have been placed upon these stories by scholars, psychics and romantics, what the myths are basically telling us is that as a result of some drama played out between the Earth, the Moon and the starry night sky, the calendar system had to be changed, and that it was Thoth, a *lunar* deity, who effected the alteration. In other words, a change in the Earth's orbit involving the Moon, which coincided with the sinking of the island continent of Atlantis, was responsible for the extra days we now have in our calendar.

Reaching a Conclusion

And so we have examined the accounts rendered by Plato and other early scholars and sages, drawn together the evidence for the possible existence of an advanced prehistoric culture that left its indelible mark on the legends of many lands, and selected a precise spot for its location based on the evidence from many different sources and scientific disciplines. Although much of this could be viewed as purely conjectural in the opinion of some, there is, I believe, sufficient data to warrant the assumption that an island continent did once exist in the region of the Atlantic Ocean and that it was destroyed in some major cataclysm, the shock waves of which were felt (and recorded) around the whole globe. Many tenable theories have been put forward as to the precise nature of the catastrophe, most of which favour an external, rather than a terrestrial, cause that altered the position of our planet in relation to both its lunar satellite and its parent star, the Sun.

Equally important is the psychological aspect, of which Richard Heinberg writes:

It is worth noting briefly the existence of physical evidence — signs of ocean level changes and of the simultaneous extinctions of large numbers of plant and animal species — that suggest that relatively recent, worldwide destructions have indeed taken place. Geologists and archaeologists are generally undecided about the interpretation of this evidence and often refer to it as 'mysterious'. But for the mythologist and psychologist, there can be no question: the *memory* of catastrophe is universal, and the terror persists.[20]

As to the part played by humankind in the courting of these catastrophic events, philosophers and mystics are ever wont to quote the adage: 'As above, so below', about which Heinberg has this to say:

.... nearly every tradition ascribes the loss of Paradise to the appearance of some tragic aberration in the attitude or behavior of human beings. While in the Golden Age they had been 'truth-speaking' and 'self-subdued,' living 'with no evil desires, without guilt or crime,' they now succumbed to suspicion, fear, greed, mistrust, and violence.

But how did this change of character come about? Though purporting to describe a historical event, the ancients' descriptions of the cause of the Fall were nearly always cast in metaphors and allegories. As noted earlier, among these stories the most frequently encountered themes are disobedience, the eating of forbidden fruit, and forgetting (spiritual amnesia). [21]

The final two words in that phrase strike me as being of particular significance.

Bearing all this in mind, we will cautiously proceed with

the premise that Atlantis was indeed a reality, the knowledge of which lies deeply locked within the human collective unconscious, into which we are, at times, permitted to delve.

CHAPTER 8

Atlantis and Her Peoples

How many goodly creatures are there here!
How beauteous mankind is! O brave new world
That has such people in't.

SHAKESPEARE, *The Tempest*

When examining the history of Atlantis and her peoples there are two factors that must be borne in mind. Firstly, although there are a few pieces of evidence that might be acceptable by some authorities as proof of the existence of the Atlantean culture, the main body of information has been gleaned from myth, legend and ancient tradition, and would not therefore be acceptable to those who demand the sort of proof usually associated with empirical methodological research and tangible archaeological evidence. This does not mean, however, that it is less valid or authentic, many scholars, sages and people of erudition over the ages having seen fit to accept the overall premise if not the surmised detail.

Secondly, assuming that there were two cataclysms, the first of which took place several thousand years earlier and related to the Mu, or Lemuria, episode and the second to the Atlantean cataclysm, the Atlantean culture must have taken a comparatively long period to develop and mature. It is therefore logical to suppose that its earlier history, customs and religion probably differed considerably from those of the latter days, which the priests of Sais so vividly described to Solon. After all, were some time traveller of the future to look in on our lands around the year 400 BC, he or she would see a very different social structure, system of religious beliefs and standard of ethics from that which is prevalent now.

The Continent Described

In order to establish the background against which the population of the island continent thrived, we need to take a look at the estimates given for its size and climatic conditions. Working on the figures given by Plato, Atlantologists have tended to consider the island continent as being roughly 600,000 square miles (1,553,994 square kilometres) in area, about the size of present-day Iran. Moscow physicist and mathematician Professor N. Lednev is of the opinion that ancient historical documents and other antiquities suggest that Atlantis was 'a huge island extending for hundreds of kilometres, situated west of Gibraltar'.[1]

According to the mythological sources of some American Indians, their original home was a large island in the ocean that was destroyed by a calamity. The fact that over 130 tribes have this legend of a world catastrophe would seem to lift it beyond the realms of tribal superstition and fanciful thinking and, I hope, clear the names of Plato and Solon once and for all; but this is still not the case.[2]

Plato describes Atlantis as 'larger than Asia and Libya together', but, as Muck points out, Plato's Asia is the Asia Minor of today; Libya, according to Plato, is that part of North Africa that was known to the ancients. Muck tells us:

In view of the lack of geodetic knowledge in antiquity and preantiquity, we cannot get very much help from Plato's statement about the size of the island. All we can deduce from it is that the island must have been a large one. But Plato's general statement is supplemented by a passage giving details about the large plain in the southern part of the island. The area of this plain is given as 3,000 by 2,000 stades. Six million square stades is equivalent to 77,000 square miles (200,000 sq.km). If we assume that this large plain occupied about half of the entire island, we arrive at a total area of 154,440 square miles (400,000 sq.km).* An estimate derived from the pattern of the seabed contours in the Azores region results in a size not very different to this.[3]

The topography on Muck's map (see Figure 20) suggests that the high mountains would have protected the southern plain from wintry storms and snow in the same way that northern Italy is protected by the Alps. The large plain would therefore have enjoyed a climate similar to that of Lombardy. Basing his estimates on the isobaths, Muck judges the plain of Atlantis from north-east to south-west to have been some 370 miles (600 kilometres) and the average width 230 miles (370 kilometres), which he sees as commensurate with Plato's 3,000 and 2,000 stadia (see footnote on p. 20). Following on this, and taking into account Plato's text, the whole region would have been very high and rising steeply from the sea with the main city probably enclosed by a protective range of mountains.

If Muck's theory regarding the Gulf Stream is correct, a never failing supply of warm water would have flowed around the island, bringing to its western coast a hot, damp climate, caressed by gentle west and south-west winds. Here the rise in sea-bed was less dramatic than on the eastern coastline, with air and water temperatures being identical, making a paradise for lovers of the sun and sea. But because of the cooler air from across the mountains from the north,

* Slightly smaller than Spain.

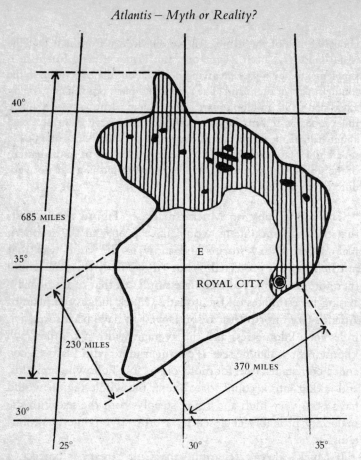

Fig. 20. Large scale map of Atlantis, 1:10,000,000. The outline plotted from the isobaths obtained by surroundings shows a large island extending 685 miles (1,100 km) from north to south, sufficient to deflect the Gulf Stream from its eastward course. A range of high mountains towered over the northern portion with ten tall peaks, among them Mt Atlas (today Pico Alto), which was then more than 16,400 ft (5,000 m) high. The south-western part of the island, which enjoyed a Gulf Stream climate ideal for vegetation, comprises the 'Great Plain' (E) mentioned by Plato and occupying an area of about 77,000 square miles (200,000 sq.km). The Royal City, according to Plato, is situated near the south-east coast. *Hatched:* mountainous area.[4] Observe the position of the capital, which accords with my own impressions; see Chapter 13.

the general climate would have been subtropical rather than tropical. Muck claims:

The Gulf Stream, diverted by the west coast, pushed the isotherms northwards toward the pack ice cap. Icebergs drifted southward from this cap and cold water currents flowed toward the northern tip of the island. This explains the abnormal crowding together of the isotherms, a crowding which indicates an extremely steep climatic gradient. In only 15° latitude the climate changes from subtropical warm to arctic cold.[5]

There is, however, something that worries me about all this: the many reports we have, notably in the *Oera Linda Book*, that in their part of the world, which was considerably farther north and should, by Muck's reckoning and other geological facts, have come well within the ice belt, the climate was mild! It was only *after* the cataclysm that it turned cold and inhospitable. The only possible answer to this would be that the Earth was in a different position in relation to the Sun and Moon in those times, which brings us back to the axis tilts described in Chapter 6 and the various scientific theories that have been offered in their support.

Tracing the Atlanteans' Genealogy

Let us assume, then, that the peoples of Atlantis enjoyed a fine, warm climate that provided them with two harvests a year and ample scope for outdoor recreation and the healthy life. What sort of people were these upon whom nature had bestowed such bounty? Legend and tradition appear to furnish us with details of three main races:

    1. Tall, white, gentle, bearded strangers with fair or auburn hair, who were the bringers of knowledge, law, science and medicine;

2. A red or copper-skinned people, akin to the American Indians, who possessed features not dissimilar to those depicted in Aztec art;

3. Shorter, dark-haired people with fair skins and hazel or brown eyes.

However, the *Popul Vuh* asserts that in the island paradise to the east, from which the forefathers of the Quiché hailed in some remote period of the past, 'the white, yellow and black men lived altogether in harmony under the beneficent rule of the white men.'[6] And it is logical to assume they did so, especially in the later period of Atlantean history when the races became mixed as a result of extensive overseas trading, immigration and colonization.

Donnelly notes how many of the ancient cultures made prolific use of the colour red in their art forms. It is commonly known that red is associated with blood and therefore the life force, but Donnelly seems to see more in it than that. The ancient Egyptians, he informs us, recognized four racial colours – red, yellow, black and white – as did the originators of the *Oera Linda Book*. The Egyptians themselves claimed to be *Rot*, or red men; the yellow people, which included the Asiatic races, they called *Namu*; the black men were called *Nahsu*, and the white men, *Tamhu*. Donnelly emphasizes that the Egyptians of later dynasties were so anxious to preserve their red skin colour that they would insist on being represented as an exaggerated crimson in all artwork.

These colour distinctions, he tells us, are also to be found in other cultures. Ancient Aryan writings divided mankind into four races – white, yellow, red and black – and the four castes of India were founded on these differentiations. In fact, the word for colour in Sanskrit (*varna*) means caste. According to the *Mahabharata*, the Kshatriyas, or warrior caste, who later engaged in combat with the whites, or Brahmins, were red men. Few whites survived the conflict, and from their stock Buddha was born.

The Cushites and Ethiopians were also red men according to Donnelly. *Himyar*, the prefix of the Himyaritic Arabians, is also said to mean red, and illustrations of Arab people on Egyptian monuments were often painted red. The Phoenicians, a Semitic race, called themselves the 'people of Carou', the name 'Phoenicians' having been bestowed upon them by the Greeks. There are two suppositions as to why: the first derives from the Greek word *phoinix* (red), and the second from the legendary bird, the phoenix, which was believed to be reborn every 500 years from its own funeral ashes. The latter reference no doubt arose from the Egyptian legend of the bennu bird, which flew singing out of a burning tree and symbolized resurrection. Either way, the intimation would seem to be that the Phoenicians belonged to a red-skinned race who lived through some past catastrophe to tell the tale.

Not all 'red' Indians, it seems, were red-skinned. Many of the Menominee, Dakota, Mandan and Zuni tribes were fair, with auburn hair and blue eyes. The prominent theosophist, Colonel Scott-Elliot, writing towards the end of the last century, quoted Professor Retzius as stating that the primitive dolichocephalae of America are closely related to the Gaunches of the Canary Islands and to the population of the seaboard of Africa, which racial type was categorized in those days as *Egyptian Atlantidae*. The same form of skull is found in the Canary Islands and the Caribbean Islands, the colour of the skin in both cases being reddish-brown.

The results of the search for genetic identification among short sequences of DNA that have survived 7,000 years in bodies preserved in a marshy bog in what is now Little Salt Spring, Florida, have baffled scientists. By examining the DNA in minute detail and comparing it with that of present-day human races the bog people's genealogy could be partly traced. One piece of the ancient DNA matched that found in more than half of today's Indians living in the south-western United States and most modern Asians, which marks the bog people out as the Asian-Indian stock from which all Amerindians are believed to have descended. However, also present was a portion of DNA, extremely rare in modern world-wide populations, indicating that they had an ancestry unknown in the New World. The scientists hope that further research will throw light on both the origin of the enigmatic genetic 'stranger' and how these people migrated to their marshy corner of America from some distant home in Asia.[7] The Asian DNA tracing could be seen as being of Lemurian or Gondwanian origin, and the unidentified strain, Atlantean, although the scientific establishment will no doubt render its own interpretation in due course.

Colonel Braghine sees European culture as inherited from some western race of the dolichocephalic type, who arrived in the Mediterranean basin from somewhere beyond Gibraltar during the Neolithic period. He tells us:

Almost all mysterious nations of the Mediterranean basin were remarkable for the reddish colour of their skin and scantiness of the beard except the Jews and Arabs. The pre-Egyptians, Pelasgi, Lycians, Crete-Egeans, Phoenicians, Philistines, the Biblical 'Kaftorim', i.e. the inhabitants of Kaftor (Crete), the enigmatical 'Masinti' of the old Egyptian frescos, and on the other side of the ocean, the Toltecs, Mayas, etc. were reddish. The Aryan peoples, on the contrary, are rich in facial hair and are white skinned and brachicephalic.[8]

Since Cro-Magnon people are believed to have been a reddish-brown colour, some scholars have been tempted to consider that the first humans might have been red-skinned. The name Adam is said to mean 'the red', so maybe some-where along the line the idea of a very early race whose peoples were reddish-skinned gave rise to the Adamic myth in the Christian Bible.

On the other hand, recent research has tended to show that the first *Homo sapiens* were black and originated in Africa. According to a report in the *Guardian*, Professor Allan Wilson, a biochemist at the University of California at Berkeley, produced genetic evidence that all present-day humans are related to an African woman who lived 200,000 years ago. Journalist Tim Radford, commenting on the 1989 American Conference for the Advancement of Science in San Francisco, tells us that 'by measuring the diversity of maternally inherited genes in modern racial groups, Professor Wilson and other Berkeley scientists concluded that the oldest lineage was Africa dating back 140,000 to 290,000 years. This is partly supported by fossil evidence.'

Interestingly, the *Oera Linda Book* creation myth tends to confirm the findings of modern science. The first beings to be created from the joint energies of the god Wr'alda and Mother Earth, it tells us, were three daughters. The first of these was black, with 'hair curled like a lamb's'; her name was Lyda. The second was yellow, with 'hair like the mane of a horse'; her name was Finda. The third was white, and 'the blue of her eyes vied with the rainbow ... Like the rays of the sun shone the locks of her hair ...'. She was named Frya, whom the Frisians claimed as the founder of their race.[9]

Stories of 'white men who came from the gods' are, on average, more frequent than those concerned with red men. The Aztec and Inca oral traditions spoke of men who were tall, white-skinned and bearded, who hailed from the land of the sunrise, which accounted for the attitude adopted by these peoples on the arrival of the Spaniards. Believing them to be the benign white beings who had visited their shores centuries earlier and taught them fine and gentle arts, the people of Montezuma and Atahualpa received the new white arrivals with open arms. The red-skinned element in Atlantis, which doubtlessly existed, probably derived from the old Muan or Lemurian stock, which would figure had the Atlantean land mass once been attached or easily accessible to the American coast.

Tribal legends of white visitors who were great reformers, leaders and missionaries, who preached a doctrine of pacifism, non-violence, brotherly love and law and order seem to number eight. Braghine lists them as follows:

In Peru, Manco Capac, Viracocha and Pachacamac; in Columbia, Bochica, among the Tupis, Tupan; in Yucatan, It-Zamna, or Zamna; in Mexico, Quetzal-Coatl (called in Guatemala, 'Gucumatz', and in Yucatan, 'Cuculcan'): and in Brazil and Paraguay, Zume (called by the Caribs 'Tamu', by the Arovacs 'Camu' and by the Carayas 'Caboy'). The Peruvian myth concerning Viracocha resembles the Columbian myth concerning Bochica.[10]

All these teachers, he tells us, were sages who came from some unknown land to the east of the Americas. Features they shared in common included long beards, white skin and blue eyes, and they were clothed in white or pale blue garments. Their philosophical and spiritual messages were identical.

The brown people of Atlantis can be easily accounted for. They came from the east, and probably resulted from inter-breeding between white Atlanteans and the indigenous populations of Egypt, Spain and other parts of Europe and the Mediterranean area. It is debatable, however, where the white Atlanteans came from, and a lot of fanciful speculation and science fiction has been written and channelled to account for them. But more of that when we come to the metaphysical aspects of this inquiry.

Blood Groups and Genes

A study of blood groups throws even more light on to the ethnological aspects of Atlantis. The Basques, often presumed to be the descendants of the Atlanteans, show a high incidence of the rhesus-negative factor, which they shared with the Mayans, the Ossets of the Caucasus and certain Berber tribes. They have a high frequency of the O group, up to 75 per cent, in fact, the A group appearing only very rarely. They are believed by some authorities, notably Louis Charpentier, to represent an almost pure survival of Cro-Magnon man, and skeletal remains would appear to show evidence of facial similarities. The Basques are unlike the aboriginals of France and Spain either in genetic type or culture. They share many similar beliefs and rituals with the ancient Egyptians and Incas, notably the practice of flattening the head of children in infancy, the effect of which may be observed in ancient Inca art.

Lemesurier tells us that the percentage of O blood group is as high as 94 among mummies exhumed in the Canary Islands, from where, Spence and others believe, Cro-Magnon people spread to Europe and the Americas, and 100 among various isolated Central and South American native populations.[11] What he does not tell us, however, is whether they, like the Basques, contained a correspondingly high incidence of the rhesus-negative factor and other genetic markers of significance that would aid further identification and classification. After all, the O group is the most common, and is to be found in many parts of the world.

According to Muck there is no lack of evidence that the Cro-Magnon race, which he called *Homo sapiens diluvialis*, lived in Europe between 20,000 and 10,000 BC. Prehistoric skeletons have been found in large numbers in the valleys of Guadalquivir, the Tejo, the Douro, the Charente, the Dordogne and

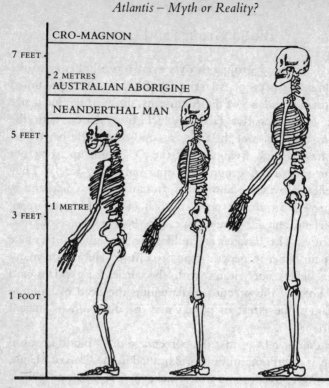

Fig. 21.

Garonne. A skeleton estimated as being 10,000 years old was found in the 'Tomb of Palli Aike' in Tierra del Fuego in 1969–70 and has been identified as Cro-Magnon, which indicates that this race also spread to South America. Muck considers Neanderthal man as the proto-European, and Cro-Magnon a later arrival, probably from the west. He also sees the Cro-Magnons as bearing many similarities to the North American Indians, being tall, muscular, athletic and agile.

Muck produced an illustration of three skeletons to prove his point (see Figure 21). European Neanderthals, he tells us, were plump, strong-boned 'pygmies' averaging less than 5 feet 3 inches (1.6 metres) in height: the dwarfs and troglodytes of old European folklore. The Cro-Magnons, on the other hand, averaged 6 feet 7 inches (2 metres), which could well have given rise to the 'giants' referred to in Classical and biblical texts. Not all scientists agree with Muck's measurements, but there is greater accord on the conclusion that the Neanderthal and Cro-Magnon races existed side by side at some time in the distant past.

We may speculate as to how the Cro-Magnons arrived in Europe. Was it from the east or the west? Atlantologists tend to favour the idea that they were proto-Atlanteans, while other authorities believe that they came from the east. Either way, their superior intelligence and weaponry no doubt helped them to push the Neanderthals back to the Alpine regions and hinterlands of central Europe. Braghine makes the interesting observation that the Basque language bears a striking resemblance to Japanese. Since the Mongolian stock from which the Japanese are descended is of Tungus origin, and the Tungus are known to have migrated eastwards, this is hardly surprising. My own feeling is that the Cro-Magnons were the remnants of an advanced Muan or Lemurian root-race, a branch of which later evolved (or mutated?) into Plato's latter-day Atlanteans. As I am unable to substantiate this, however, for the time being it is anyone's guess.

Blood groups have fascinated me for many years, and in the 1970s I made a detailed study of the subject. Obviously one cannot make too broad a statement in this respect, especially as modern travel facilities have enabled people to interbreed world-wide, with the result that certain blood groups are now likely to appear in places where they were not hitherto encountered. However, let us say that populations with a high frequency of blood group O tend to have a peripheral distribution, and are to be found in north-eastern Europe (Wales, Scotland, Ireland, Iceland), south-west Africa, parts of Australia, and most notably Central and South America. North American Indians also have a high frequency of the O gene, although the A gene is found amongst them. The B group features strongly in eastern Europe, among the Mongolian and oriental races, as well as in the peoples of central Asia and the Indian subcontinent. Frequencies of A gene are particularly high in Scandinavia and parts of Central Europe, among the Aborigines of southern Australia and the Indian tribes of western North America. Regarding the A gene, geneticist A. E. Mourant has this to say:

. . . if we consider only the broad distribution of A in the world as a whole and disregard minor details, it becomes obvious that a higher frequency of A is something especially European. The high A people may have come into Europe from the east in late prehistoric times, but if so, they do not appear to have left any extensive roots behind, for nowhere in Asia, except Anatolia and Armenia, do we find any large populations with A frequencies as high as in parts of Europe. In North Africa, which lies on another route for early man into western Europe, frequencies of A are notably low.[12]

When writing on the subject of the Celts I had recourse to a book entitled *Genetic and Population Studies in Wales*, which, I think, throws additional light on blood groups in relation to Atlantis. Ancestral origins can be ascertained from the information provided by the genetic frequencies in blood groups. In Wales there are three main genetic groupings. The eldest of these, which is found in the moors and moorland fringes of western Wales and in areas of megalithic significance associated with prehistoric settlement, carries the B gene but without certain of the genetic identities usually found in the B blood group in the Far East. This genetic feature was not, therefore, imported from eastern Europe or adjacent Asia in historical times as was generally suspected, but probably formed part of the aboriginal frequency.

Those carrying the *B* gene are few in number, however, when compared to the carriers of the *O* gene which occurs in much of central and northern Wales and is generally associated with the Goidelic Celts. Similar frequencies of the genetic code found here can be traced to tribes in the western Caucasus and Transcaucasia, the Mediterranean islands and parts of northern Africa – all places from which the ancient Celts were reputed to have come. Physical anthropology, linguistics and archaeology all offer support for human migration from the eastern Mediterranean to Britain in Neolithic times, and inform us that the fundamental physical type in most of Wales is the long-headed brunette, universally belonging to the fair-skinned Berbers or Mediterranean race of Sergi.[13]

Finally, we come to the *A* gene, high frequencies of which occur mainly in southern Wales and that southern part of Pembrokeshire known as 'Little England'. High incidences of this gene also occur in Cornwall and Brittany and would appear to go hand in hand with the Brythonic tongue. Although these high levels of *A* were formerly attributed to the Viking influence, recent genetic evidence suggests that they more likely derived from either the Belgae or the Flemish weavers who arrived in Britain around AD 1500, since it has been established that the Vikings did not appear to have the high frequency of *A* gene common to most Scandinavian peoples, but, like the Celts, were predominantly of the O blood group.[14]

From the aforegoing we may deduce that there is a connection between blood groups and the colour of skin pigment, hair, eyes, etc., although there are obviously other genetic markers to be taken into account.

Blood tests on five Inca mummies in the British Museum showed that three of them possessed traces of blood group A, which is utterly foreign to the South American Indian. None of them displayed the rhesus-negative factor dominant in the

Basques and Berbers, however, but one did have substances *C* and *D* with the absence of *E*, a rare combination among Indians. From this we may deduce that the Inca kings did not belong to the aboriginal population of South America. I recall watching a television programme in the early 1980s that dealt with similar blood tests carried out on Egyptian mummies. Those belonging to royalty also displayed the A group with somewhat unusual genetic variations, but only up to a certain point in history, the early Eighteenth Dynasty, after which it appeared to be overtaken by the more common O.

The pale-skinned, fair-haired Atlanteans probably carried a high incidence of the *A* gene, and the fact that this gene was also identified in mummies from both the Inca and ancient Egyptian ruling classes suggests that the A blood group might have been the dominant one among the kings of Atlantis, while other Atlantean tribes, such as the red-skinned people, the brown-skinned Berber-types and the red-haired Celts, were of the O blood group. Since the South American continent appears to show a higher incidence of the O gene than any other part of the world, one may surmise that if Mu/Lemuria had lain to the west of, and was at one time connected to, that land mass, it might conceivably have been the cradle of the O blood group peoples.

Those interested in specific genetic groupings are recommended to the appropriate medical literature (see Bibliography). Should the Genome project (a proposed scientific survey of the peoples of the Earth based on an analysis of their personal genetic code) go ahead, its findings could serve to throw considerably more light on all of our origins and on the peoples of Atlantis.

Bearing all this in mind, it would be easy to suppose that there was some form of caste system in Atlantis that was based on colour, but I do not believe this to have been the case. What probably happened was that when Atlantis broke away from the land mass to which it was originally attached at the time of the upheaval that caused the sinking of Mu, the tribes occupying the newly formed island whose members survived the catastrophe were predominantly white with a smattering of red. It is logical to assume that once they had reorganized themselves, the most technologically and culturally advanced would have assumed leadership.

Whether the island was last attached to the American or European continent is still hotly debated by scholars, some seeing in the Cro-Magnon settlements along the west coast of Europe and the Mediterranean evidence of the European connection, and others insisting that these pockets of Cro-Magnon activity resulted from early attempts at colonization. However, much of this is pure conjecture, as we do not have Atlantis above water and handy for geological comparisons and carbon-14 datings. I am inclined to think that there was once a chain of smaller islands between the European mainland and the Atlantean island, which made for easy access either way. In later times, after the civilization had established its maritime connections, Atlantean sailors probably took wives from their various ports of call and the strain became mixed – the Biblical 'sons of God and the daughters of men' being nothing more esoteric than that!

Evidence from Art, Artefacts and Language

Lewis Spence, who devoted much of his life to studying the subject of Atlantis and its peoples, writes of the arrival in Spain and southern France of a race of men known as the Azilian-Tardenoisian. The Abbé Breuil, considered by many as the greatest authority on the prehistory of France and Spain, believes these people to have come from 'circum-Mediterranean' sources about 10,000 years ago. The name

Azilian is derived from a cave or tunnel known as Le Mas d'Azil in the Pyrenean department of Ariége, where its deposits were unearthed by Edouard Piette.[15] From remains that were discovered on the site it became apparent that the Azilians were markedly vegetarian and fruitarian, while the presence of barley seeds suggested that they also cultivated cereal. As harpoons featured in their culture, we may also assume them to have been people of maritime habits.

One of the most interesting details featured in Azilian art was a collection of pebbles, each painted red with a mixture of peroxide of iron and some resinous substance and displaying strange marks or symbols. These consisted of zigzags, crosses, circles, vertical strokes and ladder-like patterns, some of which resembled the letter E while others appeared to be nothing more than a series of random lines. Various authorities have debated their meaning, some suggesting that they were alphabetic characters while others saw them as a kind of game. It was also noted that they bore a resemblance to the fetishes and totemic symbols displayed on the churingas of the Australian aborigines.

This theme was the subject of a BBC television programme in 1989, which showed cave paintings exhibiting almost identical designs that were found in Spain and have been dated to 15,000 years ago. The researchers had also noted similar designs in the art of the African Bushmen in the mountains north of Cape Town, while shamanic animal forms also feature prominently in the art of both cultures. These geometric patterns, it seems, appear in art forms that go back 20,000 years or more, and are seen as belonging to the Upper Palaeolithic period. Some authorities have designated them as relating to the spirit, or after world, wherein dwell the souls of the ancestors.

That they are connected with altered states of consciousness (ASCs), however, there seems to be little doubt, since psychologists undertaking experiments in ASCs have noted that there is a certain cerebral frequency at which people claim to see mental pictures of geometrical designs that are almost identical to those displayed in these ancient caves and pebbles. From this we may conclude that the artists of old were probably either shamans themselves, or those who had experienced some level of ecstasy or paraphronesia under their ministrations which causes the cerebral mechanisms to register this particular kind of phenomenon. On the other hand, our modern-day experimenters could simply be tuning into the collective unconscious, either psychically or genetically. Whether this has anything to do with Atlantis, however, I very much doubt, in spite of scholarly opinion to the contrary.

A body of information regarding the root-races and sub-races of Atlantis has also come to us from psychic sources, but rather than confuse this here with the findings of empirical research on the one hand, and scientifically viable hypotheses on the other, I will confine it to the latter part of my inquiry.

If we are to lend any credence to Plato's account and the legendary chronicles that have come down to us from other sources, it must be agreed that whoever these Atlanteans were, and regardless of their genetic or racial type, they were a highly ingenious race who achieved a great deal both culturally and technologically. This naturally made for a pleasant and easeful life-style with comfortable dwellings, grand temples, good public utilities, and probably a system of state support for all. They must also have possessed an efficient system of communication and record keeping aside from oral tradition. Donnelly collected the following snippets of information regarding pre-Flood writing:

The Hebrew commentators on Genesis say, 'Our rabbins assert that Adam, our father of blessed memory, composed a book of precepts, which were delivered to him by God in Paradise.' (Smith's 'Sacred Annals,' p. 49.) That is to say, the Hebrews preserved a tradition that the Ad-ami, the people of Ad, or Atlantis, possessed, while yet dwelling in Paradise, the art of writing. It has been suggested that without the use of letters it would have been impossible to preserve the many details as to dates, ages, and measurements, as of the ark, handed down to us in Genesis. Josephus, quoting Jewish tradition, says, 'The births and deaths of illustrious men, between Adam and Noah, were noted down at the time with great accuracy.' (Ant., lib. i, cap. iii, sec. 3.) Suidas, a Greek lexicographer of the eleventh century, expresses tradition when he says, 'Adam was the author of arts and letters.' The Egyptians said that their god Anubis was an antediluvian, and 'wrote annals *before* the Flood.' The Chinese have traditions that the earliest race of their nation, prior to history, 'taught all the arts of life and wrote books.' 'The Goths always had the use of letters;' and Le Grand affirms that before or soon after the Flood 'there were found the acts of great men engraved in letters on large stones.' (Fosbroke's 'Encyclopaedia of Antiquity, vol. i, p. 355.) Pliny says, 'Letters were always in use.' Strabo says, 'The inhabitants of Spain possessed records *written before the Deluge*.' (Jackson's 'Chronicles of Antiquity,' vol. iii, p. 85.) Mitford ('History of Greece,' vol. i, p. 121) says, 'Nothing appears to us so probable as that it (the alphabet) was derived from the antediluvian world.'[16]

In spite of this emphasis on some kind of written language or alphabet being essential to the preservation of knowledge, the Incas used *quipus*, or knotted cords, to explain the fate of their people, while it is also the belief of many (not all of whom are metaphysicians or psychics) that information can be stored in stones or 'time capsules' to be released at appropriate times in our planet's history.

The word 'paradise' has some interesting connotations if taken in the Atlantean context. Aside from the normal religious explanations, the *Reader's Digest Great Illustrated Dictionary* defines it as '. . . from, Avestan *pairi-daēza*, circumvallation, walled-in park: (*pairi* around + *daēza* wall)'; in other words,

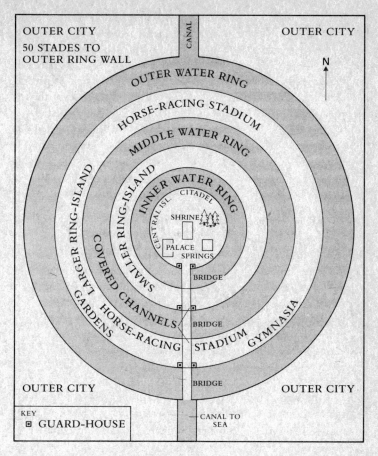

OUTER CITY
50 STADES TO
OUTER RING WALL

CANAL

OUTER CITY

N

OUTER WATER RING

HORSE-RACING STADIUM

MIDDLE WATER RING

LARGER RING-ISLAND

SMALLER RING-ISLAND

INNER WATER RING

CENTRAL ISL.

CITADEL

SHRINE

PALACE SPRINGS

BRIDGE

COVERED CHANNELS

LARGER HORSE-RACING GARDENS

STADIUM

GYMNASIA

BRIDGE

OUTER CITY

BRIDGE

OUTER CITY

KEY
▣ GUARD-HOUSE

CANAL TO SEA

Fig. 22. The capital city of Atlantis. Source: Christopher Gill; *Plato: The Atlantis Story*, Bristol, Bristol Classical Press, 1980

some kind of circular enclosure. Now let us compare this with Plato's city, the first illustration of which (Figure 22) is from Christopher Gill's *Plato: The Atlantis Story*, and the second (Figure 23) from David Wood's *Genisis*, illustrating

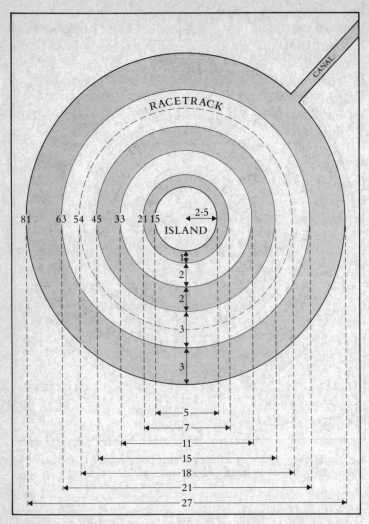

Fig. 23. The ground plan of Atlantis.
Source: David Wood, *Genisis*, Tunbridge Wells, Baton Press, 1985

the author's own sacred geometry based on the 'goddess' content of his book. The paradise of the Bible appears to have an uncomfortable number of points in common with the capital of old Atlantis!

Richard Heinberg's book *Memories and Visions of Paradise*, which provides a comprehensive survey of the 'paradise' theme, contains many gems of wisdom that could certainly apply to Atlantis and all those other legendary Edenic civilizations of the past. I find his attention to the psychological and transcendental aspects of the study particularly interesting, since the material manifestation of the Atlantean episode would appear to have strong metaphysical connotations. I particularly liked his comment:

Paradise myths do seem to imply the primordial existence of a unified mind encompassing all of humanity. The Hebraic, Indochinese, and Mayan traditions, for example, speak of the one original language, which was shared with the animals as well. The Hopi legend of the First People says that they 'felt as one and understood one another without talking.' The original mind seems to have been a kind of living, pulsating web of telepathic interconnectedness, through the strands of which flowed a current of universal love.[17]

The above passage suggests a state of being to which I can most certainly relate. No, I do not think Atlantis was that perfect, but I do believe that all living things are part of the One Whole, and our spiritual fall lies in the fact that we have been programmed to disregard this basic truth, which is the main cause of our suffering on this planet. Our path to freedom from life's afflictions lies in severing the bonds that separate us by thought and language from the rest of creation, and shedding the scales that blind our eyes to the spiritual truth.

But to return to the Atlantis that was. Aside from a luxuriant growth of trees, flowers, herbs, fruits and other bounties of nature, the Atlanteans enjoyed the presence of many species of animals. Horses, it seems, were among the favourites, while lions, dogs, sheep and goats were also present on the island. Plato's elephants seem to have suffered the heavy hand of scholarly critique, although in the ruined city of Palenque one of the palaces has a stucco bas-relief of a priest whose elaborate headdress or helmet is a faithful representation of the head of an elephant. Donnelly tells us that the decoration known as 'elephant trunks' is found in many parts of the ancient ruins of Central America, projecting from above the doorways of buildings. In fact, there are many representations of elephants from ancient Mexican and surrounding Central American cultures, which implies that these animals must either have existed there in antediluvian times, or people who were familiar with their presence in other climes must have carried their impression to these places. One is tempted to consider that animals might have been seen as preferable to more mechanical forms of transport, since in Central and South America in those early times the wheel appears to be conspicuous by its absence. The fact that the people must have known about it, however, is evident from wheeled toys that have been excavated in those parts.

Of the creatures of the sea, seals seem to have played some part in Atlantean life. Aelian, a Classical writer of the third century AD, wrote of 'rams of the sea' (seals) in his work entitled *The Nature of Animals*.

... the male ram has around his forehead a white band. One would say it resembled the diadem of Lysimachus or Antigonus or some other Macedonian king. The inhabitants of the shores of the ocean tell that in former times the kings of Atlantis, descendants of Poseidon, wore on their heads, as a mark of power, the headband of the male rams, and that their wives, the queens, wore, as a sign of their power, headbands of the female rams.[18]

It is reasonable to question why this writer and his informants should assume that the Atlantean priesthood or aristocracy wore headbands made of seal skins. The answer to this probably lies in the fact that these seafaring people, observing the white headbands on the seals in question, likened them to the mode of attire described to them by their ancestors and passed orally from generation to generation until, like the story at the party, the original meaning becomes obscured. After all, headbands have formed part of the priestly regalia in many ancient tribes and cultures, so why not Atlantis? One esoteric tradition has it that the type of headband worn by Atlantean priests denoted their rank and occult abilities, certain metals and stones being reserved for wear by high initiates only.

Much has been written and debated about Atlantean linguistics, successive scholars and researchers supplying impressive catalogues of similarities between languages both sides of the Atlantic and world-wide that they believe indicate a single point of origin. The following comparisons were noted by Donnelly:

ENGLISH	CHINESE	CHALDEE
To shine	Mut	Mul
To die	Mut	Mit
Book	King	Kin
Cloth	Sik	Sik
Right hand	Dzek	Zag
Hero	Tan	Dun
Earth	Kien-kai	Kiengi
Cow	Lub	Lu, lup
Brick	Ku	Ku[19]

Here is another, more up-to-date variation, from information supplied by Charles Berlitz:

ENGLISH	AMERINDIAN	EURO—ASIAN—AFRICAN
King	Aimara: *malku*	Arabic: *melek*; Hebrew: *melekh*
Priest	Maya: *balaam*	Hebrew: *bileam* (magician)
Home	Guarani: *oko*	Greek: *oika*
Butterfly	Nahuatl: *popalo-tl*	Latin: *papilio*
Cloud	Nahuatl: *mixtli*	Greek: *omichtli*
To blow	Klamath: *pniw*	Greek: *pneu*
High mountain	Quechua: *andi*	Ancient Egyptian: *andi*
Heron	Quechua: *llake llake*	Sumerian: *lak lak*
Lie	Quechua: *llu llu*	Sumerian: *lul*
Sun	Araucanian: *anta*	Ancient Egyptian: *anta*
Ax	Araucanian: *bal*	Sumerian: *bal*[20]

Berlitz continues:

An unusual example of a word that sounds and means the same in a number of languages scattered throughout the Old and the New World is the word for 'father' — *aht, tata, ata*, with slight modifications. It is especially interesting in that this is not a natural sound comparable to the variants of *ma, mama, mu, um*, etc. for 'mother'. One is led to wonder whether these recognizable variants of what is essentially the same word for 'father' represent an echo of one of the world's first languages.

AMERINDIAN & POLYNESIAN	EURO—ASIAN—AFRICAN COUNTERPART
Quechua: *taita*	Basque: *aita*
Dakotah: *atey*	Hungarian: *atya*
Zuni: *tatchu*	Tagalog: *tatay*
Seminole: *tati*	Russian: *aht-yets*
Eskimo: *atatak*	Ancient Egyptian: *aht*
Nahuatl (Aztec) *tatli*	Turkish & Turkic languages: *ata*

AMERINDIAN & POLYNESIAN	EURO–ASIAN–AFRICAN COUNTERPART
Central Mexican Indian dialects: *tata*	Old Gothic (variant): *atta*
Fujian: *tata*	Latin (colloquial): *tata*
Samoan: *tata*	Romanian: *tata*
	Slovak: *tata*
	Maltese: *tata*
	Sinhalese: *tata*
	Yiddish: *tatale*
	Cymric: *tad*[21]

Although these comparisons are not conclusive proof of an Atlantean origin, it would appear that at some time in the dim and distant past mankind shared a single language, which became split into different dialects and ultimately altered over long periods of time following cataclysms when people found themselves living in isolated pockets away from the original collective of which they had once formed an integral part. Perhaps the biblical myth of the Tower of Babel is not so far-fetched after all. But then, surely, all myth must contain some element of truth.

CHAPTER 9

Religion and Science in Atlantis

The knowledge and the science of one long-dead age
  Becomes the mystery, the theurgy of the next;
Until the fires of reason rise to burn the superstitions
  That offend their logic.
Yet, from the embers of their holocaust, the Phoenix
  Stretches forth its wings in flight,
Bearing aloft the gods of future years.

There has been much speculation regarding the religion of old Atlantis, most of which has been based on the beliefs encountered in her colonies. Plato has rendered us one account, which seems to echo the old Cretan religious practices, and one cannot help wondering if Solon, or Plato himself for that matter, was not influenced by the myths of his own people when pronouncing on the religion of Atlantis. Many of the names he mentions, for example, have a decidedly Greek ring about them, while the bull rituals could surely pass as Minoan. One point that most observations on this subject seem to have in common, however, is the idea that towards what are referred to as the 'latter days', a sizeable rift occurred in the morals and ethics of both priesthood and people, one side adhering rigidly to the 'path of light', or ways of goodness, caring and love, while the opposition chose to tread the left-hand path of darkness and use their powers for evil ends.

Over the years I have spent studying the Atlantis saga I

have heard and read what I feel to be a load of codswallop from both academic and metaphysical sources. It would seem that some people are more anxious to hoist the pennants of their pet postulations than compare notes or pool their knowledge with other areas of research in a profound effort to seek the truth. The Atlantean catastrophe has been attributed to genetic engineering gone haywire, the misuse of crystal power and atomic energy, magical rites that exercised hypnotic powers over the populace, battles with beings from outer space; and all this against the gentleness, piety and spirituality of the adherents to the right-hand path. What seems more likely is that towards the end of any great empire or civilization the rot sets in, decadence prevails and law and order fly the coop. This may be evidenced on a smaller scale in the latter days of Imperial Rome, while some authorities point the finger at both Europe and the United States as heading in that direction at present.

One of the first things I was taught when I began my metaphysical studies over forty years ago was that the world was heading for an 'evolutionary quantum jump', a term that is guaranteed to produce a negative effect on the blood pressure of many a loyal son or daughter of the scientific establishment! At those times in the history of the Earth when these events occur (as they have indeed in the past), there is much sorting of the wheat and chaff in the arena of human choice of experience, people tending to opt for either a more spiritual, sensitive, caring and loving way of life, or the hedonistic, selfish, materialistic opposite. I will leave my readers to judge for themselves as to how we stand today where these theories are concerned, but suffice it to say that we are believed to be well on course for the impact that will constitute the physical counterpart of the spiritual shake-up (as above, so below). Working on this premise, we may assume that the coordinates of the latter-day Atlanteans were set for a similar trajectory, sufficient negative/destructive energy having been generated by their actions and thoughts to attract a correspondingly destructive force: 'As ye sow, so shall ye reap.'

In order to gain a clearer picture of what these negative–destructive powers were, whether they emanated from the misuse of science and technology, magico-religious practices or political skulduggery, it is necessary to examine what information we do have regarding the government, beliefs and technology of the Old Country.

The Atlantean State

I have always understood Atlantis to have been essentially a theocracy or sacerdotally-ruled society, which has caused me to question Plato's 'kings' and their nepotistic practices. Donnelly postulates that the Olympus of the Greeks was none other than Atlantis, wherein the old sea-god dwelt with his wife, Tethys, while Muck and others have suggested that the legend of Oceanus encircling the Earth was synonymous with the Gulf Stream encircling the old Atlantean land mass. The references to the gods of the Greeks living on nectar and ambrosia are seen as appertaining to a degree of civilization and some species of food and liquid refreshment superior to those imbibed by other, more barbarous tribes with whom the Atlanteans came in contact. In the 'Islands of the Blessed' dwelt the god-kings, the highest peak being allocated to Zeus. The twelve Olympians were Zeus, Hera, Poseidon, Demeter, Apollo, Artemis, Hephaestus, Athene, Ares, Aphrodite, Hermes and Hestia.

Plato, however, emphasizes the number ten: ten kings or rulers of Atlantis. But Donnelly reinforces his argument with allusions to the division of the year into twelve parts and other references from Classical and historical literature. Diodorus Siculus, for example, mentions that among the Babylonians there were twelve gods of the heavens, each personified by one of the signs of the zodiac and worshipped in a *certain month of the year*. The Hindus had twelve primal gods, 'the Aditya'; Moses erected twelve pillars at Sinai; the Mandan Indians celebrated the Flood with twelve zodiac-like characters who danced around an ark; the Scandinavians had their twelve gods, the Aesir, who dwelt on Asgard. Donnelly further asserts that the human-type characteristics bestowed upon the Greek gods were simply a carry-over from the way they and their families actually behaved in Atlantis.

The colonies of Atlantis, notably Peru and Egypt, favoured Sun and planetary worship. The Babylonians also looked to the skies for guidance, and the Phoenicians were Sun worshippers. In addition to celestial considerations, most of the ancient peoples acknowledged the life force in nature and animism was widespread.

The concept of dualism is found in many archaic beliefs, as exemplified in Baal and Moloch of the Phoenicians, although not all of the opposites were malign; some simply represented different aspects of the same deity; the Egyptian lion-headed goddess Sekhmet, for example, embodied the burning heat of the Sun, while the cat-goddess, Bast, exemplified the gentler rays of that orb. Likewise, the Celts acknowledged the bright countenance of Llew/Lugh, while Gwyn-ap-Nudd, the Dark Tanist who was equally powerful, kept court in the chthonic regions, or 'fairyland', according to some schools of belief.

Viewed in the light of Donnelly's conjectures, the Age of Cronus, known to the Greeks as the Golden Age, would have represented an era in Atlantean history when things ran particularly smoothly. The Atlantean genetic pool had not been tainted by the influx of immigrants from other lands, people were spiritually aware, cognizant of the beauty of the world around them and the need to nurture it with love and respect,

and their particular brand of civilization and culture was working well for all concerned. Friendship and fellowship were
prized above all worldly possessions, which suggests a form
of socialism in which the competitive spirit either did not
exist or was not encouraged. According to Virgil's *Georgics*
and Tibullus's *Elegies*, there was a time in the distant past
when all land was held in common. Memories of an archaic
democracy are seen by some authorities as perpetuated in the
ancient festivals of Cronia and Saturnalia, when masters and
slaves dropped rank and enjoyed the festivities on an equal
footing. The long lost Golden Age of earthly bliss is recalled
in the 5,000-year-old Engidu and the lines of Uttu of Sumer,
which lament the passing of a lost social system in which
'. . . there were no liars, no sickness, nor old age'.[1]

The name Cronus can, of course, be seen as representing
time, and his swallowing of the stones as the encapsulation of
an epoch that was destined ultimately to be superseded by the
patriarchal Zeus. The Silver Age, with its matrist overtones,
must surely have coincided with the Age of Cancer, which
would suggest that the Golden Age was Leo's (the kingly
sign), in which case this must have represented the last period
of Atlantean history when the affairs of the Atlantean state
were reasonably stable. It also suggests to me that it was
during the Age of Leo that the wise priests foresaw what the
ultimate fate of the island was likely to be, and made their
records in stone, that being the only material they judged
durable enough to survive a major cataclysm.

Let us return for one moment to the nomenclatures given
to us by Plato. Gill remarks that many of the names accorded
to the Atlantean royal family simply imply magnificence or
strength, and cites Evenor – good or brave man; Cleito –
famous or splendid; while Leucippe is evocative of those fabled
Atlantean horses that were sacred to Poseidon. Gill sees the
reference to 'divine ancestry' as helping to account for the

fabulous luxury and technical know-how, but '. . . when the divine genetic element weakens by successive breeding, this godlike wealth tends to (human) moral problems.'[2]

Referring again to the *Critias*, it would appear that for a long period (the Golden Age of Cronus?) the laws of the land were dispensed according to the statutes of Poseidon, the founding ruler and deity. But when the divine genetic element in the nature of the rulers (one is tempted to broaden this reference to include the people as a whole) became diluted, they gave themselves up to unjust greed and love of power, which caused conflict at all levels of society. It has been suggested that this 'divine gene' of Poseidon came from a genus external to this planet, Sirius being a favourite spot on the celestial dial. Visions of aliens carrying out genetic engineering is guaranteed to evoke a negative response in many thinking people, which is quite understandable in the light of current scientific opinion. However, Professor Fred Hoyle's panspermia theory, which conceives of alien mico-organisms distributed throughout interstellar space and penetrating the Earth's atmosphere, puts a slightly different slant on the matter – Hoyle's answer as to whether life originated on Earth being a decided NO![3]

What is not made very clear, however, is the type of genetic dilution to which Plato refers. After all, excessive interbreeding can produce as many recessive genes as random genetic dilution. It is commonly agreed that our genes are related to our temperament and abilities; mathematical and musical skills, for example, frequently running in families. The final question on this issue that I find myself asking, and which has, no doubt, been posed by countless researchers over the centuries, is who was Poseidon?

Gods, Goddesses and Cults

What we now need to establish is the basic nature of Atlantean worship. Was it patrist or matrist orientated, or neither? It would be safe to assume that the Sun featured prominently in the state religion of the Old Country, while there was obviously a healthy respect for the deity, or deities, of water, Atlantis being an island continent and reliant to an extent upon the stable behaviour of the surrounding currents. Bull cults I find difficult to accept, but then it all depends on which era in the long history of the continent we are considering. In the solar Age of Virgo, blood sacrifices would have been unheard of and offerings to the gods or goddesses would have consisted of fruit, grains and the produce of the earth. Solar worship would probably have predominated, but with a feminine slant. The preceding Ages of Libra and Scorpio could be suspect, however, since according to some schools of thought the Lemurian, or Muan, catastrophe occurred during the transition from the latter to the former, and the old pre-Atlantean cultures are believed to have been noted for their barbaric sacrificial practices.

Most of the primeval creation myths favour a creatrix rather than a creator, and it should be remembered that not all of the early civilizations or tribal cultures acknowledged the Sun as a masculine force. Among the ancient Germanic peoples, for example, the Sun and solar power were considered to be of a feminine nature, as represented by the goddesses Sól and Sunna. Dominant Sun-goddesses were also to be found in Egypt, while among the deities of the Eskimos, Japanese and the Khasis of India the solar goddesses were accompanied by subordinate brothers who were symbolized by the Moon. David Wood writes of the antiquity of the goddess Neith, the Mighty Mother who gave birth to Ra, which naturally raises questions since the Sun-god was

believed to have been self-begotten and therefore androgynous. Wood refers to Isis (Sothis – Sirius?) as being the mother
of Rat, the female Sun, which he sees as entitling her to the
role of creatrix. This would make her another aspect of Neith
of Sais, but since most of the later Egyptian god-forms can be
dissolved into their earlier equivalent archetypes this is hardly
surprising.

The Atlanteans of the Age of Virgo probably did acknowledge a female essence in the Sun or, if they had any common
sense at all (and one is inclined to credit them with a modicum
of that faculty), an androgynous or father/mother presence.
The feminine aspect may possibly have dimmed during the
Leonine Age, only to return to dominate the Age of Cancer.
Regarding the Age of Leo, some interesting fragments from
that era appear to have filtered down over the centuries via
the traditions of Egypt: the *Emerald Tables of Hermes* and the
Hermes Trismegistus (see Chapter 10).

The Atlanteans do not appear to have been overtly poly-
theistic, although certain archaeological, anthropological and
allied data collected from the legends and annals of those
countries that were considered to have been Atlantean colonies
suggest that they worshipped a Lord or Lady of Light and
paid due deference to the progenitor of their race, referred to
as Poseidon by Plato and other authorities. This tends to
indicate that they attributed some kind of unusual or 'divine'
qualities to their distant ancestor. Whether the name of the
Greek sea-god has any bearing on this or not cannot be
vouched for. Perhaps the legend dates back to the time when
the island of Atlantis broke away from a continental mainland
and the survivors saw fit to give thanks for their safety to the
watery element. Or perchance there was some culture-hero
who took charge during the catastrophe and helped his fellow
men and women to lay the foundations of the new Atlantis.

It has been proposed by certain adherents to the Western

mystery tradition that although a form of Sun worship constituted the exoteric religion of the Atlantean peoples, there was
also an esoteric tradition based on sea and star worship that
was observed only by priestly initiates of a high order. While
the former was basically patrist, the latter dealt with the
mysteries of the Great Mother, and its magical practices were
believed to be infinitely more powerful than those of the
solar religion. Numerous psychics have also claimed knowledge of what really took place in the Old Country, and
although I shall be featuring some of these views in Chapter
13, in the final analysis one has to admit that no one really
knows for sure. Perhaps one of those fabled time-capsules will
suddenly make a convenient appearance and put us straight
once and for all!

Most students of Atlantology who have applied their researches to the area of ancient myth and legend seem happy
to agree that the Titans and the Atlanteans were one and the
same. The story of the chequered life of the Titan Prometheus
always strikes me as having some bearing on the Atlantean
saga. According to the Greek myths, Prometheus played an
important role in the legendary history and origins of humanity. During the revolt of the Titans he observed a prudent
neutrality and was actually admitted into the circle of im-
mortals. However, he entertained a silent grudge against the
destroyers of his race and constantly favoured humankind
rather than the gods.

Legend tells us that Prometheus, using clay and water –
and, according to some, his own tears – fashioned the first
people in the likeness of the gods, into whom Athene breathed
life. A similar account occurs in Jehovah's creation of Adam
and Eve, which suggests that both stories derived from the
same source. The Archangel Michael is seen by some authorities as the counterpart of Prometheus, while those enigmatic couplings engaged in by some exalted race of beings

and the womenfolk of Earth have already received comment. Prometheus, whose name is said to mean 'forethought', was believed by some to have assisted in the birth of Athene (Athens?), in payment for which she taught him architecture, astronomy, mathematics, navigation, medicine, metallurgy and other useful arts, which he duly passed on to the beings he created. He is also reputed to have given humankind the gift of fire, which, according to one story, he stole from the forge of Hephaestus. Another myth, however, informs us that from the Sun's chariot he lighted a torch from which he broke a glowing fragment of charcoal which he thrust into the hollow of a giant fennel stalk (narthex). After extinguishing the torch he stole away undiscovered to pass on the narthex containing his gift to the race he had created. Either way, he incurred the wrath of Zeus, who gave vent to his annoyance by letting Pandora and her box of ills loose on mankind.

According to the Egyptians, Prometheus was a son of Poseidon, which is another way of saying that he represented a person or persons who hailed from across the sea. In view of the gifts he supposedly bestowed on the then uncivilized world, he is probably representative of a race or culture – the civilization of Atlantis – rather than a singular being, while genetic inferences could also be read into the role he played in the birth of Athene, Goddess of Wisdom. If, however, there was such a person as Prometheus, the kindly Titan would surely qualify as a leading figure in the history of Atlantis, along with the goddess who was his teacher and benefactor.

Lewis Spence wrote at some length on the religion of Atlantis, exploring all the possible avenues of interest via the many ancient cults and beliefs of the countries and islands that bordered Atlantis to the east and west. Bull cults may be observed in many of these, but I do not see this as a sure indication of the accuracy of Plato's account when it comes to the blood sacrifices. What strikes me as being more likely is that immigrants from North Africa, Spain, the Mediterranean islands and parts of the Americas, intent upon obtaining a slice of the 'good life', took their bull cults with them and slowly infiltrated the Atlantean religious establishment. It is very easily done, and may be seen in missionary practices past and present. People have ever fashioned their gods after their own image and likeness, and according to their own needs, the prevailing climate of opinion among both rulers and ordinary people demanding divinities whose attributes they could both relate to and understand.

Spence sees the Atlantean pantheon as consisting of Atlas, his nine brothers, his mother, Cleito, and his brother Saturn (Cronus). These twelve he relates to the constellations, Atlas being by reputation an astronomer of some distinction. In other words, the religion of Atlantis was stellar orientated. Man's need to work in harmony with the celestial spheres was therefore seen as imperative, which betokens the importance of the role played by priestly astrologers. The study of star lore could be seen to greatly antedate the civilization of the Euphrates, the fixed stars, in particular, suggesting some divine celestial significance (see p.210). The fact that astrology (and astronomy, as the two were not seen as separate studies in the distant past) features so strongly in the credos of all of the races who are believed to have had Atlantean origins surely says something for this premise. While I cannot go all the way with Spence on his bull cult theory, I am totally with him when it comes to star lore. It is my belief that the Atlanteans knew a lot more about the universe outside this planet than we might imagine, which notion future scientific discoveries will only serve to reinforce.

In summary, the religion of the Atlanteans in its most pristine form was gentle, non-sacrificial and concerned mainly with a universal creative force which manifested via the agencies of extraterrestrial phenomena such as the Sun, planets and fixed stars. It later degenerated into a more bloody reality due to the influx of sacrificial cults from outside its homeland. Many of its citizens, both priestly and otherwise, succumbed to the false pleasures and values of this hedonistic input, and the degeneracy that ensued precipitated the horrendous end.

Science and Technology

There are some schools of thought that see the scientists of Atlantis, rather than the priests, as the transgressors in the manipulation of 'dark' energies, although I have always been given to understand that in those days one had to be a priest to be a scientist, but perhaps in the latter days the religious and scientific branches were separate. But were the Atlanteans really that technologically advanced? Are the stories of space ships, atomic power, submarines, crystal energy and so forth simply flights on psychic imagination or wishful thinking on the part of honest channellers? After all, many of us are at loggerheads with the values of today's world: the desecration of Gaia, the abject materialism and lack of fundamental spirituality engender a sense of cosmic belonging in the more sensitive among us. Psychologists might therefore argue, and not without good reason, that when we humans are faced with something we find too difficult to handle, but about which can do little or nothing, we create our own Utopias amongst whose rosy bowers we may indulge our need for peace, security and love unsullied by the 'real' world around us. Our spiritual needs aside, however, are there any concrete or logical indications from the past that the Atlanteans might conceivably have spawned a race of fine scientists whose expertise rivalled (or even surpassed) that of our present generation?

Over the past few years there has been a deluge of books

on the subject of technological achievements in prehistory, which usually have E.T. over- (or under-) tones. We have been treated to a circus of Vimanas, believed to have been the flying machines of prehistoric India, portrayals of space rockets and astronauts in ancient South and Central American art, what are believed to be electric batteries from the Euphrates area, ancient computers and a host of allied phenomena the authenticity of which does not constitute part of this inquiry. On the question of the exodus from Atlantis, however, we must give ear to other opinions if we are to make a fair assessment of the Atlantean situation in the latter days of the island's history. An inclusion of an illustration in the *Interplanetary Travel Encyclopaedia*, compiled by Professor N. A. Rynin of the Soviet Union, depicts Atlantean high priests being picked up by an aircraft against the background of the sinking continent. Andrew Tomas, in commenting on this rather extraordinary deviation from the rigidly scientific approach by a man of such erudition, suggests that although the latter-day Atlanteans might well have mastered the technique of flight, such vehicles might have been available only to priests and officials and not in service to the public generally.

The Babylonians, it seems, preserved the memory of prehistoric astronauts or aviators in their myth of Etana, the flier. The Berlin Museum has in its possession a cylinder seal that shows him soaring through the sky astride an eagle's back, between the Sun and Moon. Tomas tells us that the Samsaptakabadha scripture of India mentions airships powered by 'celestial forces' and speaks of a missile that contained the 'power of the universe', the power of its explosion being compared to 'ten thousand suns'. The Sanskrit *Mausola Purva* refers to 'an unknown weapon, an iron thunderbolt, a gigantic messenger of death that reduced to ashes the entire race of the Vrishnis and the Anhakas'. The corpses were so badly burned as to be unrecognizable. Hair and nails fell out, pottery was shattered, birds turned white, and foodstuffs were rendered inedible.

The radiation inferences here are obvious, but the evidence is insufficient to convince the sceptic that the ancients possessed atomic weapons. Tomas tells of a case cited in Alexander Gorbovsky's *Riddles of Antiquity* where a human skeleton found in India was radioactive fifty times above normal readings, which leads Tomas to wonder if the *Mausola Purva* is history rather than legend. Berlitz also mentions that a number of skeletons on the street levels of the prehistoric Indian cities of Mohenjo-daro and Harappa were found to be highly radioactive.

Although these and similar cases cited are taken as firm indications of the use of atomic energy in prehistoric times, it could equally be argued that the descent of some extraterrestrial object, such as a meteor or comet, might well have generated radioactivity. Things are not always what they seem. Muck, for example, suspected the magnetic properties in his sunken 'asteroid' of being the culprit in the Bermuda Triangle mystery.

Tomas does give some helpful and encouraging quotes from Nobel Prize winner and pioneer nuclear physicist Professor Frederick Soddy, however, which I feel justified in including. Speaking of the traditions that have been handed to us from prehistoric times, Soddy wrote in 1909:

Can we not read into them some justification for the belief that some former forgotten race of men attained not only to the knowledge we have so recently won, but also to the power that is not yet ours . . . it may be an echo from one of the many previous epochs in the unrecorded history of the world, of an age of men which have trod the road we are treading today.[4]

Of course, when Soddy wrote those words nuclear power was as yet undiscovered, although some great minds, like Soddy's, doubtless retained a far-memory of it in their deep unconscious. Perhaps it was some vague reminiscence that prompted Soddy to add:

'A race which could transmute matter would have little need to earn its bread by the sweat of its brow. Such a race could transform a desert continent, thaw the frozen poles, and make the whole world one smiling Garden of Eden.'[5]

I am personally not too happy about Atlantean A- or H-bombs, nor can I conceive of the Atlantean landscape pock-marked by giant nuclear reactors of the sort that are viewed with apprehension by many people today. But then we are talking fission rather than fusion, so I suppose an open mind is called for. What does seem more plausible is that the Atlanteans had discovered *some other form of energy*, which was more economical (and probably free!) and did not constitute an environmental eyesore.

During a sojourn in Moscow, Andrew Tomas, a Russian by birth, reports hearing of a biography of Albert Einstein in which the great scientist expresses a similar idea that nuclear power was merely rediscovered. The editor of the manuscript, however, abstained from publishing the statement that was apparently made by Einstein shortly before his death, on the grounds that 'the old man must have lost his mind.'[6]

While on the subject of Nobel Prize winners, in 1978 I was privileged to be taken to lunch by a scientist who had received this acknowledgement for his work some years earlier. During the course of the meal he confided to me that he had clear memories from his youth of being a sonics scientist in Atlantis, which he referred to affectionately as the 'Old Country', the recollection of which brought tears to his eyes. I questioned him as to why he had not researched sonics in his present life and he replied that he had been warned subconsciously against pursuing this line of scientific enquiry as 'the world was not yet ready to handle that kind of power'. Strangely enough, although scientists as a body are often openly hostile to anything even vaguely approaching the paranormal, in private many of them share the same views as Professor Soddy and my own contact. In fact, I have engaged in deep discussions with some highly qualified men 'on the condition that none of this is repeated publicly – one has one's career to think of, and all that.' Shortly after the aforementioned incident I left the UK to live in Canada for a brief period during which the correspondence that had passed between my learned freind and myself became lost, and therefore also that valuable contact. More's the pity, as I would be grateful for his assistance and advice with this book although, since he was quite elderly at the time of our meeting, he has, no doubt, long since returned to another universe wherein his former knowledge of sonics is readily available to him.

Tomas spends several chapters of his interesting and informative book giving us possible examples of scientific knowledge possessed by ancient civilizations, including what appeared to be an ancient electric battery, which was discovered by Wilhelm Konig, a German archaeologist and engineer engaged on excavation work near Baghdad in Iraq. Replicas were duly made and tested by the General Electric Company at Pittsfield, Massachusetts; they worked perfectly. Tomas also gives details of similar finds that have appeared in China and India, while legends of 'perpetual lights' are to be found on both sides of the Atlantic.

While I am happy to concede that these discoveries provide evidence of a technology that does not appear in our history books, I cannot see them as any proof of the existence of Atlantis, unless we are being given to understand that Atlantean colonists took their technology with them to these diverse sites. What seems to be more logical is that there have been several pockets of civilization in prehistoric times aside from those of Atlantis and Lemuria, in which men and women have made their own rudimentary discoveries. However, when it comes to similar cases in ancient Egypt, then the Atlantean implication does call for consideration.

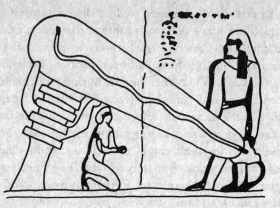

Fig. 24.

Charles Berlitz writes of strange illustrations on the walls of the temple at Denderah which appear to be:

... five-foot [1.5-metre] light bulbs, each one with an elongated 'serpent' filament inside, held up by high-tension insulators and attached to braided cables which in turn are connected to a transformer [see Figure 24]. The overwhelming majority of Egyptologists interpret these apparent bulbs as 'lotus offerings', 'snake stones', or 'cult offerings'.[7]

How the ancient Egyptians managed to illuminate their sub-terranean chambers sufficiently to carry out some of the intricate artwork contained there has never been satisfactorily explained, however. Torches or lamps would have left tell-tale signs on the walls and ceilings, but there are none. Another theory is that it was executed with a series of mirrors. But surely, by the time the reflected light reached deep into the cavernous depths of some of these ancient structures, it would have diminished to such an extent as to render the execution of fine artistic detail almost impossible. And so the mystery remains.

Which brings us round to the question of the movement of Cyclopean objects such as enormous statues, pyramidic blocks, giant stones and other monolithic erections! One theory is that the Atlanteans were cognizant of the *modus operandi* for utilizing the Earth's own gravitational or magnetic forces, either by some process of neutralization or repulsion/attraction. It has even been postulated that the misuse of Gaia's natural energies could have caused her to rebel and cast off the perpetrators of her torment – man! I heard the same point emphasized as regards our present misuse of Gaia's energies and resources at the opening lecture given by actor and ecologist Dennis Weaver at the 1989 'Whole Life Expo' in San Francisco.

My Noble Prize-winning friend mentioned above was convinced that the motive power used by the Atlanteans for lifting heavy objects was sonics, and that by learning the basic 'keynote' of any substance one could effect a degree of control over it. The destructive possibilities of this are, of course, horrendous, especially if one thinks in terms of the personal 'keynote' of every human being! On the other hand, its potential for healing, for making life easier and for the conservation of Gaia's natural resources and energies are also noteworthy. One cannot help asking why all of these energies that contain such a great potential for human happiness are inevitably double-edged swords? The answer to this must surely lie in the metaphysical concept that we need to attain spiritual maturity (or mature humanistically, as some may prefer to view it) before we can be trusted with such powerful forces.

Nikola Tesla, the genius who invented alternating current and after whom the Tesla coil was named, was engaged in some strange tests involving the conveyance of electrical currents without wires while also exploring the relationships between the harmonic sound and power. During the course of this work at his laboratory in Manhattan violent lightning and thunderstorms occurred in the immediate vicinity with such force that the local residents approached the authorities to have his experiments halted. On another occasion, harmonic vibrations that he had induced produced seismic-type effects on the whole neighbourhood. It was generally accepted that Tesla's experiments had shown that sonics could affect the atmosphere and move objects. When it comes to scientific knowledge in Atlantis, sonics seems to ring true, while it is only logical to assume that if the Atlanteans were cognizant of the Gaia potential, they would have been aware of crystal energy in both its natural and amplified (laser) forms.

One of the questions that I am frequently being asked concerning Atlantean temple practices is what methods of healing did they employ? Were there hospitals for the sick and establishments for medical training? Was the treatment allopathic, homoeopathic or psychic/spiritual, or were other methods used? Once again we must separate psychic impression and past-life memories from facts, although the former may ultimately be proven correct. What we do know from Clement of Alexandria (AD 150) and Iamblichus (AD 363) is that certain antediluvian medical textbooks, which could have carried a strong Atlantean influence, contained the following information concerning the healing knowledge possessed in ancient Egypt. The healer priests, or 'shrine bearers', learned their medical arts from six different books, which were among forty-two works purportedly brought to Egypt by a different race of people *before the Flood*. These scrolls were shown to Iamblichus, who was informed that Thoth or Tehuti was their author. Some Egyptologists have suggested that the *Papyrus Ebers* may be a fraction of these lost works. Of the first thirty-six we need not concern ourselves, as they related mainly to priestly procedures, but those numbered 37–42 were titled as follows.

37. The Constitution of the Body.

38. Diseases

39. Instruments

40. Drugs

41. Eyes

42. The Maladies of Women.[8]

Information gleaned from healing methods employed in places thought to be colonies of Atlantis would also tend to indicate that the Atlantean healer priests were well-versed in surgery, psychology and psychic healing. They understood the mind/body relationship and the need for this to be in balance in order for the individual to enjoy good health. They were probably also familiar with bionics. The Irish mythological cycles relate how the Tuatha de Danaans, a 'magical' people who were 'wafted into the land on a magic cloud' in western Connaught, were engaged in combat by the local inhabitants, the Firbolgs. The Firbolgs were led by their king Mac Erc, and the Danaans by Nuada of the Silver Hand, who received his name following an incident in this very battle. His hand was severed during the affray, and one of the many Danaan artificer/healers made a silver replacement which worked 'just like a normal hand'. A corresponding legend is also found in the Arabian folk-tale of a famous pre-Islamic rain god called Hobbal, who lost an arm, which was replaced by a mechanical limb, this time made of gold! The Irish scholar Bob Quinn tells us that E. L. Ranelegh, who had devoted his researches to the study of folklore, regarded the affinity between Irish and Arabian epics as remarkable 'because the early stories did not appear to have been mediated through normal Roman–Greek–Latin channels, i.e. through continental Europe'.[9]

The Danaans have one point in common with the Atlanteans. Following their disappearance from Ireland, about which there are several legends but no tangible evidence, they assumed the role of benevolent genii, having employed their magical powers to effect a veil of invisibility from behind which they guide the initiated, wise and pure of heart. Hesiod, speaking of a 'golden race of men' who came first, whom we may presume to be the Atlanteans of the Golden Age of Cronus, wrote:

> But now that fate has closed over this race,
> They are holy demons upon earth,
> Beneficent averters of ills, guardians of mortal men.[10]

The Greek use of the term 'demon' or 'daemon' does not carry the same connotations as the later Christian meaning, being employed in Classical times to describe the spirits of demi-gods, devas and, latterly, the souls of the great heroes of the Hellenistic past.

Although in his book *Atlantean* Quinn does not tackle the subject of Atlantis itself, but the peoples of the Atlantic coast-lines of whose musical traditions he has made a study, he does leave us with this thought:

Possibly the most important myth in the context of Atlanteans is that of Atlantis, the drowned continent. I agree with Robert Graves that it is a pity that the term 'myth' has come to mean 'fanciful, absurd, unhistorical'. The poet maintained that myths are all 'grave records of ancient religious customs or events, and reliable enough as history once their language is understood.' *Once their language is understood*: that is the key phrase. Our lately acquired rationalist dialects probably make us quite illiterate in the language of myth.[11]

Thank you, Bob Quinn, for those words of wisdom.

Colonies, Missions
and Safe Havens

I have come from the house of the Leonine One,
I left there for the house of Isis,
I saw her hidden mysteries in that she let me see the birth of the
    Great God.

              ANCIENT EGYPTIAN COFFIN TEXT

Prior to the disappearance of their island, the Atlanteans are believed to have established colonies both east and west of the motherland and it is to the myths, legends and ancient practices of these places that we must now turn for further information concerning the 'visitors from afar' who arrived on their shores. However, care should be taken to distinguish between those major centres of Atlantean religion, learning and commerce that were well established prior to the cataclysm, and the lesser known shores that provided a haven for Atlantean survivors fleeing the approaching inundation.

Egypt

Several places have been suggested by scholars as possible Atlantean colonies based on similarities in myths and customs. The best known of all of these colonies is believed to be Egypt, whose history can be traced back many thousands of

years. There are, however, conflicting reports and a wide divergence of opinion regarding early civilization in pre-
dynastic Egypt that need to be aired and analysed. According
to Cyril Aldred, during late Palaeolithic times the retreating
ice-cap affected the climate of North Africa, causing it to
become progressively drier. In Egypt the early pre-dynastic
period, calculated from around 5000 BC to 3600 BC, encompasses the Neolithic and Chalcolithic periods. The Middle
and Late pre-dynastic period is reckoned as 3600 BC to 3200
BC, after which we enter the realms of history. From archaeological finds, we know that during the Amratian period
there was an influx of broad-headed (brachycephalic) peoples,
the indigenous population of Hamites belonging to the long-
headed (dolichocephalic) type. All the evidence points to the
fact that this spread of foreign influence in the fourth millennium BC came from the north.[1]

Spanuth agrees with this, asserting that in the Egypt of
8000–9000 BC there was no Egyptian state, no temples with
inscriptions and no papyrus texts. The Nile Valley was un-
inhabited (the first few remains in the area date from the fifth
to sixth millennia BC and were found on the nearby heights)
while the Libyans make their first appearance in the records
of Merneptah around 1227 BC. In Greece there was no Athens
to be conquered, no Acropolis, no Greek states and no Athenian armies. Nor had the Bronze Age made its appearance
in weaponry or artefacts. And yet all these things are mentioned by Plato, and confirmed by other sources, so what is
the answer?

According to Herodotus, who received his information
from the Egyptian priests, their written history dated back
11,340 years before his era, or nearly 14,000 years prior to the
present. A degree of support for this can be found in Ignatius
Donnelly's quotation of other sources:

'At the epoch of Menes,' says Winchell, 'the Egyptians were already a civilized and numerous people. Manetho tells us that Athotis, the son of this first king, Menes, built the palace at Memphis; that he was a physician, and left anatomical books. All these statements imply that even at this early period the Egyptians were in a high state of civilization.' (Winchell's *Preadamites*, p. 120.) 'In the time of Menes the Egyptians had long been architects, sculptors, painters, mythologists, and theologians.' Professor Richard Owen says: 'Egypt is recorded to have been a civilized and governed community *before* the time of Menes. The pastoral community of a group of nomad families, as portrayed in the Pentateuch, may be admitted as an early step in civilization. But how far in advance of this stage is a nation administered by a kingly government, consisting of grades of society, with divisions of labor, of which one kind, assigned to the priesthood, was to record or chronicle the names and dynasties of the kings, the duration and chief events of their reigns!' Ernest Renan points out that 'Egypt at the beginning appears mature, old, and entirely without mythical and heroic ages, as if the country had never known youth. Its civilization has no infancy, and its art no archaic period. The civilization of the Old Monarchy did not appear with infancy. It was already mature.'[2]

The Alsatian philosopher R. A. Schwaller de Lubicz assembled a great deal of Egyptian material over a period of ten years following a sojourn of fifteen years at Luxor (1936–51). His stepdaughter, Lucie Lamy, made detailed measurements and drawings of the stones and statuary of the great temple at Luxor that showed that the ancient Egyptians possessed a hitherto unsuspected knowledge of mathematics and cosmic form, which she later incorporated into her book *Egyptian Mysteries*. Schwaller de Lubicz himself was the author of several published works, notably *Le Temple de l'Homme*, which also deals with the more esoteric aspects of early Egyptian culture.

The ancient Egyptians possessed a solar, lunar and Sothic calendar. In fact, Sothis, the binary star we know as Sirius, featured strongly in their earliest history. It is my fervent belief that the Egyptians derived this information from the Atlantean priests, which goes to confirm the standard of knowledge that the scientific community of the Old Country had attained. Schwaller de Lubicz tells us:

The Sothic cycle is established on the coincidence every 1,460 years of the *vague year* of 365 days with the *Sothic* (or *Sirian*) *year* of 365¼ days. All civil acts were dated according to the vague year, composed of exactly 360 days plus the five epagomenal days consecrated to the *Neters*: Osiris, Isis, Seth, Nephthys and Horus.

The Sirian, or *fixed year*, was established according to the heliacal rising of Sirius, yet the interval between two heliacal risings of Sirius corresponds neither to the tropical year, which is shorter, nor to the sidereal year, which is longer. For it is remarkable that *owing to the precession of the equinoxes, on the one hand, and the movement of Sirius on the other, the position of the sun with respect to Sirius is displaced in the same direction, almost exactly to the same extent.*

Calculations established by astronomers have demonstrated that between 4231 and 2231 BC, the approximate duration of the reign of the Bull, *Hap*, the Sirian year was almost identical to our Julian year of 365¼ days. This period would cover the entire Ancient Empire, 'and we cannot but admire the greatness of a science capable of discovering such a coincidence because *Sirius is the only star among the "fixed stars" which allows this cycle*. It can therefore be supposed that Sirius plays the role of a center for the circuit of our entire solar system.'[3]

Enter another character in the *dramatis personae* of the Atlantis drama, and it is ancient Egypt we have to thank for the preservation of this knowledge. Sirius was known as the 'Great Provider' and as such was constantly evoked in pyramid texts:

Isis comes to thee [Osiris] joyous in thy love;
Your seed rises in her, penetrating [*spd.t*]★ like Sirius [*spd.t*].

> The penetrating [*spd*] Horus comes forth from thee in his
> name of Horus-who-is-in-Sirius.[4]

Although a history is claimed for Egypt that dates back to 36,620 BC (see p. 214), the Pharaonic calendar is established as being introduced only in 4240 BC. The five epagomenal days are related to the birth of the five Neters, and since the whole arrangement revolves around Sirius, the only star to return periodically every $365\frac{1}{4}$ days, does this imply that whichever energies were responsible for the loss of the Atlantean civilization were orchestrated from Sirius? Should this prove to be the case, it would be reasonable to inquire as to whether the five Neters were, as Donnelly and others suggest, Atlantean leaders, priests/priestesses or leading personalities on the Atlantean political scene, or were they from somewhere else?

When I wrote my epic poem *The Story of Isis and Osiris* I referred to the Egyptian god Ra as relating to the Sothian system and not to our own Sun, the latter being represented by Ra's legendary 'eye'. It was not until I encountered the following statement, and other aspects of Schwaller de Lubicz's work, that many of my own 'memories' began to fall into place.

It took our own discoveries in atomism and astronomy to suggest yet another characteristic of Sirius which coincides with what we are beginning to know about the atomic nucleus, made up of a positron (a giant star of very weak density) accompanying a neutron whose volume is exceedingly small in relation to the atom, but where all its weight is concentrated (a dwarf star of incredible density) . . .

The double star of Sirius – which for Pharaonic Egypt played the role of a central sun to our entire solar system – today suggests the existence of a cosmic system of atomic structure whose *nucleus* is

---

★ *spd.* and *spd.t* represent the Egyptian hieroglyphics for Sothis (Sirius), the 't' indicating the feminine gender.

this 'Great Provider', the Sothis [*spd.t*] of the ancients. There might well be a need to revise our cosmology in the not-so-distant future.[5]

Details of my studies of Sirius, from both an astronomical and a metaphysical viewpoint, are to be found in my books *The Lion People* and *Ancient Egypt – The Sirius Connection*. The fact that during the whole historical period of Pharaonic Egypt the heliacal rising of Sirius, which marked the New Year's Day, always took place when the Sun was in the constellation of Leo confirms my suspicion that the arrival of the first colonists from Atlantis would have been connected with both the constellation of the lion and the binary system of the fixed star Sirius (longitude 13° 34′ of Cancer).

Schwaller de Lubicz also sees Sirius as having some bearing on the climate of our planet and comments on the fact that climatological variation, if only a few degrees, can affect all life on Earth. A drop in temperature drives peoples towards other, less hostile zones, while higher temperatures witness the birth of new plant and animal life. Some of the principal movements within our solar system are well known, others not so, and since climatological modifications appear to obey sidereal variations, he sees Sirius as being responsible for both our climate and that of the entire solar system.[6]

It may be deduced from a study of the Sothian calendar that the precession of equinoxes, the discovery of which was hitherto attributed to Hipparchus in 134 BC, was known to the ancient Egyptians (and Atlanteans), the heliacal rising of Sirius being associated with the beginning of the Nile's flooding and the birth of Ra in the zodiacal sign of Leo. Schwaller de Lubicz tells us:

Yet it was always *Nun*, the primordial, indeterminate state (or ocean) which receives the characteristic impulse of the celestial influence, and this impulse varies according to the precessional month.

Thus it is that Pharaonic prehistory was dominated by The Twins *Shu* and *Tefnut*, whose nature consists in separating Heaven from Earth. This has been interpreted as representing the two crowns of the Empire, as yet dualized. At that time there existed the kingdom of the South with its double capital, *Nekhen* and *Nekheb*, and the kingdom of the North with its dual capital, *Dep* and *Pe*. The vestiges of this period show a pronounced double character and it is certainly at this time that the Heliopolitan mystery of primordial dualization was revealed.

At Memphis, under the Ancient Empire, there was the domination of Hap, the Bull, who precipitated celestial fire into terrestrial form. The Bull, the great *Neter* of the historical period extending from 4380 to 2200 BC, commands the Cretan civilization as well.

From the Middle Empire to the beginning of the Christian era, we see the domination of Amon the Ram. It is in Thebes, under the predominance of Amon, that the generating fire is 'extracted,' so to speak, from its terrestrial gangue-matrix, Khonsu, by the grace of Djehuti (Thoth), master of Hermopolis.

Nun is invariable, while the receptive milieux, or environments, are generative, and hence feminine. They are successively: *Nut* in Heliopolis, *Sekhmet-Hathor* in Memphis, and then *Mut* in Thebes.

What was elaborated at Heliopolis was Shu and Tefnut as creation; in Memphis it becomes Nefertum, issue of the couple Ptah-Sekhmet, while at Thebes, the product of Amon and Mut is Khonsu.

But succession means generation and not juxtaposition, although the philosophical legend must situate the principles as if coexisting personages were involved.

Finally, toward the year 60 BC, with the end of the political empire of Egypt under Cleopatra, our Christian era of Pisces begins.[7]

As I have always intimated, the prevailing ethos colours the overshadowing influences, each respective culture moulding the Neters, or gods and goddesses, according to its own needs or image and likeness.

Schwaller de Lubicz's researchers coincide with, and give credence to, the eighteenth-century scholar Bacstrom's estimate that the *Emerald Tables* were written in circa 2500 BC, falling somewhere between the Memphian and Middle Empires. Plato's bull cults also assume a new reality in the light of later datings, which show how either Solon or the Egyptian priests mixed up their historical facts somewhere along the line. I am inclined to suspect Solon, as the works of Schwaller de Lubicz and Lucie Lamy tend to confirm that the Egyptians had retained the earlier knowledge with some degree of accuracy.

A deeper look at the contents of the *Emerald Tables* gives us an even clearer picture of the profundity of early Egyptian knowledge, both esoteric and exoteric:

True it is, without falsehood, certain, and very real:

What is below is as that which is above, and what is above is as that which is below, in order to perform the Miracle of one thing only.

And just as all things have been and have come forth from One, so all things have been born of this sole-singular thing, by adaptation.

The Sun is its Father, the Moon is its Mother and the Wind has carried it in its belly; the Earth is its nurse. The Father of the entire Teleme of the whole world is here. Its force of puissance is entire if it be converted into Earth.

Thou shalt separate the Earth from the Fire, the Subtile from the Dense, gently, with great ingenuity. It rises from Earth to Heaven, and again descends into Earth, and it receives the strength of things above and below. By this means thou shalt have the glory of all the World, and through it, all obscurity will flee from thee.

This is the strong Strength of all strength, for it will vanquish any subtile thing and penetrate any solid thing.

Thus has the world been created.

From this there shall be and there will come forth marvellous adaptations, the means of which is here.

Therefore, I have been called Hermes Trismegistus, possessing the three parts of the Philosophy of the entire world.

What I have said concerning the operation of the Sun is accomplished and perfected.[8]

These words have both scientific and metaphysical connotations, such as the idea of the oneness of the universe and the unity of all matter, the mirror-like similarity between the quantum or subatomic worlds and the greater universe, the nature of interpenetrative and generative energy fields, the mastery of atomic power, and the cycle of learning through which all living creatures progress – the refiner's fire of experience – which ultimately leads us back along the road to the One. The Greek philosopher and scientist Democritus (c. 460–370 BC) expounded a theory that the universe is made up of minute particles (atoms) multifariously arranged to account for the differing properties of matter. Moschus the Phoenician is believed to have communicated this ancient knowledge to Democritus. Moschus's atomic theory, however, was nearer the truth in that it also accommodated the concept of the divisibility of the atom.

In view of the Sirius connection it is little wonder that Plato, who was schooled in the strict discipline of Greek logic, was unable to comprehend or effect an accurate account of events that were simply the play-out of some extraterrestrial or cosmic drama with much greater implications than the deeds of humankind on Earth.

What else can we learn from prehistoric Egypt that might help us to place the arrival of the Atlantean colonists? Egyptian chronological tables that take the records back many thousands of years have been found in the course of excavation, but unfortunately there are too many inconsistencies among them and therefore no tangible evidence for their accuracy. The various sources, however, postulate a long period during which Egypt was ruled by the Neters, or gods, followed by an equally long time when it came under the rulership of the

Shemsu Hor, the Companions of Horus, also translated as the Followers of Horus (see p. 45).

Schwaller de Lubicz asserts the most valuable document concerning the prehistory of Egypt is the *Royal Papyrus of Turin*, which gave a complete list of kings who reigned over Upper and Lower Egypt from Menes to the New Empire, including the duration of each reign. The first columns of the papyrus, however, were devoted to the prehistoric period, which preceded Menes, and consisted of a list of ten Neters (gods), each name inscribed in a cartouche preceded by the bulrush and bee – the royal symbols of Upper and Lower Egypt – and followed by the number of years of each reign. Unfortunately, most of these numbers are missing. It was followed by a list of kings who reigned before Menes and the duration of each reign, while the remaining fragments establish that nine dynasties were mentioned, among which, Schwaller de Lubicz tells us, were:

. . . the (venerables) of Memphis, the venerables of the North, and finally the *Shemsu-Hor*, usually translated as the 'Companions of Horus.' Fortunately, the last two lines have survived almost intact, as have indications regarding the number of years:

'. . . venerables Shemsu-Hor, 13,420 years
'Reigns up to Shemsu-Hor, 23,200 years (total 36,620)
King Menes'.[9]

It could be speculated, of course, that the Neters were the original Atlantean colonists, and the Shemsu Hor were the descendants of matings between them and the indigenous population. But one cannot help feeling that there are some ends here that are not quite neatly tied, and I, for one, would like to have some further evidence from a source other than psychism to set the Egyptian pre-dynastic books in order.

As regards the chronology, with so little to go on the tendency has been for researchers to adjust the figures that are available from various sources (some of which are highly suspect) to accommodate their theories, which has resulted in a series of suggested dates for the beginning of civilization in Egypt and the arrival of the first Atlantean colonists on those shores, which range from 30,000 BC to 15,000 BC. According to Herodotus, who was thus informed by one of his Egyptian guides, 'the sun had risen twice where it now set, and twice set where it now rises', a passage that is seen by subsequent scholars as relating to the precessional cycles. This would place the foundation of Egypt at about 36,000 BC, in keeping with the *Royal Papyrus of Turin*, which is, no doubt, guaranteed to strain the credulity of many an establishment of orthodox learning. However, according to an article in the *National Geographic* entitled 'The Search for Modern Humans', a carved body of a man – the world's earliest known anthropomorphic figure, which pushes back in time evidence of human ability to create symbols – has been excavated at the 32,000-year-old level in a cave in Hohlenstein, West Germany. Years later museum officials were presented with a beautifully carved ivory lion muzzle that had been found in the same cave: it fitted the statuette perfectly![10]

It should be borne in mind, however, that prior to the arrival of the Atlantean missionaries, Egypt (and indeed the whole of Africa) could have come under Lemurian influence.

The presence of shell fossils from the sea around the base of the Great Pyramid has been seen by some researchers as evidence that the structure has experienced one or more major inundations, although sceptics will no doubt counter with the suggestion that the shells were probably there when the pyramid was built. Schwaller de Lubicz maintains that the erosion of the Sphinx was due to the action of water, not of wind and sand. Were this to be confirmed, however, the accepted chronological history of civilization would be overthrown. As John Anthony West, a researcher into ancient knowledge and a disciple of Schwaller de Lubicz, succinctly points out:

In principle, there can be no objection to the water erosion of the Sphinx, since it is agreed that in the past Egypt has suffered radical climatic changes and periodic inundations – by the sea and (in the not so remote past) by tremendous Nile floods. The latter are thought to correspond to the melting of the ice from the last ice age. Current thinking puts this date around 15,000 BC, but periodic great Nile floods are believed to have taken place subsequent to this date. The last of these floods is dated around 10,000 BC.

It follows, therefore, that if the great Sphinx has been eroded by water, it must have been constructed prior to the flood or floods responsible for the erosion.[11]

Of course, Schwaller de Lubicz is by no means the first to believe that the Sphinx pre-dates the Flood and was probably constructed by the Atlanteans centuries earlier. Mystics down the ages have intimated a similar belief, while more recently several metaphysical schools, unorthodox philosophers and teachers, notably G. I. Gurdjieff, have reiterated it.

When Napoleon arrived in Egypt in the late eighteenth century the Sphinx was buried up to the neck in sand, while the temple adjacent to it was invisible. Its body, anyway, had therefore been protected for thousands of years. In 1819 it was excavated by Cavaglia, and again in 1853 by Mariette. The ever-moving sands buried it yet again for Maspero to clear in 1888, and in 1916 it was reported in a fashionable guidebook as once again being covered. Periods when it was covered can be assessed from lack of references to its existence in various periods of Egyptian history.

From the time of Pharaoh Chephren (*c.* 2700 BC) onwards Egypt underwent a period of political stability that lasted some four centuries. (It then entered a period of chaos, a pattern that was repeated over many centuries and seems to bear out the Chaos theory of the perpetual pendulum.)

It has been suggested that because the sculptors of Egypt were past masters at producing the faces of Pharaohs exactly and in all mediums, the original face of the Sphinx might well have been exchanged for the likeness of Chephren, a deception that has continued to play its role down the pages of history. It strikes me that, in spite of suggestions made by Atlantologists and others as to the symbology of the human face and in the light of the importance of the sign of Leo to the priests and scholars of the earliest dynasty, and the information concerning Sirius, the original face might well have been leonine.

The importance of the lion symbology may be evidenced in the *Stobaeus*, one of the sacred books of the *Hermes Trismegistus*. (Thrice Greatest Hermes) which features the *Minerva Mundi* (translated as the Virgin of the World). In this treatise Isis (representing the teacher) instructs her son Horus (the student) in the sacred mysteries. Referring to those souls who have reached an advanced stage of evolution and are all but ready to ascend to higher planes, she tells him:

But the more righteous of you, who stand upon the threshold of the change to the diviner state, shall among men be righteous kings, and genuine philosophers, founders of states, and lawgivers, the real seers, and true herb-knowers, and prophets of the Gods most excellent, skilful musicians, skilled astronomers, and augurs wise, consummate sacrificers — as many of you are as worthy of things fair and good.

Among winged tribes [they shall be] eagles, for these will neither scare away their kind nor feed upon them; nay more, when they are by, no other weaker beast will be allowed by them to suffer wrong, for what will be the eagles' nature is too just [to suffer it].

Among four-footed things [they will be] lions — a life of strength and of a kind which in a measure needs no sleep, in mortal body practising the exercises of immortal life — for they nor weary grow nor sleep.*

And among creeping things [they will be] dragons, in that this

---

* There was an old belief that the lion always slept with its eyes open, being ever wary of what went on around it.

animal will have great strength and live for long, will do no harm, and in a way be friends with man, and let itself be tamed; it will possess no poison and will cast its skin, as in the nature of the Gods.*

Among the things that swim [they will be] dolphins; for dolphins will take pity upon those who fall into the sea, and if they are still breathing bear them to the land, while if they're dead they will not even touch them, though they will be the most voracious tribe that in the water dwells.[12]

Certain schools of esoteric thought maintain that there are planets in the universe that house highly evolved life forms other than hominids. The Siriun system, for example, is believed to be the home of a race of leonids, while lizard-like beings are thought to reside in the region of Capella in Auriga; likewise, there is said to be a planet of dolphins in another part of the galaxy. A similar doctrine is also to be found in the traditions of the Dogon of Mali. These life forms are believed to be much more spiritually advanced than *Homo sapiens*, and there is therefore much to be learned from them before we can make the ascent to the finer frequencies of the spiritual universe.

Shamanism often observes these distinctions in one form or another, and seeks the assistance of animal spirits to help its followers. The degrees of the Mithraic mysteries also acknowledged these beliefs as spiritual facts, their *mystae* passing through one or other of the grades associated with the four leading types of animals connected with the souls of highest rank, during which rites they would take on the persona of the animal in question (which would vary according to the individual nature of the initiate), imitating their calls, roars or communicatory sounds.[13]

---

* The allusion to 'dragons' is believed to refer to the lizard family rather than the creatures of mythology.

Nor are the Egyptians the only ones to have this knowledge. In Hindu mythology, the fourth incarnation of the god Vishnu is the man-lion, known as the 'Tawny One'.

The aforegoing suggests that the inner mysteries of many earlier cults and religions, the Egyptian in particular, accommodated the knowledge of other worlds. And since these mystery schools are assumed to have been inherited from the Atlanteans, one may also assume that a broad knowledge of life in the universe outside our own solar system was not unknown to the priesthood of the Old Country.

Greece

As I have mentioned earlier, certain passages in the unabridged versions of the *Timaeus* and *Critias* have caused some concern to scholars because of the discrepancy between the dates given by Plato and the generally accepted historical picture of prehistoric Athens. In order to comment on this, we need to see what was actually said.

Once upon a time the gods divided up the Earth between them – not in the course of a quarrel; for it would be quite wrong to think that the gods do not know what is appropriate to them, or that, knowing it, they would want to annex what properly belongs to others. Each gladly received his just allocation, and settled his territories; and having done so they proceeded to look after us, their creatures and children, as shepherds look after their flocks. They did not use physical means of control, like shepherds who direct their flock with blows, but brought their influence to bear on the creature's most sensitive part, using persuasion as a steersman uses the helm to direct the mind as they saw fit and so guide the whole mortal creature. The various gods, then, administered the various regions which had been allotted to them. But Hephaestos and Athene, who shared as brother and sister a common character, and pursued the same ends in their love of knowledge and skill, were allotted this land of ours as their joint sphere and as a suitable and natural home for excellence and wisdom. They produced a native race of good men and gave them suitable political arrangements. Their names have been preserved but what they did has been forgotten because of the destruction of their successors and the long lapse of time. For as we said before, the survivors of this destruction were an unlettered mountain race who had just heard the names of the rulers of the land but knew little of their achievements. They were glad enough to give their names to their own children, but they knew nothing of the virtues and institutions of their predecessors, except for a few hazy reports; for many generations they and their children were short of bare necessities, and their minds and thoughts were occupied with providing for them, to the neglect of earlier history and tradition. For an interest in the past and historical research come only when communities have leisure and when men are already provided with the necessities of life. That is how the names but not the achievements of these early generation come to be preserved. My evidence is this, that Cecrops, Erectheus, Erichthonios, Erusichthon and most of the other names recorded before Theseus, occurred, according to Solon, in the narrative of the priests about this war; and the same is true of the women's names. What is more, as men and women in those days both took part in military exercises, so the figure and image of the goddess, following the custom, was in full armour, as a sign that whenever animals are grouped into male and female it is natural for each sex to be able to practise its appropriate excellence in the community.[14]

Plato then proceeds to describe the life-style of the Athens of those times; the temples, the original Acropolis and the communal life-style of the people. Men and women enjoyed equal status, gold and silver was never used, and most classes of citizen were concerned with manufacture and agriculture. Only the military lived apart, in quarters where they were provided with what was necessary for their maintenance and training. The climate then, he tells us, was different, and rich soil covered the plains and the mountain sides abounded with thick woods. There was an adequate rainfall, which was absorbed by the soil, any excesses flowing down to the fertile valleys to form rivers and springs.

The destruction of the original city of Athens by the sea is an acknowledged historical fact, and is related in the myths as a battle between Athene and Poseidon for the possession of Attica (the land versus the sea). However, as discussed previously, Plato's statement that Athens was founded 9,000 years earlier tends to suggest that he does not take the historical status of his account too seriously.

Among the names mentioned by Plato in this passage one in particular caught my eye – Cecrops. According to the *Oera Linda Book*, Athens was founded by the Frisian warrior princess Min-erva* (Greek: Athene), in whose honour the Acropolis was built. Min-erva, like the other Frisian people, was fair-haired and blue-eyed, the physical attributes normally accorded to the goddess Athene, who, like many Frisian women, bore arms alongside her menfolk. After the death of Min-erva, the local people of the Hellenes established her as a goddess, an act that did not meet with the approval of their Frisian colonizers, who were monotheists. This resulted in the people of the newly founded Athenian state accusing the Frisians of envy, because Min-erva had bestowed such affection upon them. The altercation that ensued was, however, resolved in the following manner: 'Then, lo and behold! an Egyptian high priest, bright of eye, clear of brain, and enlightened of mind, whose name was Cecrops, came to give them advice.'[15]

The ensuing narrative, which appears to complement the known history of the period, then goes on to describe how Cecrops helped the Frisians and the peoples of old Athens to sort out their differences. According to Scrutton:

... Min-erva founded Athens, shortly after the Mycenae sacked Troy (probably *c.* 1250 BC), and before the Dorians invaded from

---

* The Romans adopted a goddess of this name from the Etruscans, whom some believe also had Atlantean ancestors.

the north and founded what has come to be known as historical Greece. Therefore, the people from the sunken land beyond the Pillars of Hercules must have been the Frisians who founded Athens.

No doubt Egyptians – a branch of Finda's people – did flee across the Mediterranean to proto-Greece when the Nile delta was flooded.

But stories of (a) the deluge and (b) the tall race of Frya's people who colonized Greece, undoubtedly became muddled over the centuries. The *Oera Linda Book* goes on to relate later how Cecrops, the son of a Frisian girl by an Egyptian priest, brought wild Finda soldiers and drove the Frisians from Athens.[16]

May we therefore assume that Plato's 'Atlanteans' who waged war on the Athenians and were defeated were none other than the Frisians? The facts would certainly seem to fit.

The character of Cecrops also appears to have mythic associations. The Spanish psychologist and metaphysician J. E. Cirlot, commenting on the cult of the 'hero' in his *Dictionary of Symbols*, refers to Cecrops as being 'half man and half serpent', a legend which was, no doubt, based on someone's assessment of his character, serpents being associated with both cunning and wisdom.[17]

Plato's reference to Hephaestus and Athene as being the founders of the ancient Athenian state calls for analysis. If the account rendered by the *Oera Linda Book* is correct, many of the gods of ancient Greece were, as Donnelly contends, real people – conquerors or colonizers from another land, but not necessarily, it would seem, Atlantis. As the Greek god forms lend themselves so easily to identification with major Jungian archetypes, we may look at it in another way: Hephaestus was essentially a god of craftsmen, or divine artificer, and Athene a warrior goddess whose preference really lay in the execution of arts and crafts, such as weaving. Could the myth therefore be telling us that ancient Athens was founded by a

people who were skilled smiths, artisans, weavers, agriculturalists and so forth, whose skills stood out against the stark
simplicity of a people who were shepherds, goatherds and
country folk?

While I do not see all the ancient Egyptian gods as having
been Atlantean settlers, I am inclined to think that there is
some connection between the twelve Greek Olympians and
the latter-day kings of Atlantis. The characters of the Classical
pantheon are all too human to be divine. What probably
happened is that the original Atlantean visitors to those parts
did not settle the country districts, but implanted the story of
their native land, with its lofty peaks and twelve rulers, upon
the folk of the coastal areas and it later became fused with the
archetypal gods and indigenous deities of the region. The
demi-gods and heroes who came later were probably the descendants of the children they begat with native women,
being described in the myths as fathered by a god on a mortal
woman. The Frisians, who came later and with whom the
early Athenians did battle, no doubt resembled the Atlanteans
in appearance and skills, being a tall, fair people who worked
in bronze.

The various tales of the exploits of Poseidon should not,
therefore, be attributed to the deeds of a single deity, but
rather to those enigmatic 'sea peoples', be they Atlanteans or
Frisians, who imposed themselves upon the natives of Corinth,
Aegina, Naxos, Delphi and other Mediterranean locations.
Working on this assumption, Poseidon's famous 'sea monsters'
would have been nothing more than large and unfamiliar
ships, probably sporting animal figureheads or gargoyle-like
decorations. Likewise, Poseidon's association with the horse
probably arose from the fact that the Atlanteans were among
the earliest people to domesticate that animal and, as we shall
see, many of the peoples who claim Atlantean ancestry count
equine skills among their accomplishments.

Sumeria/Chaldea

The Mesopotamian area was, until recent times, thought of as being the cradle of civilization and home of the biblical Adam and Eve. The Chaldeans feature prominently among the peoples of those parts who claimed to have received their instructions in such subjects as astronomy, metaphysics and ethics from a strange, foreign source. Berossus, a Babylonian priest of the thirteenth century BC, rendered the following account of the early history of those parts:

At first they led a somewhat wretched existence and lived without rule after the manner of beasts. But, in the first year, appeared a monster endowed with human reason, named Oannes, who rose from out of the Erythaean sea, at the point where it borders Babylonia. He had the whole body of a fish, but above his fish's head he had another head which was that of a man, and human feet emerged from beneath his fish's tail; he had a human voice, and his image is preserved to this day. He passed the day in the midst of men without taking food; he taught them the use of letters, sciences and arts of all kinds, and rules for the founding of cities, and the construction of temples, the principles of land and surveying; he showed them how to sow and reap; he gave them all that contributes to the comforts of life. Since that time nothing excellent has been invented.[18] (See Figure 25.)

The reference to a monster arising from the sea has often been taken to suggest that Oannes emerged from a submarine. I am inclined to the opinion that this band of civilizers – for I believe there had to be more than one person to accomplish all these things – were conveyed to their destination by a vessel, the like of which was totally unfamiliar to the natives. Maybe a hovercraft? The clothing they wore would have been of a protective nature and probably made of some kind of waterproof material, while the fish motif would indicate that they were either mariners or travelling in the aquatic

Fig. 25.

mode. The fact that Oannes refrained from sharing the food enjoyed by the natives suggests that he and his band obviously followed a strict, and probably priestly, diet, supplies of which they kept on board their ship. The allusion to 'a day' is also misleading, and suggests a people who had no concept of time as it is known and allocated in civilized society.

Somehow I cannot conceive of Oannes and his band of followers as being Frisians or sea people from the north, and am therefore inclined to view them as Atlanteans. The astronomy they taught to the Chaldeans was certainly highly advanced, as may be seen in the Chaldean knowledge of the solar system and the ninth planet in particular (excluding the Sun and Moon), the existence of which is only just receiving credence from the scientific establishment.

Initially the biblical version of the Flood was not taken seriously outside the bastions of Hebraic and Christian fundamentalism. Numerous legends and other archaeological finds in Mesopotamia changed that. In 1872 scholar and Assyriologist George Smith, while studying the ancient cuneiform texts from the library of King Assurbanipal IV unearthed in the ruins of Nineveh, found what is referred to as the Gilgamesh epic. This story of Gilgamesh, the legendary hero of the Chaldeans whose exploits featured so prominently in Sumero-Babylonian mythology, relates the event of the Flood and subsequent changes to the world. Archaeologists investigating the ruins of Nippur at a later date discovered a more ancient Sumerian version of the Creation and Flood myths, which adds credence to the biblical texts, although I strongly suspect that the latter was borrowed from the former.

There are two versions of the Deluge story, unequally developed but exhibiting a remarkable agreement. The shorter of these was extracted by Berossus from the sacred books of Babylon, and later introduced into the history he wrote for the Greeks. Nine kings are mentioned as having ruled over Sumeria and Mesopotamia prior to the Flood, then:

Obartès Elbaratutu being dead, his son Xisuthros (Khasisatra) reigned eighteen sares (64,800 years). It was under him that the Great Deluge took place, the history of which is told in the sacred documents as follows: Cronos (Ea) appeared to him in his sleep, and announced that on the fifteenth of the month of Daisios (the Assyrian month Sivan – a little before the summer solstice) all men should perish by a flood. He therefore commanded him to take the beginning, the middle, and the end of whatever was consigned to writing, and to bury it in the City of the Sun, at Sippara; then to build a vessel and to enter it with his family and dearest friends; to place in this vessel provisions to eat and drink, and to cause animals, birds and quadrupeds to enter it; lastly, to prepare everything for navigation. And when Xisuthros inquired in what direction he should steer his bark, he was answered 'toward the gods,' and enjoined to pray that good might come of it for men.

Xisuthros obeyed, and constructed a vessel five stadia long and five broad; he collected all that had been prescribed to him and embarked his wife, his children, and his intimate friends.

The Deluge having come, and soon going down, Xisuthros loosed some of the birds. These, finding no food nor place to alight on, returned to the ship. A few days later Xisuthros again let them free, but they returned again to the vessel, their feet full of mud. Finally, loosed the third time, the birds came no more back. Then Xisuthros understood that the earth was bare. He made an opening in the roof of the ship, and saw that it had grounded on the top of a mountain. He then descended with his wife, his daughter, and his pilot, who worshipped the earth, raised an altar, and there sacrificed to the gods; at the same moment he vanished with those who accompanied him.

Meanwhile those who had remained in the vessel, not seeing Xisuthros return, descended too, and began to seek him, calling him by his name. They saw Xisuthros no more; but a voice from heaven was heard commanding them piety toward the gods; that he, indeed, was receiving the reward of his piety in being carried away to dwell thenceforth in the midst of the gods, and that his wife, his daughter, and the pilot of the ship shared the same honor. The voice further said that they were to return to Babylon, and, conformably to the degrees of fate, disinter the writings buried at Sippara in order to transmit them to men. It added that the country in which they found themselves was Armenia. These, then, having heard the voice, sacrificed to the gods and returned on foot to Babylon. Of the vessel of Xisuthros, which had finally landed in Armenia, a portion is still to be found in the Gordyan Mountains in Armenia, and pilgrims bring thence asphalte that they have scraped from its fragments. It is used to keep off the influence of witchcraft. As to the companions of Xisuthros, they came to Babylon, disinterred the writings left at Sippara, founded numerous cities, built temples, and restored Babylon.[19]

One is tempted to think that Xisuthros and his crew met with an accident shortly after alighting. With so much mud and debris around it would have been easy to slip down a concealed crevice or into some newly formed quagmire. One thing that did catch my eye in this narrative is the date given, which is near enough to Muck's estimate of 5 June (see Chapter 6).

Flood legends the world over seem to agree on one point – that the inundation was visited upon humanity because of its transgression against the gods (misuse of cosmic laws or possibly the laws of nature?). We do not have the space to include all of these for comparison, but suffice it to say that the Sumero-Babylonian version is standard and, taken in context with other data relating to the early days of that culture, does suggest both an Atlantean influence in the founding of civilization in those parts and a confirmation of the events that precipitated the Atlantean continent's final sinking.

North America

I have already commented on how the legends of several tribes of North American Indians complement and confirm similar tales from European and African sources. Whether the Atlanteans actually established colonies in the North American continent, however, is open to debate. Many researchers suggest that a colonization took place farther south, with those tribes of Indians who had come under Atlantean influence making their way north after the cataclysm.

In a letter dated August 1683 the Quaker colonist William Penn gave this graphic description of the Indians of Pennsylvania:

The natives . . . are generally tall, straight, well built, and of singular proportion; they tread strong and clever, and mostly walk with a lofty chin . . . Their eye is little and black, not unlike a straight-looked Jew . . . I have seen among them as comely European-like faces of both sexes as on your side of the sea; and truly an Italian complexion hath not much more of the white, and the noses of several of them have as much of the Roman . . . For their original, I am ready to believe them to be of the Jewish race — I mean of the stock of the ten tribes — and that for the following reasons: . . . I find them to be of the like countenance, and their children of so lively a resemblance that a man would think himself in Duke's Place or Berry Street in London when he seeth them. But this is not all: they agree in rites, they reckon by moons, they offer their first-fruits, they have a kind of feast of tabernacles, they are said to lay their altars upon twelve stones, their mourning a year, customs of women, with many other things that do not now occur.[20]

If these Indians were of Semitic origin, they could either have crossed America from Lemuria or made their way there by boat from Atlantis. Information regarding their blood group might help solve the question, but as much interbreeding has, no doubt, taken place since Penn's time, an accurate assessment would be difficult, if not impossible. The majority of North American Indians share the same type O blood group as the Semites, although a small incidence of the *A* gene has been observed among certain tribes, which would appear to go hand in hand with the fair or auburn-haired colouring (see Chapter 8).

The Mandan Indians, of whose tribe there seem to be few if any survivors, are considered by some authorities as being likely candidates for Atlantean ancestry. Not only did the history of this tribe contain a detailed Flood legend, but until the last century its peoples had also preserved an image of an ark-like vessel, around which was performed a religious cere-mony that clearly referred to the destruction of Atlantis. Many of the Mandans were white people with hazel, grey or blue eyes, and hair varying from dark-brown to ash-blonde. The Mandans lived in fortified towns and manufactured earthen-ware pots, which they used for boiling water – a custom unique to their tribe. Ignatius Donnelly quotes the following report of a Mandan ceremony written by George Catlin, who visited the Mandans in the mid-nineteenth century:

In the centre of the village is an open space, or public square, 150 feet [46 metres] in diameter and circular in form, which is used for all public games and festivals, shows and exhibitions. The lodges around this open space front in, with their doors towards the centre; and in the middle of this stands an object of great religious veneration, on account of the importance it has in connection with the annual religious ceremonies. This object is in the form of a large hogshead, some eight or ten feet [$2\frac{1}{2}$ or 3 metres] high, made of planks and hoops, containing within it some of their choicest mysteries or medicines. They call it the Big Canoe . . .

On the day set apart for the commencement of the ceremonies a solitary figure is seen approaching the village.

During the deafening din and confusion within the pickets of the village the figure discovered on the prairie continued to approach with a dignified step, and in a right line toward the village; all eyes were upon him, and he at length made his appearance within the pickets, and proceeded toward the centre of the village where all the chiefs and braves stood ready to receive him, which they did in a cordial manner by shaking hands, recognizing him as an old acquaintance, and pronouncing his name, Nu-mohk-muck-a-nah (*the first or only man*). The body of this strange personage, which was chiefly naked, was painted with white clay, so as to resemble at a distance *a white man*. He enters the medicine lodge, and goes through certain mysterious ceremonies.

During the whole of this day Nu-mohk-muck-a-nah (the first or only man) travelled through the village, stopping in front of each man's lodge, and crying until the owner of the lodge came out and asked who he was, and what was the matter? To which he replied by narrating *the sad catastrophe which had happened on the earth's surface by the overflowing of the waters*, saying that 'he was the *only person saved from the universal calamity*; that he landed his big canoe on a high mountain in the west, where he now resides; that he has come to open the medicine lodge, which must needs receive a present of an edged tool from the owner of every wigwam, that it may be sacrificed to the water; for,' he says, 'if this is not done there will be another flood, and no one will be saved, as it was with such tools that the big canoe was made.'

Having visited every lodge in the village during the day, and having received such a present from each as a hatchet, a knife, etc. (which is undoubtedly always prepared ready for the occasion), he places them in the medicine lodge; and, on the last day of the ceremony, they are thrown into a deep place in the river – 'sacrificed to the Spirit of the Waters.'[21]

Catlin then described how twelve men danced around the ark, having arranged themselves according to the four cardinal points, and coloured themselves black, red or white. The dance they executed was called Bel-lohck-na-pie, and the horned headdresses they wore reminded Catlin of those used in Europe as symbolical of Bel, or Baal.

From the aforegoing, one might suppose that a single man or group of men escaped the Flood and fled to those parts, but other Mandan tribal legends related by Donnelly prompt me to think that the Mandans, and several other tribes of Indians, originally lived along the eastern seaboard of America on a series of islands that ultimately sank during the great cataclysm, but were previously only a short journey by sea from the Atlantean mainland. Atlantean traders calling in those parts would account for the introduction of new blood groups and colourings. What their ceremonies do provide us with, however, is verification of the Flood and the loss of a large land to the east of the American continent where their ancestors lived in 'cities with inextinguishable lights' – Atlantis!

I have always maintained that Atlantis was at one time joined to the American continent and, interestingly, confirmation for this is to be found in the legends of the Okanagaus, which tell of a time when the Sun was no bigger than a star, and the land was ruled by a strong medicine woman (matriarchal system?). Much to her chagrin, however, her subjects fell out among themselves and created a noisy war, which angered her so much that she broke off the piece of land upon which they dwelt and pushed it out to sea to drift whither it would. It was later afflicted by some giant catastrophe from which only a man and woman escaped in a canoe and arrived on the mainland, and it is from these two survivors that the whole Okanagaus tribe was descended.

In spite of the wealth of Flood legends that are to be found among the North American Indians, I cannot conceive of an actual Atlantean colony in those parts. Trade, perhaps, and a degree of intermarriage, but nothing on the scale of Egypt, or even South and Central America.

The discoveries in Bimini in the 1960s have caused quite a stir, especially as they coincided with a time given for the finding of Atlantis by the American seer Edgar Cayce. The entire area of the Bahama Banks is believed to have been above sea-level during the last glaciation, but disappeared beneath the waters when the sea-level rose following the melting of the ice. Dr Manson Valentine, a palaeontologist, geologist and underwater archaeologist of Miami, who had been studying the underwater Bahama Banks for some twenty-five years, became convinced that this area held the clues to a civilization that existed before the Flood.

Investigating the area between Orange Key and Bimini off the Florida coast, he discovered a series of giant rectangles along the sea bottom connected by straight lines. In fact, the ocean bed in that area abounded with architectural patterns that could not be attributed to nature. It was in 1968 that Valentine first saw the enormous stones that were obviously the remnants of a man-made causeway. In an interview with Berlitz, Valentine explained:

Many of the stones are of flint-hard micrite, unlike soft beach rock. The lines of closely fitted stones are straight, mutually parallel, and terminate in cornerstones. The stone avenue does not follow the curving beach rock-line, which follows the shape of the island, but is straight. The long avenue contains enormous flat stones propped up at their corners by pillar stones like the dolmens of the coast of Western Europe. Perfect rectangles, right angles, and rectilinear configurations are unaccountable in a natural formation. One end of the complex swings into a beautifully curved corner before vanishing under the sand. No one has yet dug underneath it, so we don't know how far down the stones go.[22]

Valentine believed the causeway was a ceremonial road leading to a special site, and that further investigation might well uncover buildings, but feared that more orthodox archaeologists might fight shy of such research in case it upset their anticataclysmic opinions. During the course of a later expedition a grooved building block was brought up together with a stylized head believed to be that of a giant feline and weighing between 200 and 300 pounds (90 and 136 kilogrammes).

All in all, there seems little doubt that a prehistoric civilization specializing in monolithic building occupied those lands prior to their submergence, but whether these people were Plato's Atlanteans, or pre-Atlantean Lemurians/Muans, is still open to conjecture.

Central and South America

The character of Atlas is to be found among the Chibchas of Bogota. Bochica, their leading divinity in ancient times, spent many years elevating his subjects. He dwelt in the Sun while his wife occupied the Moon. A lesser divinity in the Chibchas pantheon named Chibchacum, in a fit of pique, brought a Deluge on the people of the tableland, for which act he was severely punished by Bochica, who obliged him to bear the burden of the Earth upon his back. When he occasionally shifts the burden from one shoulder to the other for comfort, earthquakes are caused. When answering the prayers of the people to quell the Deluge, Bochica appeared seated on a rainbow.

According to Braghine, the last representatives of a strange white-skinned Indian tribe are still to be found in Venezuela.

They are called Paria, and some years ago inhabited a village called Atlan, in the virgin forests between Apure and Orinoco, but are now almost extinct. They possessed traditions of a certain catastrophe which destroyed their fatherland, a large island in the ocean inhabited by a prosperous and 'wonderful' race. Their descendants lived for a long time among the Venezuelan Indians as a separate tribe.[23]

The Toltecs claimed to have originated in a land called Aztlan or Atlan; the original home of the Nahautlacas was Aztlan; the Aztecs also tell of their ancestors having come from Aztlan. According to the *Popul Vuh*, after their migration from Aztlan the three sons of the king of the Quichés, upon the death of their father, '. . . determined to go as their fathers had ordered to the East, on the shores of the sea whence their fathers had come, to receive the royalty, "bidding adieu to their brothers and friends and promising to return." '[24] The information gleaned from blood samples taken from Inca mummies tends to suggest that the royal families, anyway, hailed from the Old Country, and the lands over which they ruled could certainly be classed as Atlantean colonies of the first order (see Chapter 8).

Donnelly saw the Atlantean colonies of Central and South America as stretching from the shores of Mexico to the peninsula of Yucatan, from Brazil to the heights of Bolivia and Peru, and from the Gulf of Mexico to the headwaters of the Mississippi River. Perhaps he was right, but I am inclined to see some of the ancient peoples of those parts as more Lemurian or Muan than Atlantean, which would suggest that their coastal lands were inundated in earlier times when the Atlantean island originally separated from the American mainland.

Lewis Spence conceived of Atlantis as originally being a much larger land mass than Plato described, which split into two sections, the second of which he named Antillia (see Figure 26). Assuming Wegener to be correct, this was possibly true, and as Spence places Antillia closer to the American coastline than Plato's location for Atlantis, it would accommodate many of the aforementioned legends of the Americas, and the Mandan, Yucatan and Bimini connections. Spence assumes Antillia to have encompassed the region of the West Indies. Regarding timing, he tells us:

. . . that these two island continents and the connecting chain of islands persisted until late Pleistocene times, at which epoch (about

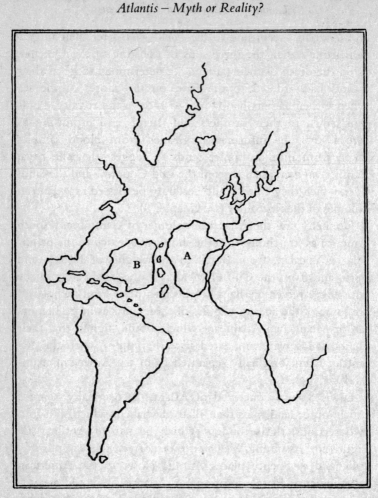

Fig. 26. Map showing probable relative position of Atlantis (A) and Antillia (B) according to Lewis Spence.

25,000 years ago, or the beginning of the post-glacial epoch) Atlantis seems to have experienced further disintegration. Final disaster appears to have overtaken Atlantis about 10,000 BC. Antillia, on the other hand, seems to have survived until a much more recent period, and still persists fragmentally in the Antillean group or West India Islands.[25]

As may be gathered from my earlier comments, I am not in agreement with Spence on this issue. I tend to see Plato's Atlantis as being the later survivor, and the Antillian fragment as relating to an earlier cataclysm that left a series of islands stretching into the Atlantic between the American coastline and the Atlantean mainland. American Indian and South and Central American legends tend to support this theory.

Africa

A possible Atlantean connection with the Berbers of North Africa has already been shown (see p. 171) and further evidence is found in their myths. Bob Quinn emphasizes that part of their home territory is a range of mountains known as the Atlas, while Ouzzin, a modern Berber scholar, discovered an old Sumerian legend of a drowned civilization that contained names that were familiar to him and his own culture. The legend told of a princess called Tangis, who gave her name to the city of Tangier, who was overtaken by a storm at sea and drowned. Her grieving husband instituted a search for her, which involved attacking an island called Atlantis by means of an underground cavern. So strong was his attack that it precipitated an earthquake which caused the whole island to disappear. The husband later became a hermit and spent his time sitting on a rock looking out to sea until the spirit of Tangis finally called him to join her. Quinn was particularly intrigued by the name of the husband – Lugal – which is ever-present in Celtic mythology. The Irish Sun-god-hero was called Lugh, his Welsh equivalent being Llew. He gave his name to the major Celtic feast of Lughnasa or Luguasad, which was celebrated on 1 August. The cities of

Leyden, Lyons (*Lug-dunum*), London and, in London, Ludgate Circus are among the places reputedly named after him.

The Canary Islands are believed to form part of a land complex that was originally attached to the African continent, as it is still connected to Africa's continental shelf. This led Spence and others to believe that Atlantis might have been considerably closer to Africa than Plato suggested, but I am inclined to the view that although the western coast of Africa did, no doubt, extend much farther into the ocean and encompass many smaller islands, it was not connected to the Atlantean mainland. The evidence suggests that Atlantean culture and learning probably found its way into central and even north-west Africa via Egypt and the trade routes from the north-eastern regions. Where else could tribes such as the Dogon of Mali, the Bambara and the Bozo have gained their detailed knowledge of the Sirius system?

Mooney insists that there was little trace of occupation in Africa south of the present Sahara until less than 10,000 years ago, which he sees as being the period *following* the catastrophe. However, I hardly see this as compatible with the currently favoured 'Black Eve' hypothesis, which views Africa as the ancient motherland of *Homo sapiens*, nor with the legends and history of the Bushmen and other tribes of the south. Either way, however, the peoples of that continent, wherever they lived, do not appear to have been exposed to the Atlantean influence until just prior to, or immediately after, the catastrophe, and then indirectly, which might be what Mooney is implying.

Ireland

Irish legends concerning the arrival of the Tuatha de Danaans are often believed to relate to Celtic landings in those parts.

But since the references in question, which were originally orally transmitted and later appeared in the mythological cycles, refer to physical and geographical changes in the contours of that country, the dating for the arrival of the earliest visitors still needs to be questioned.

When the legendary Partholan arrived on the shores of Ireland, there were 'but three lakes, nine rivers and one plain'. But during the reign of Partholan and his queen, Dealgnaid (pronounced Dalny), the land changed contour and a new lake was formed, which was named after Partholan's son, Rury, as it was said to have burst from the Earth during the digging of Rury's grave. The Partholanians were eventually wiped out by what the legends describe as a 'pestilence', which could mean anything in those days, but may have been caused by the release of bacteria during some seismic upheaval.

The indigenous population who faced these presumed Atlantean arrivals were the Formorians, who were by all accounts not the most prepossessing of people. How they fared during those violent climatic and geological changes, however, we are not told.

Next came Nemed and his people, whom we are given to believe were also of Atlantean stock, being in some way related to Partholan. The Nemedians had sailed for Ireland in a fleet of thirty-two barks, each of which contained thirty persons, but because of appalling weather conditions only nine survived the journey. In time they, too, died mysteriously. The next person to arrive in Ireland was Semion, son of Stariat, from whom descended the Firbolgs and two other tribes that persisted into historic times.

The most mysterious of all Irish visitors, however, were the Tuatha de Danaans, or fairy people, whom we have already discussed and 'from whom all Irishmen of learning are sprung'. It would seem logical to assume that the

Partholanians and Nemedians could have been ordinary folk who escaped the shores of Atlantis either just prior to the Flood, or during that period of chaos that reigned directly after, when the Earth was in the process of settling down to its new orbit. The Tuatha de Danaans, on the other hand, sound to me like Atlantean priests and artificers from one of the more advanced colonies, possibly Egypt, Spain or Gaul, who had embarked on a mission of enlightenment. I shall be dealing with the Celtic connection in the next chapter.

Wales

The Reverend Edward Davies, whose book *The Mythology and Rites of the British Druids* first appeared in 1809, expressed his famous 'Arkite' theory, in which he stated that Wales had its own Noah in the person of Hu Gadarn. According to Davies, Hu Gadarn appeared on the western shores of Wales around the time of the final sinking of Atlantis and, with the help of a magic rite involving a team of oxen, contained the Flood and saved the lives of his people. In fact, the Hu Gadarn legend would appear to complement Plato's story regarding Atlantean bull cults, so whether Hu's arrival on Welsh shores actually followed the Atlantean inundation or whether he was simply fleeing from the aftermath of the Thera, or similarly dated seismic disturbances, is open to speculation. The similarity between Hu's name and that of the Sphinx (in Egyptian Hu, 𓉗𓏤𓂝),[26] would seem to suggest an Egyptian connection; since Davies was apparently of the opinion that the Celts originally hailed from North Africa, this is hardly surprising.

Scandinavia and the Northern Regions

As we have already discussed the *Oera Linda Book* and Spanuth's *Atlantis of the North* in some detail, all that needs to be decided at this juncture is whether the Atland described in these documents was an Atlantean colony or a culture that had developed along enlightened lines without external influence. The descendants of the ancient Frisians would, no doubt, argue the latter, but the blood groups concerned could be seen as too much of a coincidence on the one hand (see p. 171), while the descriptions of those 'tall fair strangers' would appear to fit the ancient Frisians perfectly. No doubt it could also be argued that there were no tall, fair Atlanteans – only Frisians who were the colonizers and bringers of civilization and learning. But much as the morals and ethics of the ancient Frisian matriarchal system are to be admired, I do not see the culture as being synonymous with that of Plato's Atlantis. The religious and technological differences were too accentuated to start with, while the disparity between the dates rendered in the *Oera Linda Book* and the latest geological findings off the Scandinavian coast in the North Sea must be taken into account. The Atlantean influence in those parts would seem to me to be obvious, and probably dates back to the Age of Virgo, when Atlantis was, in my opinion, at its best. So, 'good on' the Frisians, for preserving its pristine quality and ethics for so long!

In Summary

Our examination of those countries that appear to have been most deeply affected by the Atlantean influence, or which I believe were imbued with a goodly portion of both the virtues and vices of the Old Country, has certainly yielded up some interesting information. From Egypt, for example, we have learned that the Atlanteans were probably not only aware of the nature of our own solar system, but also of other star systems within our galaxy. This is also confirmed in the legends and writings of the Chaldeans, who, for many centuries, kept alive the story of the arrival of the Wise Ones who were their original teachers and instructors, whom they believed to have been of a different genus from themselves.

The giant monoliths from the past suggest the existence of a people who possessed an advanced knowledge of mathematics, geometry, physics and sonics, and who also understood both the general pattern of universal evolution and the nature and energy of time. In the light of the *Oera Linda Book* many of the myths of ancient Greece could be seen as having some basis in fact and, like the oral traditions and legends of other early cultures, may now be viewed as distorted records of long-lost history or cosmological events rather than pure fairy-tales. Other information gleaned from rites and folk memories collected from both sides of the Atlantic provides evidence of a strong ethnic and genetic relationship between the peoples concerned. Descriptions of visitors from a 'land across the seas', who brought with them a message of love and hope, and taught the natives the finer arts of civilization, occur in all the lands that surround the Atlantic Ocean. In other words, there was a very real connecting link, and that was the now sunken island continent of Atlantis.

We have considered that the Atlantean missionaries, colonists, traders and those fleeing from the rising waters could have established links all along the western coastlines of Central, South, and parts of North America and Europe, and that some scholars, experts and researchers are of the opinion that the Basques, Etruscans and Phoenicians were either of pure Atlantean blood or the descendants of intermarriages between the Atlantean visitors and the local population.

The next question is how much, if any, of the old ways, beliefs, knowledge and personal characteristics of the ancient Atlanteans has filtered through to us today.

CHAPTER 11

Atlantean Heritage

Weep with me, my children, as I search
   The wild wastelands and the azure seas
Of the Blue Planet, wherein lie
   The fourteen pieces of my love.
And I, Isis, will recall those tears
   When Sothis shows her final hand.

Leaving aside the view of those mystics, occultists and metaphysicians who assert that *all* Western tradition can be traced back to Atlantis, there are some more tangible enigmas that have survived to this day, the origins of which are believed to lie in the culture, religion or science of the lost continent.

Pyramids and Other Monoliths

The pyramids of Egypt have provided a source of dialogue and polemic among historians, scientists, mystics and alchemists over the centuries. Were these monolithic structures really erected by thousands of perspiring slaves? Diodorus Siculus seemed to think so; 360,000 men, he tells us, were employed on the project for twenty years. Herodotus, however, claims it was 100,000 men who flexed their muscles in that arduous task over the proposed twenty-year period, and that the extravagant venture all but bankrupted Cheops

(Khufu), who saw fit to expose his daughter to the rigours of a house of ill-repute in order to set his bank account right again. The lady must have been proficient at her task, however, for not only did she obtain the sum needed by her father, but also collected a stone for her future memorial from each of her 'visitors'! One rather suspects that dear old Herodotus was either spun a tall yarn by the Egyptian priests, who, no doubt, chuckled to themselves after he had left, or that he deliberately embroidered the incident to amuse his readers.

Several books written recently state the exact measurements of the Great Pyramid, the mathematical precision of which evidences an advanced knowledge of that science. The angle between each of the sides and the plane of the foundation is almost exactly 51°51′14″. The original pinnacle being missing, the height was calculated by geometry, while mathematics applied to the perimeter of the base, divided by double height, rendered the surprising figure of 3.14149, or pi (π). The mean distance of the Earth to the Sun is, we are told, about 93 million miles (149.5 million kilometres). The height of the Cheops pyramid is 485 feet (147.8 metres), which equals the astronomical distance to the Sun reduced by a thousand million, with an error of only 1 per cent.

The basic unit of measurement employed in the construction of this edifice was the 'sacred cubit', equivalent to 25 'primitive inches' − in modern measurements 25.0265 inches (635.66 mm). The radius of the Earth from the centre to the pole is 3,950 miles (6,357 kilometres) − the sacred cubit multiplied ten million times. The length of the pyramid side at the base is 365.25 (365.242 to be exact) pyramid cubits, a figure identical to the number of days in the solar tropical year − and the same figure is also to be found in other features of the design. Peter Lemesurier points out yet another 'coincidence':

Yet from the slightly indented shape of the base of the core-masonry alternative measurements of 365.256 and 365.259 of these units can be derived – figures which turn out to be the length in days of the sidereal year (the actual time the earth takes to complete a circuit of the sun) and of the anomalistic year (the time taken by the earth to return to the same point in its elliptical orbit, which is itself revolving slowly about the sun). Meanwhile further measurements appear to give exact figures for the eccentricity of the orbit, for the mean distance of the earth from the sun, and for the period of the earth's full precessional cycle (a period of over 25,000 years). If one wished to have an architectural symbol for the planet Earth itself one could scarcely do better than to take the Great Pyramid of Giza.[1]

The Great Pyramid is built on solid bedrock, which makes it virtually invulnerable to the severest earthquake. The shape of the pyramids also suggests a function other than a tomb, being ideally suited to withstand almost any kind of shock.

Egyptologists tell us that there is no evidence of an advanced technology in pre-dynastic Egypt. If this is the case, from where or whom did the ancient Egyptians obtain this obvious knowledge of mathematics and astronomy? Surely, they cannot have landed on such precise figures by accident. This is one of many questions that had led even sceptical researchers to consider that there must have been another civilization of considerable technological advancement who actually built the pyramids or supplied the know-how to the indigenous population of those parts. Perhaps the Egyptian priests knew more than they were prepared to say, although they were inclined to let slip the odd snippet of information that could be picked up by anyone sharp enough to catch it.

The Egyptian Manetho (Beloved of Thoth), who lived in the last years of the fourth and first half of the third century BC, was a priest of Heliopolis and historian of veracity and reliability. He wrote not only on historical subjects, but also on the mystic philosophy and religion of his country and it is

generally believed that his books were the source of knowledge on all things Egyptian from which Plutarch and later
writers derived their information. It is to Manetho that we
owe the scant writings and other fragments contained in the
Thrice Greatest Hermes that were assembled and published by
the great theosophical scholar G. R. S. Mead in the earlier part
of this century. According to Manetho, Thoth, the Egyptian
god of letters, Keeper of the Akashic Records, Divine Advocate and Time Lord, produced 36,525 books of ancient
wisdom – *a figure identical to the number of 'primitive inches' in
the Great Pyramid's designed perimeter!*[2]

Manetho is believed to have derived his information from
the hieroglyphic inscriptions in the temples and other priestly
records, but unfortunately only fragments of his original writings remain. Mead considered the most important of these to
be the fragment, preserved by Georgius Syncellus, from a
work by Manetho entitled *Sothis*, which has otherwise
disappeared. The passage, with an introductory sentence of the
monk Syncellus, runs as follows:

It is proposed then to make a few extracts concerning the Egyptian
dynasties from the Books of Manetho. [This Manetho] being high
priest of the Heathen temples of Egypt, based his replies to [King
Ptolemy] on the monuments which lay in the Seriadic country. [These
monuments,] he tells us, were engraved in the sacred language and in
the characters of the sacred writings of Thoth, the first Hermes; after
the Flood they were translated from the sacred language into the then
common tongue, but [still written] in hieroglyphic characters, and
stored away in books by the Good Daimon's son, and the second
Hermes, father of Tat – in the inner chambers of the temples of Egypt.[3]

The King, it seems, had been acquainted with Manetho's
vast knowledge of the past and asked the priest if he could see
some of these records, and whether, in fact, Manetho's powers
of perception could equally be applied to probing the future.
Mead continues the story:

In the *Book of Sothis* Manetho addresses King Philadelphus, the second Ptolemy, personally, writing as follows word for word:

'The letter of Manetho, the Sebennyte, to Ptolemy Philadelphus.

'To the great King Ptolemy Philadelphus, the venerable: I, Manetho, high priest and scribe of the holy fanes of Egypt, citizen of Heliopolis but by birth a Sebennyte, to my master Ptolemy send greeting.

'We must make calculations concerning all the points which you may wish us to examine into, to answer your questions concerning what will happen to the world. According to your commands, the sacred books, written by our forefather Thrice Greatest Hermes, which I study, shall be shown to you. My lord and king, farewell.'[4]

From the aforegoing we may deduce that the name Thoth or Hermes is purely titular and relates to an order in the priestly castes that deals with history and records. We may also be permitted to conclude that the first Hermes, or earliest order of priesthood, used a sacred language – probably archaic Egyptian or perhaps the old Atlantean tongue – which in the time of the second Hermes was no longer spoken. Two successions of priests and prophets were separated by a 'flood', which was, no doubt, one and the same inundation that the priests of Sais had mentioned to Solon years earlier. All in all, Manetho's text would appear to be implying that the archaic civilization of Egypt, which was apparently badly hit when Atlantis went down, was regarded as one of great excellence – the time of the gods, divine kings or demi-gods. There were, naturally, the usual flock of scholars who loudly proclaimed the *Book of Sothis* as a Neoplatonic forgery, but the apology subsequently given by Mead and other later authorities more than satisfies all but the deliberately biased.

In more recent times Moscow engineer A. K. Abramov made an intensive study of the geometrical dimensions of the Khufu Pyramid, which prompted him to conclude that the structure holds the answer to the squaring of the circle. The ancient Egyptians, he believed, had successfully coped with it through the use of the septenary system in defining π as $\frac{22}{7}$, while also using a 'radian' or $\frac{\pi}{6}$ as a basic unit of measure. In an interview with Atlantologist Andrew Tomas in Moscow, Abramov told him:

One must, of necessity, consider the historical background which determined the appearance of the quadrature of the circle in actual practice. Let us drift into the depths of the ages for 4,500 years to the time of the construction of the Great Pyramid. Long before its erection rational minds of antiquity cognized many objective facts. The most important among these was the discovery of the relation of the length of the circumference to its diameter – equal to $\frac{22}{7}$ in the septenary system. About the same time discoveries of certain relative truths were also made. To these belong the straightening of the circumference, three sections of an angle, doubling of a cube without modifying its form, conversion of the volumes of cubes into volumes of spheres, etc. It is but natural that the discovered facts were put into objective reality. After all, it has been ascertained that the Khufu Pyramid is so constructed that the perimeter of the base is equal to the circumference, drawn with a radius equal to the pyramid's height. From the dimensions of the pyramid, expressed in 'radians', this equality of the perimeters of the square and the circle becomes apparent in the following equation where the first shows the length of the four sides of the Khufu Pyramid and the second – that of a circumference drawn with the radius equivalent to the pyramid's height $(2\pi r)$: $440 \times 4 = 1760$ $2 \times \frac{22}{7} \times 280 = 1760$.[5]

A project set up by the United Arab Republic to X-ray the Chephren Pyramid in search of some hitherto undiscovered burial chamber yielded up some strange results.

Normal X-rays not being considered powerful enough to penetrate the stonework, Dr Luis Alvarez, a Nobel prizewinner for physics and director of the Lawrence Radiation Laboratory at the University of California, suggested his equipment might fit the bill. This technology was developed to measure the radiation particles bombarding the Earth from outer space, so it was logically assumed that, if it were placed in the existing burial chamber in Chephren's pyramid, the amount of radiation reaching the chamber through the stonework could be recorded on tape and any deviation in the solidity of the structure could be noted. This would make it comparatively easy to trace any additional burial chambers that had not, as yet, come to light.

The complicated radiation apparatus, operating at some 10,000 volts, was duly installed and a considerable amount of cosmic ray information collected as a result; there was certainly enough to answer the original query. Lauren Yazolino of California University stated, 'We have run two tapes through the computer and are satisfied that our equipment is functioning correctly.' Dr Alvarez visited the pyramid to collect the recorded tapes from his apparatus and then promptly left without making any comment on his findings. Dr Amir Gohed, of El Shams University, Cairo, was left in charge of the equipment once the Americans had left and his only significant comment was, 'It defies all the known laws of science and electronics; in fact, the taped results are scientifically impossible. The tapes we had hoped would reveal a great discovery are a jumbled mass of meaningless symbols. Two tapes which should be exactly the same are totally different. Either the geometry of the pyramid is substantially erroneous, which we know it is not, or there is a mystery which is beyond explanation. Call it what you will – occultism, the curse of the pharaohs, sorcery or magic – there is some force at work in Chephren's pyramid that defies all the known laws of science.'[6]

None of this, however, tells us whether or not the pyramids were erected by thousands of workmen labouring with trolleys, as is popularly supposed, although there are certain legends that might afford us some clues. According to one Arab source the huge stone blocks were wrapped in some kind of papyrus and then struck with a rod by a priest, which appeared to have the effect of rendering them weightless.

They could then be moved through the air effortlessly and placed precisely in position. Babylonian tablets also affirm that sound could lift stones, but what we are talking about here is basically a firm knowledge of the manipulation of sonic energy, which I somehow feel really *was* understood and practised in the Old Country although whether the Atlantean colonists employed it to build the pyramids cannot be proven either way. What the old legends may be recalling, however, is that such things could be done in the past and, there being no other acceptable explanation available when it comes to the riddle of the pyramids, sonics seem to fit the bill.

Another aspect of the pyramids that is hotly debated is whether they were constructed as tombs, places of religious worship, safe harbours during the cataclysm or time-capsules. Andrew Tomas cites the following interesting snippets of information that have seeped through from the historical past:

Herodotus saw the inscriptions on the sides of the pyramids in the fifth century before our era. Ibn Haukal, an Arab traveller and writer in the tenth century, states that the writing on the pyramid casings was still visible in his time. Abd el Latif (twelfth century) writes that the inscriptions on the exterior of the pyramids could fill ten thousand pages.

Ibn Batuta (fourteenth century), another Arab scholar, writes that: 'The pyramids were constructed by Hermes to preserve the arts and sciences and other scientific acquirements during the Flood.' The Dictionary of Firazabadi (fourteenth century) states that the pyramids were supposed to 'preserve the arts and sciences and other knowledge during the deluge.' The Coptic papyrus from the monastery of Abou Hormeis has the following passage: 'In this manner were the pyramids built. Upon the walls were written the mysteries of science, astronomy, geometry, physic, and much useful knowledge, which any person who understands our writing can read.'

Ibn Abd Hokm, ninth-century Arab historian, left a rare account of the building of the pyramids, an extract from which is cited below: 'The greatest part of chronologers agree that he who built the pyramids was Surid Ibn Salhouk, king of Egypt, who lived three hundred years before the Flood. The occasion of this was because he saw in his sleep that the whole earth was turned over, with the inhabitants of it, the men lying upon their faces, and the stars falling down and striking one another with a terrible noise: and being troubled, he concealed it. Awakening with great fear, he assembled the chief priests of all the provinces of Egypt, one hundred and thirty in number, the chief of whom was Aclimon, and related the whole matter to them. They took the altitude of the stars and making their prognostications, foretold of a deluge. The king said: "Will it come to our country?" They answered: "Yes, and will destroy it." But there remained a certain number of years for it to come, and he commanded in the meantime to build the pyramids with vaults. He filled them with talismans, strange things, riches, treasures and the like. Then he built in the western pyramid thirty treasuries, filled with store of riches and utensils, cartouches made of precious stones, instruments of iron, vessels of clay, arms which did not rust, and glass which could be bent and yet not broken.'[7]

The Egyptian Copt historian Masudi, writing during the Middle Ages, also recounts a tradition that the Great Pyramid was built by a king named Surid, who lived three hundred years *before* the Flood, to safeguard the ancient knowledge. The priests had apparently forewarned him of an impending catastrophe, connected in some way with the constellation of Leo, that would involve the Earth in both flood and fire. The walls and ceiling in the pyramid were engraved with astronomical, mathematical and medical knowledge, and strange beings (probably artificial elementals) were placed there by the priests to prevent this knowledge falling into the hands of those unworthy to handle it. Another Coptic legend confirms this, but adds that Surid ordered the inscription to be engraved in words together with 'other matters' on the pyramid casing. As this casing has completely disappeared, we are unfortunately denied the knowledge the worthy monarch saw fit to leave to posterity.[8] It could, of course, be argued that all these reports were derived from one original text, which was included in the standard syllabus of education extant in the Middle Eastern countries during the periods cited, while the fact that none of the references concerned makes any mention of the methods employed in the construction of the pyramid could also be seized upon as fuel for the 'anti' camp. Personally, I do not think the Great Pyramid was built as a tomb, temple of worship or safe haven from the Flood. A time-capsule? Now that is more like it!

The evidence from the pyramids alone should be sufficient to convince us that someone, somewhere in the distant past possessed a knowledge of mathematics, geometry and astronomy on a par with, or perhaps in advance of, our own. However, this idea seems to tread all too firmly (and no doubt painfully) on the egos of some people, to the extent that they will blindly refuse to accept the type of empirical evidence that normally satisfies them. It matters not, though, as truth will out in the fullness of time.

One is often asked why, if the Atlanteans were so scientifically advanced, were there people around during the time of Atlantis, and just after, who erected giant monoliths that appear to have no connection with the kind of geometrical precision associated with the pyramids?

First of all, we have to consider the fact that the Atlantean island continent was obviously the home of peoples of all classes, colours and grades of intelligence. After all, not all of us are scientists, engineers, doctors or mathematicians. Some of us are, however, artists, stonemasons, smiths, tillers of the land – or even writers! People escaping the Flood in vessels of all kinds would have been required to adapt to the lands upon which their ships were cast by the unsettled weather of the times. Those who were fortunate enough to find themselves in the safe harbours of Egypt, Greece, Spain, Portugal, Etruria (Tyrrhenia) or even the northern shores of Hyperborea (Thule) would have found conditions not dissimilar to those they had known at home. The less fortunate, however, would have been faced with the rigours of a possibly hostile environment where the only shelter was caves, and the only building material available was wood! This might well have given rise to the tree cults or, as Muck puts it '. . . the tree of life – or of knowledge, or fate, or time, or space'. The symbol of the Tree of Life was an essential feature of the megalithic civilization that grew up in those areas where the ice had retreated. Muck sees these people as being of the red-skinned, Cro-Magnon type, who settled on the virgin land and erected the vast structures such as Stonehenge and Karnac: 'Avenues of huge stone pillars point the way to coasts long since vanished. They point to the sea, to the west where lay their own first home.'[9]

The lack of 'civilized' artefacts dating from the prehistoric period is frequently used to demolish the concept of an Atlantean civilization having existed in antediluvian times. However, had there been such tools or technological equipment made of the kind of substances we use today, they would hardly be around some ten thousand years later. After all, how many of our modern-day cars will be intact or even recognizable to archaeologists some ten to fifteen thousand years hence? A glance at any scrap-metal yard will soon supply the answer. The only material to last would be stone, and that is precisely what has happened!

Although there is a popular belief that the old stone sites and monoliths obey certain magnetic rules that accord with lines of power that run in grid-like formation across our planet, which is believed to imply a deeper knowledge of the workings of nature on the part of the builders, I tend to dispute the fact that all this knowledge was Atlantean. After all, there are also monolithic edifices in other parts of the world, such as Easter Island, which would seem to me to have far more in common with the ancient culture of Lemuria/Mu than that of Atlantis. Nor can I accept that the Cro-Magnon race was necessarily proto-Atlantean, as there would appear to be just as many, if not more, 'red' men on the American side of the Atlantic.

What seems more logical to me is that one of the racial groups from which both the Cro-Magnons and red Atlanteans originated became scattered over a period of time *prior* to the Flood and ultimate end of the Atlantean continent. The Cro-Magnons might not, in fact, have found their way into Europe from across the Atlantic as I suggested in an earlier chapter, but might have migrated from the north while there were still land-links between Atlantis and Lemuria/Mu. Another suggestion is that Altantis was, as Spence proposes, joined to Europe and Africa rather than the Americas at a time in its primitive past, and when the cataclysm occurred that split it from the matrix some of its peoples were left behind in the caves of Europe, to use what little material there was around them – i.e., stone and wood – in order to survive.

Many strange and incredible legends have surfaced from time to time concerning the survivors of past cataclysms, notably the story related to Dr Ferdinand Ossendowski of the Académie Française by Prince Chultun Beyli and his chief lama in Mongolia some sixty years ago. Two continents, he was told, had formerly existed in the Atlantic and the Pacific, which latterly sank into the sea-depths. Some of their inhabitants, however, found refuge in vast underground caves that are flooded with a strange light. Plants and people are sustained by this luminous transmission, which has also enabled the people to advance to the highest levels of science.[10]

One cannot fail to be struck by the similarity between this

legend and certain extraterrestrial 'information' that has been 'recalled' under hypnosis, or brought through by any of several psychic channels. In other words, someone here 'has his wires crossed'!

Aside from the pyramids and other monoliths, there are other strange coastal phenomena that have puzzled researchers from time to time. My late guardian, who was a scholar of some distinction, drew my attention to the *nuraghi* towers of Sardinia, which he had examined in some detail during the course of his world travels. They had, he pointed out, many features in common with the *chullpa* towers of pre-Inca Peru and other structures he had duly noted that seemed to be of a similar age. He and I arrived at the joint conclusion that these singular round towers were post-Atlantean, and probably held some maritime significance during a later period. Donnelly noted that Diodorus Siculus, in writing about Ireland, and describing it as 'an island in the ocean over against Gaul, to the north, and not inferior in size to Sicily, the soil of which is so fruitful that they mow there twice in the year', also commented on 'their sacred groves, *and their singular temples of round form.*' The remainders of similar round towers are also to be found in the Orkneys and Shetlands.[11]

Talents and Traits

Let us now turn our attention to people. Surely, some of us must have inherited Atlantean genes, which suggests that the knowledge of the Old Country and its ways might conceivably be locked within our genetic code. Since it is generally accepted by 'believers' that the Atlanteans understood the use of the right-brain hemisphere – in other words, they had mastered the mental process of moving outside the barriers of time and space – then must not that ability come just as naturally to those alive today who carry the Atlantean genetic blueprint? One has to tread warily where this subject is concerned, however, as it does tend to have ego-bruising inferences.

Attitudes toward PK (psychokinesis) and ESP (extrasensory perception, clairvoyance, telepathy, precognition, far memory, astral travel and allied phenomena) can be broadly categorized as follows:

1. Those adopted by adherents to certain religious persuasions, who tend to view any preternatural gifts, other than those exhibited under the auspices of their particular brand of faith, as manifestations of 'the works of the devil' (whoever *he* might be!).

2. Those held by people who see in these abilities the chance to prove themselves as something out of the ordinary or better than their peers or contemporaries, and pretend to possess them if they are not thus gifted.

3. Those held by persons suffering from psychological disturbances or inadequacies who tend either to lay false claim to great occult or psychic powers, or systematically go about denegrating or invalidating those who do.

In other words, the subject of this particular Atlantean gift carries a tribal taboo either way, as many who genuinely possess it have found to their cost.

Certain races, however, have been credited with inheriting what are believed to be Atlantean talents, notably the Celts, whose musical, psychic and medical skills are evident to this day. Some writers and researchers are also of the opinion that the Celts inherited the stature and colouring of their Atlantean ancestors from the time when Britain fringed the Atlantean empire. As I (and others) see it, however, the term 'Celts' can be confusing, to say the least. The popular conception of the tall, statuesque, vainglorious warriors who swept across Europe in the fifth and fourth centuries BC hardly equates with the shorter, dark-haired people who share the same blood group as the Berbers of North Africa; so which Celts are we talking about?

The Roman writer Dio Cassius described the Icenian Queen Boudicca in some detail: 'She was huge of frame and terrifying in aspect with a harsh voice. A great mass of bright red hair fell to her knees.'[12] Strabo and others mentioned the long, flowing blonde hair of the Celts, their blue eyes and fine, tall frames. These people, so carefully defined by writers and historians of repute, appear to have more in common with the tall, fair peoples of the *Oera Linda Book*. The Druidic cult, however, received just as bad a press from the Frisians as it did from the Romans. The chroniclers of the *Oera Linda Book* referred to the Druids as *Golen*, and *Triuwenden* – 'abstainers from the truth' – and alluded to 'all sorts of vile and monstrous festivals' which constituted part of their religious activities. According to the Frisians, Tyre and Sidon were the original home of the Golen, which would tend to confirm the writings of Robert Graves, the Reverend Edward Davies and others who see this particular branch of the Celts as having originated in North Africa or the Mediterranean region:

A numerous race, and fierce, as fame reports them,
Were thy first colonists, Britain, chief of Isles:
Natives of a country in Asia, and of the region of the Grafis,
A people said to have been skilful; but the district is
    unknown,
That was mother to this progeny, these warlike adventurers on
    the sea.
Clad in their long dress, who could equal them?

Atlantean Heritage

> Celebrated is their skill; they were the
> Dread of Europe.
>
> *The Pacification of Lud*[13]

The historian Timagenes, writing in the first century AD about the Gauls, mentioned that at least some of these tribes preserved legends concerning their remote fatherland in the middle of the ocean. Apparently the ancients gave the name 'Gauls' to three different races, which, according to Braghine, were the Aryan Gauls, who hailed from Asia; the descendants of the autochthons of western Europe; and the descendants of the colonists who emigrated to Europe from a country in the western ocean. Timagenes, it seems, considered the terms 'Gauls' and 'Celts' should be applied only to the refugees from Atlantis, and not to the Aryans and other eastern European or northern tribes who were later designated as Celtic. The shorter, dark-haired Celts, or Goidels, and the tall, fair Celts, or Brythons, appear to represent different genetic strains. As I have come across members of both clans who are psychically, musically and otherwise highly gifted, it would be logical to assume that those who were not directly from Atlantis might conceivably have picked up the Atlantean gene from traders, missionaries and other travellers; or from inter-marrying into other Celtic tribes, such as the fairer peoples who are believed to have come from the area of the Danube; or the Berber, Sergi and other peoples of North Africa and Spain with whom the Welsh and Irish share strong genetic affinities (see Chapter 8).

But were any of these Celtic tribes actually one of the races of Atlantis? Ignatius Donnelly certainly thought so. He tells us:

According to the ancient books of Ireland the race known as 'Partholan's people,' the Nemedians, the Fir-Bolgs, the Tuatha-de-

Danaans, and the Milesians were all descended from two brothers, sons of Magog, son of Japheth, son of Noah, who escaped from the catastrophe which destroyed his country. Thus all these races were Atlantean. They were connected with the African colonies of Atlantis, the Berbers, and with the Egyptians. The Milesians lived in Egypt: they were expelled thence; they stopped a while in Crete, then in Scythia, then they settled in Africa (see MacGeoghegan's *History of Ireland*, p. 57), at a place called Gaethulighe or Getulia, and lived there during eight generations, say two hundred and fifty years; 'then they entered Spain, where they built Brigantia, or Briganza, named after their king Breogan: they dwelt in Spain a considerable time. Milesius, a descendant of Breogan, went on an expedition to Egypt, took part in a war against the Ethiopians, married the king's daughter, Scota: he died in Spain, but his people soon after conquered Ireland. On landing on the coast they offered sacrifices to Neptune or Poseidon' – the god of Atlantis.[14]

Donnelly's information would seem to receive confirmation in the recent researches of the Irish writer and film-maker Bob Quinn. When Quinn first heard *sean-nõs* singing in Connemara, he became fascinated by a musical form that seemed to bear no relationship to the European tradition. The similarity between *sean-nõs* and Arab music was the first of a series of discoveries that led Quinn to connect Ireland with the Middle East. He also found archaeological, musical, religious, linguistic and artistic parallels between the inhabitants of the coastal regions of western Ireland and other isolated groups in Brittany, Galicia and the Middle East. These parallels extended from prehistoric megalithic times through all periods of history to the twentieth century. Quinn's former notion of a land-diffused Celtic culture was replaced by a culture diffused by the sea – a common inheritance of the people living on the western seaboard of Europe and the Mediterranean. This he saw as Atlantean, which is the title of his book.

Quinn's fascinating deductions are too lengthy to embark

upon in any detail, although he does raise some cogent points that call for comment. For example, he mentions the Aran Islanders as having a different blood group 'not only from that which is deemed "Celtic" [the O blood group] but from the bulk of the population of Ireland'.[15] He does not tell us what these differences are, however, which is a pity, as it would have helped me to render a more accurate assessment of my own subject matter. The conclusions he drew from his researches led him to proffer the following questions and conclusions:

If the Irish are not 'Celts' then, logically, neither are the Scots, Welsh, Manx, Bretons, Cornish or Galicians. So what are, who are, these people? If Liam de Paor is correct in describing the so-called 'Celtic' attributes as romantic inventions of the nineteenth century, then what are the links that undoubtedly bind these people into some kind of felt unity?

The peoples of the Atlantic seaways are isolated by modern communication systems: to visit each other they must travel uncomfortably by secondary routes. These areas form what has already been described as a cultural archipelago, having more in common with each other than with the centralized governments that control them – and have written their history.

It is difficult and unwieldy to describe these people, their culture and language without falling back on the vague, if convenient title of 'Celts'. That is why I have opted for the term 'Atlantean'. At least it has some realistic maritime connotation and suggests a less jaded perspective from which to examine the subject. Logically, though, if the essence of this perspective is sea-based, then one must extend the catchment area further north to Iceland and western Scandinavia – areas which have admitted links with Ireland. But – and this is the hard part – it must also be extended southward, to those other people bordered by the Atlantic, the Moroccan Berbers.[16]

I am rather glad it has been an Irishman who has said all

this (and, for those interested in the Celtic enigma, much more)! There are, I feel, certain unhealthy signs in the current spate of 'Celtomania' that do not exhibit the kind of spirituality one would associate with those who stayed on the Path of Light in the latter days of Atlantis. As one such 'Celt' (or Atlantean, if Mr Quinn prefers), on both sides of my family, who has seen fit to assume a less tribal attitude, I have encountered a deal of bigotry, egotism and prejudice beneath this cloak of 'Celtomania' that has more in common with the less desirable aspects of Cancerian latter-day Atlantis than with the earlier, more spiritually orientated mysteries of the Old Country. Enough said.

Ancient Maps

Braghine quotes the famous naturalist Buffon as suggesting that America was once connected to the Azores group and Ireland by a narrow strip of land, remains of fossil animals and shells peculiar to America having been found in Ireland but nowhere else in Europe! In this, Buffon is in agreement with the work of the scientist Lamettrie, published at the end of the eighteenth century. Legends of other lost lands, such as Ys off the coast of Brittany, and Lyonesse off the south-western coast of England, obviously relate to a time when the Atlantic seaboard of both countries stretched much farther out into what is now the realm of Poseidon. Were we to see the shape of our land masses in antediluvian times, we might be surprised; which brings me to the subject of ancient maps.

During the past few decades a series of ancient maps have surfaced, some of which show Atlantis, while others give an outline of the coast of Antarctica *prior to its glaciation*. A great deal has been made of these maps both by Atlantologists and those who subscribe to the theory that our planet has been visited by beings from other parts of the universe. As objective students of biblical myth will be only too aware, however, one can shape facts to fit any theory, so whether these finds are either relics or copies of relics from the antediluvian world is still open to conjecture. Either way, those who drew them up must have possessed knowledge of pre-Flood times, otherwise how would they have been able to make such precise observations of a coastline that is completely ice-bound and has been for hundreds of centuries? So, what are these maps, and what is the story behind them?

In his book *Maps of the Ancient Sea Kings* Professor Charles H. Hapgood appears to have unearthed important evidence that substantiates the claim that civilization existed long before Egypt and Sumeria. The 'Oronteus Finaeus' world map was drawn in 1531, during which time the Antarctic continent was hidden under a sheet of ice 2 miles (3 kilometres) thick, which in some places stretched well out into the ocean. There is no way in which the cartographer could have known what lay beneath that ice, yet he produced a map giving the correct shape of the hidden continent – its concealed bays and estuaries, rivers and other details of the coastline, all of which modern research has shown to be correct. Since Oronteus Finaeus had no knowledge of such matters, it is only logical to assume that he copied his map from an earlier edition, which must have originated thousands of years before, when both the northern and southern hemispheres were warm and ice-free. This map also shows the broad, level north coast of ancient Scotland, including islands that have since submerged and land that has been reclaimed by the sea. The east coast of England is shown to cover what is now the Dogger Bank, while the Cornish extension embraces the lost lands of the 'mythical' Lyonnesse!

Muhiddin Piri Re'is, a Turkish admiral (1470–1554), published a navigation atlas, *Bahriyye*, in 1520. Another map

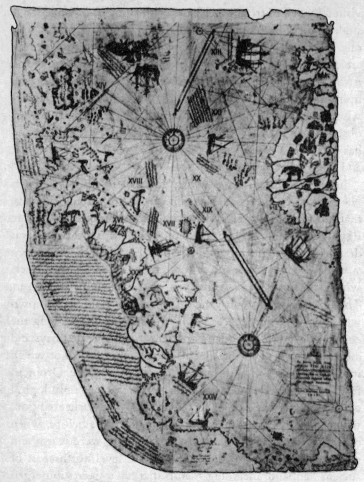

Fig. 27. The Piri Re'is Map.

drawn by him, on roe-skin with marginal notes and dated in the Muslim year 919 (AD 1513), was discovered at the palace of Topkapi in Istanbul on 9 November 1929 by Halil Edhem,

Director of the National Museums. This map, which is believed to be the fragment of a world map extant in the library of Alexandria 2,000 years ago, indicates ancient knowledge of spherical trigonometry as applied to maps, which was not rediscovered in Europe until the reign of George III. It, too, shows the accurate outline of the Antarctic continent. Hapgood became so enthusiastic about the details shown in this and other ancient maps that he decided to approach the American government for help and permission to search for underwater cities in the region of the St Peter and St Paul Rocks, as the Piri Re'is map indicated that there once had been a large island in that area. By October 1963 Hapgood had succeeded in obtaining an interview with President Kennedy to discuss the matter and put forward his evidence, but circumstances, the details of which are all too familiar, intervened, and the Old Country was left once again to defer behind a curtain of silence.

Robert Scrutton draws our attention to the Ibn ben Zara map in support of the *Oera Linda Book* records (see Figure 28). This map shows the remains of glaciers and great lakes in parts of the British Isles and which seem to cover some of the northern parts of Europe now clear of ice and water. Note the islands north of Ireland, now vanished, the different coastline of Britain, and also the ice which covers the land which was once adjacent to Atland.[17]

Science and Religion

The suggestion that the Atlanteans were adept in the utilization of crystal power has often been viewed with scepticism bordering on humour by certain members of the scientific establishment. Assuming there was such a race as the Atlanteans (which they very much doubt), how could a people

Fig. 28. The Portolano of Ibn ben Zara, 1487.

living all those thousands of years ago (who must, of course, have been primitive!) have mastered the control of an energy source that eludes us to this day? Like the ouroboros, things have a habit of going full circle and ending up at their starting point, albeit an octave or so higher. An article by Anthony Tucker, a portion of which is reproduced below, appeared in the *Guardian* in 1989, under the title of 'The incredible shrinking alloy':

Laboratory curiosities have an intriguing habit of metamorphosing into crucial technologies. The laser, for example, seemed pretty useless for a decade or two, was dubbed dismissively as a solution in search of problems but then burgeoned into a huge family of related technologies capable of answering questions which could not sensibly have been asked in the pre-laser era . . .

One other such curious phenomenon is known as magneto-striction (let's call it mag-S) in which solid materials change their dimensions when subjected to a magnetic field. It has been around the text books for decades, became something more than a curiosity in the hands of the US military about 25 years ago, and has been looking for problems ever since.

The point about the mag-S effect is that it is extremely powerful and exquisitely controllable. It rests on the fact that some metallic crystal structures change their phase instantly on the application of a magnetic field.

This can mean, for example, that a solid metal rod becomes longer and thinner, or shorter and fatter (by more than 1,000 parts per million) as the applied magnetic field changes. An oscillating field whose frequency is coupled to the natural acoustic frequency of the rod creates a solid metal oscillator of enormous power.

. . . One intriguing thing is that such a short solid rod can be so highly and simultaneously responsive to a huge range of frequencies.

Another is that it can produce sound best when firmly bolted between heavy metal clamps. What emerges is the extraordinary power of the mag-S effect. *It could, quite certainly, move buildings* [my italics] . . .

What is evident is that some local limits of technology are about to be pushed back rapidly. Oh yes, and when was this amazing new magnetostrictive effect first observed? Give or take a year or two, *it was a century and a half ago* [my italics].[18]

According to Berlitz, fishermen and pilots had reported seeing underwater pyramids on or off the Bahama Banks and rising from the ocean floor. One very large pyramidic structure was sighted in outline on the depth finder of a boat south-west of the Cay Sal Bank in 1977, and was initially dismissed by geologists as being a natural formation. However, in 1978 an expedition was organized by Ari Marshall, a Greek industrialist, with some strange results. Marshall recounted the following details to Berlitz:

The first thing we noticed when we got near the area was that all the compasses were going berserk. We spent eight hours making tapes, starting at 700 feet to 1,500 feet [213 to 457 metres] deep. We would go about a mile [1.6 kilometres], then make a 90° turn and go back again. Finally I saw it coming up on the sonar screen. I told the captain to stop and then to proceed slowly. We were right over the pyramid. The top seemed to be about 150 feet [46 metres] from the surface, with the total depth about 650 feet [198 metres]. We lowered the camera and high intensity lights down the side of the mass and suddenly came to an opening. Light flashes or shining white objects were being swept into the opening by turbulence. They may have been gas or some sort of energy crystals. Further down, the same thing happened in reverse. They were coming out again at a lower level. It was surprising that the water in this deep area was green instead of black near the pyramid, even at night.[19]

Did we inherit the Bermuda Triangle from the Atlanteans? Otto Muck and others seem to think so; perhaps they have something after all!

Finally, we come to the question of whether vestiges of the old Atlantean religion are still to be found in our world today. Most occult fraternities would reply in the affirmative, but one should also remember that although the Atlanteans are reputed to have worshipped Helios, the Sun, or Poseidon, god of the sea, it is generally accepted among esotericists that they saw the waters that surrounded them, our own yellow star and other celestial bodies only as manifestations of the different aspects or facets of one creative source. Sometimes that source appeared as feminine – Sothis, the blue Lady of Heaven, whose son, the Lord of Light, was their champion. Her symbol, the Serpent of Wisdom (uraeus), was later derided as a sort of Pandora's box that contained the evils that knowledge could bring. Perhaps the Atlanteans were aware that wisdom emanated from the feminine principle, which is why they paid so much attention to Sirius A, which, according to ancient Egyptian tradition, was either the great goddess Isis or Rat, also known as Sekhmet or Hathor, the daughter of Ra (Sirius B), from which our own solar system is believed to have been seeded. Well, some of us like to think so anyway!

CHAPTER 12

Torch-Bearing
Collectives

Follow me, he said.
   And, having no place else to go
I trod the path laid out before me,
   And was glad
Until the precipice appeared –
   I could not fly!

In order to make a comprehensive appraisal of the subject matter, it is essential that our inquiry is not limited to any one school of thought or avenue of research. This, perforce, demands an examination of other, more rationally questionable sources of Atlantean information, which necessitates the inclusion of those views held by established theosophical, philosophical and religious groups, impressions received by sensitives during demonstrations of psi or channelling, details that have surfaced during meditation, hypnotherapy and any other procedures that allow access to the subconscious mind or the collective unconscious.

The Atlantean general theme comprises an important part of the teachings of several world-wide organizations, each of which appears to present a slightly different picture. Non-psychics or sceptics usually tend to view these discrepancies with suspicion, and not without just cause in many cases, so the question that needs to be asked at this juncture is, why is this so? Psychics and occultists will naturally argue that when one is receiving impressions of a civilization that lasted for several thousands of years, there is no guarantee that every sensitive is going to 'tune' in to the same period, any more than those using the psi faculty to probe the past episodes of known history necessarily relate the same story. Families, circumstances, locations, can all vary considerably over a comparatively short period of time. I recently experienced a dream in which I returned to a part of London where I lived with my nanny in the 1930s – it was entirely different, unrecognizable, in fact. To satisfy my curiosity I paid it a visit. Gone was the friendly little corner shop, the old Co-op and other features of my childhood, all of which had been replaced by a large, enclosed shopping mall, just as I had seen in my dream.

In the early years of my metaphysical studies I was given the following analogy to account for the lack of accurate minute detail so often encountered in psychic practice: if one were to climb to the top of Nelson's Column in central London, one would have a fair view of the surrounding thoroughfares. Were one to ascend in a balloon, one would naturally observe even more of the city, which, in addition to the beautiful gardens and fine buildings, would also include the gas works, power stations, slum areas and corporation rubbish dumps. From an even greater height one would perceive a far wider panorama, *but in considerably less detail*.

Speaking as a psychic, I have often been able to gain what can broadly be described as *impressions* of events that took place during certain periods of history with sufficient accuracy to pass school examinations with comparative ease (in fact, on one occasion I was severely reprimanded for being out of bounds – stealing from textbooks that I never knew even existed – and lying about it when I was totally innocent). But were someone to have asked me why Farmer Giles's cattle were sick, or whether Mrs Jones's expected child would be a girl or boy, I would not have had a clue, and would doubtless have been dubbed a fake!

I can hear my critics say, 'Well, that argument may apply as far as clairvoyance is concerned, but what about all this "channelling" nonsense that gullible people see fit to believe?' Fair comment. But then we are up against several psychological factors here. After all, leaving the subject of Atlantis aside, the mythology upon which some of the major religions are founded would hardly stand up to close scrutiny if exposed to the microscope of empirical research, yet fundamentalists choose to adhere to these rigid doctrines in the face of irrefutable evidence of the errors involved. What we really have to face up to is the fact that *people believe exactly what they want to believe, and will follow any credo that accords with their own particular pet theories*. This affords them a degree of personal mental security, which is why so many people feel happier under the umbrella of large collectives. The more people they know who view this life and the after-life in the same light as themselves, the better they feel about it. What we are talking about basically is the 'might is right' philosophy or, as a journalist friend of mine once put it, 'When the world adopts the fool's beliefs, he is no longer the fool!'

On the esoteric or metaphysical side, of course, the dimensions of one's view are decided by one's stage of spiritual maturity. Thus the young psyche, like the climber of Nelson's Column, is acutely aware of its immediate surroundings, whereas he or she who has the more comprehensive view of the universe, in addition to observing the broader panorama, is also likely to apprehend the causes and effects that have resulted in its formation.

Therefore, when it comes to assessing the validity of channelled communications, each of us will apply our own interpretations to what we hear, accepting what pleases us and rejecting that which does not accord with our own inner feelings. Likewise, the channeller will either submit elements of his or her own subconscious, or attract communicators who are at the same level of spiritual development as him or herself. Whether or not the channeller's view of the universe and its extra-terrestrial inhabitants, Atlantis, or other eras from the Earth's past is accurate will very much depend on the frequency at which the picture is being viewed. But it is always worth remembering that evidential and verifiable details are best seen from *close up*, whereas the truths of the broader view, although less impressive to those whom Pythagoras would doubtless refer to as *acusmatici*, would be fully comprehended by his *mathematici*. Those interested in a comprehensive psychological analysis of the channelling phenomenon are referred to *The Psychology of Ritual*.

In the light of the aforegoing, the deciding factor in the differing views of those major organizations whose tenets incorporate the Atlantean drama may be seen to depend on:

1. The outcome or results of research undertaken by the original founder;

2. The quality and accuracy of the information channelled or communicated to the founder or founders;

3. The spiritual level or external source from which such information emanated and the cosmic maturity (or otherwise) of the receiver.

Theosophy

Bearing all this in mind, let us deal first with the beliefs of the Theosophical Society. Theosophical teachings conceive of our present race being the Fifth, or Aryan, Race. The Fourth

Race was the great race of Atlantis. Catastrophes such as those experienced by the Fourth Race have not as yet made their appearance on Fifth Race horizons, although many people (other than Theosophists) are of the opinion that we will shortly be bidding a fond farewell to the period of stability we have enjoyed since the Old Country went down (but more of that in Chapter 14). The Theosophists opine that the destruction of Atlantis was accomplished by a series of catastrophes varying in character from great cataclysms in which whole territories and populations perished, to comparatively unimportant landslides of the type that occur on coastlines to this day.

Four great catastrophes are conceived of: the first took place in the Miocene Age, some 800,000 years ago; the second, which was less important, occurred about 200,000 years ago; the third, which destroyed all of Atlantis except the island of Poseidon mentioned by Plato, 80,000 years ago. The fourth, and final catastrophe, they see as having occurred around 9564 BC. Colonel W. Scott-Elliot, to whom the task of presenting the Atlantis and allied data seems to have fallen in the 1890s, included in his book four maps that purport to show the world prior to each of the four events. Where the worthy gentleman obtained these maps we are not told, but I am inclined to suspect that they have been 'put together' by early scholars within the Theosophical movement to illustrate their beliefs. Scott-Elliot tells us:

The first map [see Figure 29] represents the land surface of the earth as it existed about a million years ago, when the Atlantean Race was at its height, and before the first great submergence took place about 800,000 years ago. The continent of Atlantis itself, it will be observed, extended from a point a few degrees east of Iceland to about the site now occupied by Rio de Janeiro, in South America. Embracing Texas and the Gulf of Mexico, the Southern and Eastern States of America, up to and including Labrador, it stretched across the ocean to our own islands – Scotland and Ireland, and a small portion of the north of England forming one of its promontories – while its equatorial lands embraced Brazil and the whole stretch of ocean to the African Gold Coast. Scattered fragments of what eventually became the continents of Europe, Africa and America, as well as remains of the still older, and once wide-spread continent of Lemuria, are also shown on this map. The remains of the still older Hyperborean continent, which was inhabited by the Second Root Race, are also given . . .

As will be seen from the second map [see Figure 30] the catastrophe of 800,000 years ago caused very great changes in the land distribution of the globe. The great continent is now shorn of its northern regions, and its remaining portion has been still further rent. The now growing American continent is separated by a chasm from its parent continent of Atlantis, and this no longer comprises any of the lands now existing, but occupies the bulk of the Atlantic basin from about 50 degrees north to a few degrees south of the equator. The subsidences and upheavals in other parts of the world have also been considerable – the British Islands for example, now being part of a huge island which also embraces the Scandinavian peninsula, the north of France, and all the intervening and some of the surrounding seas. The dimensions of the remains of Lemuria, it will be observed, have been further curtailed, while Europe, Africa and America have received accretions of territory.

The third map [see Figure 31] shows the results of the catastrophe which took place about 200,000 years ago. With the exception of the rents in the continents both of Atlantis and America, and the submergence of Egypt, it will be seen how relatively unimportant were the subsidences and upheavals at this epoch, indeed the fact that this catastrophe has not always been considered as one of the great ones, is apparent from the quotation already given from the sacred book of the Guatemalans – three great ones only being there mentioned. The Scandinavian island, however, appears now as joined to the mainland. The two islands into which Atlantis was now split were known by the names of Ruta and Daitya.

The stupendous character of the natural convulsion that took

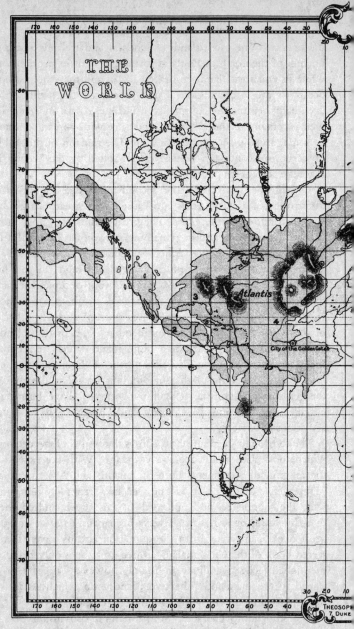

Fig. 29. The world about one million years ago, during many previous ages, and up to the catastrophe of about 800,000 years ago.

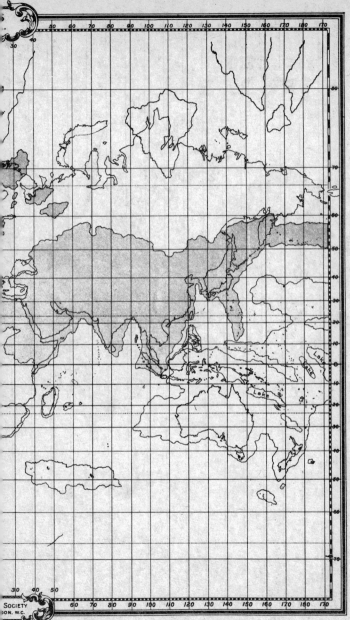

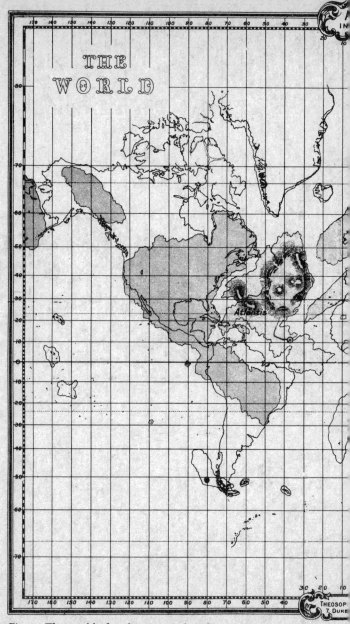

Fig. 30. The world after the catastrophe of 800,000 years ago and up to the catastrophe of 200,000 years ago.

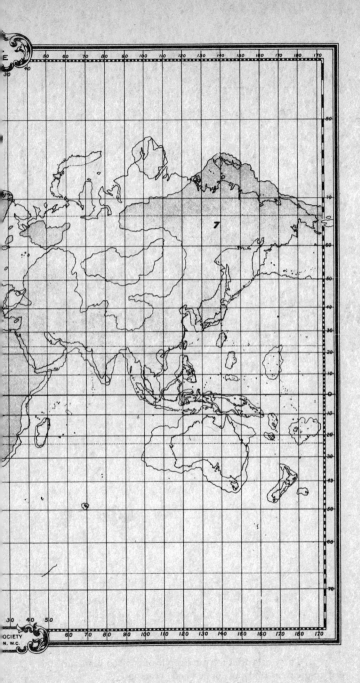

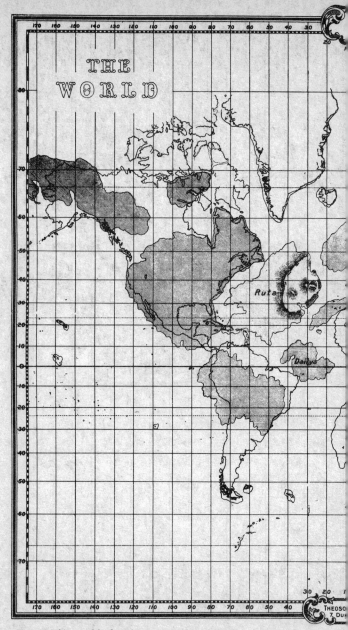

Fig. 31. The world after the catastrophe of 200,000 years ago and up to the catastrophe of about 80,000 years ago.

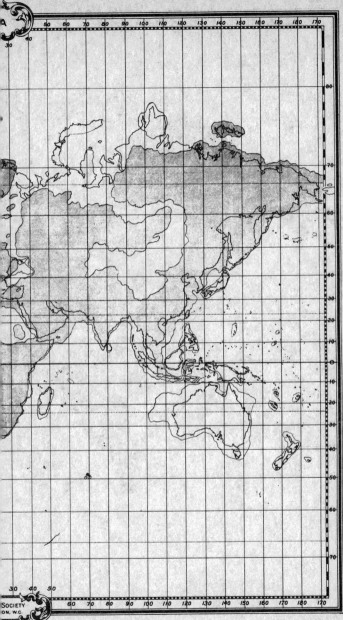

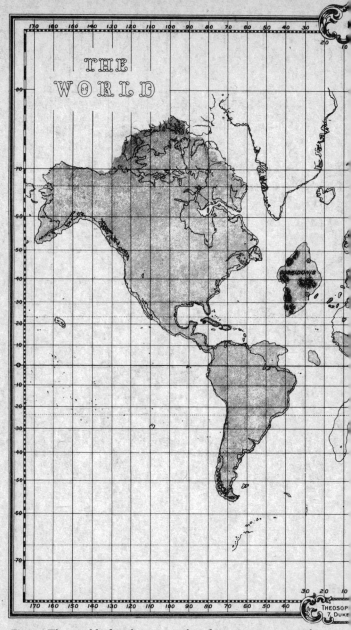

Fig. 32. The world after the catastrophe of 80,000 years ago and up to the final submergence of Poseidonis in 9564 BC.

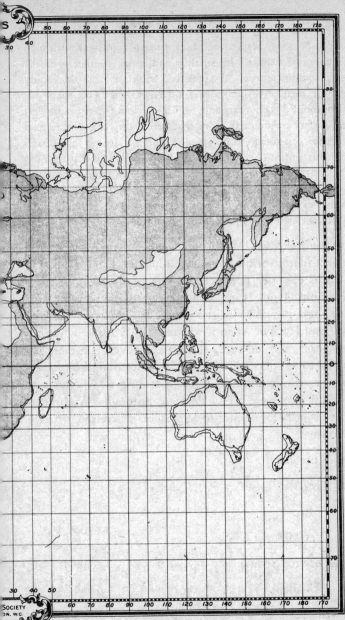

place about 80,000 years ago will be apparent from the fourth map [see Figure 32]. Daitya, the smaller and more southerly of the islands, has almost entirely disappeared, while of Ruta there only remains the relatively small island of Poseidonis. This map was compiled about 75,000 years ago, and it no doubt fairly represents the land surface of the earth from that period onwards till the final submergence of Poseidonis in 9564 BC, though during that period minor changes must have taken place. It will be noted that the land outlines had then begun to assume roughly the same appearance they do today, though the British Islands were still joined to the European continent, while the Baltic Sea was non-existent, and the Sahara desert then formed part of the ocean floor.[1]

As the complexities of Theosophical beliefs do not comprise the subject matter of this book, we must limit our inquiry to the Atlantis episode. The race that preceded that of Atlantis was the Third Root Race, which occupied the continent of Lemuria, and it was from the peoples of this race that the Fourth Root Race of Atlantis was apparently formed. Within Atlantis itself, we are told, there were seven sub-races, to which the theosophist teachers applied the following names, which were chosen ethnologically according to where traces of these sub-races have been identified, although it is admitted that there is little for science to seize upon where the first two are concerned:

1. Rmoahal

2. Tlavatli

3. Toltec

4. First Turanian

5. Original Semite

6. Akkadian

7. Mongolian

The Rmoahals, who originated in Lemuria, were a dark people who averaged some 10 to 12 feet (3 to 3.6 metres) in height, although their stature dwindled over the following centuries. They ultimately emigrated to the southern shore of Atlantis, where they were engaged in constant warfare with the sixth and seventh sub-races of the Lemurians. Most of the tribe eventually moved north, while the remainder settled down and intermarried with the black Lemurian aborigines. The remainder of the race travelled to the extreme north-eastern promontories contiguous with Iceland, and after many generations their colour lightened until they became a relatively fair people.

The Tlavatli originated on an island off the west coast of Atlantis (see Figure 29). From there they eventually spread into Atlantis proper, chiefly across the centre of the continent and tending towards the northern stretch facing Greenland. A strong and hardy race of mountain-lovers, red-brown in colour, the Tlavatli were not so tall as the Rmoahals, whom they drove still farther north.

The Toltecs are spoken of as a 'magnificent development'. These people ruled the continent of Atlantis for thousands of years, during which they paid much attention to material power and glory. Remnants of this race were to be found among the ruling families of Mexico and Peru before their degenerate descendants eventually were conquered by the fiercer Aztec tribes from the north. These people were also red-brown, but more copper coloured than the Tlavatli. Their height averaged around 8 feet (2.4 metres) and their features were straight, after the style portrayed by the ancient Greeks. These first three sub-races are spoken of as the 'red races'. The following four are referred to as 'yellow'.

The Turanian sub-race had its origin on the eastern side of the continent, south of the mountains inhabited by the Tlavatli people. These people were great colonists and travellers, although Theosophical teaching does not see them as being particularly dominant as far as the mother country is concerned.

Ethnologists are somewhat confused, we are told, when it comes to the Semite sub-race. These people had their origin in the mountainous country that formed the more southerly of the two north-eastern peninsulas, now represented by Scotland, Ireland and some surrounding areas (see site 5 on Figure 29). It seems these were a turbulent, discontented people, always at war with their neighbours, the Akkadians in particular, who eventually gained ascendancy over them.

The birthplace of the Akkadian, or sixth, sub-race is shown on Figure 30, for it was after the great catastrophe of 800,000 years ago that this race first came into existence. After defeating the Semites, the Akkadians set up a dynasty that ruled the country wisely for several hundred years. These were a great trading, seafaring and colonizing people, who established many centres of communication with distant lands.

According to Scott-Elliot, the Mongolian, or seventh, sub-race had absolutely no touch with the mother continent, having its origin on the plains of Tartary, which I think rather strange. This sub-race spawned the ancestors of the majority of the Earth's inhabitants, although many of its divisions are also genetically related to earlier races to the extent that it is seldom seen in its purest form today.

In those early days humanity was still, for the most part, possessed of psychic attributes, which were carefully nurtured and trained according to the prevailing occult disciplines. In later times the Atlanteans developed engineering skills and were able to produce airships. Regarding the method of propulsion, we are told that in earlier times personal *vril* ('occult power' – what we would probably refer to today as PK) supplied the motive power. Later, when the demand exceeded the number of adepts able to exercise this phenomenon, a new type of energy was employed, which, from Scott-Elliot's description (he assures us it is part etheric and part mechanical), sounds somewhat like a prehistoric jump-jet! However, the contraption was evidently capable of speeds up to 100 miles (160 kilometres) an hour, which no doubt inspired the early Theosophists but would be dismissed as unimpressive by today's standards. These vehicles were, however, able to achieve a height of only a few hundred feet (100–200 metres), which obliged them to circumnavigate mountains or any other tall objects that might obstruct their paths.

Men and women were, we are informed, equal in those ancient times, although some branches of the sub-races were polygamous. Others allowed two wives, and some only one, which sounds rather like a contradiction of facts. Many women were occult adepts with full knowledge of the *vril* power. Equality was recognized from infancy and there was no separation of the sexes in schools and colleges. The diet of the adept kings, initiated priesthood, sages and scholars was strictly vegetarian and differed considerably from that of the ordinary people. Strong drink was known, but because it caused those who partook of it to lose their sense of propriety and become violent, its consumption was forbidden by law.

Weapons of war naturally altered over the long period involved, although explosives were in use from very early times and poison gas was also employed in warfare. As regards a system of exchange, originally there was no coinage as such, although a system of tokens was later developed. During the most prosperous epochs a system of barter prevailed, although the produce of the whole district or kingdom was divided among the inhabitants, each person receiving his or her just portion. Children were selected very early for their destined trade or calling, the assessment being made by a

gifted psychic or what sounds to me like the Atlantean equivalent of a 'transpersonal psychologist'! The state provided care
and all necessities of life for every inhabitant. This included
food and shelter, education for all, and care of the sick and
infirm. Retirement began at 45, this being deemed the age
when hard work should cease and leisure and enjoyment take
over, 'except for the governing class, for whom there was no
cessation of work'. (Fantastic! When does the next plane
leave?)

To be serious, however, the Theosophists also believe that
towards the latter days degeneration on a mass scale took
place, with only a few initiates, priests of learning and
wisdom, and pursuers of the Right-Hand Path holding firmly
on to the banner of Light.

And that, in a nutshell, is the Theosophical picture of
Atlantis. Those wishing for more detail are referred to Scott-
Elliot's book, or to the headquarters of the Theosophical
Society in the major city nearest them. The fact that these
teachings set a pattern for future psychics is evident in that
much of their information, and dates in particular, has
appeared with striking regularity in subsequent revelations,
albeit differently presented and coloured by the personal bias
of the channellers.

Strangely, when I was living in Devon recently, my husband and I chanced upon an elderly, aristocratic neighbour
with the surname Scott-Elliot. Could there, I wondered, be
any possible connection between this lady and the Theosophical
colonel of the same name? In time she invited us to tea and
we returned the compliment. I put the question to her and she
replied in the affirmative: 'Oh, you mean our dear old nutty
uncle! Well, that's how we used to refer to him when I was a
girl, but now I know better.' She then embarked on a lengthy
dissertation on matters metaphysical, in respect of which her
erudition and psychic perception were unquestionable.

Perhaps this is a good place for me to state categorically that I do not necessarily concur with all or, in fact, any of the views expressed in this and the following chapter, not that I would dare to pass judgement on any of them, because, after all, any or all of us may be partially or entirely either right or wrong. Also, I am no different from other people in that my beliefs are governed by my own subjective experience and spiritual/cosmic limitations, although what I have learned and do believe (and that, I may add, is in a constant state of change, as one is ever learning) will become increasingly obvious before the end of this book.

Anthroposophy

Rudolf Steiner, founder of the Anthroposophical Society, seems to have shared many views with the theosophists prior to setting up his own organization. In his book *Cosmic Memory*, Steiner devotes a chapter to what he refers to as 'our Atlantean ancestors', who, he assures us, differed considerably from present-day people. This difference was evident not only in physical appearance, but also in spiritual faculties. Logical reason, arithmetic, mathematics and all those faculties we have now come to associate with left-brain hemisphere activity, he tells us, were totally absent. But by way of compensation, the Atlanteans were gifted with exceptional powers of *memory*. In other words, Steiner's Atlanteans had no need to learn their arithmetical tables because they could remember the results from previous occasions, and in defence of his statement he offers the premise:

One need only realize that each time a new faculty develops in an organism, an old faculty loses power and acuteness. The man of today is superior to the Atlantean in logical reasoning, in the ability to combine. On the other hand, memory has deteriorated. Nowadays man thinks in concepts; the Atlantean thought in images. When an image appeared in his soul he remembered a great many similar images which he had already experienced. He directed his judgement accordingly. For this reason all teaching at that time was different from what it became later. It was not calculated to furnish the child with rules, to sharpen his reason. Instead, life was presented to him in vivid images, so that later he could remember as much as possible when he had to act under particular conditions.[2]

Steiner concurred with the Theosophists on the matter of root races and their subdivisions, and recommended his pupils to Scott-Elliot's book for the details. He claimed to have gathered his information concerning the past of the Earth and other planets in the solar system from the Akashic records, which he incorporated in a series of essays entitled *From the Akasha Chronicle*. Referring to how the Earth looked in ancient Atlantean times (meaning, I think, that period as indicated by the Theosophists rather than Plato's Atlantis), he states:

It was said that at that time the air was saturated with water mist vapours. Man lived in the water mist, which in certain regions never lifted to the point where the air was completely clear. Sun and Moon could not be seen as they are today, but were surrounded by coloured coronas. A distribution of rain and sunshine, such as occurs at present, did not exist at that time. One can clairvoyantly explore this old land; the phenomenon of the rainbow did not exist at that time . . .[3]

This question of 'exploring the Akasha' is ever a thorny one for the sceptic and I have to confess that there are times when the whole concept bothers me. With so many people claiming access to this supposed infinite library of universal information with such contradictory results, from a psychological standpoint one has to consider both the 'wishful thinking' and 'frustrated story-teller' syndromes as possible answers to much of this purported viewing. On the other hand (and I am more inclined to this view), one can *unconsciously* tune in to the collective unconscious, the data banks of which must obviously contain the memory of all that has taken place in the history of our planet from the very beginning. Therefore, the open-minded writer, artist, scientist or philosopher is more likely to stumble upon the truth than the person who undertakes a calculated search of the Akasha during altered states of consciousness, the latter being more inclined to present the seeker with what he or she is *wanting* to see rather than what actually is or was. Sudden flashes of ancient memories, the fabric of a dream, or *déjà vu* would seem to provide more accurate information and a great deal of inspiration. Although the question of parallel universes and all time existing simultaneously at a given point or universal frequency, can be seen to apply to the Atlantean phenomena as exhibited via so many psychic channels, an in-depth analysis of its potentialities is not really called for within the present context.

The idea of Atlanteans functioning entirely on the right-brain hemisphere also worries me, since they are credited with scientific discoveries that are believed by many to have been superior to those possessed in modern times, and science is definitely a left-brain activity. However, intelligence is now known to exist on several levels. People who are able to handle standard IQ tests with ease are not necessarily gifted creatively, while there are those who have experienced difficulty with their basic school arithmetic who have contributed more to our society than many an 'intellectual' specialist! Ideally we should all be able to utilize both brain hemispheres – and I think many of us do. As I have previously explained, I learned a lot of my school history by simply 'thinking about' what happened around the time in question, and visualization and memory have certainly featured strongly in my education both in school and post-school studies. I think that standard IQ tests prove nothing in the long run. So whether the Atlanteans of old were much, if any, different from ourselves I have my doubts.

The Rosicrucians

This is a difficult one since there are several orders that have adopted this name, each with its own flavour. The European orders, for example, incorporate different views in their teachings than their American counterparts. Where the Atlantean question is concerned, however, there is general agreement that such a place existed, that its peoples went off the rails somewhere along the lines, and that it was obliterated by a giant cataclysm that shook the whole planet and altered the Earth's evolutionary course. I have talked with several Rosicrucians from different schools/traditions. To represent all their views would be impossible, but suffice it to say that we are aware of their Atlantean connections, and acknowledge the fact that they do have a definite set of teachings on the subject.

The Pegasus Foundation at Runnings Park (incorporating The Atlanteans)

As I had a hand in founding the original Atlantean Society back in 1957, I must be careful not to show them too much favour, although I left them amicably in 1975. Since then, my own studies have taken me along somewhat different lines. A fair amount of the Atlantean teaching is based in the mediumship (today it is more popular to refer to this as 'channelling') of Tony Neate, whose guiding entity is one Helio-

Arcanophus, a former high priest of Atlantis during the zodiacal Age of Virgo. This was prior to the period when the continent was split into kingships and many of the scientific innovations later credited to the peoples of Atlantis had appeared on the scene.

The Atlanteans, like myself, have broadened their activities since we parted company. Tony Neate is now Chairman of the Wrekin Trust, Council Member of the College of Psychic Studies, Chairman of 'New Approaches to Cancer', founder of/tutor at The College of Healing, founder member of the Runnings Park Community, Chairman of a company manufacturing vitamins and minerals, and a practising psychic counsellor. Runnings Park, which houses the Atlantean headquarters, is one of the major conference centres in Britain specializing in workshops and seminars on psychology, alternative therapies and various metaphysical inquiries.

The Atlantean teaching differs from others in that the date given for the catastrophe, around 5000 BC, is much nearer our time than Plato's estimated 9000 BC. An alteration between the position of the Moon as related to Earth is given as an explanation for the catastrophe, while the island continent of Atlantis is seen as being in the generally accepted Atlantic position, but *with the Earth's axis at variance with its present bearings*, which would make for a different positioning of what we now acknowledge as the northern and southern hemispheres. Interestingly, this is confirmed in Hapgood's maps of the pole shifts (see Chapters 5 and 6).

The story of Mu or Lemuria appears much as it does in the teachings of similar philosophies, while the early Atlanteans are seen as Lemurians who accommodated a more advanced strain of incarnating psyches to allow for the evolutionary quantum jump that was designed to forward the overall advancement of the life forms on this planet. Towards the latter days, however, newly discovered powers, both material and occult, were grossly misused, not by the main body of the priesthood who had by that time withdrawn to the comparative safety of their temple precincts and grounds, but by renegade practitioners of the occult – the genetic product of Atlanteans interbreeding with other people of less spiritual understanding and younger soul-age.

Prior to the last days, the reigning high priest, or Arcanophus, gathered the energies that were used by the priests of Light and, by the execution of a certain powerful rite, encapsulated them so that they could not be called upon again until such a time as the people of Earth would be wise enough to handle them with love and care. Many Atlantean members connect this encapsulation with the stories of King Arthur and the sword Excalibur, which was returned to the Lady of the Lake (Gaia?).

Atlantean teachings also conceive of the Earth today being faced with a situation similar to that which occurred towards the latter days of Atlantis, another evolutionary quantum jump precipitating, perhaps, yet a further change in the angle of the Earth's axis. Since this prophecy is shared by numerous other groups, societies and individuals throughout the world, one is inclined to think that there might well be something in it after all. I recall a long conversation on the subject with psychiatrist Dr Charlotte Wolff, who told me many people had confided in her that they experienced recurring dreams of some world-wide catastrophe; too many, in fact, for it to be the subjective ramblings of any one person's frustrated unconscious. Her conclusion? That the subconscious mind programmes major catastrophic events into the conscious mode via the dream sequence as a form of preparation for forthcoming events – a view that has since been endorsed by other qualified workers in her field.

Regarding the date favoured by the Atlanteans for the final inundation of the Old Country, we have already verified that the time of the sinking of the lands identified in the *Oera Linda Book* and Spanuth's *Atlantis of the North* was somewhere between 5000 and 4000 BC. Spence, Mooney and others have also suggested that the final episode of the Atlantean drama may have taken place much nearer to the onset of recorded history than was previously supposed (see Chapter 7). So, until such time as the question is empirically resolved one way or another, one person's conjecture is as good as another's.

The Edgar Cayce Foundation

The American psychic Edgar Cayce is acknowledged by many to have been one of the world's most gifted seers. Cayce was born on 18 March 1877 on a farm near Hopkinsville, Kentucky, and from an early age he displayed powers of perception that seemed to extend beyond the range of the normal five senses. Following a psychosomatic illness that occurred in his early twenties, with the help of a friend he managed to effect a kind of hypnotic sleep, or self-induced trance, that he had used as a child to memorize his school books. During this and subsequent altered states of consciousness Cayce was able to render accurate clinical diagnoses both for himself and later for a group of local physicians who took advantage of his unique talent. He died on 3 January 1945, leaving behind him over 14,000 documented stenographic records of the telepathic-clairvoyant statements he had given for more than 8,000 people over a period of forty-three years. These are referred to as his 'readings'. In June 1954 the University of Chicago held Cayce in sufficient esteem to accept a PhD thesis based on a study of his life and work.

However, what we are concerned with are his pronouncements on the subject of Atlantis, which appeared regularly in many of these readings both in the context of reincarnation and with regard to the early days of our planet and its ultimate future. Cayce stated clearly that the Atlantean continent occupied a position between the Gulf of Mexico and the Mediterranean, and pointed to evidence for this that could be found in the Pyrenees, Morocco, British Honduras, Yucatan and America. The West Indies were also highlighted, and the Bimini area alluded to.

In Chapter 6 we discussed axis tilts and possible reversions of poles and Equator. The teachings of the Atlanteans encompass this idea, as did Cayce's. When asked about the early days of the Earth, he is recorded as saying:

The extreme northern portions were then the southern portions, or the polar regions were then turned to where they occupied more of the tropical and semi-tropical regions; hence it would be hard to describe the change. The Nile entered into the Atlantic Ocean. What is now the Sahara was an inhabited land and very fertile. What is now the central portion of this country, or the Mississippi basin, was then all in the ocean; only the plateau was existent, or the regions that are now portions of Nevada, Utah and Arizona formed the greater part of what we now know as the United States. That along the Atlantic seaboard formed the outer portion then, or the lowlands of Atlantis. The Andean, or the Pacific coast of South America, occupied then the extreme western portion of Lemuria. The Urals and the northern regions of same were turned into a tropical land. The desert in the Mongolian land was then the fertile portion. . . .

You see, with the changes when they came the uprising of the Atlantean land, and the sojourning southward with the turning of the axis, the white and yellow races came more into that portion of Egypt, India, Persia and Arabia. (364–13; 1932)[4]*

* Reprinted by permission of Warner Books/New York from *Edgar Cayce on Atlantis* by Edgar Cayce. Copyright 1968 by the Association for Research and Enlightenment, Inc.

Cayce's contact insisted that there were originally five races: white, black, red, brown and yellow. These are referred to in his readings as 'five projections', which, we are told, occurred on this planet simultaneously, a statement that appeared to have caused some consternation among evolutionists! Cayce's readings also contain a deal of information concerning other evolutionary features in early man, some of which, like the theory that the original inhabitants of our planet were androgynous, the separation of the sexes having occurred at a later date, appear to accord with other ancient esoteric teachings. Whether or not Cayce had access to such information prior to giving his readings, however, we are not told.

Overlays of Cayce's own religious upbringing and social conditioning are obvious in his readings, and any psychologist worth his or her salt will have no problem distinguishing this programming from the kind of information that would not normally have formed part of the educational vocabulary of a man of Cayce's background. Of course, the same criticism can be levelled at any psychic, for we are all, to an extent, the product of our environment, and therefore reliant upon the prevailing semantics of the era in which we live, limited though these may be, to express our concepts of other times, places or abstracts for which our existing vocabulary offers us no suitable terms of reference.

Cayce refers to a perfect race of beings appearing in the early days of this planet's history who were faced by soul-entities who had taken on a variety of grotesque bodies from giants to pygmies, including many freakish abnormalities that had resulted from interbreeding with animals. As long as the strain was kept pure, he tells us, all went well, but then the inevitable 'sons of god and daughters of men' situation seems to have arisen, degeneracy being the anticipated outcome. Eventually, this mixed race, which Cayce refers to as that of

Lemuria, disappeared beneath the Pacific Ocean, after which a new era commenced in Atlantis.

Unlike the Theosophists and Anthroposophists, Cayce saw the Atlanteans as a highly scientific people who made great strides in mechanics, chemistry, physics and psychology. Electricity and atomic power were known to them, while they were also adept in the manipulation of lasers and other light-rays. Cayce assessed the most noble of their achievements, however, as the harnessing of the Sun's energy:

Developed originally as a means of spiritual communication between the finite and the infinite, the huge reflective crystals were first known as the *Tuaoi* Stone. Later, as its use was improved upon over the centuries, it expanded to become a generator of power and energy, radiating across the land without wires. Then it became known as the *Firestone*, or the *Great Crystals*.

Set in the Temple of the Sun in Poseidia, the Firestone was the central power station of the country. Basically, it was a large cylindrical glass or stone of many facets, capped with a mechanism at one end. It was suspended in the centre of the building and insulated with a non-conductive material akin to asbestos but resembling bakelite. Above the stone was a dome which could be rolled back for exposure to the sun.

The concentration and magnification of the sun's rays through many prisms was of tremendous intensity. So powerful was it that it could be regenerated and transmitted throughout the land in invisible beams similar to radio waves. Its energy was used to power ships at sea, aircraft and even pleasure vehicles. This was done by remote control through induction methods to the apparatus in the craft. Cities and towns received their power from the same source.

The human body could even be rejuvenated through the moderate application of the rays from the crystals, and man often rejuvenated himself. Yet by mis-application, the Firestone could be and was turned to destructive uses as well as the means for torture and punishment. Tuned too high – not intentionally – it contributed to the cause of the second catastrophe. The rays combined with other electrical forces to start many fires deep within the earth, and volcanic eruptions were precipitated from nature's powerful storehouse of energy.[5]

In addition to submitting yet a further explanation for the final sinking of the lost continent, the aforegoing gives us a pretty clear picture of Cayce's general Atlantean data, although there is obviously far more of it available for those who feel drawn to his particular interpretation of antediluvian phenomena. It contains rather too much biblical myth and allegory for my taste, although I do understand the need felt by many to align their psychic findings with the religious convictions currently favoured by the larger collectives. More's the pity, however, as I have usually found that a lack of commitment to any one dogma makes for a more open-minded approach where the utilization of the psi faculty is concerned. But safe harbours appear to be essential to some people, so who am I to argue?

There are, of course, many other metaphysical organizations in our world that support the belief in Atlantis. Some of these are known to me, while others have not formed part of my studies. This is no reflection on the quality of their communications, however, but rather on my own time limitations (and the need to keep this book within the confines of the publisher's requirements).

CHAPTER 13

Akashic Anomalies

Trismegistus! Three Times Greatest!
How thy name sublime
Has descended to this latest
Progeny of time.

   LONGFELLOW, *Hermes Trismegistus*

In many ways I have found the subject matter of this and
the previous chapter the most difficult to treat. Having dealt
with the theories, viewpoints and explorations of those Atlantologists who have tended to lean on the results of their
own researches and calculations, it now falls to me to examine the subjective experiences of certain individuals and
provide some kind of guideline or judgement for my
readers.

  As I have already explained, I make no claims to having all
(if any) of the answers, and am therefore obliged to have
recourse to a combination of psychology, healthy scepticism
and open-mindedness when analysing the material. In addition, I must make it quite clear that I shall be mentioning the
visionary experiences of only a few better known personalities
from the world of psychism and occultism, although I am
quite convinced that there are many others who might conceivably represent a more psychologically balanced viewpoint
and contain a higher degree of accuracy. However, this is all

pure conjecture, as none of it can be proven or disproven, and as such it should not be taken as a serious contribution to the resolution of the Atlantis enigma.

Much could be said on the subject of ESP and allied studies, and the attitudes adopted by people generally towards these phenomena. Rather than embark on a lengthy psychological explanation I will refer to the Gnostic view, which saw humankind divided into three classes. G. R. S. Mead tells us:

(a) the lowest, or *hylics*, were those who were so entirely dead to spiritual things that they were as the *hyle* or unperceptive matter of the world; (b) the intermediate class were called *psychics*, for though believers in things spiritual, they were believers simply, and required miracles and signs to strengthen their faith; (c) whereas the *pneumatics* or spiritual, the highest class, were those capable of knowledge of spiritual matters, those who could receive the Gnosis . . . It is somewhat the custom in our days in extreme circles to claim that all men are 'equal'. The modern theologian wisely qualifies this claim by the adverb 'morally'. Thus stated the idea is by no means a peculiarly Christian view – for the doctrine is common to all great religions, seeing that it simply asserts the great principle of justice as one of the manifestations of the Deity. The Gnostic view, however, is far clearer and more in accord with the facts of evolution; it admits the 'morally equal', but further asserts difference of degree, not only in body and soul, but also in spirit, in order to make the morality proportional, and so to carry out the inner meaning of the parable of talents.[1]

In my youth it was Dr Mona Rolfe, the Osirian communicators of H. C. Randall-Stevens, Mary Long's contacts, and the Atlantean high priest who guided Diana of the Golden Triangle Fellowship whose inspired words championed the Atlantean cause. There were others, of course, with whose work I was not familiar, however, so my limited contacts will become obvious as this chapter progresses.

Dion Fortune and Gareth Knight

Violet Mary Firth, alias Dion Fortune, was born on 6 December 1890 in Llandudno, Wales, of Yorkshire parentage. One of her biographers, Alan Richardson, has rendered a sensitive account of her childhood and how she came to adopt the mystical name that was to feature so strongly in the magical world for years to come. To this day, many students of the esoteric consider her to have been the greatest occultist of our times. But she is also acknowledged as possessing shamanic powers, which removes her from the essentially directive role of magician. Her work with the famous Fraternity of the Inner Light is also well documented by Richardson in his book *Dancers to the Gods*, and, no doubt, many members of that organization both past and present will share some, if not all, of her beliefs concerning the Old Country.

Richardson recounts how, at the tender age of 4 years, Dion experienced a constantly recurring dream-like image of

... a sandy foreshore with a level plain behind it and mountains rising abruptly in the distance. A sluggish river made its way across the plain; a few queer-looking trees like feather dusters straggled at intervals along its banks, but it was not safe to go near these trees because there were dangerous beasts in the river that might gobble you up. For the same reason it was not safe to go too near to the waters of the shallow sea that rippled over the sands; things like giant jellyfish were believed to swim there, and fat, shiny, porpoise-like backs could sometimes be seen further out.

There was glowing warmth, a lush grassy vegetation, the sky was a very dark indigo blue; and the sun, strangest of all, was copper-coloured. The copper-coloured sun made a great impression.[2]

Richardson comments that this could have been a vision of a life in Atlantis, as some psychic sources – Steiner, for example – suggest that the atmosphere of Atlantis contained far more water vapour than any climate known to us today.

There were also cannibalistic fisherfolk in Fortune's vision, and sudden storms that rose with little warning, while 'home' to her was some distance inland in a cave at the base of mountains, where she dwelt with her animal skin-clad companions.

I have listened to a tape recording made by the well-known occultist, Qabalist and Tarot specialist Gareth Knight, entitled *Visions of Lost Atlantis*, in which he claims that the information he was about to impart concerning the lost continent had been obtained by Dion Fortune and her immediate associates and had remained unpublished to this day. He emphasized its fragmentary nature and the fact that much of it derived from memories of former lives, with an occasional insight afforded by those 'inner planes' communicators who are aware that a higher arc of the evolutionary spiral is approaching and will be instrumental in instructing humankind in harnessing the potential of the human will.

I must confess that the association of Dion Fortune with some of the following material does concern me, as one is given to understand that she was a reasonable, logical-minded person, well capable of making both scientific and metaphysical cross-checks. However, the evidence must speak for itself; besides, how much of it was actually approved by Dion herself we are not told.

The term 'inner planes' can be confusing to the uninitiated (and to yours truly, to be honest). My kind of logic demands that I consider anything of an expansive nature as moving *outwards*; the inward approach tending to impose psychological limitations that imprison one within one's own subjective experiences, which incline one to believe whatever one *wants* to believe.

I, and several other metaphysicians I know, prefer to think in terms of energy frequencies of a finer, faster or more subtle nature, which constitute levels of perception that can be accessed only by those minds, intelligences or essences whose personal wavelengths are of a similar, complementary or compatible quality. But leaving all this aside, let us see what information about Atlantis Dion and her associates gleaned from these so-termed 'inner planes'.

It is agreed by most mystics and psychics that it was the cream of the Lemurians who were the founders of Atlantis following the Lemurian cataclysm. It is in this area of the following data that the anomalies occur.

According to Knight's information, the average Atlantean was 7 feet (2 metres) tall, whereas the Lemurians had been much taller. Atlantean bodies were also more porous than ours are today. There were several racial types, including black ape-like people who matured at the age of 9 and who are described as being more animal than human. There were also yellow, Mongolian-type people of extremely low intellect. Slaves were taken from both these groups, which constituted the lower of three social tiers or castes. The former group lived in sheer filth and the latter did not fare much better, there being no sanitation.

The upper tier consisted of a king, the priestly castes, the scribes and artificers, and the warriors. As Atlantis was a theocracy, the king was directly responsible to the High Priest of the Sun. The religion of the Sun represented the secular worship of the people, rather after the style of our modern churches, whereas the Sea Mysteries and Stellar Mysteries were exclusively for the initiated and therefore kept secret from the profane masses. The priests were vegetarian; the warriors ate meat; and, if I am to understand Knight correctly, the animal-type people lived on filth, excrement and the bodies of their own dead! The society was primitive in one sense, but highly evolved esoterically.

Defective children were put down at birth, although mothers would frequently cheat the law by borrowing another's child and concealing their own. If a child from one of the lower tiers showed talent, he or she was brought to the temple to be educated. Genetic selection was practised and people were bred to intensify characteristics of social value. The technology of the artificers was kept strictly secret, and it was customary for each man or woman to present the tools of his or her trade regularly at the high temple for blessing. The system of exchange was one of barter, and there was a form of phonetic writing.

The sacerdotal caste consisted of priests and priestesses; the latter manipulated a magical 'Hall of Mirrors'. There were two main temples, the High Temple of the Sun in the City of the Golden Gates, which was built on a mountain to the west of the continent, and one referred to as 'The Sun behind the Sun', which was nearer to the sea. (Could this perhaps be an arcane reference to the binary star system Sirius?) Although the priests of the former temple were reputed to have suc-cumbed to the dark forces towards the latter days, those of 'The Sun behind the Sun' never wavered from the Path of Light. The latter were also totally non-political, whereas the former were very much concerned with the machinations of the power game. It was at the second, or Mystery Temple, that the Seeresses were initiated. These priestesses of the sea had the final say in all matters – even the High Priest of the Sun could not argue with their judgements.

Among the occult rites practised were strange magical matings that took place on those enigmatic 'inner planes' and were involved with the ensoulment of 'higher forces'(?). The Stellar Mysteries derived from the knowledge of a strange, radioactive force, the nature of which was understood by only a few high initiates. This was related to energies emitted from the stars and those stellar forces, in particular, that are destined to manifest in the approaching Aquarian Age. Knight draws a comparison between these energies and those of the

Qabalistic Sephirot Chokmah and Binah, which are accessible only to initiates of high grade. He also refers to a 'Hall of Images', which was concerned with elements of water, the power of which was closely allied to the science of sonics. Those members of the priesthood adept at controlling this particular branch of the elemental family were, we are told, responsible for loosing the waters that produced the final inundation. One mention that caused me to prick up my ears concerned an ancient legend of a White Emperor from the distant Atlantean past, whom, we assume, was an incarnate being of Light, whose statutes constituted the earlier, more spiritual basis of the Atlantean system that later collapsed under the power of the dark forces.

In the latter days the priesthood of the Sun became so corrupt that the powers they possessed were grossly misused and all that was good was withdrawn by the priesthood of Light to rest for ages until recalled on a higher arc at the appropriate time. One Atlantean colony, which was set up in Britain, gave birth to Stonehenge and other monoliths later associated with Druidism, which is indicated as being of At-lantean origin! Many of the good priests who managed to escape the cataclysm are said to have landed on the now sunken lands of Lyonnesse, off the coast of Brittany.

Knight also deals with the visions of Margaret Lumley-Brown, whom he describes as a psychic of some integrity. It seems that Lumley-Brown's interpretation of the whole scen-ario took on a Christian flavour rather than an Eastern one. (Why does it have to be one or the other?) From her work we learn that the Sea Mysteries of Atlantis were considerably more powerful and older than those of the Sun, being con-cerned with the origins of primordial life itself as manifest through the element of water, the Great Mother of birth and death and the feminine cosmos.

Well, well, comment is irresistible! First of all, Dion Fortune's childhood memories: why should these be seen as relating to Atlantis? While Mooney and others have commented on the possibility of the atmosphere containing more water vapour were our planet positioned slightly nearer to the Sun, surely this could equally apply to any of several earlier periods in the Earth's history. What about Lemuria or Gondwanaland, for example, or even some parallel world or environment external to our solar system?

Now to the fragments of information derived from various ESP sources: black, ape-like men who matured at the tender age of 9. In Atlantis? Hardly. In Lemuria? Well, I will keep an open mind on that one! The same applies to the descriptions of corpse- and sewage-eating slaves, which is hardly consistent with Plato's highly evolved and beautiful people who were skilled traders, artisans, metal-workers and warriors, or those documented accounts of scholarly priests who taught a doctrine of service, discipline and brotherly love wherever they landed (the Oannes and Quetzalcoatl stories, for example).

A tall people? Yes, I find that credible. But a hostile environment filled with prehistoric monsters and cannibalistic fisherfolk hardly relates to Otto Muck's description of the kind of coastline Atlantis would have enjoyed when it was encircled by the Gulf Stream.

Strange and evil rites? In the latter days, perhaps. But then there are some pretty gruesome things going on in today's world, a fair degree of which masquerades under the guise of modern civilized society.

Genetic engineering? We have been using this on animals and crops for some years now, and research indicates that DNA can cross the genetic barriers between the animal and fungus kingdoms. Professor George Sprague, a molecular biologist at Oregon University, and Jack Heinneman, a student, have shown that bacteria that colonize the human gut can transfer their genes to yeast.[3] This discovery has enormous potential implications for genetic engineering, and for the possible dangers of releasing 'test-tube' bacteria and plants into the environment. Some genetic engineers believe that transfers to other species would be impossible, or at least extremely unlikely. Sprague, on the other hand, sees this discovery as having a number of implications, the foremost of which is for evolution. But it also raises the possibility that barriers to the transfer of DNA between species are not as solid as we might have supposed. In fact, such transfers may be a lot more frequent than we have thought. Sprague cautions: 'It highlights that we need to remain cautious about how we deal with recombinant organisms [creatures altered by genetic engineering] in the laboratory, and in commercial ventures, to make sure they don't escape into the environment.' All this, plus the Genome project (see p. 172), would seem to indicate that we may be in for a repeat performance of the Atlantean drama.

As to the question of Atlanteans landing in England and founding the Druidic order in these isles, there is ample historical, archaeological and ethnological evidence that points to the Druidic cult having other, more shamanic beginnings. Besides, the Celts, for whom Druidism comprised the essence of their sacerdotal establishment, can be proven by blood groupings and other genetic factors to have originated elsewhere, although it must be conceded that Atlantean colonists are believed to have settled in the regions of Tyre and Sidon, which, according to the *Oera Linda Book*, were strongholds of the Druids in days long past. As far as the Celtic/Druidic controversy is concerned, I feel more inclined to trust the scholarship of Bob Quinn and other Irish authorities, whose conclusions concerning the Atlantic sea peoples seem far more feasible to me.

Sea worship – yes. This was, as Knight suggests, closely related to the worship of the Great Mother and therefore akin to the matriarchal Age of Cancer, which seems a likely time for a major inundation.

I must confess I do have a problem when it comes to the statement that the ancient Atlanteans were 'primitive in one sense, but highly evolved esoterically'. I have come across the same kind of thinking in some contemporary esoteric groups, whose members appear to suffer from the 'holier than thou' syndrome: they feel they are too highly evolved or spiritually exalted to acknowledge a letter, say 'thank you', attend to the cleanliness of their bodies, or exhibit other courtesies common to civilized people. In my book of rules spirituality goes hand in hand with understanding, caring and respecting the views of others.

With regard to the supposed Atlantean sanitary arrangements enumerated in the 'impressions' related by Mr Knight, my nanny always used to say 'cleanliness is next to godliness', which may sound Victorian, but when applied to the occult principle that 'like attracts like' inclines one to think she had something!

Christine Hartley

In her book *A Case for Reincarnation*, Christine Hartley, an acknowledged adept, whose work with fellow magician Charles Seymour is well documented in Richardson's *Dancers to the Gods*, afforded Atlantis a degree of coverage. She recalls vividly her clairvoyant impressions of a life in the latter days:

Because I was a young priestess and had work to do in another place, when the destruction of Atlantis was known to be approaching I was put into a small boat with F.P.D. [her teacher in this life] and a few other people – sailors, I think, and we were eventually washed up on the coast of Lyonnesse after being tossed about on a raging sea.[4]

She reiterates the belief of others that 'Atlantis fell because her mental faculties outstripped her spiritual advancement; evil powers were invoked and the priests used their knowledge for self-advancement and not for the benefit of humanity.'[5]

Phyllis Cradock

Non-fiction is by no means the only representative of the Atlantean drama. The Phyllis Cradock trilogy *Gateway to Remembrance*, *The Eternal Echo* and *The Immortal Hour* also deals with the years leading up to the latter days. Although written in novel form, they actually recount Ms Cradock's own experiences in those times, as shared with her husband, Johnny (the Johnny and Fanny Cradock who graced British TV screens during the 1950s and 1960s). These books are well written and certainly throw a different slant on the Atlantean period they portray.

Daphne Vigers

Among the hotch-potch of clairvoyant impressions that have filtered through down the ages, however, a few have fitted the known facts and added credence to the logical deductions of men such as Spence, Donnelly, Braghine, Muck, Tomas and Berlitz – glimmers of truth that cannot be proven, but that seem to ring the right bells for many people.

One such work is *Atlantis Rising* by Daphne Vigers. Published in 1944, when Miss Vigers was in her middle twenties, it comprises a series of 'astral' experiences and includes an understanding of the element of time, something that had received little if any consideration in her day aside from the work of Dunne and Bergson. I was impressed when I first came across it in the late 1950s, and found it more than a coincidence that the name of Miss Vigers's Atlantean High Priest, Helio-Arkhan, bore such a close resemblance to Tony Neate's contact, Helio-Arcanophus. Neither Tony nor any of us with whom he worked closely had encountered Miss Vigers's book until after H.A., as he is affectionately known, had established himself as a spiritual teacher.

Aside from certain nationalistic emphases, which are logical in the light of the hostilities extant at the time, Vigers's book contains a simplicity that is neither tainted by abstruse metaphysical dogmas nor cluttered by the megrims of currently fashionable occult semantics. One could not do justice to it in a few paragraphs, but suffice it to say her descriptions complement much of what has been written about in the earlier parts of this book. Her Atlantis, as seen at the height of its glory, boasted a common-sense economy and an efficient system of public utilities, which made adequate provision for the welfare of all of its peoples. Her descriptions of the latter days could be seen as somewhat exaggerated, however, and she, too, alludes to the Druids as having arrived in Britain from the Old Country. I think the mistake here lies in confusing Caesar's Druids and those described in the *Oera Linda Book* with the secret cults of Quinn's 'sea people', who were, undoubtedly, the true Atlanteans.

One of the problems of pinning a national bias on the Atlantean theme is that everyone else does it. While British mystics fervently claim Atlantean roots in the belief that the good priests of Atlantis landed on these shores, wherein they buried the sacred power of the old priesthood, I have encountered the same belief elsewhere. Many Americans, for example, are convinced that the encapsulated energies of the Light were left in their safe keeping, and I have been entrusted with a similar 'occult secret' by mystics from France, Spain, Scandinavia and North Africa. Perhaps generosity is the kindest (and probably the more truthful) answer to all this, as there were undoubtedly both 'goodies and baddies' among the many who did manage to escape, either prior to, or around the time of, the final cataclysm. Therefore, the Cauldron of the Graal, the Sword of Arthur and other Atlantean memorabilia that form part of the mystique of British magic are no more exclusively ours than Sun or sea worship.

Those of us who feel Atlantean kinship or who have experienced recall of past lives ('fragments in other time zones', in my terminology) should refrain from indulging in the kind of xenophobic jingoism that is guaranteed to limit our spiritual progress. The ultimate brotherhood of the Old Country cast its seed far further afield than we might imagine. Within which race the new priestly order will arise (assuming that it does) is still anybody's guess, much as this may bruise the egos of certain occult (I refuse to use the term 'spiritual') snobs among us!

Like that other great seer, Edgar Cayce, whom we have already mentioned, Daphne Vigers conceived of the continent of Atlantis rising from its watery depths at some future date. Cayce specified the years 1968 and 1969 as being significant in the discovery of Atlantis. His prophecy, made in 1940, says:

And Poseidia will be among the first portions of Atlantis to rise again. Expect it in '68 or '69 – not so far away . . . A portion of the [Atlantean] temple may yet be discovered under the slime of ages of seawater – near what is known as Bimini, off the coast of Florida.[6]* (See Chapter 14.)

Vigers is less specific, but I am sure that her message has given hope to many a faint-heart who has despaired of the direction in which our world would appear to be heading.

*Reprinted by permission of Warner Books/New York from *Edgar Cayce on Atlantis* by Edgar Cayce. Copyright 1968 by the Association for Research and Enlightenment, Inc.

Brad Steiger

The American writer Brad Steiger devotes the whole of his book, also called *Atlantis Rising*, to exploring the various facets of the Atlantean legend and the conflicting views concerning it that have arisen over the centuries. Included in his analysis is the 'people from outer space' concept, which is used by some researchers to explain many of the myths that have been attributed to the arrival of Atlanteans. The Chaldean's Oannes, for example, is seen as an alien astronaut rather than an Atlantean priest, and the five epagomenal gods of Egypt as space visitors. There is also a school of thought that associates the rise of the wise priest–initiates of Atlantis with civilizing missions, and perhaps a tad of genetic engineering from some other part of the galaxy. Sirius is a popular target because of the Egyptian references on the one hand, and Robert K. Temple's fascinating book *The Sirius Mystery* on the other.

Steiger also provides a wealth of psychic information received through well-known American mediums, notably Joseph W. Donnelly and his associates, which covers such subjects as the ancient Atlantean language, why Atlantis sank, the true symbolism of the pyramid, which was completely misunderstood by the ancient Egyptians, other sunken lands such as Mu, Lemuria, and two at the North and South Poles, and how axis tilts are caused by the accumulation of ice at certain spots. The destruction of Thera, Pompeii and later cataclysms were brought about by natural causes, while the destruction of Atlantis and Lemuria were purely mankind's doing, or so said Donnelly's psychic contacts.[7]

Varying Psychic Views

I have had the privilege of working with a few American psychics – quiet, responsible people, several of whom are also highly qualified in psychology, sociology and medicine. I found their standards of psychism extremely high, a factor that was enhanced by their ability to express what they 'saw' in the semantics of the scientific, social and medical community of which they were a part. The younger people also showed an open-minded and dogma-free approach that enabled them to project both back and forward in time unfettered by the preconditioning of the kind of medieval hocus-pocus so often encountered in Britain, where either Eastern mysticism or the Qabalah seem to rule supreme amongst the occult fraternity.

I must be among the very few who not only refuse to associate with Qabalistic practices, but positively dislike the Qabalah. However, because it constitutes such a firm basis for dialogue within the Western tradition, I spent several years grappling with its complexities as part of my general training. This experience served only to strengthen my conviction that it was *not* for me. I mention this specifically because I cannot in all honesty see any connection between the mystical symbology of the Qabalah and the old Atlantean occult system. Others may sense a compatibility here; I do not.

In the United States, a country of extremes, there exists – in contrast to the gifted group I have just mentioned – a body of American seers who qualify for less complimentary comment. However, I will not embark on some of the more way-out ideas I have encountered in the American psychic scene, especially in relation to Atlantis, for no matter what I say, people will inevitably be drawn to that which complements their own inner beliefs and I can only trust my readers to make their own judgement of any literature that comes their way.

Frank Alper

One man who has an enormous following in the United States, and whose special theme is Atlantis, is Dr Frank Alper, who founded the Arizona Metaphysical Society in 1974. Alper is one of a crop of popular American channellers whose contact goes by the name of Adamis, and who, according to the back cover of his book, has appointed himself '. . . the spiritual name of "Christos", which means "The Enlightened One" '. (I always understood the word 'Christos' to mean 'anointed'!). Alper has published three books on the Adamis teachings. However, as I found myself at variance with so much of what I read in the first volume, notably Alper's observations concerning animals, I saw no sense in pursuing the study further, and therefore cannot comment on the contents of the other two books.

Alper refers to Mu and an ancient Atlantean land mass as having been destroyed by cataclysms around 85,000 BC, when both continents sank beneath the waves. In the year 77,777 BC, he claims, the first ships from alien worlds landed off the coast of what is now Florida, to begin to resettle and reconstruct Atlantis *beneath the sea*! There is lots more along this line, some of which makes sense, some of which does not. But then, perhaps, I am looking for the kind of left-brain logic that does not appear to belong to this kind of scenario. Alper does refer to crystals as being the source of power in Atlantis, which, as we have discussed in a previous chapter, is quite logical and could also find a place in the energy scheme of our own future. In the final analysis it all depends on whether you like your Atlantis presented in a hypothetical manner that lacks practical substantiation of any kind, or prefer the rational theories of Donnelly, Muck, Scrutton, Spanuth and other, more orthodox scholars. As to who is correct in their Atlantean assumptions, however, only time will tell.

Personal Experiences

Since I have tended to distance myself from most of the views expressed, it is only fair to point out before I cite my own experiences that I do not feel my psychic observations qualify as being any more valid than those of the next person. My psychic abilities were tested under laboratory conditions by Dr Carl Sargent in 1977 and I fared well, but that does not make me an expert on Atlantis.

However, I have been gifted with 'far memory' since early childhood, and, although that statement in itself proves nothing, I was aware of the Old Country long before I had ever heard of Plato or even encountered the name Atlantis.

The Atlantis I knew (if indeed it was Atlantis, and I am inclined to think it might have been) had more in common with the place described by Daphne Vigers. There were certainly no ape-men, slaves, gross experiments in genetic engineering or unhygienic living conditions – quite the contrary, in fact. It was a theocracy, the high priest/priestess having the final say, although there were state administrators who looked after the more practical aspects of life. The state was a form of socialism, with resources being shared by all. The method of exchange was barter, so anyone who wanted to increase his or her possessions simply worked a little harder to achieve the required exchanges. Medical care was free to all. Children were selected for their role in life at the age of 3. People were certainly very tall, but I do not recall their being 'porous'. In character they were much like people are today, having the same faults, jealousies, depravities, power struggles, and so forth. Only in those times, which I think must have been many centuries before the 'latter days', everything was well under control. Wrong-doers were submitted to the healers rather than to prisons and were obliged to make restitution via community service in much the same way as they do in some countries today.

Do I recall crystals? Not really, although there was one extremely large blue stone, possibly a blue diamond, that was worn on a chain around the neck of the High Priest on ceremonial occasions. When not used for this purpose, it reposed on an altar that was positioned to catch the rays of the Sun at certain times, when it emitted powerful energies. This was, no doubt, the prototype of the later energy crystals mentioned by so many other psychics. The main source of energy was sonics, but its use was kept highly secret and was available only to the Masonic branch of the priesthood, who were the scientists. The people were either fair-haired and blue-eyed, or copper-skinned with green or brown eyes, although I seem to recall some with dark hair and blue eyes, a combination that doubtlessly resulted from interbreeding between the two types. Slanted eyes seemed to predominate, giving the face a Mongolian sort of appearance; the skin colour, even of the 'white' people, inclined to a yellowish or golden tone and freckles were not unknown. Among the foreigners who came from afar to trade there were people of all colours from ebony black to pinkish white. As I led a somewhat sheltered life in those times, however, I had little to do with any of them.

My memories also differ in that the capital I knew was on the eastern side of the continent (as suggested by Plato and Muck – see Figure 20, p. 160), about 30 miles (48 kilometres) distance from the coast that I visited frequently with my family. On that beach there were no tides – the water-level always seemed to remain fairly static – and there were bushes similar to rhododendrons, and other highly colourful flowers that grew almost to the water's edge. I do not recall seeing a moon in the night sky; the daytime sunlight was very brilliant, but somehow different from our present sunshine. It had a hazy, silvery appearance, which could be seen as consistent with the water-vapour phenomenon that some psychics and researchers have suggested might result from our planet being slightly nearer to its Sun (see Chapter 6, end-note 21). Another strange thing: it was the north that was warm, whereas the mountainous regions in the *south* were temperate, which seems to indicate that the poles and Equator did not occupy their present positions.

I also remember being part of a close family unit that had its spiritual origins in some place other than Earth (which I *do* recall), and that it was my first time here. I am not familiar with any other episode in Atlantean or Lemurian history, nor have I made a point of 'searching the Akasha' to take stock of what did actually occur. My energies have been employed in other directions during this incarnation, and since many other psychics have engaged in that little exercise I see no reason to add to the confusion!

My childhood learning processes were not calculated: I simply allowed my mind to wander across the canvas of my subject matter, as it were, and the pictures appeared as and when I needed them. I had not heard of the Akashic records or any such state of timelessness in those days. My own subjective experiences, however, incline me to the idea that much of what is served up by psychics as Atlantis or Lemuria could, in fact, relate to environments external to this planet, as in the case of Dion Fortune's childhood memory. As we mature and are subjected to the conditioning of the society in which we live, the tendency is subconsciously to rationalize our 'memories' in the light of the knowledge and terms of reference available. In Dion Fortune's time the 'alien' time-bomb had not yet exploded, so Atlantis or Lemuria was the obvious answer. In years ahead our successors will, no doubt, laugh at our ignorance and fail to understand why we did not use our supposed logic to deduce that we are not alone in this vast universe.

True to the laws of chaos science, Atlantis seemed to rise

from the chaos that followed the Lemurian disaster to achieve a state of order, balance or equilibrium. But the pendulum was destined to return to its chaotic extreme sooner or later, which is exactly what happened. Is it, therefore, a definite scientific law that stability *is not*, *cannot* ever be a permanent fixture in our society? A sobering thought, and one that is the subject of the final chapter.

CHAPTER 14

Is Chaos Returning?

> There will come a time in the late age of the world
> When the ocean will relax its bonds over what it holds,
> And land will appear in its glory.
> Thetis will uncover new continents
> And Thule will no longer be at the end of the world.
>
> SENECA, *Medea*

In my search for answers to the Atlantean enigma, I seem to have uncovered many other strange prehistoric phenomena that are not accounted for in the textbooks of academe. Nor am I alone in my findings; other Atlantologists have been quick to note that there is more to the prehistoric world than might previously have been imagined, while eminent scholars engaged in unrelated fields of research also appear to have stumbled on a myriad of clues that have led them to question the closed attitudes of their calling. Scientists in the Soviet Union appear to be more open-minded regarding the prehistory of our planet, giving credence to the myth and legend that for many years constituted the history of the past for ordinary and unlettered people. In parts of Africa the oral traditions are passed from generation to generation, and although missionaries and subsequent Western educationalists endeavoured to block these transmissions, researchers are now being forced to eat humble pie and treat these and other ancient legends as folk memories of facts.

Is Chaos Returning?

Highly respected stalwarts from recognized scientific disciplines are slowly applying themselves to sorting and analysing the mounting pile of evidence that is now facing the academic world. Among those who have seen fit to question their original programming is Professor Charles Hapgood, who has this to say regarding those mysterious days of prehistory that have, for so many centuries, remained the domain of mystics and occultists:

The evidence presented by the ancient maps appears to suggest the existence in remote times, before the rise of any of the known cultures, of a true civilization, of an advanced kind, which either was localized in one area but had worldwide commerce, or was, in a real sense, a *worldwide* culture. This culture, at least in some respects, was more advanced than the civilizations of Greece and Rome. In geodesy, nautical science, and mapmaking, it was more advanced than any known culture before the 18th century of the Christian Era. It was only in the 18th century that we first developed a practical means of finding longitude. It was in the 18th century that we first accurately measured the circumference of the earth. Not until the 19th century did we begin to send out ships for exploration into the Arctic or Antarctic Seas and only then did we begin the exploration of the bottom of the Atlantic. The maps indicate that some ancient people did all these things.

Mapping on a continental scale suggests both economic motivations and economic resources. Organized government is indicated. The mapping of a continent like Antarctica implies many exploring expeditions, many stages in the compilation of local observations and local maps into a general map under a central direction. Furthermore, it is unlikely that navigation and mapmaking were the only sciences developed by this people, or that the application of mathematics to cartography was the only practical application they made of their mathematical knowledge.

Whatever its attainments may have been, however, this civilization disappeared, perhaps suddenly, more likely by gradual stages. Its disappearance has implications we ought to consider seriously. If I may be permitted a little philosophizing, I would like to suggest that there are four principal conclusions to which we are led.

1. The idea of the simple linear development of society from the culture of the palaeolithic (Old Stone Age) through the successive stages of the neolithic (New Stone Age), Bronze, and Iron Ages must be given up. Today we find primitive cultures co-existing with advanced modern society on all the continents – the Aboriginals of Australia, the Bushmen of South Africa, truly primitive peoples in South America, and in New Guinea; some tribal peoples in the United States. We shall now assume that, some 20,000 or more years ago, while palaeolithic peoples held out in Europe, more advanced cultures existed elsewhere on the earth, and that we have inherited a part of what they once possessed, passed down from people to people.

2. Every culture contains the seeds of its own disintegration. At every moment forces of progress and of decay co-exist, building up or tearing down. All too evidently the destructive forces have often gained the upper hand; witness such known cases as the extinctions of the high cultures of ancient Crete, Troy, Babylon, Greece, and Rome, to which it would be easy to add twenty others. And, it is worth nothing that Crete and Troy were long considered myths.

3. Every civilization seems eventually to develop a technology sufficient for its own destruction, and hitherto has made use of the same. There is nothing magical about this. As soon as men learned to build walls for defence, other men learned how to tear them down. The vaster the achievements of a civilization, the farther it spreads, the greater must be the engines of destruction; and so today, to counter the modern worldwide spread of civilization, we have atomic means to destroy all life on earth. Simple. Logical.

4. The more advanced the culture, the more easily it will be destroyed, and the less evidence will remain. Take New York. Suppose it was destroyed by a hydrogen bomb. After some 2,000 years, how much of its life could anthropologists reconstruct? Even

if quite a few books survived, it would be quite impossible to reconstruct the mental life of New York.[1]

In the light of point number 4, the thought suddenly occurred to me that some future civilization investigating the ruins of New York, upon discovering the Statue of Liberty might assume that its present inhabitants were worshippers of the Goddess!

After commenting on the sad story of the desecration of past knowledge executed under the cloak of religious 'enlightenment' – the destruction of the great libraries, which, for example, set medical knowledge back centuries and consequently caused unnecessary suffering to millions of people – Hapgood goes on to highlight some of the covert efforts to hide the truth today. Book burning, he cogently reminds us, is not the prerogative of the early Christians or the Nazis of recent times:

The libraries of America are combed relentlessly by gimlet-eyed agents of various self-appointed saviours of morality and religion. The books just disappear off the shelves! Thousands of them, every year! And of course, American libraries have recently been the particular objects of anti-American mobs in several countries.[2]

More recently the Salman Rushdie affair has served to remind us that the world is still greatly influenced by powerful collectives that strive to dictate set codes of belief that conflict with the need for spiritual and psychological freedom, and the right of personal expression felt by many serious seekers after the truth.

All this has an uncomfortable feel about it, and I do not think it is my imagination. In fact, I can confirm the findings of Hapgood and others from personal experience. In the late 1980s I was travelling on a bus in London perusing a copy of a book I had been sent to review for a well-known newspaper.

A man, a complete stranger, leaned over me and said: 'A nice lady like you should not be reading a book like that. Let me take it away and burn it.' I assured him I knew exactly what I was about and before he could embark on a tirade of abuse, missionary work or whatever, I anticipated the imminent approach of my alighting point and made my way to the exit and the protection of the friendly conductor.

The next incident occurred in my own home. My husband and I engaged a young lady to give a helping hand with the housework one morning a week. She duly arrived and seemed to be doing an efficient job – until she espied one of my books that dealt with the religion of ancient Egypt. That did it! She offered to take it away to her pastor so that it could be ceremonially burned, an action that, she assured me, would purge me of its evil influences! I could cite a page of such instances – and we are supposed to live in a *free* world! Freedom, it would seem, is confined to those large 'collectives' who toe one or other of the great 'lines' – political, religious or humanitarian.

Atlantologists, like many others whose research extends beyond the bounds set by the major collectives, would appear to be poised between two opposing camps. As one journalist recently observed, knowledge has become debatable, a matter of public consensus, a relationship between people and propositions and not a relationship between sense, impressions and the way our minds work; science and religion have collapsed in the ring, leaving the audience at a loss to know who won. This labyrinth of confusion does have its exits, however, and just as myth is slowly dissolving into history, the science fiction of one age tends to become the science fact of the next. We can only hope that there is a corresponding broadening of general understanding of the transcendental.

For those sceptical individuals who demand empirical proof, I recommend Hapgood's book *Maps of the Ancient Sea*

Kings, especially from page 188 onwards. Nor is he the only scientist of repute to concede that civilization did *not* commence in Mesopotamia around 4000 BC. As he points out, the history of archaeological research in the nineteenth century consisted mainly of the rediscovery of ancient civilizations. Jacquetta Hawkes, in her anthology of archaeological works covering all periods, devotes an entire section to those who have found lost civilizations: Claudius Rich's rediscovery of Babylon; Paul Emile Botta, Henry Layard and Henry Rawlinson, who reinstated Assyria in the annals of history; Champollion's breaking of the hieroglyphic code, which brought Egypt back into focus; Schliemann's discoveries, which elevated Troy from the mists of myth; and the work of Sir Arthur Evans, who gave substance to the tales of ancient Crete. In more recent times an advanced culture that existed on the banks of the Indus River some 5,000 years ago, and which obviously enjoyed luxuries up to a modern standard, has been counted among the 'lost and found', while Geoffrey Bibby's *Looking for Dilmun* details the rediscovery of civilizations that pre-date the Indus culture, extending back at least 6,000 years.

Among the many fascinating works germane to this study, Hapgood cites Dr William F. Warren's *Paradise Found: The Cradle of the Human Race at the North Pole* (published in 1898) in which the writer, a distinguished scientist of his day and president of Boston University, postulates that the north polar region was once, in times when it was not the ice-ridden expanse we see today, inhabited by an ancient race. The theme was later taken up by the Vedic scholar B. G. Tilak, whose book was titled *The Arctic Home of the Vedas*. This was first published in 1903 and republished in 1925 and 1956. Tilak believed that the Vedas were forced to abandon their polar home because of the coming of the last Ice Age, or 'Wisconsin Glaciation', in North America.

Hapgood, however, challenges this theory on the grounds

that radiocarbon and other evidence suggests that this ice age began at least 50,000 years ago, while geology indicates that there is no land at the North Pole. The South Pole, however, suggests a different picture. There is an abundance of land in Antarctica, and Hapgood has demonstrated in his book *The Path of the Pole* that the arrival of the present ice-sheet can be dated at between 10,000 and 15,000 years ago. The likelihood is therefore that it was from this polar region that the Vedic peoples originally came.

Hapgood also comments on the astronomical details possessed by the Dogons of Mali and other African tribes, which I discussed in an earlier chapter. In addition to their precise knowledge of the binary system of the star Sirius, and their belief that this star accommodates the souls of the dead, these people also inherited the following facts from some advanced civilization of the past:

1. The Moon is a dry, dead sphere.

2. Saturn (which they refer to as 'the star of limiting the place', which will, no doubt, prove of great interest to students of astrology) has a system of rings.

3. The planets revolve around the Sun.

4. The Milky Way is composed of distant stars.

5. The four moons of Jupiter; all this information was brought to Earth by non-hominid space beings.

The Dogon believe that their tradition can be traced back to ancient Egypt, but the odds are that it goes back considerably further than that. How about Atlantis?

In view of this formidable array of evidence that, much as it may bruise our egos, we have been preceded by civilizations that surpassed us in scientific knowledge, technology and a metaphysical and practical comprehension of the universe, and that it disappeared into the smoke of myth and superstition, what is to stop our own world experiencing the same exit to anonymity? And should this be the case, what immutable universal law decrees such matters? Must we, as thinking beings with some modicum of intelligence (at least that is how we like to see ourselves), stand by and watch it happen all over again? Are we so utterly powerless? After all, the Atlanteans were supposedly intelligent, thinking people, with powerfully developed minds capable of the kind of PK that could manipulate natural forces like gravity and sonics. So where does that leave us?

In his recent book *The Cosmic Blueprint*, Paul Davies refers to James Lovelock's Gaia Hypothesis as:

An even more dramatic example of a complex system exercising a seemingly unreasonable degree of self-regulation . . . Gaia is a way of thinking about our planet as a holistic self-regulating system in which activities of the biosphere cannot be untangled from the complex processes of geology, climatology and atmospheric physics.[3]★

After rendering a complicated and highly technical analysis of Lovelock's theory, Davies concludes the relevant chapter with the comment:

The apparently stable conditions on the surface of our planet serve to illustrate the general point that complex systems have an unusual ability to organize themselves into stable patterns of activity when *a priori* we would expect disintegration and collapse. Most computer simulations of the Earth's atmosphere predict *some sort of runaway disaster* [my italics], such as global glaciation, the boiling of the oceans, or wholesale incineration due to an overbalance of oxygen

★ Reprinted by permission of William Heinemann Limited. Copyright Paul Davies, 1987.

setting the world on fire. The impression is gained that the atmosphere is only marginally stable. Yet somehow the integrative effect of many interlocking complex processes has maintained atmospheric stability in the face of large-scale changes and even during periods of cataclysmic disruption.[4]*

In other words, it is on the cards that disaster is calculated to strike somewhere or somehow. However, owing to the resilience of the entity we call 'Gaia', life as we know it will not cease but, as the survivors of the Atlantean and earlier disasters found, will simply adjust to the new conditions.

As the aforegoing could be seen to indicate that Atlantis and similarly highly advanced prehistoric cultures that have proved a thorn in the side of the establishment for so many years are part of an ongoing process, this seems as good a point as any for me to summarize the preceding chapters and cast a few thoughts regarding what the pendulum of Chaos might hold for us in the future.

There is, I feel, a sound psychology behind the Atlantis hypothesis that is based on genetic information, albeit subconscious; and what have been classified as 'psychic impressions', that is, those gained from accessing the collective unconscious on the one hand, or the data of individuals' personal memory banks on the other. The latter, of course, presupposes an acceptance of reincarnation, an analysis of which is not an essential contribution to this inquiry. Suffice it to say that I do not subscribe to the popularly accepted linear concept nor to the Eastern idea that our psyches (or essences) started as stones and worked their way up to the exalted stage of *Homo sapiens*! Anyone wishing to pursue this line of thought is referred to *The Lion People*, *The Psychology of Healing* and *Time: The Ultimate Energy*.

* Reprinted by permission of William Heinemann Limited. Copyright Paul Davies, 1987.

Is Chaos Returning?

As Dr Wolff suggested, coming events cast their shadows and, as thinking human beings, many of us must be aware in some concealed department of our psychic economy that sooner or later the pendulum of chaos is bound to swing the other way. It is only natural that our subconscious fears will be coloured by our social, religious, and ethnic programming, so that one faction of society will be thinking in apocalyptic or eschatological terms, while others envision the dreaded nuclear holocaust, a holy war to end all wars, the acceleration of the 'greenhouse effect', or an ending of the old order by a cataclysm precipitated by some agency external to our earthly environment that will result in the rising of Atlantis from her watery bed, just as Seneca suggests.

In fact, the 'Atlantis rising' theme has grown apace over the last fifty years; I have come across several books that feature this as a title, and many, many more that foster the idea within their pages. Nor have all of these come from the pens of psychics. It has been known for a long time that science-fiction writers, for example, frequently utilize their craft as a vehicle through which to express those personal views and impressions that, if mentioned in a different context, might ruin their careers or relegate them to the lunatic fringe. Likewise, gentlemen of the cloth have confided in me their beliefs in Atlantis and similar 'myths' on the strict understanding that I do not make their views known in established circles. After all, Athanasius Kircher, famed for his map of Atlantis, was a Jesuit.

Atlantis is therefore deeply embedded in the human psyche and, try as we may to rationalize it away, it has the habit of reappearing again and again under different guises. On this occasion it has recruited stauncher allies from the bastions of science, which makes it, perhaps, a little easier for those like myself, to whom falls the onerous task of presenting the pros and cons, to proffer an adequate appraisal of the facts and fiction.

From the evidence available from all sources it would seem that there was more than one advanced culture occupying our planet in prehistoric times. Some authorities may go back as far as 85,000 BC in their estimates as to when the initial cultural thrust was made, but the more conservative tend to go along with the geological facts and view the Atlantean civilization as having commenced around 17,000 BC and ended somewhere between 9000 BC and 5000 BC. Atlantis, in turn, derived from another prehistoric culture that flourished in the Pacific Ocean in the vicinity of the South American western seaboard. In fact, there are many who believe that the old continent of Lemuria was at one time attached to South America and to Asia, but whether this idea is accommodated by the break-up of the original land masses as postulated by Wegener, or whether there were other geological changes that were cataclysmically precipitated, is still open to conjecture.

Many of the ancient ruins attributed to Atlantean colonists, notably those cities that both research and logic tell us could not possibly have been built at certain altitudes, were not, as I see it, Atlantean at all, but Lemurian. Some researchers are of the opinion that those Cyclopean ruins of cities that straddle the Andean heights were actually elevated to those positions at the time of the Lemurian cataclysm.

Similarly, I do not agree with those psychics who think of every prehistoric past life as having been in Atlantis. After all, in view of what science has recently discovered, there are so many places to choose from! Why, for example, do we not hear of 'my exciting past life in Antarctica'? After all, someone must have lived there since, according to the ancient mapmakers, it enjoyed a moderate climate within the memory of mankind. And if the poles have changed places, as our learned friends affirm, then what about a life sunbathing in the lush pastures of Siberia, or living in an igloo in freezing California?

I have always thought along these lines, as those who have known me for some years will attest, so I cannot be accused of showing knowledge after the event!

There have undoubtedly been advanced civilizations in the early days of our planet's history, in addition to those of Lemuria and Atlantis. Whether or not these accord with the information given in channellings by psychics such as Frank Alper, the teachings of Theosophy, or the readings of Edgar Cayce, I do not feel qualified to judge. Perhaps some day we will know for sure, but meanwhile I do not see the arguments for or against as anything to get excited about. It is only insecurity that causes us to become upset when our pet theories come under fire, and that applies to both the pro- and anti-Atlantean factions. From a psychological point, it is unwise to become too fixed in one's views; we all know what happens to the 'reed that bends not in the wind'. Inner security should therefore involve a peace of mind as expressed in the attitude, 'Well, I do (do not) believe in Atlantis, and having investigated the matter thoroughly, I feel satisfied with the results of my decision. But should I be presented with evidence to the contrary, then fair enough, as it may well highlight areas of prejudice in my own psyche that call for adjustment.'

What might the swing of the chaos pendulum entail in terms of world changes? On the purely rational side we are faced with the 'greenhouse effect', the outcome of which we really know very little about, being reliant mainly upon those 'mechanical psychics', the computers, for simulations and projections.

It has also been suggested that the chaos principle is equally manifest in the human psychology. Those who, during their youth, have been involved in antisocial behaviour or rebellion, provided their hedonism has not resulted in physical or mental disintegration, frequently turn to religion in later years or become pillars of society. Likewise, the severe morality of one generation slowly gives way to the hedonism of the next, while the children born to the hedonists have been noted to despise their parents' attitudes and opt for a more disciplined and orderly existence. The traumas of war beg for the stability of peace, which in turn is shattered by outbreaks of violence among those who find themselves with no outlet for their pent-up aggressions and no enemy upon whom to focus their irrational anger. So they embark on a career of mugging, rape and other equally horrendous antisocial activities. It has been speculated that in wartime conditions such people would excel as pilots, commandos or whatever, but whether that is true of the present generation I would not care to hazard a guess. In fact, the military life has been known to bring out the worst in some people, but this is viewed in a different light when executed under the appropriate, if convenient, banner of freedom. I mention this because, world events are, to a degree, determined by the people who live on this planet, so although Gaia might make constant adjustments to accommodate her errant progeny, sooner or later she is likely to either pack them off to a detention centre for reprogramming or dispossess them entirely! In other words, she will precipitate a calamity that will have that effect.

There is a theory that because of the way we are desecrating the Earth we are making Gaia ill, and should the point arise when she is no longer able to heal herself, she will seek external help, which might be what happened in the Atlantean context. By 'external help' I mean the intrusion of a foreign body calculated to rid her of the virus that is afflicting her and causing her so much pain – humankind!

This brings me round to the question of future axis tilts. Some thirty years ago I can recall being told through a channelling that the axis of the Earth would tilt again as it did at the time of the sinking of Atlantis, and that this event would take place in the lifetimes of some of those present. Some of us, in the eagerness of our youth, looked forward to the event as though the proof of the prophecy were the most important thing. But others among us, myself included, viewed this future cloud with apprehension. Visions of a world without public utilities, food, clothing, or communications, in which cold places became suddenly warm and sunnier climes experienced extremes of cold for which they were totally unprepared had a nightmarish quality about it. As the years rolled by, many of us slipped into complacency. It was, we rationalized, one of those psychic 'misses' that sometimes occur, even with the best mediums. And then, quite suddenly, we found we were no longer alone in our knowledge. Others, all around the world, had also received it. Dr Wolff was right.

Edgar Cayce had foretold that in 1968 a segment of old Atlantis would be discovered. American author Brad Steiger tells us:

On August 23 1968, Robert Cummings, Canadian broadcast journalist, excitedly tore the following news item from the studio teletype and put it in an envelope addressed to me:

ATLANTIS
MIAMI, FLORIDA — A NOTED ARCHAEOLOGIST REPORTS WHAT HE CALLS 'EXCITING AND DISTURBING' DISCOVERY IN BAHAMIAN WATERS OF AN ANCIENT 'TEMPLE'. DR MANSON VALENTINE SPECULATES IT MIGHT BE PART OF THE LEGENDARY LOST CONTINENT OF ATLANTIS . . .[5]

In fact, Cayce made several prophecies concerning the eventual reappearance of the Atlantean land mass including:

Poseidia will be among the first portions of Atlantis to rise again — expect it in '68 and '69 — not so far away . . .

As to the physical changes again: The Earth will be broken up in the western portion of America. The greater portion of Japan must go into the sea. The upper portion of Europe will be changed as in the twinkling of an eye. Land will appear off the east coast of America.

There will be upheavals in the Arctic and in the Antarctic that will make for the eruption of volcanoes in the Torrid areas, and there will be the shifting then of the poles – so that where there have been those of a frigid or semitropical [sic] will become the more tropical, and moss and fern will grow . . .

. . . lands will appear in the Atlantic as well as in the Pacific, and what is the coastline now of many a land will be bed of the ocean. Even many of the battlefields of the present [1941] will be ocean, will be the seas, the bays, the lands over which the new order will carry on their trade as one with another . . .

Portions of the now east coast of New York, or New York City itself, will in main disappear. This will be another generation, though, here; while the southern portions of Carolina, Georgia, these will disappear. This will be much sooner.

The waters of the lakes [Great Lakes] will empty into the Gulf [Gulf of Mexico] rather than the waterway over which such discussions have been recently made . . . [St Lawrence Seaway].

Then the area where the entity is now located [Virginia Beach] will be among the safety lands – as will be portions of what is now Ohio, Indiana and Illinois and much of the southern portion of Canada, and the eastern portion of Canada; while the western land, much of that is to be disturbed in this land, as, of course, much in other lands.

The earth will be broken up in many places. The early portion will see a change in the physical aspect of the west coast of America. There will be open waters in the northern portion of Greenland. There will be new lands seen off the Caribbean Sea and dry land will appear – South America shall be shaken from the uppermost portion to the end, and in the Antarctic off Tierra Del Fuego, land, and a strait with rushing waters.[6]*

Other seers, well-known and otherwise, have also added

their weight to the Atlantis rising/future cataclysm theory, including Daphne Vigers, whose enchanting book was mentioned in Chapter 13; the noted American seeress Jean Dixon, and numerous other psychics and channellers in the UK, USA, Australia, New Zealand, Ireland, France, Germany, Holland, Italy, Spain, India, and even the Soviet Union. In fact, the belief in these future events appears to be firmly established in world consciousness, its timing lending credence to Jung's 'Law of Synchronicity'.

Nor are the modern seers alone in their prognostications. They are joined in their beliefs by many famous names from the past, including Nostradamus and Mother Shipton, while that all-time best-seller, the Christian Bible, is more than generous with its forecasts of doom and destruction. There are, however, several books on the subject to which the interested reader may refer, notably *The Story of Prophecy Fulfilled* by the late Justine Glass, and *After Nostradamus: Great Prophecies for the Future of Mankind* by the Italian writer A. Woldben, translated by Cambridge scholar Gavin Gibbons. The legends of many countries are also as rich in references to the future as they are to the past. The Berbers, for example, who acknowledge that their ancient homeland originally lay off the coast of Africa, have among their legends a prophecy that it will one day reappear, while many Amerindian tribes firmly believe that the island in the ocean from which their ancestors originally came is destined to see daylight once again at some unspecified future date.

I am reminded of the words of the Greek historians that I recounted in the final two paragraphs of Chapter 4; that cataclysmic ends to great civilizations occur every 10,000

---

* Reprinted by permission of Warner Books/New York from *Edgar Cayce on Atlantis* by Edgar Cayce. Copyright 1968 by the Association for Research and Enlightenment, Inc.

years. Taking, for example Muck's estimated date of 8498 BC for the Atlantean inundation or, better still, the later dates proposed by Mooney, Ivimy, Spence and others, it would seem that we are uncomfortably close to the extreme arc of the pendulum's swing. Panic talk? Maybe. The increase in minor seismic disturbances in certain parts of California are hardly guaranteed to put one's mind at rest. However, as one Australian recently replied to a television interviewer when questioned about the 'greenhouse effect', 'Don't believe a word of it. Nutty professors have been coming up with this kind of rubbish for years and we're still here!' Whereupon he downed his can of lager and lit another cigar! In the final analysis I can only reiterate my earlier words that people believe what they want to believe. Perhaps our Australian friend may one day be in for a rude awakening, or maybe it will be the seers, who for once are in the reassuring company of the scientists, who will eat their words. *Quien sabe?*

I can already hear some of my readers/critics saying, 'She has given us all these various views, backed by a barrage of confusing and often contradictory facts and figures, of what other people see as the cause of the Atlantean disaster. But she doesn't tell us which one is correct.'

That is something I would not presume to do, for although I may have my own thoughts on the subject, I have absolutely no proof as to their accuracy or reliability. There certainly seems to be plenty of evidence to suggest that our planet was hit by some object, be it a comet, planetesimal or asteroid, in the past, as it might well be again in the future; but I cannot help thinking that somewhere, somehow, the Moon had a hand in it all. I am convinced, however, that at the time of the Atlantean cataclysm the axis of the Earth was altered, the poles shifted, the planet moved ever so slightly away from the Sun, and the year gained five extra days as a result. I am also of the opinion that the major evolutionary developments that take place on this planet are closely tied in with the binary star Sirius and its dark companion, Sirius B.

And as a final parting shot: no, I do not think Gaia will take much more from her unruly and destructive brood. She may well deem a good shake-up to be the only answer, although as regards the final outcome, perhaps there is some comfort to be found in the prophetic words of Plutarch:

. . . there will become a fated and predestined time when the earth will be completely levelled, united and equal, there will be but one mode of life and but one form of government among mankind who will all speak of one language and will live happily.

Isis and Osiris[7]

One must, however, keep an open mind to allow for logical adjustments in the face of new evidence, and with that I will rest my case.

Notes on Sources

Where an abbreviated reference is given below, full details of the work referred to will be found in the Bibliography

CHAPTER 1. *The Atlantis Legend*
1 Berlitz, *Atlantis*, p. 20.
2 Lemesurier, pp. 272–3.
3 Spanuth, p. 31.
4 Muck, p. 97.
5 Graves, *vol. 1*, p. 281.

CHAPTER 2. *Plato's Atlantis*
1 Donnelly, pp. 6–21.

CHAPTER 3. *Question Marks*
1 Bellamy, *The Atlantis Myth*, p. 15.
2 Muck, p. 299.
3 Gill, p. 53.
4 Ibid., p. ix.
5 Ivimy, p. 96.
6 Jung, p. 17.
7 Scrutton, p. 167.
8 Ibid., pp. 16–17.
9 Bramwell, pp. 69–70.
10 Donnelly, p. 299.
11 Ivimy, p. 52.
12 Tomas, A. *Atlantis – From Legend to Discovery*, p. 25.
13 Ibid., p. 105.
14 Berlitz, *Atlantis*, p. 135.
15 Emery, pp. 39–40.
16 Donnelly, p. 125.

17 Spence, *The History of Atlantis*, p. 32.

CHAPTER 4. *Alternative Sites*

1 Donnelly, p. 37.
2 1 Kings 10:22–3.
3 Spanuth, p. 30.
4 Ibid., p. 21.
5 Mooney, pp. 133–4.
6 Scrutton, p. 25.
7 Braghine, pp. 30–31.
8 Ibid., p. 31.
9 Berlitz, *Atlantis*, p. 70.
10 Ibid., p. 71.
11 Donnelly, p. 34.
12 Berlitz, op. cit., p. 74.

CHAPTER 5. *The Atlantic Ocean*

1 Berlitz, *Atlantis*, p. 74.
2 Eysenck and Sargent, p. 184.
3 Tomas, A., *Atlantis – From Legend to Discovery*, p. 95.
4 Donnelly, pp. 46–9.
5 *Science*, no. 181, 31 August 1973, pp. 803–9.
6 Goodman, p. 166.
7 Muck, p. 137.
8 Muck, *The Secret of Atlantis*, p. 144.
9 Ibid., p. 145.
10 Berlitz, op. cit., p. 159.
11 Ibid., pp. 78–9.
12 Ibid., p. 84.
13 Ibid., pp. 83–4.
14 Ibid., pp. 84–5.
15 Ibid., p. 85.
16 Ibid., p. 86.
17 Ibid., p. 86.
18 Donnelly, p. 173.
19 Wood, p. 262.

CHAPTER 6. *Asteroids, Moons and Axis Tilts*

1 Tomas, A. *Atlantis – From Legend to Discovery*, p. 133.
2 Muck, p. 151.
3 Ibid., p. 183.
4 Ibid., p. 183.

5 Tomas, op. cit., p. 31.

6 Ibid., p. 30.

7 *New Scientist*, 24/31 December 1988, p. 6.

8 Muck, pp. 167–8.

9 Ibid., p. 169.

10 Allaby and Lovelock, p. 31.

11 Moore, pp. 204–13.

12 Scrutton, p. 48.

13 Hapgood, p. 178.

14 Muck, p. 220.

15 Scrutton, p. 50.

16 Hapgood, pp. 174–5.

17 Hapgood, p. 175.

18 Goodman, pp. 161–2.

19 W. K. Hartmann, 'Piecing Together Earth's Early History' *Astronomy*, vol. 17, no. 6, June 1989, pp. 24–34.

20 Horton E. Newsom & Stuart Ross Taylor, 'Geochemical implications of the formation of the Moon by a single giant impact', *Nature*, vol. 338, 2 March 1989, pp. 29–34.

21 Braghine, p. 105.

22 Ibid.

23 Muck, p. 176.

24 Saurat, p. 11.

25 Mooney, p. 109.

26 Goodman, pp. 160–61.

CHAPTER 7. *Cycles, Time Scales and Dates*

1 Donnelly, p. 8.

2 Mitton, p. 171.

3 Gauquelin, p. 105.

4 Guirand, p. 98.

5 Ibid., p. 99.

6 Berlitz, *Atlantis*, pp. 193–4.

7 Gleick, p. 7.

8 P. Davies, p. 19.

9 Ibid., p. 20.

10 Tomas, *We Are Not the First*, p. 71.

11 Ibid., p. 117.

12 West, pp. 113–14.

13 Muck, p. 247.

14 Ibid., p. 253.

15 Spence, *The History of Atlantis*, p. 210.

16 Scrutton, p. 44.

17 Taylor and Dee, pp. 38–9.

18 Mooney, pp. 95–6.

19 Ibid., p. 97.

20 Heinberg, p. 111.

21 Ibid., p. 89.

CHAPTER 8. *Atlantis and Her Peoples*

1 Tomas, *Atlantis – From Legend to Discovery*, p. 20.

2 Ibid., p. 30.

3 Muck, p. 86.

4 Ibid., p. 109.

5 Ibid., p. 111.

6 Mooney, p. 105.

7 Paul Simons, 'Picking their brains 7,000 years later,' *Guardian*, 1 December 1989.

8 Braghine, p. 148.

9 Scrutton, p. 28.

10 Braghine, pp. 31–2.

11 Lemesurier, p. 278.

12 Mourant, p. 62.

13 I. Morgan Watkins, 'ABO Blood Group Distribution in Wales in Relation to Human Settlement', in Harper and Sunderland, pp. 118–40.

14 Mourant, p. 67.

15 Spence, op. cit., p. 76.

16 Donnelly, p. 236.

17 Heinberg, p. 205.

18 Berlitz, *Atlantis*, p. 175.

19 Donnelly, p. 432.

20 Berlitz, op. cit., pp. 60–61.

21 Ibid., pp. 60–61.

CHAPTER 9. *Religion and Science in Atlantis*

1 Tomas, *Atlantis – From Legend to Discovery*, p. 18.

2 Gill, p. 59.

3 Hoyle, p. 158.

4 Tomas, op. cit., pp. 44, 47.

5 Tomas, op. cit., p. 76.

6 Tomas, loc. cit.

7 Berlitz, *Atlantis*, p. 129.

8 Mead, *Thrice Greatest Hermes*, vol. 3, p. 225.

9 Quinn, p. 128.

10 Donnelly, p. 290.

11 Quinn, p. 134.

CHAPTER 10. *Colonies, Missions and Safe Havens*

1 Aldred, p. 70.
2 Donnelly, pp. 131–2.
3 Schwaller de Lubicz, pp. 26–7.
4 Ibid., p. 27.
5 Ibid., p. 28.
6 Ibid., p. 62.
7 Ibid., pp. 177–9.
8 Ibid., p. 170.
9 Ibid., p. 86.
10 John J. Putnam, 'The Search for Modern Humans', *National Geographic*, vol. 174, no. 4, October 1988, p. 467.
11 West, pp. 198–9.
12 Mead, *Thrice Greatest Hermes*, vol. 3, pp. 111–13.
13 Ibid., pp. 180–81.
14 Plato, pp. 131–3.
15 Scrutton, p. 125.
16 Ibid., p. 107.
17 Cirlot, p. 141.
18 Maspero, p. 546.
19 Donnelly, pp. 75–6.
20 Ibid., p. 185.
21 Ibid., pp. 111–12.
22 Berlitz, *Atlantis*, pp. 96–7.
23 Braghine, p. 39.
24 Donnelly, p. 106.
25 Spence, *The History of Atlantis*, p. 64.
26 Budge, vol. 2, p. 361.

CHAPTER 11. *Atlantean Heritage*

1 Lemesurier, p. 8.
2 Ibid., p. 15.
3 Mead, *Thrice Greatest Hermes*, vol. 1, p. 104.
4 Ibid., pp. 104–5.
5 Tomas, *Atlantis – From Legend to Discovery*, pp. 91–2.
6 Hope, *Practical Egyptian Magic*, p. 62.
7 Tomas, op. cit., pp. 114–15.
8 Mooney, p. 198.
9 Muck, p. 104–5.
10 Tomas, op. cit., p. 48.
11 Donnelly, p. 417.

12 Rolleston, p. 37.
13 E. Davies, p. 3.
14 Donnelly, p. 411.
15 Quinn, p. 93.
16 Ibid., pp. 95–6.
17 Scrutton, p. 248.
18 Anthony Tucker, 'The incredible shrinking alloy', *Guardian*, 4 July 1989.
19 Berlitz, *Atlantis*, p. 101.

CHAPTER 12. *Torch-Bearing Collectives*
1 Scott-Elliot, pp. 17–19.
2 Steiner, p. 43.
3 Ibid., p. 253.
4 Cayce, *Edgar Cayce on Atlantis*, pp. 53–4.
5 Cayce, *Edgar Cayce's Story of the Origin and Destiny of Man*, pp. 58–9.

CHAPTER 13. *Akashic Anomalies*
1 Mead, *Fragments of a Faith Forgotten*, pp. 139–40.
2 Richardson, *Priestess*, p. 31.
3 Jack A. Heinemann and George F. Sprague Jr, 'Bacterial conjugative plasmids mobilize DNA transfer between bacteria and yeast', *Nature*, vol. 340, no. 6230, 20 July 1989, pp. 205–9.
4 Richardson, *Dancers to the Gods*.
5 Ibid.
6 Cayce, *Edgar Cayce on Atlantis*, p. 157.
7 Steiger, p. 116.

CHAPTER 14. *Is Chaos Returning?*
1 Hapgood, pp. 188–9.
2 Ibid. p. 190.
3 P. Davies, p. 131.
4 Ibid., p. 132.
5 Steiger, p. 147.
6 Cayce, *Edgar Cayce on Atlantis*, pp. 159–60.
7 Tomas, *Atlantis – From Legend to Discovery*, p. 133.

Bibliography

Aldred, Cyril, *The Egyptians*, London, Thames & Hudson, 1961.

Allaby, M. & Lovelock, J., *The Great Extinction*, London, Paladin Books, 1985.

Alper, Frank *Exploring Atlantis*, Phoenix, Arizona Metaphysical Society, 1981.

Bellamy, H. S., *The Atlantis Myth*, London, Faber & Faber, 1948.

Bellamy, H. S., *Moons, Myths and Man*, London, Faber & Faber, 1950.

Berlitz, Charles, *The Mystery of Atlantis*, London, Souvenir Press, 1969.

Berlitz, Charles, *Atlantis*, London, Macmillan, 1984.

Bonewitz, R. A., *Cosmic Crystals*, Wellingborough, Northants, Turnstone Press, 1986.

Braghine, A., *The Shadow of Atlantis*, Wellingborough, Northants, Aquarian Press, 1980.

Bramwell, James, *Lost Atlantis*, Los Angeles, Newcastle Pub. Co. Inc., 1974.

Braude, Stephen, *The Limits of Influence*, London, Routledge & Kegan Paul, 1986.

Budge, E. A. Wallis, *The Gods of The Egyptians*, New York, Dover Publications, 1969.

Cayce, Edgar, *Edgar Cayce on Atlantis*, New York, Warner Books, 1968.

Cayce, Edgar, *Edgar Cayce's Story of the Origin and Destiny of Man*, New York, Berkeley Books, 1972.

Charpentier, Louis, *La mystère basque*, Paris, La Font, 1975.

Cirlot, C. E., *Dictionary of Symbols*, London, Routledge & Kegan Paul, 1961.

Cumont, Franz, *Astrology and Religion Among the Greeks and Romans*, New York, Dover Publications, 1960.

Bibliography

Davies, Edward, *The Mythology and Rites of the British Druids*, London, 1909.

Davies, P., *The Cosmic Blueprint*, London, Unwin Hyman, 1989.

Donnelly, Ignatius, *Atlantis – The Antediluvian World*, London, Sampson, Low, Marston & Co. Ltd, 1882.

Drake, W. Raymond, *Gods and Spacemen Throughout History*, London, Sphere Books, 1977.

Emery, W. B., *Archaic Egypt*, London, Penguin Books, 1971.

Eysenck, Hans & Sargent, Carl, *Explaining the Unexplained*, London, Weidenfeld & Nicolson, 1982.

Forman, Joan, *The Mask of Time*, London, Corgi Books, 1978.

Gauquelin, Michael, *The Cosmic Clocks*, St Albans, Granada Publications, 1980.

Gill, Christopher, *Plato – The Atlantis Story*, Bristol, Bristol Classical Press, 1980.

Gleick, James, *Chaos: Making a New Science*, London, Heinemann, 1988.

Goodman, Jeffrey, *The Earthquake Generation*, London, Turnstone Books, 1979.

Graves, Robert, *The Greek Myths*, Vols. I & II, Harmondsworth, Penguin Books, 1984.

Guirand, Felix (ed.), *Larousse Encyclopedia of Mythology*, R. Aldington and D. Ames (trs.), London, Hamlyn, 1968.

Hapgood, Charles, *Maps of the Ancient Sea Kings*, London, Turnstone Books, 1979.

Harper, P. S. and Sunderland, E. (eds.), *Genetic and Population Studies in Wales*, Cardiff, Cardiff University Press, 1986.

Heinberg, Richard, *Memories & Visions of Paradise*, Los Angeles, Jeremy Tarcher Inc., 1989.

Hone, Margaret, *The Modern Textbook of Astrology*, London, Fowler & Co. Ltd, 1975.

Hope, Murry, *The Story of Isis and Osiris*, Enniscorthy, Eire, Cesara Publications, 1974.

Hope, Murry, *Practical Egyptian Magic*, Wellingborough, Northants, Aquarian Press, 1984.

Hope, Murry, *Practical Celtic Magic*, Wellingborough, Northants, Aquarian Press, 1987.

Hope, Murry, *The Psychology of Ritual*, Shaftesbury, Element Books, 1988.

Hope, Murry, *The Lion People*, Chichester, Thoth Publications, 1988.

Hope, Murry, *The Elements of Greek Tradition*, Shaftesbury, Element Books, 1989.

Hope, Murry, *Ancient Egypt – the Sirius Connection*, Shaftesbury, Element Books, 1990.

Hoyle, Fred, *The Intelligent Universe*, London, Michael Joseph, 1983.

Iamblichos, *The Egyptian Mysteries*, London, Rider and Sons Ltd, 1911.

Ivimy, John, *The Sphinx and the Megaliths*, London, Abacus Books, 1976.

Jung, C. G., *Memories, Dreams and Reflections*, London, Routledge & Kegan Paul, 1963.

Lamy, Lucie, *Egyptian Mysteries*, London, Thames and Hudson, 1981.

Lee, Dal, *A Dictionary of Astrology*, London, Sphere Books, 1969.

Lemesurier, Peter, *The Great Pyramid Decoded*, Tisbury, Wiltshire, Compton Russell Elements, 1977.

Luce, J. V., *The End of Atlantis*, Book Club Associates, London, 1973.

Maspero, Gaston, *The Dawn of Civilization*, London, The Society for Promoting Christian Knowledge, 1910.

Mead, G. R. S., *Thrice Greatest Hermes*, London, Theosophical Publishing Co., 1906.

Mead, G. R. S., *Fragments of a Faith Forgotten*, London, John M. Watkins, 1931.

Mitton, Simon (ed.), *The Cambridge Encyclopedia of Astronomy*, Cambridge, CUP, 1977.

Mooney, Richard, *Colony Earth*, London, Souvenir Press, 1974.

Moore, Patrick (ed.), *1987 Yearbook of Astronomy*, London, Sidgwick & Jackson, 1986.

Mourant, A. E., *Distribution of Human Blood Groups*, 2nd edn, Oxford, OUP, 1976.

Muck, Otto, *The Secret of Atlantis*, Fred Bradley (trs.), London, Collins, 1978.

Pauwels, Louis and Bergier, Jacques, *The Morning of the Magicians*, St Albans, Granada Publishing, 1979.

Plato, *Timaeus and Critias*, Desmond Lee (trs.), London, Penguin Books, 1977.

Quinn, Bob, *Atlantean*, London, Quartet Books, 1986.

Richardson, Alan, *Dancers to the Gods*, Wellingborough, Northants, Aquarian Press, 1985.

Richardson, Alan, *Priestess*, Wellingborough, Northants, Aquarian Press, 1986.

Rolleston, T. W., *Myths and Legends of the Celtic Race*, London, George G. Harrap, 1911.

Saurat, Denis, *Atlantis and the Giants*, London, Faber & Faber, 1957.

Scott-Elliot, Col. W., *The Story of Atlantis*, Benares, India, Theosophical Publishing Co., 1896.

Scrutton, Robert, *The Other Atlantis*, Jersey, Neville Spearman, 1977.

Schwaller de Lubicz, R. A., *Sacred Science*, Rochester, Vermont, Inner Traditions International, 1961.

Spanuth, Jergen, *Atlantis of the North*, London, Sidgwick & Jackson, 1979.

Spence, Lewis, *The History of Atlantis*, New York, University Books, Inc., 1968.

Spence, Lewis, *Will Europe Follow Atlantis?*, London, Rider, (undated).

Steiger, Brad, *Atlantis Rising*, New York, Berkeley Books, 1981.

Steiner, Rudolf, *Cosmic Memory*, San Francisco, Harper and Row, 1969.

Taylor, Stephen and Dee, Nerys, *Atlantis, Past and to Come*, Malvern, Atlanteans Association Ltd, 1968.

Tomas, Andrew, *We Are Not the First*, London, Souvenir Press, 1971.

Tomas, Andrew, *Atlantis – From Legend to Discovery*, London, Robert Hale, 1972.

Tomas, Andrew, *Beyond the Time Barrier*, London, Sphere Books, 1974.

Vigers, Daphne, *Atlantis Rising*, London, Andrew Dakers, 1944.

Watson, Lyall, *Lifetide*, London, Sceptre Books, 1987.

West, John A., *Serpent in the Sky*, New York, Julian Press, 1987.

Wilber, Ken, *Quantum Questions*, Boston, Mass, New Science Library, 1985.

Wood, David, *Genisis*, Tunbridge Wells, Baton Press, 1985.

Index

Page numbers in *italic* refer to the illustrations and captions

Abd el Latif, 251

Aborigines, 170, 174, 322

Abou Hormeis papyrus, 140, 251

Abramov, A. K., 248–9

Academician Petrovsky, 83–8

Adam, 164–5, 175–6, 192, 224

Adamis, 315

Adonis (asteroid group), 98, 99

Adriatic Sea, 51

Aelian, 10, 180–1

Africa: Atlantean colonies, 237–8; blood groups, 169, 171; earliest man, 165; ice sheets, 110; and Lemuria, 116; oral tradition, 320; racial types, 163; as site for Atlantis, 53; tribal names, 6

Agadir earthquake, 150

Age of Cronus, 187–8

'Ages of Man', 132–4, 139

Aidos, 134

airships, 286

Akashic Records, 2, 153, 247, 290–1, 318

Akeru, 140

Akkadians, 284, 286

Aksyonov, Andrei, 86–7

Alcinous, 39–40

Aldred, Cyril, 206

Alexandria, 265

aliens, 138, 188–9, 313

Allaby, Michael, 100–1

Alper, Dr Frank, 315, 331

Alpha Draconis, 129

alphabets, 176

altered states of consciousness (ASCs), 174–5

Alvarez, Dr Luis, 249–50

American Geophysical Union, 97

Amerindians, 158, 164, 171–2, 182, 335

Ammianus Marcellinus, 44

Amon, 211

Ampere seamount, 84, 85–7

Amphitrite, 52

Amratian period, 206

Andes mountains, 60, 63, 330

Angkor Thom, 37

animals, 180

Antarctica, 330; axis tilts, 56,
109; glaciation, 146, 326;
maps, 147, 262, 263, 265,
321; as site of Atlantis, 61;
South Pole, 56, 106, 109,
313, 326

Anthroposophy, 122, 289–91

Anubis, 176

Aquarian Age, 131, 142, 305

Aquarius, 142

Arabia, 115

Arabs, 7, 163, 203, 260

Aran Islanders, 261

Aravacs, 117

Arcadia, 5

archaeology, 325

Arctic, 9, 106; North Pole, 56,
106, 107, 108, 109, 129,
313, 325–6

Argentina, 111

Argonauts, 51

Arian Age, 130, 131

Ariége, 174

Aries, 129, 130

Aristophanes, 32

Aristotle, 12

Arnobius, 46

art, 173–5

Arthur, King, 294, 312

Aryabhatiya, 151

Aryans, 151, 162–3, 164, 259,
273

Asia, 164, 170, 330

Assurbanipal IV, King of
Assyria, 43, 226

Assyria, 43, 226, 325

asteroids, 9, 93, 94–102, 114, 115,
144, 145, 147, 197

astral travel, 257

astrology, 129–32, 139–42, 194

astronauts, 196, 313

astronomy, 93–102, 134–5, 194,
226, 242, 326

Astronomy (magazine), 112–13

Atahualpa, 165–6

Athene, 35, 192, 193, 219–20, 221

Athens, 33, 34, 55, 219–23

Atlantean Society, 292–5

Atlantes, Lake, 52

Atlantic Ocean: *Academician
Petrovsky* photographs,
83–8; continental drift,
68–76, 73–5; *Jesmond*'s
evidence, 79–82; map of
Atlantis, 69; sea-bed
evidence, 67–8;
underwater volcanoes,
76–9

Atlantic Ridge, 74, 75, 76, 84, 89

Atlas, 8–10, 20, 194, 234

Atlas Mountains, 237

atomic energy, 197–8

atomic theory, 213

Australia, 111, 170

Avalon, 5, 6

Avebury, 151

axis tilts, 72, 93, 95, 102–12,
119–25, 150, 161, 293, 294,
296, 313, 332–5

Azilian-Tardenoisian men, 173–4
Azores, 6, 68, 78–9, 87, 89–90, 90, 159, 262
Aztecs, 7, 87, 162, 165–6, 234–5, 285

Baal, 187, 231
Babel, Tower of, 183
Babylonians, 134, 143, 151, 153, 187, 196, 226–8, 251, 325
Bacon, Francis, 58
Bacstrom, Dr Sigismund, 139, 212
Bahama Banks, 82, 232–3, 267–8
Baikal, Lake, 106
Bambara tribe, 238
Barinov, M., 84
Basques, 6, 88, 167, 169, 172, 242
Bast, 125, 187
BBC, 174
Bellamy, H. S., 112
Berbers, 6, 167, 171, 172, 237, 258, 259, 261, 335
Bergson, Henri, 310
Berlin Museum, 196
Berlitz, Charles, 60–1, 62, 64, 79, 81, 84, 86, 87, 89, 181–2, 197, 200, 233, 267–8, 310
Bermuda, 89
Bermuda Triangle, 197, 268
Berossus, 134, 224, 226–7
Berry, Adrian, 138

Bias, 34
Bibby, Geoffrey, 325
Bible, 51, 121, 165, 179, 226, 335
Bible of the Mayas, 100
Big Bang theory, 137
Bimini, 232–3, 235, 296, 312
'Black Eve', 238
Black Sea, 51, 63
Blandford, 116
Blessed Isles, 5, 186
blood groups, 167, 169–73, 229–30
Bochica, 234
Bogota, 234
Bohica, 117
Bolivia, 60, 235
Book of Sothis, 247–8
Borchard, Dr Paul, 52
Botta, Paul Emile, 325
Boudicca, Queen, 258
Bowles, Reverend, 151
Bozo tribe, 238
Braghine, A., 59, 94, 115–17, 147–50, 164, 166, 169, 234, 259, 310
Brahma, Year of, 138
Bramwell, James, 40
Brasseur de Bourbourg, Abbé, 59, 60, 68–71
Brazen Age *see* Bronze Age
Brazil, 60–1, 111, 166, 235
Breuil, Abbé, 173
Britain, 63, 106, 109, 306, 308
British Honduras, 296
British Museum, 81

Brittany, 171, 260, 262, 306
Bronze Age, 81–2, 133, 206, 322
Bryusov, V., 83
Buddha, 163
Buffon, Comte de, 262
bull cults, 190, 193–4, 211, 212,
    240
Bushmen, 117, 174, 238, 322
Byrd, Richard, 147
Byron, Lord, 48

Cadiz, 87–8
calendars, 151–4, 207–10
California, 336
Calypso, 38, 40
Canadian shield, 76
Canary Islands, 6–7, 89, 163,
    167, 238
Cancer, Age of, 114, 130,
    131–2, 139, 188, 191, 309
Cape Verde Islands, 89
carbon-14 dating, 144
Caribbean, 82, 94, 163
Carthage, 52
caste system, 162–3
Catlin, George, 230–1
Caucasus, 167, 171
Cavaglia, 216
cave paintings, 174–5
Cay Sal Bank, 267
Cayce, Edgar, 232, 295–9, 312,
    331, 333–4
Cecrops, 221–2
Celts, 308; ancestors, 6, 238–9;
    blood groups, 170–1, 172;
    Hu Gadarn, 142, 240;

inheritance from
    Atlanteans, 257–62;
    magical powers of number
    nine, 153; religion, 187,
    237
Central America, 7, 58–60, 118,
    167, 170, 180, 196, 234–7
Ceres (asteroid), 98
Chalcolithic period, 206
Chaldeans, 127, 224–8, 242, 313
Chaldee language, 181
Challenger, HMS, 70, 71
Champollion, Jean François, 325
channelling, 272–3, 292–3, 331
chaos science, 136, 318–19,
    331–2
Charente valley, 167
Charpentier, Louis, 167
Cheops, 244
Chephren, Pharaoh, 216–17
Chibcha Indians, 117, 234
Chilam Balams, 100
Chilon, 34
China: calendar, 152, 153;
    changes to coast-line, 63;
    comets, 102; evidence of
    axis tilts, 103, 111;
    giant fossils, 121; language,
    176, 181; technology, 199
Christianity, 165
Chultun Beyli, Prince, 255
Cicero, 143
Cirlot, J. E., 222
clairvoyance, 257
Cleito, 188, 194
Clement of Alexandria, 202

Cleobulus, 34
climate: Atlantis, 159–61;
    changes in, 93, 97, 103–11,
    119–21, 127–8, 147, 210
Codex Chimalpopoca, 118
Codex Troanus, 59, 60, 144
collective unconscious, 2, 175,
    291
Colombia, 117
colonies, 205–42
Columbia, 166
Columbia (space shuttle), 62
comets, 101–2, 147, 197
Companions of Horus, 214
conquistadores, 7
consciousness, altered states of,
    174–5
constellations, 129–30
continental drift, 68–76, *73–5*
Copts, 252
Cornwall, 171, 263
Costa, J. de, 152
Cox, Dr Allan, 72
Cradock, Johnny, 310
Cradock, Phyllis, 310
Crantor, 44
creation myths, 190, 226
Cretaceous period, 100–1
Crete, 35–6, 49, 55, 184, 211,
    322, 325
Critias, 12–29, 32–3
Cro-Magnon man, 165, 167–9,
    173, 254, 255
Croesus, 33
Cronus, 57, 132, 134, 154, 187,
    188, 194

cross of Atlantis, *23*
crystal power, 202, 265–7, 315,
    317
Ctesias, 151
Cummings, Robert, 333
Cumont, Franz, 42–3
Cushites, 163
Cuvier, Georges, 74
cycles of periodicity, 126–9
Czechoslovakia, 97

Dakota Indians, 163
Dalrymple, Dr Brent, 72
Danaans, 203–4
Danube, River, 259
dates, 142–51
Davies, Rev. Edward, 240, 258
Davies, Paul, 137, 327–8
Dee, Nerys, 150–1
Deevey, Edward S., 105
Deluge *see* Flood legends
Democritus, 32, 213
Denderah, 200
Denderah Zodiac, 111, 140–1,
    141
dendrochronology, 144
Denmark, 106
Diana of the Golden Triangle
    Fellowship, 301
Dio Cassius, 258
Diodorus Siculus, 44–5, 186–7,
    244, 256
Diogenes Laertius, 143
Dioscuria, 51
Dixon, Jean, 335
DNA, 163–4, 307

Doell, Dr Richard, 72
Dogger Bank, 263
Dogon tribe, 138, 218, 238, 326
Dolphin, USS, 70
Dolphin's Ridge, 71
Donnelly, Ignatius, 7–8, 11, 50,
    63, 67–8, 71, 82, 87–8,
    162–3, 175–6, 180, 181,
    186–7, 206–7, 222, 230, 232,
    235, 256, 259, 310, 315
Donnelly, Joseph W., 313
Dordogne, 167
Douro valley, 167
dreams, 294
Druids, 38, 258, 306, 308, 311
Duke University, 79
Dunne, J. W., 310

earthquakes, 150–1
East Africa, 53
Easter Island, 255
Ebers papyrus, 151, 202
eclipses, 127, 128
Eddas, 8
Edgar Cayce Foundation, 295–9
Edhem, Halil, 264–5
Efremov, Professor, 96, 114
Egypt, 35, 40, 50, 62, 167, 254;
    as Atlantean colony, 11,
    43–5, 54, 55, 59, 205–19;
    blood groups, 172;
    calendar, 151, 153–4; and
    date of Atlantis, 139–42;
    evidence of axis tilts, 105,
    122–5; medicine, 202;
    pyramids, 244–53; racial

types, 162; religion, 187,
    190–1, 193; technology,
    199–200; written histories,
    176
Einstein, Albert, 67, 88, 198
El-Baz, Farouk, 97
elephants, 180
Emerald Tables of Hermes, 139,
    191, 212–13
Emery, W. B., 45
energy sources, 197–202, 298–9,
    317
English language, 181–2
epagomenal days, 151–4, 209
equinoxes, precession of, 129,
    210
Eratosthenes, 37
Erewhon, 5
Eskimos, 103, 190
ESP (extrasensory perception),
    257, 301
Ethiopians, 163
Etruria, Etruscans, 51, 62, 242,
    254
Euclid, 34
Euphrates, 194, 196
Eurasia, 76
Euripides, 32
Europe: blood groups, 170;
    continental drift, 75–6; Ice
    age, 61, 109
Eusebius, 37
Evans, Sir Arthur, 325
Eve, 192, 224
Evenor, 188
Ewing, Dr Maurice, 84, 88

Excalibur, 294
'Experimenter Effect', 88
Eye of Ra, 124
Eysenck, Hans, 2, 66–7

'fairy people', 132, 239–40
far memory, 257, 316
Filipoff, L., 139
Firazabadi, Dictionary of, 251
Firbolgs, 203, 239, 259–60
Flood legends, 7, 43; and axis
        tilts, 103, 105; biblical
        version, 226; in Egyptian
        accounts, 252; Gilgamesh
        epic, 226–8; Mandan
        Indians, 230–2
Formorians, 239
Fortune, Dion, 302–9, 318
France, 6, 89, 106, 167, 173–4
Fraternity of the Inner Light,
        302
Frisians, 8, 37–9, 54–8, 61, 165,
        221–3, 241, 258
Frobinius, Leo, 53
Gabes, Gulf of, 52
Gaia, 135, 195, 201, 294, 327–8,
        332, 337
Galanopoulos, A. G., 49
Galicia, 260
Gamov, George, 128
Garonne valley, 168
Gattefossé, R. M., 147–50
Gaul, 6, 259
Gaunches, 163
Geb, 153
Geikie, Professor, 50

Gemini, Age of, 130, 131
Genesis, Book of, 146, 175–6
genetic engineering, 188–9, 305,
        307–8, 313
genetics, 161–73, 188–9, 256–9
geography of Atlantis, 158–61,
        160
Germany, 58, 106
giants, 121, 169
Gibbons, Gavin, 335
Gibraltar, 85
Gilgamesh epic, 143, 226–8
Gill, Christopher, 34–6, 177,
        188–9
glaciation, 106, 110–1
Gladstone, William, 68
Glass, Justine, 335
Gleick, James, 1
Gnosticism, 301
gods and goddesses, 186–9,
        190–5, 223
Gohed, Dr Amir, 250
Golden Age, 5, 132, 155, 187–8
Golden Triangle Fellowship,
        301
Gondwanaland, 71, 116, 164
Goodman, Jeffrey, 72, 110
Gorbovsky, Alexander, 197
Goths, 176
Graves, Robert, 10, 204, 258
Great Pyramid, 215, 245–6,
        248–53
'Great Year', 129, 130, 134
Greece, 117, 242, 254; as
        Atlantean colony, 219–23;
        calendar, 153, 154; gods,

186, 187; Plato's legend of
Atlantis, 12–29, 30–6
'greenhouse effect', 63, 331,
336
Greenland, 61, 75–6, 104
Guadalquivir valley, 167
Guardian, 165, 266–7
Guatemala, 100
Guyana, 117
Gulf Stream, 93–4, 159–61, 186,
307
Gurdjieff, G. I., 216

Hades, 42, 46
Haeckel, Ernst, 71, 116
Halley's comet, 102
Hamites, 206
Hapgood, Dr Charles, 56, 61, *89*,
95, 103, 104, 105, 106–9,
116, 147, 263, 265, 293,
321–3, 324–6
Harappa, 197
Harris Papyrus, 111
Hartley, Christine, 309–10
Hartmann, William K., 113
Hartung, 78
Hasted, John, 138
Hathor, 124, 268–9
Hatshepsut, Queen, 111
Hawaii, 63
Hawkes, Jacquetta, 325
Hawking, Stephen, 136
healing, 202–3
health, influence of Sun and
Moon on, 129
Hebrews, 53, 175–6

Heezen, Dr Bruce, 63–4, 79, 84,
101, 102
Heinberg, Richard, 155, 179
Heinneman, Jack, 307
Heligoland, 54
Heliopolis, 211
Helios, 118
Helmholtz, Hermann von, 67, 136
Hephaestus, 219–20, 222
Hercules, Pillars of, 51
Hermann, Dr Albert, 52–3
Hermes, 139, 247–8
Hermes Trismegistus, 45, 139,
191, 217–18
Hermitage Papyrus, 111
Hermocrates of Syracuse, 32–3
Herodotus, 37, 42, 51–2, 124,
144, 206, 215, 244–5, 251
Hesiod, 52, 55, 132, 133, 134,
204
Himyaritic Arabians, 163
Hindus, 138, 151, 187, 218
Hindustan, 115
Hipparchus, 210
Hippocrates, 32
Hobbal, 203
Hoerbiger, Hans, 112, 113, 115,
117
Högbom, 78
Hohlenstein, 215
Homer, 30, 35, 39–40, 66
Hopi Indians, 122, 179
horses, 180, 223
Horseshoe Archipelago, 83–4
Horus, 142, 154, 209, 214, 217
Hoyle, Fred, 188–9

Hu Gadarn, 142, 240
Hudson Bay, 108, 109
Hyperboreans, 55

Iamblichus, 202
Iberians, 6, 88, 143
Ibn Abd Hokm, 252
Ibn Batuta, 251
Ibn ben Zara, 265, *266*
Ibn Haukal, 251
Ice Age, 56, 61, 64, 101, 102,
    105–6, 108–11, 120, 128,
    325–6
ice-caps, polar, 101, 106–10
Iceland, 169, 261
Incas, 152, 165–6, 167, 171–2,
    176, 235
India, 7, 110, 138, 162–3, 170,
    190, 196, 199
Indian Ocean, 115
Indians: Amerindians, 158, 164,
    171–2, 182–3, 335; North
    American, 7, 163, 164,
    168, 170, 229–32
Indus River, 325
'inner planes', 303–4, 305
Institute of Oceanography
    (USSR), 85
intercalary days, 151–4, 209
Ipuwer Papyrus, 111
Ireland: ancestor legends, 6, 132,
    203–4, 259–61; as Atlantean
    colony, 238–40, 256;
    blood groups, 169, 261;
    Bronze Age, 82; fossils,
    262; gods, 237

Iron Age, 133–4, 322
Isis, 154, 191, 217–18, 268
Islands of the Blessed, 5, 186
Isles of the Blest, 133
Ivimy, John, 36, 41, *336*

Japan, 169, 190
Java, 121
Jehovah, 192
Jesmond, S. S., 79–82
Jews, 229
Josephine (underwater
    mountain), 84
Josephus, 45, 176
Jung, Carl Gustav, 2, 37, 67, 335
Jupiter (god), 46
Jupiter (planet), 98, 150, 326
Jutland, 106

Kampuchea, 37
Karnac, 254
Kennedy, John F., 265
Kepler, Johannes, 98
Khasis, 190
Kircher, Athanasius, 90–1, *90*,
    329
Klenova, Dr Maria, 79
Knight, Gareth, 303–9
Knopoff, Dr Leon, 72
Konig, Wilhelm, 199
Krakatoa, 51
Kuhn de Porok, Count Byron,
    62

Lalande, Count Carli de, 94
Lamettrie, Julien de, 262

Lamont Geological
    Observatory, 84
Lamy, Lucie, 207, 212
Landa, Bishop Diego de, 147
language, 175–6, 181–3
lasers, 298
Layard, Henri, 325
Le Danois, 127–8
Lednev, N., 158
Leed, Dr A., 72
Le Grand, 176
Lemesurier, Peter, 7, 167, 245–6
Lemuria, 60, 215, 229, 255, 293,
    304, 330; cataclysm, 112,
    116, 157; legends of, 116;
    location, 71, 115–6; maps,
    275; racial groups, 164,
    166, 169, 172, 285
Leo, 111, 140, 142, 210, 217, 252
Leo, Age of, 130, 132, 188, 191
Le Plongeon, Auguste, 59
Lesser Antilles, 94
Leucippe, 188
Libran Age, 190
libraries, 323
Libyans, 206
lion symbolism, 122–4, *123*,
    140–2, 217, 218
lithosphere, 71–2, 108
Little Salt Spring, Florida, 163
Long, Mary, 301
Longfellow, Henry Wadsworth,
    300
Lovelock, James, 100–1, 327
Lubbock, Sir John, 82
Luce, J. V. 35–6, 49

Ludendorff, H., 143
Lugh, 237–8
Lumley-Brown, Margaret, 306
Lurasia, 71
Luxor, 207
Lyell, Sir Charles, 73
Lyonnesse, 262, 263, 306, 309

Mac Erc, 203
Madagascar, 111, 116
Madeira, 87, 89
magnetic field, Earth's, 72,
    106–9
magnetostriction, 266–7
Magyars, 58
Mahabharata, 7, 162–3
Makritzi, 140
Mali, 138, 238, 326
mammoths, 104–6
Mandan Indians, 163, 187,
    230–2, 235
Mandelbrot, Benoit, 136
Manetho, 45, 207, 246–8
Manilius, Gaius, 139
maps, 147, 262–5, 274–84, 321
Mariette, Auguste, 216
Marinatos, Dr Spiridon, 49
Mars, 98, 113, 131
Marshall, Ari, 267–8
Martini, Martinus, 111
Marukuyev, Vladimir
    Ivanovich, 85, 87
Le Mas d'Azil, 174
Masefield, John, 5
Maspero, Sir Gaston, 216
Masudi, 252

mathematics, 245–6, 248–9
Mauritania, 90
Mausola Purva, 196–7
Mayas, 59, 100, 117, 143–4, 147,
    152, 167
Mead, G. R. S., 247–8, 301
Mecklenburg, 106
medicine, 202–3
Medinet Habu, 54
Mediterranean, 164, 171, 296
memory, 257, 289–90, 291–2,
    316
Memphis, 211
Menes, King of Egypt, 207, 214
Menominee Indians, 163
Mercury, 139
Merezhkovski, Dmitri, 83
Merneptah, 206
Mesopotamia, 81, 224–8, 325
meteors and meteorites, 95,
    96–8, 100–1, 197
Metternich Stele, 138
Mexico, 7, 59, 82, 152, 166, 180,
    235, 285
Mexico, Gulf of, 296
Michael, Archangel, 192
Midas, King of Phrygia, 10
Milankovitch, M., 128
Milesians, 260
Milky Way, 326
Min-erva, 38, 221–2
Minoan civilization, 35–6, 51,
    184
Minoan period, 133
Minos, King, 38, 49
Miocene period, 116, 274

Mississippi River, 106, 235, 296
Mitford, 176
Mithraism, 218
Mohenjo-daro, 197
Moloch, 187
Mongolia, 255
Mongolians, 169, 170, 284, 286
monoliths, 244–56
monsters, sea, 223
Montezuma, 165–6
Montigny, Alan H. Kelso de, 94
Moon, 326; 'absent Moon'
    myths, 116–17, 122;
    Cancerian Age, 131;
    captured asteroid, 144, *145*;
    eclipses, 127, 128; effect on
    health, 129; effects on
    height, 121; and the
    epagomenal days, 152–4;
    and sinking of Atlantis,
    111–17
Mooney, Richard, 56, 106,
    114–15, 121–2, 146, 151,
    152–3, 238, 295, 307, 336
Moore, Patrick, 135
Moravia, 121
Moreux, Abbé, 147–50
Morocco, 51–2, 121, 296
Moschus the Phoenician, 213
Moses, 187
Mouhot, A. H., 37
Mourant, A. E., 170
Mu, 60, 61, 71, 112, 157, 166,
    169, 172, 173, 255, 293
Muck, Otto, 8–10, 74–6, 77–8,
    93–4, 96, 98–100, 101, 104,

Index

105–6, 114, 115, 116, 143,
144, 145–6, 158–9, 167–9,
186, 197, 228, 254, 268,
307, 310, 315, 336
music, 260

Nahautlacas, 234
Nahua Indians, 118
Nalivkin, D., 135–6
Napoleon I, Emperor, 216
National Geographic, 215
Nature (journal), 113, 150
Neanderthal man, 168–9
Neate, Tony, 293, 311
Neith, 190–1
Nemed, 239, 259–60
Nemesis, 134
Neolithic period, 206
Nephthys, 154
Neters, 208, 209, 211, 213, 214
New Scientist, 97
New York, 322–3
New York Post, 81
New York Times, 87
Newdick, Captain James, 81
Newfoundland, 89
Nigeria, 53
Nile, River, 128, 206, 210, 216,
296
Nineveh, 226
Nippur, 226
Noah, 240
Norsemen, 8, 105, 119–20
North Africa, 6, 206, 237
North America: Atlantean links
with, 229–34; continental

drift, 75–6, 109; Ice Age,
106, 108
North American Indians, 7, 163,
164, 168, 170, 229–32
North Pole, 56, 106, *107*, 108,
109, 129, 313, 325–6
North Sea, 39, 54–8, 104
Nostradamus, 335
Nuada of the Silver Hand, 203
nuclear power, 197–8
nuraghi towers, 256
Nut, 153–4

Oannes, 224–6, 307, 313
Oceanus, 133, 186
Odysseus, 39–40
Oera Linda Book, 8, 37–9, 40, 54,
56–7, 102–3, 119, 121,
147, 161, 162, 165, 221–2,
241, 242, 258, 295, 308,
311
Okanagaus tribe, 232
Olukun, 53
Olympus, 134, 186
Ophir, 53
Orange Key, 233
Orkneys, 256
Oronteus Finaeus world map,
147, *148–9*, 263
Osiris, 154
Ossendowski, Dr Ferdinand,
255
Ossets, 167
Ouzzin, 237
Ovid, 43
Owen, Richard, 207

Pacific Ocean, 62–3
Palenque, 143, 180
Palongawhoya, 122
Pangaea, 71
panspermia theory, 188–9
Paor, Liam de, 261
Papagiannis, Michael, 97
Papyrus Ebers, 151, 202
Paradise, 176–9
Paraguay, 166
parallel universes, 137–8
Paria Indians, 234
Paris-Teynac, 128
Partholan, 239, 240, 259–60
Pazyrka, 37
Pegasus Foundation, 292–5
Peloponnesian War, 32
Penn, William, 229
Periander, 34
periodicity, cycles of, 126–9
Permian epoch, 116
Perrier, Edmond, 121
Persephone, 46
Peru, 166, 187, 235, 256, 285
Petersen, Dr William, 129
Petra, 37
Phaeacians, 39–40
Phaethon, 118, 126
Phanagoria, 51
Philip of Opus, 43
Philocyprus, King of Cyprus, 33
Phoenicians, 7, 45, 53, 163, 187, 242
Piette, Edouard, 174
Piri Re'is, Muhiddin, 263–5, *264*
Pisces, Age of, 130, 131, 211

Pisistratus, 33
Pittacos of Mytilene, 34
PK (psychokinesis), 88, 257, 286–7, 327
planetismals, 100–1, 113
planetoids, 95
planets, 128, 135, 150–1, 226
Plato, 11, 12–29, 30–44, 46, 48–50, 55, 58, 88, 89–90, 144, 158–9, 184, 186, 213, 219–22
Pleistocene Epoch, 108
Pliny, 37, 42, 51, 176
Plutarch, 34, 152, 247, 337
Pluto (planet), 135
Podmanen Naya Tunguska River, 97
Polaris, 129
Pole Star, 129
Polynesian languages, 182–3
Pompeii, 313
Pomponius Mela, 46
Popul Vuh, 100, 162, 235
Poqanghoya, 122
Portugal, 6, 254
Poseidon, 10, 20, 24, 27, 35, 40, 46, 52, 53, 132, 188–9, 191, 193, 221, 223, 260, 268
Poseidonius, 42
Poznansky, Arthur, 60
Prague, 97
Praha Basin, 97
precession of the equinoxes, 129, 210
precognition, 257
Preselenites, 115, 117

Index

Proclus, 43–4, 46
Prometheus, 192–3
psychic abilities, 270–3, 286–7
psychic impressions, 300–19, 328
psychokinesis (PK), 88, 257,
    286–7, 327
Ptolemy Euergetes, 151
Puerto Rico Plateau, 93
Puerto Rico Trench, 94
Punt, 53
Puranas, 7
Pyramids, 215, 244–53, 267–8,
    313
Pyrenees, 296
Pythagoras, 41, 273
Pythagoreans, 34

Qabalah, 314
Quaternary period, 93, 104–5,
    120, 135
Quetzalcoatl, 307
Quiché tribe, 100, 162, 235
Quinn, Bob, 203–4, 237, 260–2,
    308, 311
Quinternary period, 104, 144

Ra, 122–5, 138, 153, 190–1, 209,
    210, 269
racial groups, 161–73, 284–6,
    297, 304
Radford, Tim, 165
radioactivity, 196–7
Ranelegh, E. L., 203
Randall-Stevens, H. C., 301
Rawlinson, Henry, 325
reincarnation, 328

religion, 184–5, 268–9
Renan, Ernest, 207
Renne-le-Chateau, 91
Retzius, Professor, 163
Rich, Claudius, 325
Richardson, Alan, 302, 309
Rmoahals, 284, 285
Robson, Captain David, 79–82,
    84
Rolfe, Dr Mona, 301
Roman Empire, 152, 153, 185
Rosicrucians, 292
Ross Sea, 147
Royal Navy, 68
Royal Papyrus of Turin, 214, 215
Runnings Park, 292–5
Rushdie, Salman, 323
Russell, Bertrand, 136–7
Rynin, N. A., 196

Sahara Desert, 61–2, 104, 105,
    296
St Peter and St Paul Rocks, 89,
    89, 265
Sais, 13, 44, 126, 158, 248
Samsaptakabadha scripture, 196
Santa Maria, 87
Santorini *see* Thera
São Jorge, 87
Sardinia, 256
Sargasso Sea, 17, 90
Sargent, Dr Carl, 2, 66–7, 316
Saros cycle, 127, 128
Saturn (god), 194
Saturn (planet), 115, 326
Saurat, Denis, 121

Scandinavia: Atlantean colonies, 58, 241; blood groups, 170; Bronze Age, 82; gods, 187; Ice Age, 103, 106, 109; *Oera Linda Book*, 8

Scheria, 39–40

Scherzer, Dr, 100

Schliemann, Heinrich, 37, 325

Schott el Hammeina, 52

Schwaller de Lubicz, R. A., 140, 207–12, 214, 215–16

science, 195–204, 265–8, 291, 298–9

Science (journal), 72

science fiction, 324, 329

Sclater, P., 60, 116

Scorpio, Age of, 190

Scotland, 106, 169, 263

Scott-Elliot, Colonel W., 163, 274–88, 290

Scrutton, Robert, 38, 39, 56–7, 106, 147, 221–2, 265, 315

sea-levels, 63–4, *65*, 101, 102

'sea monsters', 223

seals, 180–1

Sekhmet, 124, 187, 268–9

Semion, 239

Semites, 229–30, 284, 286

Seneca, 320, 329

Senmouth, tomb of, 111

Sergi, 171

Set, 154

Seymour, Charles, 309

Shakespeare, William, 126, 157

shamanism, 174–5, 218

Shemsu Hor, 214

Shetlands, 256

Shipman, Mother, 335

Shu, 122, *123*, 153, 211

Siberia, 97, 104–6, 109

Sichota-Alin mountains, 97

Sidon, 38, 258, 308

Silenus, 10

Silver Age, 131, 132–3, 188

Sinai, 187

Sirius, 142, 153, 188–9, 207–10, 218, 238, 268–9, 305, 313, 326, 337

Smith, George, 226

Socrates, 12, 32–3, 34

Soddy, Frederick, 197–8

solar year, 125

Solomon, King, 51

Solon, 12–14, 19, 33–4, 35–6, 40, 42, 44, 50, 55, 126, 158, 184, 212

sonics, 198, 199, 201–2, 251, 306, 317

Sothic calendar, 207–9

Sothis, 207–10, 268

South Africa, 111, 121

South America, 7, 63, 110, 167, 168, 170, 171–2, 180, 196, 234–7, 330

South Pole, 56, 106, 109, 313, 326

space travel, 196, 313

Spain, 6–7, 43, 51–2, 143, 167, 254

Spanuth, Pastor Jurgen, 8, 54–5, 56, 206, 241, 295, 315

Spence, Lewis, 109, 146, 167,

173, 193–4, 235–7, 238,
255, 295, 310, 336
Sphinx, 142, 215–17, 240
Spina, 51
Sprague, George, 307–8
stars, 129–30, 194
Steiger, Brad, 313, 333
Steiner, Rudolf, 289–90, 302
Stobaeus, 217
Stokes, Dr William, 110
Stone Age, 322
Stonehenge, 254, 306
Strabo, 43, 51, 143, 176, 258
Sudan, 62
Suess, Hans, 128
Suidas, 176
Sumerians, 134–5, 146, 224–8,
237
Sun, 119; captured asteroid, 144,
145; and Earth's axis
tilts, 105, 111, 120, 121,
123–5; eclipses, 127, 128;
effect on health, 129;
harnessing energy of,
298–9; sunspots, 128, 129;
vernal equinox, 129;
worship of, 114, 187,
190–2, 304
Surid Ibn Salhouk, King of
Egypt, 252–3
Susemihl, N., 66
Sykes, Egerton, 83, 87
Syncellus, George, 247
Syria, 121

tachylites, 77

Tangier, 237
Tangis, 237
Tanis, 151
Tartessos, 43, 51–2
Tasmania, 111
Taurean Age, 130, 131
technology, 195–204, 246
Tefnut, 122, *123*, 153, 211
Tejo valley, 167
Telegraph Plateau, *69*, 76–7
telepathy, 257
Temple, Robert K., 313
Tennyson, Alfred Lord, 5
Termier, Paul, 77–9
Tertiary period, 101, 135
Tesla, Nikola, 201–2
Thales of Miletus, 34
Thames Valley, 106
Thebes, 133, 211
Theopompus of Chios, 10, 42
Theosophy, 122, 273–9
Thera, 35–6, 49–51, 240, 313
Thorpe, 84
Thoth, 45, 139, 153–4, 202,
247–8
Thrice Greatest Hermes, 217–18,
247
Thucydides, 32
Thule, 56, 254
Tibullus, 188
Tierra del Fuego, 168
Tihuanaco, 60
Tilak, B. G., 325
Timaeus, 32–3
Timagenes, 259
time scales, 134–42

Times Picayune, 80

Titans, 192

Titius-Bode Law, 98

Tlavatlis, 284, 285–6

Toltecs, 7–8, 234, 284, 285

Tomas, Andrew, 51, 140, 147, 196–7, 198, 199, 249, 251, 310

Tomaschek, Rudolph, 150–1

Tower of Babel, 183

towers, *nuraghi*, 256

Transcaucasia, 171

Tree of Life, 254

Triton, 52

Tritonis, Lake, 52

Troy, 37, 133, 322, 325

Tuaregs, 62

Tuatha de Danaans, 132, 203, 238–40, 259–60

tuberculosis, 129

Tucker, Anthony, 266–7

Tungus, 169

Tunisia, 52–3

Tupis, 117

Turanians, 284, 285–6

Tyre, 258, 308

Tyrrhenia, 62, 254

Ulysses, 38

unconscious, collective, 2, 175, 291

universe, theories of, 137–8

Upper Palaeolithic period, 174

Uranus, 150

Urey, Harold, 112

Ursa Minor, 129

USSR, 63, 83–8, 97, 106

Utopia, 5

Uttu of Sumer, 188

Valentine, Dr Manson, 233, 333

Vedas, 325–6

Venezuela, 79, 234

Venus (planet), 144

Verdaguer, Jacino, 92

vernal equinox, 129, 130

Vesta, Temple of, 38

Vetchinkin, N. S., 94–5

Vigers, Daphne, 310–12, 316, 335

Vikings, 8, 171

Virgil, 188

Virgin Islands, 79

Virgoan Age, 190, 191, 241

Vladivostok, 97

volcanoes, 49–51, 76–9, 119

Völuspá, 119–20

vril power, 286–7

Wales, 6, 142, 169, 170–1, 240

Warren, Dr William F., 325

water vapour, 121–2, 317–18

Watts, Watts and Company, 81

Weaver, Dennis, 201

Wegener, Dr Alfred, 71, 72, 73, 76, 235, 330

West, John Anthony, 140, 215–16

West Africa, 53

West Indies, 235, 296

Westbourne, S. S., 81

Wheeler, John, 137–8

Whipple, Fred L., 101
Wickramsinghe, Chandra,
    101–2
Wilkes Coast, 109
Wilson, Allan, 165
Winchell, Professor, 63, 207
Wisconsin, 7, 144
Witter, W., 55
Woldben, A., 335
Wolf, Fred A. 137
Wolff, Dr Charlotte, 294, 329,
    333
Wood, David, 91, 177–9, 190–1
Wright, Ian, 48–9, 146–7
written language, 175–6
Würm Glaciation, 56, 106
Wyston, 94

Xisuthros, 227–8
Xochicalco, pyramid of, 59

Yazolino, Lauren, 250
year: calendar, 151–4, 207–10;
    epagomenal days, 151–4,
    209; solar year, 125
'Year of Brahma', 138
Yggdrasil, 133
Yoruba, 53
Young, 84
Ys, 262
Yucatan, 58–60, 90, 166, 235,
    296

Zeus, 133, 134, 186, 188, 193
Zhirov, Nicolai, 83
Znanie-Sila, 84–5
zodiac, 129–32, 134, 139–42,
    141
Zodiac of Denderah, 111, 140–1,
    141
Zuni Indians, 163

ARKANA – NEW-AGE BOOKS FOR MIND, BODY AND SPIRIT

A selection of titles

With over 200 titles currently in print, Arkana is the leading name in quality new-age books for mind, body and spirit. Arkana encompasses the spirituality of both East and West, ancient and new, in fiction and non-fiction. A vast range of interests is covered, including Psychology and Transformation, Health, Science and Mysticism, Women's Spirituality and Astrology.

If you would like a catalogue of Arkana books, please write to:

Arkana Marketing Department
Penguin Books Ltd
27 Wright's Lane
London W8 5TZ

ARKANA – NEW-AGE BOOKS FOR MIND, BODY AND SPIRIT

A selection of titles

The Child and the Serpent: Reflections on Popular Indian Symbols Jyoti Sahi

Within the religious structure of the Indian village, Jyoti Sahi discovered a contact with symbolism reaching beyond what is specifically Hindu. Using the central figures of Hindu popular religion, *The Child and the Serpent* demonstrates that the myths of folk culture are living . . . and have a power beyond the merely rational.

The Second Ring of Power Carlos Castaneda

Carlos Castaneda's journey into the world of sorcery has captivated millions. In this fifth book, he introduces the reader to doña Soledad, whose mission is to test Castaneda by a series of terrifying tricks. Thus Castaneda is initiated into experiences so intense, so profoundly disturbing, as to be an assault on reason and on every preconceived notion of life...

Dialogues with Scientists and Sages: The Search for Unity Renée Weber

In their own words, contemporary scientists and mystics – from the Dalai Lama to Stephen Hawking – share with us their richly diverse views on space, time, matter, energy, life, consciousness, creation and our place in the scheme of things. Through the immediacy of verbatim dialogue, we encounter scientists who endorse mysticism, and those who oppose it; mystics who dismiss science, and those who embrace it.

Zen and the Art of Calligraphy Omōri Sōgen and Terayama Katsujo

Exploring every element of the relationship between Zen thought and the artistic expression of calligraphy, two long-time practitioners of Zen, calligraphy and swordsmanship show how Zen training provides a proper balance of body and mind, enabling the calligrapher to write more profoundly, freed from distraction or hesitation.

ARKANA – NEW-AGE BOOKS FOR MIND, BODY AND SPIRIT

A selection of titles

Head Off Stress: Beyond the Bottom Line D. E. Harding

Learning to head off stress takes no time at all and is impossible to forget – all it requires is that we dare take a fresh look at ourselves. This infallible and revolutionary guide from the author of *On Having No Head* – whose work C. S. Lewis described as 'highest genius' – shows how.

Shadows in the Cave Graham Dunstan Martin

We can all recognize our friends in a crowd, so why can't we describe in words what makes a particular face unique? The answer, says Graham Dunstan Martin, is that our minds are not just computers: drawing constantly on a fund of tacit knowledge, we always *know* more than we can ever *say*. Consciousness, in fact, is at the very heart of the universe, and – like the earth itself – we are all aspects of a single universal mind.

The Magus of Strovolos: The Extraordinary World of a Spiritual Healer Kyriacos C. Markides

This vivid account introduces us to the rich and intricate world of Daskalos, the Magus of Strovolos – a true healer who draws upon a seemingly limitless mixture of esoteric teachings, psychology, reincarnation, demonology, cosmology and mysticism, from both East and West.

'This is a really marvellous book . . . one of the most extraordinary accounts of a "magical" personality since Ouspensky's account of Gurdjieff' – Colin Wilson

Meetings With Remarkable Men G. I. Gurdjieff

All that we know of the early life of Gurdjieff – one of the great spiritual masters of this century – is contained within these colourful and profound tales of adventure. The men who influenced his formative years had no claim to fame in the conventional sense; what made them remarkable was the consuming desire they all shared to understand the deepest mysteries of life.

ARKANA – NEW-AGE BOOKS FOR MIND, BODY AND SPIRIT

A selection of titles

A Course in Miracles: The Course, Workbook for Students and Manual for Teachers

Hailed as 'one of the most remarkable systems of spiritual truth available today', *A Course in Miracles* is a self-study course designed to shift our perceptions, heal our minds and change our behaviour, teaching us to experience miracles – 'natural expressions of love' – rather than problems generated by fear in our lives.

Sorcerers Jacob Needleman

'An extraordinarily absorbing tale' – John Cleese.

'A fascinating story that merges the pains of growing up with the intrigue of magic . . . constantly engrossing' – *San Francisco Chronicle*

Arthur and the Sovereignty of Britain: Goddess and Tradition in the Mabinogion Caitlín Matthews

Rich in legend and the primitive magic of the Celtic Otherworld, the stories of the *Mabinogion* heralded the first flowering of European literature and became the source of Arthurian legend. Caitlín Matthews illuminates these stories, shedding light on Sovereignty, the Goddess of the Land and the spiritual principle of the Feminine.

Shamanism: Archaic Techniques of Ecstasy Mircea Eliade

Throughout Siberia and Central Asia, religious life traditionally centres around the figure of the shaman: magician and medicine man, healer and miracle-doer, priest and poet.

'Has become the standard work on the subject and justifies its claim to be the first book to study the phenomenon over a wide field and in a properly religious context' – *The Times Literary Supplement*

ARKANA – NEW-AGE BOOKS FOR MIND, BODY AND SPIRIT

A selection of titles

Weavers of Wisdom: Women Mystics of the Twentieth Century Anne Bancroft

Throughout history women have sought answers to eternal questions about existence and beyond – yet most gurus, philosophers and religious leaders have been men. Through exploring the teachings of fifteen women mystics – each with her own approach to what she calls 'the truth that goes beyond the ordinary' – Anne Bancroft gives a rare, cohesive and fascinating insight into the diversity of female approaches to mysticism.

Dynamics of the Unconscious: Seminars in Psychological Astrology Volume II Liz Greene and Howard Sasportas

The authors of *The Development of the Personality* team up again to show how the dynamics of depth psychology interact with your birth chart. They shed new light on the psychology and astrology of aggression and depression – the darker elements of the adult personality that we must confront if we are to grow to find the wisdom within.

The Myth of Eternal Return: Cosmos and History Mircea Eliade

'A luminous, profound, and extremely stimulating work . . . Eliade's thesis is that ancient man envisaged events not as constituting a linear, progressive history, but simply as so many creative repetitions of primordial archetypes . . . This is an essay which everyone interested in the history of religion and in the mentality of ancient man will have to read. It is difficult to speak too highly of it' – Theodore H. Gaster in *Review of Religion*

The Second Krishnamurti Reader Edited by Mary Lutyens

In this reader bringing together two of Krishnamurti's most popular works, *The Only Revolution* and *The Urgency of Change*, the spiritual teacher who rebelled against religion points to a new order arising when we have ceased to be envious and vicious. Krishnamurti says, simply: 'When you are not, love is.' 'Seeing,' he declares, 'is the greatest of all skills.' In these pages, gently, he helps us to open our hearts and eyes.